i

# THE POSER

## LOUISE FURLEY

# ALSO by LOUISE FURLEY

Solitar

Halo Valley

Isle of Orainn

Anastasia

The Kissing Number

Wrath of Wolf

Devil's Prince

Devil's Seed

Jungle Treasure

Adara

The Poser

His Gangster's Winnings

THE POSER

ISBN- 978-1-7357712-2-9  (Paperback)
ISBN- 978-1-7357712-1-2  (eBook)

*Cover design by Pixel Mischief Design*

The characters and events portrayed in this book are fictitious. Any similarity to real persons, living or dead, is coincidental and not intended by the author.

# THE
# POSER

# Chapter One

His smile was as hidden as he was. The last thing he needed was for Kimi Consuelo to catch his pearlies glowing in the dark before he got the upper hand. She wasn't perfect, her hair was bottle blonde and curly, she had small breasts, and her face was barely pretty.

But, she would do for this time, until he got his hands on the real thing. Later he'd get what he really wanted, right now he had a statement to make, vengeance to conduct and demons to exercise.

As she neared, he stepped back into the shadows. "Come on, baby, come closer to my car," he whispered, "just a little closer…"

The sun had settled into the horizon hours ago. Kimi was tired after working a double since four this morning as a nurse's aide at Saint Aubins General. Yet, there was a buoyancy in her step, she had a date! A real date instead of one-shot bar pickups, or just friends with benefits.

She had changed from her scrubs into her sexiest dress, a chartreuse off the shoulder with a short flouncy skirt. The fox fur jacket she'd borrowed from Ginny was pure luxurious allure. Pleased that she finally saved up enough money to buy breast implants she-

"Hey, Kimi," his husky voice reached her before he did.

Kimi spun around with her mouth open. "You're here? I thought we were meeting in front of the restaurant?" Her brow wrinkled in confusion as he approached, oddly keeping his body to her side instead of in front of her. She twisted to face him.

Now the pearlies shone with his big grin. "Yeah, hon, about that," his arm snapped out too fast for Kimi to register it.

But she did feel the sharp prick in her neck. By the time her hand splat over the shot, he had already yanked the needle out and dropped it in his pocket.

He stood back and watched her eyes round as she tried to scream, and realized she couldn't. A sound hacked from her throat when her body failed to do as she ordered it- *run*.

His chuckle macabre, the grin broadened, he caught her as she crumpled, the fright bright in her closing eyes.

Lifting her limp body in his arms, he kissed her forehead, crooned, "There's my good girl. You ready to play?" Carrying her to his van he murmured, " 'Cause I am."

# Chapter Two

In a dank alley in the middle of town, just outside Alexandria along the cold, rushing Potomac River, the two detectives in trench coats stepped around the 6X6 plastic board blocking gawkers' and reporters' views of what lay inside the alley.

After they flashed their badges to the officers standing guard they hunched their backs to pass under the yellow police tape.

Dawn was still struggling to break in the chilly night, damp atmosphere clung to grass, clothes, hair. A small unit of police officers hovered around the object centered just four or five yards inside the wide alley.

"The hell?" Detective Thomas Princeton came to a hard halt.

Moving past him, Detective Penn Hixman nodded to the sergeant he knew well. "Sarg," he hailed as he stopped beside the man the girls all swooned over with his stalwart build covered in milk-chocolate skin.

Normally, Sergeant Daron Sinclair of the Brevet Bay Police Department would have most of his teeth exposed in a broad genial smile, which also drew the women to the handsome cop. Sinclair kept his dark hair in braided scrolls tight to his head and covered with a Stetson. His brown eyes focused on the spectacle in front of them, he responded to the greeting, "Hix."

Jutting his chin as Detective Princeton joined them, Sinclair said with wry humor, "Prince, nice to see there are still some things in this world that shock you."

One side of Detective Princeton's mouth nicked up. The wind pushed his sandy blond hair into his blue eyes. While absently swatting the strands out of the way, he commented, "Can't say we see this every day."

The three men stood stoically, eyes on the object, all nodding their agreement. A unit of police officers stood at the entrance giving the detectives room to maneuver while preventing anyone else from entering the crime scene.

The sharp wind swept around them, Hix pushed the coat aside and tucked his hands in his trouser pockets to warm them. Behind him, the police gave orders and shuffled about as they worked to hold back the mushrooming crowd.

The swirling blue and white lights in the dim twilight attracted curious attention. A slash of dawn's light slicked across his black hair, Hix drew a hand up and scrubbed his fingers down his short black beard. The rest of the police stayed a distance from him, but they now crowded behind Princeton and the sergeant. Hix didn't give a damn that people steered clear of him.

He knew what the talk was. Hix's mother was fair haired and light-skinned of British descent, but his father was Egyptian. Hix had inherited his father's tall, whipcord muscular build, tanned skin, and black eyes, people said he spooked them. Said he looked like one of those ruthless villains from The Mummy movie that cuts off people's heads with a machete. Little did they know how close to the truth they were.

He wore the baggage of his past in his confident yet closed off bearing and empty dark eyes. The fact that people generally feared the very look of him helped in his line of work breaking down criminals.

Hix grew up in the Egyptian military. He had been forced to join the Quds Force; Special Forces sent to infiltrate and fight the Hezbollah militant group in Iran. Quds was an extraterritorial operation, a military operation conducted outside the territory or jurisdiction of their own country. Under international law, these activities were highly restricted, and considered a violation of a state's sovereignty. Therefore, his country would have denied any knowledge of Hix and his unit's operations if they were caught.

In Egypt, the military can recruit children younger than 8, and as a young child, Hix had been recruited, taken, against his parents' will. His career in the military had been highly dangerous, violent and bloody, he was basically one of the government's régime of trained assassins.

As soon as Hix was able to extricate himself from the army, as still a very young man, his dad grabbed Hix's mother, Hix and his siblings and they fled to the U.S. Once settled in America, the Hixmans all secured their citizenship, and Hix eased into the police force.

His voice was gravelly deep with a coarse accent, he had high, sharp cheekbones that tapered down to a narrow lower face with a strong jaw. It was his hard and rough as iron exterior, and the tales of horror he'd experienced men saw submersed in the depths of the enigmatic eyes that filled people with unease, and fright.

Women, on the other hand, the wanton ones anyway, decided as evil and vicious as he looked, with his air of mystery he'd be a rough tornado in the sack, and they flocked on him like robins on the only worm in the field.

He said to Sinclair, "Give us a rundown, Daron."

The sergeant let out a huff, shook his head. Stuffing his hands in his pockets against the shrill wind, he motioned to the front of the alley with his head. "Ah, well, a bum dumpster diving found her. He ran out screaming, actually slammed right into a patrol cop coming out of a diner down the street."

He paused and the trio stepped closer to the object in the alley.

Lowering his voice, Daron said, "We've interviewed the wit. He's agitated but cooperative. He saw nothing suspicious, saw no one else near the alley, no vehicles. John Dean is taking him to get breakfast at the diner since his meal here was interrupted."

Princeton grunted, no one smiled at Sinclair's quip.

Sinclair went on, "Ah, the vic is a Caucasian female, and clearly nude. At first we thought she was like a solid gold mannequin or something, not a real person. Body not yet the same temp as the air, she appears fairly recently deceased. I'd say she's in her mid to late twenties, no ID or personal effects around. On the short side, maybe 5'4 and around 110 to 115 pounds.

"As you can see, she's on her knees, sitting back on her heels. Her spine is arched from her hands bound tightly behind her back with what appears to be twine. Then there would be the fact that her body appears to be spray-painted in gold."

"Entire body?" Princeton asked.

"Yes. Every inch, kind of a rose-gold color. There's a steel clamp around her neck, and a unique chain as wide as my arm is what's holding her up in front of the, uh, box. The links are a mix of long rectangular, and square steel. Because their shapes are irregular, they appear to be handmade. She almost looks like some kind of sacrificial offering."

The men studied the deceased female. She was positioned partially sideways in front of a three-sided with floor and ceiling, wooden box. The 8' by 8' box had curlicues carved around the frame, and a small window with iron bars in the back wall. There was no front wall.

The chain winched up from her neck to lock onto the top of the box. Her head flopped to one side, her hair, stiff from the gold paint covered half her face.

"The, ah, odd thing is-" Sinclair started.

"What we're looking at ain't odd?" Princeton frowned, taking in the completely golden deceased woman. "I think she's kind of exhibited like a slave. On her knees, hands bound behind her back, chain around her neck."

Sinclair nodded. "Uh huh. Anyway, come over here," he beckoned the detectives to follow him as he walked around the victim to see the front of her. He crouched down, the detectives copied him.

"There," Sinclair said, gesturing to the female. "On her stomach. He cut her."

"Hmmm," Hix muttered, observing the knife marks on the woman. Standing up, he fished his phone out and walked around the victim snapping pictures of her and the box. He returned to where the detective and sergeant still squatted and joined them.

Taking close-up pictures of the cuttings, Hix said, "They are not just random stabs, there's a pattern. The puncture wounds are xs in a circle, more like a heart shape with what looks like," he leaned in to peer closer at the body, "possibly cigarette burns in the center?"

"The burn circles are too big to be cigarettes," Sinclair countered. "There's no blood, she was killed somewhere else and brought here to be...exhibited. The box isn't nailed together, it has hinges. Probably brought in sections then snapped the parts together here."

"Like this was his stage," Hix murmured thoughtfully. "A large vehicle could have blocked the entrance and hidden him while he, or she or they, put it all together. We'll check for cameras in the area."

"Signs of sexual assault?" Prince rubbed his face, blinking rapidly. The sight of the butchered golden woman was harrowing.

Sinclair shook his head. "Don't know. ME will tell us. Considering how she's displayed, I'd go on the yes side." The men all rose.

"COD?" Hix asked.

Again Sinclair shook his head. "No obvious signs of trauma, no bullet holes, just the knife wounds and they were...deep, torturous, but not enough to kill her. But, uh, enough to hurt, bad." A sad sigh rumbled out. "Her eyes are frozen wide-open, it's like we can see how she looked while he tortured her. Excruciating pain and mind-blowing terror."

"Boys," a male voice said from behind. "How 'bout ya'll get outta my way so I can do my job?" The southern drawl had the trio turning around. Seeing the medical examiner, the three lawmen stepped aside so he could get to the victim.

The doctor set his bag on the chewed up asphalt and knelt beside it.

Around them, litter cluttered the ground and more trash piled against the scummy brick walls. The smell of rotting food in dumpsters permeated every ounce of the cold air. Some poor cop or CSI is going to have to climb into the dumpster as they examine every inch and every single thing in the alley.

The fortyish, burly Dr. Burke Conway drew stares from the crowd. He had hair but shaved his head bald and wore a gold hoop in one ear. A long, scraggly beard, copious tats, and a silver chain hooked on his front belt loop to his wallet in his back pocket made him look like he spent his free time on a Harley. Already wearing paper booties and gloves, he pulled on a coverall and cap and got to work.

Hix said, "Call me when you have preliminaries, Doc, yeah?"

"You bet, son. You'll be the first call after I order my breakfast." Conway shot Hix a wink over his shoulder.

Hix, Princeton and Sinclair stepped outside the yellow tape to get out of the doctor's way as well as crime scene techs that were hustling into the area.

The lawmen maneuvered around the yellow tape and the plastic board that shielded the scene from the civilians and reporters pushing and shoving to get a peek inside, and came to a loose huddle just outside the alley.

All three sucked in a deep breath of fresh air after the stink of the damp alley that clung to their nostrils, the horrid smell of death, and the foul grime that lingered on their clothes and hair.

His hands on his hips, Hix squinted out over the crowd scanning the buildings in the vicinity. The sky was brightening, more people gathered on the cobblestone walk, the murmurings grew louder. Several reporters called out to him asking for a comment.

Hix impolitely kept his back to them. He said, "Daron, get your people started canvassing the neighborhood, including all the rubberneckers here," he nodded towards the crowd.

At the sergeant's grunt of acquiescence, squinting down the street, Hix frowned dourly. "Not going to go well. No cameras nearby, and in the dark cloak of night likely no witnesses either."

The brick-fronted shops up and down the city street were closed, there were no lights illuminating the walk or the road.

"Huh," Sinclair snorted with a grin. "Still sardonic and rude as always, eh, Hix?"

Hix didn't smile back at him because Hix never smiles, the ability to do so was beaten out of him at a very young age by his first sergeant in the boiling hot desert. He could still taste the sand he'd lived in and breathed for years, that is when they weren't in thick jungles or climbing mountains.

"And," he said as if the officer hadn't spoken, "I want every video from cameras in the area, up and down the streets, including roads coming and going by the main street. He didn't bring those huge parts of the box in a Mini Cooper."

The section of town was near Old Town Alexandria. Its streets were lined with the same kinds of quaint shops, chic boutiques, blend of high-end and casual restaurants and yuppie bars strutting along cobblestone walks. It shared the waterfront with boats sailing the churning Potomac River.

Hix said to Detective Princeton, "Prince, you and I will get on trying to identify the victim." His gaze shifted to the sergeant. "Daron, first thing I want is her prints. I'll have Mike Maverick come out with a couple of his tech guys to break down the box setup and bring it in so they can study it."

Sergeant Sinclair was already talking on his phone when Hix and Prince hopped in their car.

# Chapter Three

Laurin's head whipped to the side with a cry of pain, she staggered backwards reeling from her husband's vicious slap.

Seeing his wife's pain, Rádolfo Ajanel's sneer curled up one side of his face. "I'm warning you, Laurin, you ditch your detail again and I'll put a true whaling on you."

He tugged the sleeves of his suitcoat down his wrists and straightened the red tie with a twitch of his hand. "You've barely recovered from the last time you drew my displeasure. I would think you would be on your best behavior."

Pushing her long, straight blonde locks off her face, Laurin kept her eyes lowered in hopes of not incurring any more of Rádolfo's wrath. If he had any idea what she'd done when she ducked out on his guards, he wouldn't beat her, he'd kill her. Then there would be no one around to protect Benji.

Swallowing hard, she stuttered, "I- I, uh, it was an- an accident. I thought I was climbing onto a stationary trolley car that was there for- uh, decoration. I didn't realize it was real and that it would take me from the guards-"

Whack!

Her head snapped to the side from his backhanded slap.

"Enough of your lies, Laurin. Just remember what I said, not again. I may take it out on the boy next time, hmm?" The perpetual sneer bent into a nasty smile, winged black brows lifted in sadistic threat.

Her hand on her stinging face, Laurin cried, "No, no, please Rádolfo, don't hurt Benji, I swear I- I won't do it again, I'll be so careful. Please," she hated whimpering, begging, but she'd do anything to keep Benji from harm.

But, it had been imperative that she make contact and used the opportunity when her husband sent her with guards for a dress fitting, not to protect her but to keep her from fleeing or speaking with anyone.

Next time, she'd have to be so much more careful, sneakier, painstakingly sly. She couldn't get caught, their lives depended on her completing her task.

Rádolfo's lids lowered over dark brown, insidious eyes as his thin lips curled. "You best remember that, *darling*." Even his word 'darling' carried his sneer.

"Now," he said, the lines around those horrid eyes in his olive-toned skin creased with antagonism, he gestured with his head to the hallway. "Get in the bedroom and wait for me. I'll complete your punishment there."

He smiled at the dread that crossed her pale face. That cheered him. "It's been weeks since I've had that juicy little body and I'm going to bestow a lot of attention on it." Thankfully he often had business out of town and that gave her a lot of reprieve, as well as time to heal, in between his 'lovemaking.'

At her blanch, he smiled. "Don't worry, darling, I won't leave any marks this time. The family will be here tomorrow for dinner, and," he reached out and stroked his long tapered fingers down the side of her face, his mouth quirking at her flinch, "that silken skin will be too exposed in the dress I've chosen for you to wear next week to the charity ball. Now, get to our bedroom, I have phone calls to make, I'll be there in thirty minutes."

Dark brows lowered, threat ringing in his Portuguese-accented voice layered with a trace of South African, he warned, "And you know to be ready for me, I don't want a stitch on you when I get there. Your meagre wardrobe can't withstand another shredded outfit, can it?" Grinning at the look of despair she tried to check, he swaggered down the hall.

11

Laurin didn't move a muscle until her brutal husband had disappeared around the corner. The mansion was three stories with wings spreading out from either side. Each large room was expensively and lavishly designed, except for the boy's room. Rádolfo liked bold colors and stylish yet gaudy furnishings, including the priceless paintings that decorated the walls.

As soon as Rádolfo was out of sight, Laurin raced to the stairs and rushed up them then down the hall. Opening the door to one of the numerous rooms in the extensive house, she hurried inside.

The breath she held whooshed out in relief. Benji was sitting at his little table by the window with his tutor. His big chocolate eyes lit up when he saw her.

He leaped to his feet and scurried over to her, clutching one of his few toys, a tiny truck that Laurin had to stash away when certain maids came to clean the room. They would tell the master if they saw any of the things Laurin had managed to smuggle in for the child.

"Mommy! You here, you read to me now!" His dark curls flopped in his shining eyes as he bounced around her before throwing his little arms around Laurin's waist and hugging her.

She patted the top of his head with a smile. "Yes, sweetheart, I'll read to you for just a minute though, if you and Mrs. Wickens are done for the day?"

The tutor closed the picture workbook they'd been working on and stood up, her smile friendly. "Yes, Mrs. Ajanel, we've finished."

In her early fifties, even though the child was not yet four years old, Winifred Wickens came to the estate for two hours, two days a week to work with Benji.

Besides teaching him Portuguese, Rádolfo wanted Benji fluent in several other languages as well. Rádolfo had told Laurin that when the child reached his teens he planned on training him as an enforcer for his private businesses, and that included sending him to work in Rádolfo's home country of Brazil.

Just the thought of Benji being in harm's way like that sent pangs of dread and alarm through Laurin's heart.

Grey curly hair framed Winifred's concerned face. Placing her materials into a briefcase, she said, "It would really be good for Benji to attend kindergarten when he's of age. He has no friends to play with and he is…lonely."

The stark room void of stuffed animals or toys was glaring in its empty coldness. No shelves to hold books and games graced the all-white room, no pictures of dinosaurs or the latest children's movie characters tacked on the walls.

"Um, Benji sweetheart," Laurin said, frowning over his head at the tutor, "why don't you go check on the animals, okay? Make sure they are quiet. Marla is cleaning today and they'll have to be hidden in the big walk-in closet."

"Okay," Benji chirped, keeping his joyful agreement in a soft voice. Rádolfo Ajanel was of the mind that children should not be seen and not heard. Only three, almost four, Benji had learned that the hard way, has the scars to remind him.

He ran off towards a connecting door, threw it open and darted into the adjoining room. A woof greeted him.

When he was gone, although Laurin was less than half the tutor's age, but she was like a mama bear to the boy, she scolded Winifred. "Mrs. Wickens, please don't talk about things like that in front of Benji, it will get his hopes up and then he'll be crushed when Rádolfo doesn't allow him to go to school with the other kids."

Rádolfo doesn't permit the child to go out any more than he does Laurin.

Folding her hands in front of her slightly pouched belly in the flowered dress, Winifred's wrinkled face saddened. Her mouth drooping, she said, "I'm sorry. I just…you know, keep hoping he will relent and let the boy have a normal childhood. Heavens, he doesn't allow the child games or toys as he thinks they will make him grow up weak, a sissy. All that he has is what you've managed to smuggle in and conceal. Your husband won't let him play outside, doesn't let you take him to the park or the zoo."

Winifred's lids slit with disapproval as she regarded the petite young woman in front of her. "Heavens, Mr. Ajanel should have been arrested for sex with a minor, you had to still have been a teenager when he got you pregnant? You've only been married a little over a year, he must have come at you in the country where you lived before he brought you here. It's not right, Miss, the master is more than double your age, and you must have-"

"Mrs. Wickens!" Laurin was appalled the tutor would be so brazenly outspoken as to insult her dangerous husband. No one in the household is aware that the reason Rádolfo refuses to allow the child outside is that he fears Laurin will run with him.

Benji is an anchor for Laurin. If she managed to get away from Rádolfo, she would never be able to take Benji with her. Rádolfo made it quite clear what he'd do to the boy if she fled.

Thick brows with slivers of grey rose in question. "I just don't, I mean, why is he so cruel to his own son? Mr. Ajanel rarely speaks to the boy, and when he does it's with indifference or downright cruelness. And you, we've all seen what he does to you, why-"

"Mrs. Wickens, please," Laurin said sharply, glancing towards the bedroom door fearful of Rádolfo hearing them. Her voice softened at the tutor's hurt expression. "What goes on in this house is none of your business."

Laurin moved to her and took her hand, her tone resigned, she said quietly, "There is nothing to be done about the way things are here. He won't change. My…husband rules this roost with an iron fist, you are very aware of that. What he says goes, and…everything else here…is how he wants things done. To even bring up things like Benji attending school only…unleashes his temper."

No one in the household ever said anything out loud about the beatings Rádolfo rained upon his young, delicate wife, they'd lose their jobs, maybe their heads if anyone spoke up. It was a silent rule to keep quiet and mind their own business.

Winifred had only been tutoring the young boy for a month, she didn't know about the unspoken rules. Laurin would have to discreetly have the housekeeper explain to her that she needs to not get involved in the workings of the home.

Laurin sighed, she was grateful Rádolfo at least has the tutor brought in. As long as they keep the child, her husband thinks down the road Benji can be of some use to him. A shiver rolled across her thin shoulders at the thought. The only business Rádolfo would let the boy have anything to do with would be in his nefarious enterprises that hide behind his legitimate businesses.

Shaking the disturbing thoughts out of her head, she went to the connecting room, and her heart warmed.

Benji was hunkered down amidst a bevy of real animals. A lame black lab, three maimed cats, a damaged bird and a severely injured tortoise all clamored for his attention, including the tortoise.

Rádolfo knew about Poochie the dog, as long as he doesn't see it or hear it he forgets about him. Her husband has no inkling of the other animals. If he did, Laurin's gut clenched, he would dispose of them all. And not in a nice way, just to teach them a lesson.

She forced a smile. "Okay, peanut, a quick read, I have to be…ah, meet with Papa-Ray in a few minutes."

Her gut squeezed so hard at the awareness of what Rádolfo was going to do to her, she had to grit her teeth to keep from running hysterically into the bathroom and throwing up.

\*\*\*\*\*\*

The next evening, Laurin dabbed concealer on her cheek to cover one of the marks Rádolfo claimed he wouldn't leave. She could hear his family downstairs gathering for Sunday dinner. One of the servants had been stationed at the door waiting to hold it open as each car pulled up.

As they emerged from their vehicles, the three couples trod up the bricked steps to enter through the enormous, double front doors.

The main building of the beige colored mansion was three levels and had a white dome over the front entrance supported by five white columns.

A single-story wing led from both sides of the main building, and two more structures that were two-stories high stretched from them. No less than eight chimneys poked up around the red tiled roof. All of the windows and doors were bordered by white shutters and wide trim.

The Ajanel clan was growing loud and boisterous. They were likely on their third cocktail by now, and Laurin knew she needed to get down there before Rádolfo came to retrieve her. She would have more marks to conceal if that happened. He wasn't a patient man by any means, and to balk at his orders was signing up for a wicked thrashing.

She smoothed the pale yellow skirt, then plucked at the ruffled collar of the pale yellow, organza blouse, the material spotted with white dots. The blouse had cap sleeves and a scooped bodice that showed just a hint of cleavage. Her 48 year-old husband loved to show off his young wife. He complained she was too thin, but drooled like a dog when rampaging over her lush curves.

Rádolfo's first wife, Imena perished in a boating accident ten years ago. He had knocked Imena up when they were barely legal. He was on holiday with his family in Monaco and he had picked her out of a group of teenaged girls sunbathing. She got pregnant the one time they did it in the bathhouse.

He didn't even know her name until her parents came knocking on his parents' door with the figurative shotgun in her father's hands.

Rádolfo's three sons and their wives would be present downstairs. The youngest son, Chevalier and his wife Jewel had a baby three months ago, Laurin wondered if they'd left little Channing home again with his nanny.

The only one of the Ajanels that gave Benji the slightest acknowledgement was Chevalier who had taken over a geriatric practice from the retiring elderly owner. But, then again, Rádolfo seldom allowed the boy to come downstairs, and the only time Benji left the house was when Rádolfo felt the necessity to produce him at certain events.

"Mrs. Ajanel," a voice from the door had Laurin put away her woolgathering and turn to it.

A maid hovered, she blinked nervously, her eyes darting back and forth. She said in a quiet, conspiratorial voice, "The master has mentioned that you will be down any moment. I think he's growing perturbed."

Laurin smiled to ease the anxious maid. Everyone tiptoed around Rádolfo, terrified of incurring his wrath. "I was just coming, thank you Cynthia for telling me. Let's hurry, shall we?"

Laurin moved swiftly down the broad, curved staircase carpeted in bright ruby, her hand sliding along the polished railing, praying she hadn't stalled too long and her husband wouldn't punish her for being late.

She wasn't keen on before dinner cocktails, and the Ajanel sons' wives were always cutting and cruel to her. She would stay upstairs with Benji if she had her choice, but, she sighed, alas, she had zero choices over any aspect of her life.

Almost to the drawing room, she paused to calm herself, slow her racing pulse. Taking in a deep breath and exhaling it slowly, Laurin stepped into the drawing room with a polite smile pasted on her face.

Wallpaper with broad faint white and taupe stripes layered three walls, the fourth was a solid taupe. The fireplace was antique white, the furnishings peach and cream with gold accents. It was the only more refined, demure room in the mansion.

Blane's wife, Shona saw her first. Blane at 29 was the middle son.

Shona didn't even try to hide her disdain of the younger woman. "Well, the adulteress has arrived," her sneer could even top Rádolfo's normal snide mien. "How kind of you to deign to honor us with your presence, *Princess*."

Laurin cringed inside at the nickname that was said with derogatory sarcasm.

The three wives, Shona, Jewel, and Geraldine who was married to the eldest son, Raoul, wore identical hateful glares. Geraldine was almost simple-minded and easily led by her sisters-in-law.

They were all wealthy and Geraldine shopped at the same upper scale boutiques as Jewel and Shona, but she still managed to look like a peasant with her loose flowery dresses.

Frumpy in clumpy low-heeled pumps, and her brown hair that as soon as she left the beauty salon somehow immediately tangled itself into a mess.

On the other hand, Shona and Jewel dressed to the nines with their hair perfectly, expensively coiffed, and nothing less than six-inch Louboutin's decorated their manicured feet.

The women tonight both wore almost identical slinky sheaths. Jewel in crimson, her shimmering platinum locks in an up-twist, and Shona in light green, her blonde hair bobbed at her shoulders. So heavily glued with hairspray it moved as all one chunk when she moved her head.

Geraldine was on the dumpy side with rather saggy curves, the other two rail-thin women used padded, push-up bras and other accouterments to assist their less than curvaceous figures. All three towered over the petite Laurin and liked to intimidate her with their superior height.

Sipping his cocktail, his nose reddened from the amount of alcohol he'd imbibed all day, Blane eyed Laurin with derision. His father's wife was way younger than Rádolfo's sons. None of them wanted her nosing into their business or inheriting any of their money. He blinked away, but not soon enough for the lust to gleam in his bleary brown gaze.

Eldest son Raoul spoke with his lips on the rim of his glass, "At least Mother isn't around to see the gold digging, cheating little hussy, why the hell does Father keep her? I mean, Chevalier dodged a bullet, huh? Even as sick as Mother was-"

Blane choked on his drink. Wiping his wet chin, he snorted, "I know he'd scream a hissy fit if he heard you call him Chevalier." The two brothers kept their voices low not desiring for anyone to overhear their derisive chit chat.

"Yeah, yeah, whatever. Let him complain and I'll pants him and tie him to the flagpole like I did when we were kids. Anyway," instead of sipping his drink Raoul licked around the rim. "I can't believe Father kept the bitch. I mean, he could have fucked her once or twice and kicked her over to Chev."

"Uh, you can see the girl, right? You would kick that out of your bed? That honeypot is so fucking hot it's something you keep forever, bro. I'm still shocked over when Father bought the mail-order-bride for Chevalier since he was too busy with his practice to date, then Father kept her for himself.

"Chevy was furious, ran right out and married Jewel, and baby Channing showed up in record time. Still," Blane couldn't tear his lusting eyes from Laurin, "I can understand. That girl is one scorching piece of tail. Nothing else quite like her in this shady little town, or in all of Alexandria or Washington and beyond for that matter. Right?"

The corner of his thick lips tugged in, Raoul blatantly studied Laurin from the top of her light blonde hair, down the yellow dress over her slender yet quite curvy body and down to the tiny feet in white sandals.

A flush rolled up Raoul's flaccid face advertising his body's reaction to the lovely young woman. Unable to deny his attraction, he gulped his drink down then stalked off for a refill.

Blane and Raoul had their father's dark bold looks, well-built physiques, and were up to their elbows in Rádolfo's shadier businesses.

Chevy was slightly fairer although equally as tall and hardy, one hand holding his drink, the other tucked in his pocket, he sauntered over to Laurin while his father spoke with his major domo.

Although they spoke quietly, the brothers' voices still carried to Laurin.

Seeing the uncomfortable look on her face, Chevy said, "Hey, honey, don't let them get you down," he nudged her gently with his elbow smiling kindly. "They just like to get a rise out of you." He took a sip of his cocktail, said congenially, "Where's the boy? Father still exiling him to his room?"

Nodding sadly, Laurin's eyes were latched onto her husband. It would only be moments before he saw her, and would come to her. Then they would all go into the dining room for dinner.

The men would talk business, the women fashion, balls, shopping, all sorts of things Laurin had no interest in. That didn't matter, their conversations would never include her anyway. Laurin was the defined black sheep of the family.

Everything would start out fine, then the couples would start bickering because after liberal amounts of liquor, they would finish off bottles of wine with dinner. The brothers would argue about sports, stocks, anything just to have something to fight about. Eventually they'd all get steamed, start shouting at each other, sometimes actual brawls broke out.

Then the wives would start on gold digging, adulteress Laurin who had tricked the patriarch of the family into marrying her. King Rádolfo would sit back and watch it all like he was Shakespeare watching one of his dramatic plays.

"Oh, excuse me, Laurin." Chevy's grin huge and happy, he set his glass on a tabletop. "There's my boy." He turned from Laurin and hurried to the threshold where a nanny was holding his child. He scooped up the infant and held the sleeping baby against his chest while cooing quietly against his soft head.

His wife Jewel slid her arm under one of Chevy's and laid her head on his shoulder smiling tenderly at their baby. "He loves his daddy so much, don't you my big boy," she said softly, stroking her palm over the baby's back.

Chevy had one big hand cradling the baby's bottom, the other around the back of his neck, snuggling him to his sturdy chest and dropping soft kisses on his small head.

Laurin stared longingly at the happy couple, then stiffened when she heard her husband's voice at her ear, felt his warm breath brush her skin, smelling of cognac. She hadn't noticed him stride across the thick rug to stand beside her.

He slipped his hand around her waist tugging her against his side and bent his neck to whisper in her ear, "Ah, my sweet, I need to go away less on business so we can get more practice in to create one of our own, just like my grandson Channing, that beautiful baby boy. Or perhaps a precious daughter as lovely as her mother?"

Laurin willed her body to not quiver in anxiety as he licked the side of her face and stroked his hand around her to splay his fingers over her flat belly.

His lips sucking the side of her neck, he murmured, "As soon as they leave, we'll get right to work on making one of those, eh, darling?" His long fingers stretched down below her stomach, scarce inches from her feminine private parts. She schooled her body not to move away from him, not to shove his wandering hands off her.

Swallowing her fear, perspiration popped across Laurin's forehead. She'd had to borrow money from the minister to pay for doctor visits and the medication. If Rádolfo ever found out she got a birth control shot he would-

"Sir," a servant at the door announced to Rádolfo, "dinner is ready to serve, at your will."

# Chapter Four

A week later, as they left the limo, hard fingers tightly clinching her elbow, Rádolfo leaned over and spoke quietly yet his voice a sharp needle in Laurin's ear, "You know the drill, darling. You do not flirt with any men, you are not to be alone with any other males, you dance only with me. I find you making eyes at another man and, well, I don't have to spell it out, you know."

Trying to hold in the wince of pain at his grip, Laurin kept her voice even. "Yes, of course." She didn't say anything else, you never knew what would set the man off.

They strolled into the ballroom. Fairy lights twinkled strung from corner to corner, chandeliers cast moving diamond rainbows over the crowd.

A few people sat at white, table-clothed round tables, and the band set up towards the rear of the room played subtle dinner music. A couple clinging to each other swayed back and forth on the small dance floor in front of the band.

Rádolfo and Laurin made their way through the crowded room. The room was alive with brisk chattering, cheery and loud voices speaking over one another. Rádolfo stopped frequently to speak with people he knew, which were many.

He introduced Laurin to a few she hadn't met previously in the 18 months they'd been married. As usual, she was on the receiving end of disdainful looks and snobby judgment from both males and females, however, the males' rapt perusal of her figure had many wives jerking them away from the pair, earning a chuckle from Rádolfo.

Rádolfo's hooded eyes swept the length of his wife, his pupils glinting with desire. "Darling, I must say, if possible, you look even more ravishing than ever. The sapphire suits you, a shimmering foil for that lovely silky blonde hair and brings out the amazing deep blue of your eyes. I like it like that, pinned up on one side and rolling down in curls over one shoulder."

A bit of a disapproving frown, he remarked, "I prefer your bangs swept to the side like they are now rather than as you usually wear them hanging over your eyes like you're hiding behind a veil."

Like all the other dresses Rádolfo had custom made for Laurin, it fit to a T. Not too sleazy tight, but snug enough to show off those feminine curves. The cocktail styled dress tied behind her neck, skimmed down her torso to bell just past her knees.

The bodice was a deep slice, so narrow one had to really look hard to see the bare parts of her breasts when she moved. Realizing this, Laurin held herself even more stiffly than normal. Her husband thought it amusing to entice other men with what he could have, and they could not.

"Darling," he murmured, sliding his hand around her waist as he pulled her against his side. "Let's find a table, they appear about to start serving." He ushered her to a large round table crowded with cronies of his, and their wives.

He pulled out her chair and Laurin sank gracefully onto it, lowered her eyes against the hateful glares of the people present, and never raised them again.

After a meal of prime rib, gravy filled popovers, a variety of vegetables and salad, toasty rolls, gallons of wine and an assortment of desserts, Rádolfo pushed his chair back and stood up.

Pulling on Laurin's chair for her to rise, he bowed to his friends and said, "I am going to take my wife on a twirl of the dance floor, then I have several people I need to speak with. Please excuse us."

As they danced, more couples crowded the floor. Rádolfo's arms were punishingly tight around Laurin, her chest was smushed so hard against his she could scarcely draw a breath. When he wasn't rubbing their chests together, he was grinding his hips into her pelvis, his hands constantly sliding down to grab handfuls of her bottom.

His tongue in her ear, he whispered the filthy things he wanted to do to her when they got home. Fortunately, much of it was in Portuguese so Laurin didn't have to have a visual along with his deviant words.

Detective Penn Hixman tugged at the bowtie around his neck. "Fuckin' penguin suit," he groused.

Chuckling next to him, also in a tux, his brother Kullen pointed to the bar. "Get over it, bro, you only have to attend a few of these charity events a year for Ma. You and I got chosen for this one, our other siblings lucked out this time. Let's write out our check then get a drink and grab some hors d'oeuvres." His grin contained a leer. "I see something luscious in pink across the room I need to get to know better."

Hix snorted. "Always on the prowl, bro."

"Yeah well, variety is the spice of life, you know."

After they paid their donation, they made their way to the bar and Kullen ordered two beers. He handed one to his brother. They clinked bottles in salute.

Taking a slug, Hix complained, "I shouldn't even be here, I'm in the middle of a murder investigation."

Kullen playfully frowned at him. "Yeah, yeah, quit whining. You put in 16 hour days, you have a right to chill for a minute." He lifted his bottle and toasted, "Here's to a hot night in Pinky's bed, and maybe you'll catch a fish too. You could use a good lay to lighten up."

"Humph," Hix grunted and swigged half his beer.

"You're too goddamned picky, Penn. I know you had tough times but you didn't wear out that pecker when you were in the military. Hell, you're not the first guy whose girlfriend had an abortion than ran off with your best friend while you were away on yet another covert mission. There are good women in the world, you know."

Normal men would be scowling with grief or anger at Kullen's words, but Penn's face was as implacable as always, not a hint of expression, no tightening of his strong jaw, not a flicker of pain in his ebony eyes.

His voice lowered with compassion, Kullen said quietly, "The rest of us were lucky they could only choose one child from a family to go into the military. We very rarely saw you while growing up, they kept you fighting in other countries. We know the things you experienced were heinous and tore you up, bro. The missions in the sweltering deserts, the dense jungles, they're still eating at your soul. You-"

"Who is that tall dark fellow feeling up the blonde in the blue dress?" Hix cut him off, nodding towards the dance floor.

Kullen twisted around to see whom Hix was referring too. A lopsided smile curved up his handsome face.

With a shade of their mother's fairness faintly present, all the Hixmans were ruggedly tanned-skin from their father's genes, but Hix had darkness inside him that kept rigid walls up around his soul.

He barely let his siblings get close, he let Kullen in slightly more than the others, he always held his mother at bay. She could read his dead eyes, the disease of his past still tormenting him, he didn't want her pulling out his demons and examining them, forcing him to relive them.

Kullen told him, "That is Rádolfo Ajanel, the ambassador from Mozambique and his wife, Laurin."

"Wife? She looks young enough to be his daughter." Hix's disbelief rumbled in his broad chest. "Bastard looks like a damned pedophile the way he's got his hands all over her."

Shrugging, Kullen said, "There's that cop in you, bro. Yeah. She appears rather uncomfortable with his groping. He's got like 25 plus years on her. You haven't heard their story?"

Shaking his head, Hix finished off his beer.

Kullen glanced at his brother then turned his attention to the dance floor where another man tapped Ajanel on the shoulder and received a harsh shake of his head and a threatening glare to back off.

Kullen said, "After everything that happened, the guy is still jealous and highly possessive of the girl. Shit, look at her, I wouldn't let her out of the house, she's a man magnet. Which was the trouble to begin with."

His gaze steady on the couple, Hix commented, "What trouble could a tiny, young girl like that cause?"

Kullen barked a laugh attracting attention from people nearby. "Well, like I said, Ajanel is an ambassador but he also has many enterprises here in the U.S. that the CIA and FBI are always looking into but have never gotten an iota of evidence he's running anything illegal.

"And when they finally come up with a witness, that witness mysteriously disappears, or has a convenient accident and dies before giving a deposition." Kullen's position in aerospace and training in DC enables him to have his fingers on the pulse of the government.

Holding the bottle in one hand, Hix crossed his arms, his eyes narrowed at the smirking suave man with his big hands almost covering his wife's small yet lusciously rounded behind. "The wife doesn't seem to be enjoying the dance. She practically cringes every time he pulls her close or runs his hands over her."

Beside him, Kullen observed the couple dancing. Slipping into their own language, he said, "*Aiwa*. Yes, the word is, Ajanel purchased her as a mail-order bride for one of his sons, but then kept her for himself. Caused quite a ruckus in the family."

Hix snorted. "I bet. So a gold digging femme fatale from Russia and the ambassador from, what'd you say? Mozambique? South Africa? He doesn't look African, he's white."

Kullen replied, "Not everyone from Africa is black, bro. He's from Mozambique which was originally settled by mostly Portuguese. That's not even half the story."

"Go on." Hix didn't want to be intrigued with the beauty Ajanel held trapped in his horny embrace, but nonetheless he was.

"Well, as ambassador, Ajanel spends a lot of time in Washington. Apparently he occasionally brings the hot wife with him. So, the word is, that she was having a risqué affair with a member of the Cabinet, the Secretary of Energy, Woodrow St. Lawrence."

Hix's brows shot up. "That girl? She's barely out of diapers. St. Lawrence is fifty if a day and married, how could-"

"She's a female, Penn, men are known to throw everything they hold dear aside for a roll in the hay with an extraordinary beauty like her. A young beauty as you pointed out. Anyway, they say she got pregnant and tried to blackmail St. Lawrence, and he wanted her to have an abortion, and she got angry and tried to kill him."

"Kill him!" Hix couldn't believe the tale, his gaze stayed glued to the couple still dancing. Well, Ajanel was dancing, his wife was squirming to avoid his roaming hands. "The Secretary would have been twice her size."

"Yeah, go figure." Kullen grinned. "Sordid as hell, huh? Anyway, they claim she tried to brain him with a fireplace poker. She injured him but he fought her off."

"Why isn't she in prison?"

"There's the rub, Brother. St. Lawrence refused to press charges. And either the girl was lying about the pregnancy or she got an abortion, because she never had the baby. But," he kept going when Hix opened his mouth, "she and Ajanel supposedly have a child that is not quite four. Maybe that's why they didn't press charges."

His eyes narrowed further. "Four? She's too young, what is she 18? 19? She'd have to have been 13 when he got her pregnant."

Kullen said, "You're right. But I believe she's 22, 23 maybe? Anyway, everyone says there's something fishy about the child because the couple only met a little over 18 months ago when he bought her.

"And, she's not Russian, she's European, Welsh I think. I read her maiden name somewhere at some point and it sounded Welsh.

Perhaps the child came with her, or the husband had a twig before he met her. His first wife died in a boating accident awhile back."

Astounded, Hix expelled in harsh surprise, "Ajanel didn't kick her to the curb when she cuckolded him? She cheated on me, no matter how breathtaking she is, I'd dump her so fast she'd bounce on the sidewalk."

"I don't know, bro, that piece has a lot going on. Some guys would look the other way at her indiscretions rather than losing her. Whatever, it's their problem. Let's get some chow, you can tell me about the date Ma's forcing you to take to the Cartwright wedding."

Kullen clapped Hix on the back when he continued to stare at the couple. "Penn, come on."

Hix blinked, shook his head then followed his brother to a table.

# Chapter Five

After they ate, the brothers went in opposite directions. Kullen off to chase after the girl in pink, Hix headed for the outside balcony to smoke a Turkish thin cigar.

As he passed a hallway, he paused to look into the large room, basically a wide corridor. "Oh crap," he cursed a few foreign words when he realized what had caught his attention.

That woman, Ajanel's wife had emerged from the restroom and was closing the clasp on her purse when it slipped from her hands.

Hix told himself to keep on moving, but he was mesmerized, he couldn't make his feet move.

The hallway they were in was cream colored with burgundy accents, gilded paintings decorated the long walls. Highly polished white tile reflected the blue of the girl's high heels.

He watched as she gracefully bent her knees to pick up the purse. Right before the girl bent, two women entered the hallway heading to the restroom. Their conversation stopped when they saw her.

One of the women slapped her friend's arm and said, "Hey, it's trash day," and she hurried the few steps to Mrs. Ajanel and deliberately shoved her as she was stooping for the purse, knocking her over. The woman kept going and she joined arms with her friends and they giggled into the restroom.

"Oh!" Mrs. Ajanel gasped, as her knees slammed into the cool tile. Rubbing one knee, she went to reach for her purse when two more women seeing what the others had done, swiftly approached.

One of them called out, "Slut, adulteress!" And shoved her to slam back onto the floor, and kicked her purse several feet away from her reach.

Laughing, the woman's friend joined her and gave the girl struggling to rise a hard shove. The first woman stood on her other side so they could push the girl back and forth between them-

"Enough," Penn ordered, dropping his arms between the two women and the girl.

"Oh, poosh, honey," the first woman snickered. "She deserves everything she gets, gold digging mail-order-tramp."

"Yeah," the other woman exclaimed. "The sleaze cheated on her husband, committed attempted murder and extortion, and she has a young child at home whom she obviously cares nothing about! Just a useless bag of skin and bones, I say."

Penn moved his arms and the women were forced to stand back from Mrs. Ajanel.

"Come on, Cissy, who gives two shits about the slut, I need another drink." Their heels clacking on the tile, the women sniggered down the hall and out of sight.

Penn bent and swooped up the purse, then grasped the young woman's arm to help her to her unsteady feet. He held onto her to keep her stable, then handed her the purse.

Her face red with mortification, hair in disarray, she pushed locks back and set the back of her hand against her forehead.

After gaining some composure, Mrs. Ajanel took a breath and said softly, "Thank you, sir, for your help. I don't know what would have-"

"Save it," his snarl whiplashed like a verbal slap. "That's what happens when you whore around on your husband and try to bash in the skull of your lover. Might be best if you stayed in your ivory tower, little Miss Boutique. However, for now, we should seek your husband so he can see you safely to your car. Let's go," he gave her a tug.

Fear fired like blisters in her eyes as she dug her feet in resisting his pull. Her face suddenly stricken white, she cried, "No, I-"

An angry voice raged from the entrance to the hall, "Get your fucking hands off my wife, you son-of-a-bitch!" The ambassador came storming towards them.

Penn released the woman and cocked his head to Ajanel, said blithely, "That's Detective Son-of-a-bitch to you, Ambassador Ajanel."

As soon as Hix let her go, Rádolfo grabbed up her other arm. Winding his fingers tightly around her upper arm he squeezed so hard she started to pull at his wrist but he violently shook her.

Raising his fist to her, he ground out through grit teeth, "You flirting with this cop, Laurin? You fucking know better. You know what's going to happen."

Laurin cringed and turned her head as if to avoid his punch. He didn't hit her but crushed her arm so much harder her shoulder lifted in response to the pain.

"Hey, Ajanel," Penn frowned, "you need to let go of her. I was merely helping her pick up her purse. Trust me, there is nothing untoward between us *at all*." His tone indicated that there wouldn't be even if she was the last woman on earth.

Ajanel snarled at him, "Mind your own business, Cop," and furiously dug his fingers into her skin so hard she couldn't stifle her whimper.

Moving in close to him, Penn ordered, "That's enough, Ajanel." Turning to Laurin, he said more gently, "Come with me, I'll take you to the station. There will be a victim advocate there that can speak with you about this kind of abusive treatment."

"She's not going anywhere with you, Cop." Ajanel shook Laurin so hard her teeth clacked together. "Isn't that right, Laurin? You tell him." The harsh anger on his face, the clear threat of retribution loud his voice, he glared at his wife.

Penn reached for her. "Mrs. Ajanel come-"

She cowered back from his hand. "No, please, I need to- to go home. Leave us alone, please."

Penn had no choice. He stood helplessly watching Ajanel speaking quietly in her ear as he practically lifted her off her feet as he ushered her out the exit. Her face turned whiter at his whispered words.

Penn was concerned. The man hadn't struck her, but all the signs showed he probably would have if they'd been alone. That meant he was more than likely abusing her at home.

His gut cramped, but, he could do nothing. If he had witnessed Ajanel strike her, he could have arrested him, but without her cooperation he couldn't help her. He stood frustrated, his fists clenched in impotent anger.

Once they arrived at home, Rádolfo dragged Laurin from the limo and gave her a rough push towards the house. He grasped her arm again, painfully hard, and walked her through the house and up to their bedroom.

Laurin quivered with fear, her husband was in a blind rage and she knows it will be futile to beg for mercy.

Slamming the door closed behind them, Rádolfo hauled his arm back and fiercely slapped her. Laurin stumbled backwards from the blow, tears of pain welled instantly.

Stomping to her, he stuck his face in hers and shouted, "You want that man? You want that cop?" and he slapped her again.

The tears sprung, Laurin covered her stinging cheeks with her palms. "No! No, please, he was only retrieving my purse for me! These- these women, they knocked me over, on purpose, and he-"

Wham! Another ferocious slap and her head whipped to the side.

He bellowed while slapping her back and forth, "You whore, you slut! If I let you out of my sight for a second you would spread them for any male that comes along, wouldn't you?" Slap- slap-

Hit so callously, Laurin tumbled to the floor with a cry. She curled into a ball to protect herself.

Rádolfo bent over her cowering, sobbing form. "Well my darling, if I have to break your legs to keep you from running out on me," he laughed unpleasantly, "so be it. For now," he grasped her arm and jerked her to her feet.

"Rádolfo, please," the pleading sobs wrenched from Laurin as she forced herself not to flee from him, it would only infuriate the man more. And, she had nowhere to go, he'd catch her in two steps, as he has before.

Rádolfo spun her around and shoved her roughly at the bed, her hipbones slammed into the footboard, she cried out at the pain. Ignoring her cries, he put his hand on her back and pushed her to bend over with her palms on the bed.

Shudders rippled across her thin shoulders when she heard him unbuckle his belt, heard the leather whoosh through the belt loops. When she heard his gruesome snickers, she knew he re-buckled the belt and would swing it so the buckle would strike her.

"*Rádolfo, please,*" the sobs so wracking Laurin coughed the words out, her body shaking with terror. She could taste the blood in her mouth from his vicious slaps.

He shoved her face into the duvet and pushed the dress up, gripped her panties and ripped them ruthlessly from her body gouging cuts into her skin. He kicked her feet apart, Laurin could almost hear him grinning at the sight of her so helpless, vulnerable, trapped.

"You move and you'll get it worse, Laurin," he warned, then lashed the belt across her bare bottom. Laurin muffled her cries of pain as the buckle sliced into her.

Rádolfo leaned over her, grasped the back neckline of her dress with both hands and tore it completely apart then wailed his belt viciously up and down his delicate wife's entire body.

Her cries and pleading for him to stop urged him to strike more forcefully, more brutally, her pain turned him on. The lust for her mingled with rage that he thought she had been flirting with the detective turned him into a ferocious, punishing machine.

Huffing with exertion, he bent over her, grabbed a fistful of her hair and jerked her head up, twisting it so he could spit his enraged words in her face. "This will teach you to look at another male, my darling wife. This is gentle compared to what I'll do if I catch you flirting with a man again."

He shoved Laurin's tear ravaged face, smashing it into the duvet. Sobs wracked her shoulders, she tried to hold back the shrieks but they rambled up her throat and into the bed. And he just whipped her harder, up and down her back, her legs, arms, across the back of her head.

After what seemed like forever, he finally tired and tossed the belt to a chair. Her body heaving with agony, she heard his zipper slide open.

Shoving his trousers down to his thighs, Rádolfo pushed her legs wider apart, aimed, and rammed straight into his wife's tender channel with no preparation. Her silent screams hitched out as he drove into her again and again, deliberately slamming her hips into the footboard with each thrust.

Pausing, panting for breaths, he leaned over so she could hear him. "Buck up, darling, we have all night. I have other things planned for your screwing around with that fucking cop. So, hold on, baby, I'm nowhere near done with you," and plunged viciously over and over.

Even if anyone could hear her screams, no one would have been brave enough to try to interfere.

# Chapter Six

Eden Lombardo patted her hair admiring herself in the shop window. A cunning smile curled her full lips, feeling the rush of adrenalin making her heart beat faster, her hand went to her chest. She couldn't believe her luck!

Who would have thought that man would want to have a private rendezvous with her? The smile grew bigger, a delicious shiver rippled through her body zinging at the apex of her thighs.

When she'd met him at the club, Eden never dreamed the gorgeous hunk of man would ask her to go to his opulent cabin with him. He had promised her brunch on the deck overlooking the water. Eggs Benedict and champagne after hot heavy sex with kinky prime meat while watching watercraft whizz by, come on, what could be better? Well, shopping in France, but still, the best runner up!

She turned to the side and studied her reflection. Sliding a palm down her slightly plump figure, Eden straightened her spine so her heavy breasts would lift and bow out more, she sucked her pouchy tummy in.

"Sure," she spoke out loud, "I'm pretty enough to get any guy I want, after all, I captured a stock broker for heaven's sake. But, him...I had dreamed about him when I heard the rumors of how he is in bed. Scary rough, violent even, seriously dominant. The kind of alpha male I'm attracted to. Heck, he'd even been tossed out of the club due to complaints of his extreme sadistic roughness."

Eden sighed as a pulsating throb started between her legs. "But that's the stuff that gets me hot! My Dante is too much of a milk-toast to play on the wild, kinky side."

She glanced around with a frown, looked down at the diamond encrusted watch on her wrist. "He's late, twenty minutes. I hope he hasn't changed his mind."

One more pat on her fluffy blonde curls, she'd give him another thirty minutes, I mean, really, it was *him*, he was worth waiting for! Yet, the longer he took to get there, the less time they'd have to spend together before she had to meet her husband for dinner at the country club.

Early on a Saturday morning, most of the stores were still closed and very few people were out and about. A car door slamming had her looking down the street, and a breath of relief released the tension in her shoulders, a tingling thrill whistled through her.

There he was, standing next to a black van. Not his of course, he wouldn't get caught dead in such a cheap common vehicle. He must have parked further down the street.

Eden was about to wave when she saw him abruptly drop to one knee. "Oh! Oh dear!" She minced in her high heels down the walk rushing to help him.

When she reached him, he was still crouched on one knee. "Oh," she gushed breathless, "are you all right? Did you trip? Here, let me help you-" A gasp chopped from Eden as he suddenly stood up, grabbed her and threw her into the open side door of the van.

Before she could gather her wits and scream, he was on her. Dropping his heavier body on hers to contain her, one hand over her mouth, he jabbed the needle into her neck.

Eden squirmed, screamed against his palm, eyes wide with confusion and fear. When he felt her body slowly still, stop fighting him, he sat back on his heels and grinned down at her. All the fight left her as she passed out.

"Ah, my sweet Eden, have I got a fun day planned for us!" Just to be safe, he bound her wrists and ankles and taped her mouth closed.

Sliding backwards out of the van, he rolled the door shut with a scraping bang and climbed inside the truck through the passenger side, then slid over to sit in the driver's seat. Twisting around to look at his prize, he asked her, "Are you excited, Eden? I sure am."

Swinging around, he whistled a tune as he pulled out of the parking spot and sped off, but carefully within the speed limit, to the highway that would take them to his special little hideaway.

Her head felt tingly, it was difficult to draw a deep breath, pins and needles prickled throughout her body. Her muddled brain buzzing, Eden fought to crack open her fuzzy eyes, and then wished she hadn't. The pins and needles exploded with a vengeance. Her torso was horribly, painfully arched backwards, she couldn't move her limbs.

"Ah, you're finally awake. I've been getting antsy waiting for you to come around," he said cheerfully as he sauntered from the doorway to where she was…placed.

"How do ya like my apparatus?" He swept his hand in an arc around the room. "All handmade, my dear, are you impressed?"

The windowless room was made up of a combination of metal and wood. Tools lined the walls, a steel table was layered with all kinds of knives, each one bigger than the last.

Also on the table appeared to be vials with liquid in them, and an assembly of syringes and rags, electrical tape and twine, and a pair of scissors. And of all things, a curling iron, plugged in, the little red light was lit.

In one corner sat a huge, three-sided wooden box, a thick length of unusual chain hung from the top of it. She couldn't take in the rest of the items when her heart skipped a beat at seeing a stack of blue tarps, and one was spread out directly under her.

Eden sucked in several breaths, trying to deepen each one to get oxygen to her brain so she could comprehend what the hell was going on. Her head swiveled slowly, pulse started jamming as she became aware that she was nude, lowering her eyes, she saw her clothes in tatters on the floor.

He'd cut them off her. Her head lolled slightly to the side, her breath caught in her lungs when she saw what she was bound to. "What-" the alarmed gasp gagged out of her throat that was rapidly tightening in escalating fear.

Her spine was bent around the curved side of a giant wooden wheel. Her arms and legs were spread apart and tied behind her to the center of the wheel. If the wheel rolled, she would get squashed. The rope was tied so tight she couldn't feel her hands, it cut into her wrists and ankles, the pain was unbelievable.

She wasn't on top of the thing, but tied so if she was loose, she would be standing up straight on her feet instead of bending around the curve. A rope strung under her ribs kept some of the stress off her arm-sockets from the weight of her body.

Gulping down the fright beginning to overwhelm her, she stuttered, "H- hey, listen, this is- too- way too-"

His lips turned down in a pout. "Aw, come on Eden, you've told everyone that would listen how much you love BDSM and you want it rough. I'm only giving you what you want, except," he shrugged one shoulder apologetically. "I'm not into caning and violet wands, that hot wax shit, no," smiling, he shook his head. "I have different tastes that I'm going to share with you today, sweet Eden."

He stepped closer, between her spread legs, and pawed her fat breasts. Slapping them back and forth, at first lightly, then harder, he stopped to squeeze them roughly and smiled. "Ya like that, doncha, hon?"

He pinched her nipples then gave them a wicked twist, she yelped. "And that?" He carefully studied her reactions. Sniffing loudly, he grinned. "I can smell you, honey, you are quickly aroused aren't you?"

Eden surprised herself, she had instantly grown wet, goose bumps ruffled up her arms. "I- I- oh!" She gasped when he suddenly thrust his fingers up her. Her moan oozed ragged, sweat broke out on her bare skin.

Smiling at her body's obvious aroused response, he expertly worked her with his fingers. "Yeah, this is what you wanted, right?

A little bondage, maybe some fright to whip up the old libido, that whole pain and pleasure thing, eh?"

Her hips wriggled at his busy hand, her exhalation coarse, Eden gasped, sucked in a breath, the moan a husky scrape, "Uhng, yes, no, it's too- the ropes on my arms and legs, they're too- too tight. But, ahh," she hissed as he worked her up to a tizzy of roaring heat.

As uncomfortable as she was, she was still already on the edge, about to shoot off the cliff- "Hey," she squawked when he removed his hand and stood back from her.

Turning to the metal table next to the wheel, he rubbed his chin and frowned in concentration at the implements.

"Hey!" she barked. "Wait, you- you didn't finish, I'm not, I haven't…" She groaned with a full body writhe. Her teeth clenched at the shiver undulating through her.

"Are you going to, uh, keep me tied like this when you bang me? Are," her eyes widened when he picked up a knife. "Uh, no, really, I don't get off on knife play. I don't want to-" Mouth suddenly dry, she licked her lips, begged, "Please, no."

"Okay." He grinned at her and set the knife down. The breath of relief she expressed blew out in a rush. He picked up a syringe attached to an IV and turned to her with his cheerful smile. "I forgot the most important first part. Here, you're gonna love this, I sure will."

Her head moved to follow him as he hung the IV over a piece of wood that jutted from the back of the wheel and moved over to stand beside her.

Craning her neck at the syringe, voice trembling, she said, "You, uh, aren't going to- to stick that in me, are you? I don't do drugs, it's a hard limit with me. I'm ready for just, uh, straight vanilla sex now, okay? You can untie me, okay?"

She felt him grip her upper arm, but couldn't see what he was doing, he was moving out of her line of vision behind her. Nervously, she asked, "No, please, what is it? I don't want to, please, stop, noooo…" she wailed as he plunged the needle into the vein at the top of her hand.

Taping the needle to her hand, he murmured jauntily, "There we go, hon. Nice and easy." Giving her an award winning smile, he moved back to between her and the metal table containing the instruments.

Her eyes watered as she watched him set the tape down and pick the knife back up.

Returning to stand in front of her, he touched the end of the blade, grinning at the confusion creasing her face as the realization that her body was slowly freezing up sunk in.

"Whaa," Eden couldn't form the words, couldn't make her mouth work, couldn't even blink.

Moving the knife closer to her, he said, "Okay, this is the fun part, for me anyway. So, what I gave you is called vecuronium bromide." He smiled at her slow blink.

"Of course, you don't know what that is. Little Kimi did, but then she worked in a hospital. Well, it's used in surgery to paralyze the body so it doesn't move during an operation. Thing is, you're supposed to add a sedation so you're knocked out and don't feel the pain."

He suddenly slashed an X on her stomach, blood spurted instantly. A scream gurgled, trapped in her frozen throat.

"See?" he said with excitement. "You can feel the pain, right? But you can't move to escape it, not even a squirm or a twitch. Cool, huh?" He made another slashing X, her belly hitched, tears filled her eyes.

After several more slashes, the blood trickled down her belly to between her legs then down to pool on the blue tarp beneath her.

"Oh hell," he cursed, snapping his fingers rolling his eyes. "I forgot to mention, one also needs to provide you know, a breathing tube. Without intubation, you'll, well, die, you know, suffocate." He nodded to an oxygen tank with a tube attachment by the metal table.

"But, I got ya covered, for a while anyway. Unfortunately, I forgot about this part with Kimi, and, she was so brave, but it cut our time too short. I barely got all my carving and burning done before she passed. I had to do all the rest after she was dead. But," his sigh swooshed with a grin, "I've learned my lesson, Eden, so you and I get to spend all night together. Aren't you as thrilled as I am?"

Another slow blink was the only response she could give, but terror radiated from her blue eyes. Those eyes tracked him as he set the knife down and picked up the curling iron.

Grinning, he said, "Oh don't worry, we're not done with the knife, we're just going to take a little detour with this curling iron. It makes the biggest prettiest burn circles, ya know? Much more fun than a plain ol' cigarette. Am I right?"

She couldn't blink but her eyes seemed to widen further. He studied her, and smiled. "It's amazing that your eyes can still move. Cool."

Snickering at the horror reflecting back at him, he stuck the heated end of the iron into the center of the heart-shaped circle he was slicing on her body and crowed eagerly as her skin shriveled and blistered around the red mark.

"Oh yeah, that's it, that's great!" He leaned in close, squinting to scrutinize her face, then nodded with a smile.

"Yepper, you can feel it. Your damned eyes are seizing up, now that's new, way cool. One thing you don't need to worry your pretty little head about, it'll take quite a while before the oxygen runs out. I mean, I did promise we'd spend the whole day together. Great, huh?" And he shoved the iron into her stomach again. A gurgle of agony leaching in her chest was music to his ears.

He bent over so he could examine his handiwork, sniffing long and hard, he inhaled the rank odor of her burning flesh. "Ahh, now that's nice. That's real perfume." Grinning with delight, he watched her skin sizzle.

"Fries just like baloney, Eden, you should see it. Can you smell it? You're gonna be immortalized as one of my Gold Girls, aren't you proud?"

While he peered at the cuts and burns, he smiled sweetly up at her and asked, "You still want me to get you off, hon? I know," he grinned while shaking his head abashed, "I promised you I would. So, I'll let the meds wear down, then we can fuck, and then do this all over again. What do you say?"

# Chapter Seven

**H**ix put just his fingertips on the small of her back to guide her, he hated to even touch her that much, it would only make her think this was a real date. "Here, uh, Carmen," he motioned to a pew, "let's sit here."

The tall brunette gave him a look as she slid past him, she admonished, "That's Carmella, Penn, and that's the third time I've reminded you. You do it again and I'll think you're only bringing me to this wedding to appease your mother, when," she caught the top of his tie to pull his head down, "we both know there's red hot attraction between us, right?"

She snuggled up to him with a wide smile of red lips and blindingly white teeth declaring, "The best part will come after the reception. We going to your place or mine, Detective?"

Resisting an eye-roll which would have brought teasing laughter from his sister if she saw it, because that was something a hardened soldier did not do, he gave her a nudge pushing her to take a seat.

Carmella settled on the hard bench and slid over for him to join her. She moved to sit near the older man and woman that were already in the pew.

The church was filling up quickly. Hix stared down at his phone, texting, to avoid conversation with the exhaustingly vivacious Carmella.

At Hix's noncommittal grunted responses, she turned to the man beside her and rattled on in Spanish. Which, Hix wasn't sure if the old guy understood her or not, but it didn't seem to matter when her dress was so low cut much of her voluminous breasts were exposed.

"Huh," Hix thought to himself, he bet the old guy didn't even know what color the inflatable doll's eyes were. For that matter, neither did Hix, because he didn't care. The man's wife was busy leafing through her Bible. The wedding was taking place an hour after the regular church service had ended.

Hix's head was bowed over the phone he held in his lap, but his eyes shifted up to the bright blonde hair in front of him. He'd chosen the seat behind her on purpose. Mrs. Ajanel. Like his brother had said, the woman was a damned male magnet, and he was a chunk of male iron.

As soon as he spotted her, against his will and internal argument to stay away, his feet bee-lined to sit directly behind her.

Suddenly, a small head popped up on the left side of her and grinned at him. Surprisingly, Hix couldn't help but grin back at the cute little imp. The unnatural lift to his lips felt weird. But nice.

He occasionally played with his niece and nephew and during those times the sides of his lips lifted slightly in affection. His mother and sister could also very rarely pull a slight curve to his tough mouth that fortunately was hidden by his short dark beard. But a full grin? Never.

"Hi!" the boy about shouted, all dark curly hair and bright round eyes.

"Hey little man, what's your name?"

Chiclet teeth grinned at Hix. Clutching a tiny truck in his hand, big brown eyes twinkled with mischief, he said, "Me is Benji. Mama says I gonna be four, real soon!" He shouted every word.

Mrs. Ajanel turned to him with a gentle admonishment, "Shh, honey, we have to be very, very quiet now, like we talked about at home, remember? Now, turn around like a good boy, I brought animal crackers and a small picture book you can look at until Papa-Ray comes."

"But, Mama, he a nice man," Benji pouted then flashed his mischievous grin again at Hix. Hix winked at him bringing giggles to the boy.

"I know, sweetheart, come, face forward now, don't bother the nice-" she turned around fully to pull the boy around to sit. Her eyes popped when she saw Hix was the nice man.

"Oh, I'm so sorry, Detective, I won't let him bother you." Her face flushed as she was probably recalling the vitriolic words he had spouted so meanly to her at the charity ball.

His grin gone, Hix nodded politely and said, "Boy is no bother, Mrs. Ajanel. Please call me Hix, or Penn, my first name."

"Penn! Penn! Penn!" Benji hollered, everyone sitting around them laughed.

Hix couldn't help it, his head fell forward with his own chuckle.

"Oh dear, Benji honey, our indoor voice, remember?" She tilted her head at Hix with an apologetic half-smile. "I'm sorry, Detective Hixman, he rarely goes out. He's not allowed-" she bit the words off, a deeper blush colored her round cheeks.

Hix couldn't take his eyes off her. The girl was beyond stunning. He'd thought her eyes were black, like his, but he saw up close they were a deep blue, sapphire, riveting. Like those anime characters. Captivated, he couldn't look away, he muttered, "Hix, or Penn, please, Mrs. Ajanel."

His gaze strolled over her face. Pink and cream came to his mind, like pink peonies. "Can I, uh, call you, what's your first name?" In his mind he had called her 'Boutique' thinking she was likely high maintenance.

He had wanted to Google her, it had been a struggle to resist it. He didn't want to read about the crap she was supposedly involved in up in Washington.

The blush darkened further. Without answering she ducked her head, the long, straight blonde hair, like corn silk showered over her face.

Hix glanced at the boy who was now running his truck across the back of the pew making vroom vroom sounds. Rolling the truck back and forth he yelled, "Pa-Ray call mommy La-win." He dragged the name out with a lisp, "Wid a i i i i Pa-Ray says!"

"I see, thank you, little man. What kind of truck is that? Looks like what I drive." His eyes on Laurin, he spoke to the engaging child. People shuffled onto the seat on the other side of him.

His date was babbling at the man next to her, and the one behind, to the chagrin of their women. Carmella's dress dipped dangerously low, Hix thought it was tacky to wear such a burlesque outfit to a church. The red dress was skintight and barely covered her ass.

Hix was embarrassed to be seen with her. She reminded him of the faceless whores the military leaders brought to the camps for the soldiers to release their pent-up energy on when they weren't out in the field fighting so they wouldn't brawl amongst themselves. Good for a quick drilling and then back to practice; boxing, fencing, MMA, shooting, anything and everything to make them into perfect, indestructible fighting machines.

After his fiancée killed their baby and ditched him, he screwed anything put in front of him with a vengeance. Once he escaped the military he became much more circumspect. Picky, his brother had called him.

Benji shouted, "Mama say it a pick-up truck! Right, Mommy?"

People chuckled at the cute kid.

Laurin lifted her head with a gorgeous warm smile and ruffled the boy's dark hair. "You bet, Peanut. Listen sweetheart," she lowered her voice, "if you turn around and be very, very quiet, when we get home we'll take Poochie out for a walk, would you like that?"

The child's brow furrowed, he shook his head solemnly. "Can't, Mama. Pa-Ray won't let us outside." He turned his little face up to hers. "Can I get another truck, so this un don't get lonely?"

Hix could literally feel the sadness envelope Laurin, and pour off the boy in waves. The roses left her cheeks, the pretty plump lips turned down, and the saddest light he'd ever seen darkened her eyes.

His heart actually crimped at the sight. The loneliness in the child's voice was heartbreakingly palpable. The kid felt so lonely he thought his truck would too.

Laurin shook her head. "No, darling, you know Papa, um," aware people were listening, she said quietly, "turn around now Benji, you promised you would be good. Okay?" She whispered, but Hix heard her words, "If you don't behave, you know Papa won't let us come to church again."

The boy nodded solemnly. "Bye mister nice man," he said forlornly to Hix and reluctantly turned around.

Peeping through a wisp of straight bangs that almost hid her gorgeous eyes, again, Laurin apologized. "I'm sorry, Detective, I'll keep him busy so he won't bother you."

Keeping his face from hardening into a scowl, Hix repeated, "I said he's no bother, Laurin."

The soft music in the background started growing louder, indicating the wedding was about to begin.

Hix started to say something else to keep Laurin from turning away from him, when she was suddenly bumped, hard. Her husband slid in next to her.

Rádolfo Ajanel dropped a heavy arm around Laurin's shoulders and squeezed her against him. Hix turned his head as soon as he saw him so Ajanel wouldn't recognize him, he didn't want a repeat of the charity event. Hix leaned forward in the pretext of grasping the Bible in front of him and looked over the pew.

Benji was utterly still and silent, his head down, the truck clasped tightly in his hands in his lap, he was hiding it. Beside him, Laurin was sliding his picture book under her thigh, hiding that as well. Huh. What's that all about?

Ajanel hadn't said a word to the boy, didn't even look over at him. His big hand moved to Laurin's thigh, high up.

She set a hand between his hand and further up her thigh apparently as a block from him taking blatant liberties not only in front of the child but while they were in public at a damned wedding in a damned church for shit's sake. Hix sat and fumed.

Carmella turned towards him and set her own hand on Hix's thigh. Hell, he knew how Laurin felt with unwanted intimate touches in public. He shook his head, no he didn't. Somehow he felt Laurin was trapped, Hix was not. He brushed Carmella's hand off his leg.

"Honey," she murmured, her perfume of gardenias and roses wrinkled his nose it was so strong. She tried to snuggle into him. Thankfully the music grew louder, a sign for the maids of honor to start down the aisle. The Wedding March began, and everyone rose, thank God. Hix about jumped to his feet.

Not his favorite thing, weddings, Hix stoically bore it, his mind on other things. Like the murder. Like the blonde in front of him. His brother and those nasty women at the party had said she was an adulteress, a murderous whore. He couldn't believe that beautiful shy, sweet young woman was capable of any of it.

But, he sighed, last time he believed that about a woman his fiancée aborted their child and ran off with another man while he was in a hospital recovering from wounds incurred during a deadly covert mission. Chantal had thought he was going to be a cripple and sent him a Dear John letter telling him she couldn't deal with it.

He hadn't been allowed home much while growing up so he hadn't learned a mother's care. So, between Chantal's betrayal, and camp prostitutes, they were the only females he had contact with, he had learned his lesson. Women were conniving bitches that were good for only one thing, otherwise, he steered clear of them.

The wedding went on and on, he tried to keep his eyes open. Pushing Carmella's travelling fingers away did help keep him awake.

Finally, the bride and groom grinning foolishly, holding hands, sailed down the rose-petal covered aisle together, the maids and ushers followed. Everyone stood up clapping and cheering.

"Great," Carmella yawned. "Onto the booze, come on Penn, I gotta get a drink."

The couple beside him slid out and got up to stand in the aisle. They held hands, smiling like two lovers in love. The man lowered his head to kiss the woman but she blushed and put her hand to his chest to stop him. "Will, we're not alone," but she giggled up at him.

Will rolled his arm around her. "Sorry, babe, the wedding just made me think of ours. You remember that night, Chelsea? Remember when we-"

"Will Brown!" The blush brightened, the young woman put two fingers over her husband's mouth and scolded, "Hush now!" He laughed and hugged her to his side, then led her down the aisle.

Hix stood watching them with a slight smile. Musing on how he actually envied the couple their closeness, intimacy, how they were not too shy or too uptight to show their love for each other.

To some extent, physically they resembled Hix and Laurin, the man Will was tall and dark, his wife much smaller and fairer. *Hell,* Hix told himself, Laurin belonged to another man. The slug standing beside her.

"Chels, come on!" A small woman pushed through the throng to reach the couple. "Chels, you guys, Sammy said he'd meet me at the bar next door to the reception, hurry up, I don't want him to see I'm not there and hook up with someone else!"

Chelsea smiled with affection at her sister. "We're coming, Annalisa, Sammy's in lust, he'll wait for you, he's called you every night since Creamz," she and her husband laughed together.

Will chucked his sister-in-law's chin and popped her on the end of her nose. "Sam has the hots for you, Annsies, he'll wait. You go on to the bar, we're going to the reception. We'll catch up with you tomorrow. We'll set up a night for dinner and we can meet him."

"Yeah, yeah, okay then, come on." Annalisa grasped her sister's wrist and dragged her towards the front of the sanctuary with Will chuckling following behind.

Carmella moved out and pressed the front of her body up against Hix's. "I can't wait to dance with you, Penny, those big strong arms around me, oo," she wriggled a faux shiver. "What's Penn short for, anyway?" she asked, rubbing her chest over his.

Rolling his eyes, he replied not caring if the irritation was audible in his voice, "It's just Penn, Carmen. And knock off the Penny crap." His attention was on the people in the pew in front of them.

Ajanel leaned over and said something in Laurin's ear. Her face appeared to relax a shade. Ignoring the boy who did not look at him either, Ajanel left the pew and pushed his way through the crowd gathering in the aisle and disappeared through the door.

The reception was being held in a large room where the church held functions and special dinners. The Loud music already blared from the hallway.

Hix observed both Laurin and Benji's body language alter.

Their shoulders lowered and softened as if taut rubber bands loosened, held breaths oozed out, the boy's head tipped up, he smiled at his mother. Both of their deportments had morphed completely opposite from the frozen statues they had been when Ajanel had been present.

Holding Benji's hand, Laurin stepped into the open aisle and bumped right into Hix.

"Oh!" There went that pretty blush again. "I'm so sorry, Detective, I didn't see you. I guess this is my day of apologies." Her slender shoulders twittered elegantly with her embarrassment.

Hix had deliberately placed himself so when she turned she'd run right into him. His hands moved up to grasp her arms to steady her. He didn't let go.

"Peeennnyy," Carmella whined. She was standing behind him about to follow the crowd to the reception hall. "Come on," the whine droned, "I wanna drink."

Hix sighed, he said to her, "Carmen, why don't you go on and grab us a table. Order a bourbon neat for me. I'm gonna step outside for a smoke." He reluctantly let go of Laurin's arms.

Groaning dramatically, Carmella snapped, "That's Carmella, Penny, get it?" She pivoted and stalked down the aisle, big butt swaying side-to-side in an exaggerated strut.

Covering his sigh of relief, Hix put his hand on top of Benji's curly head and ruffled the brown locks. His head down towards the boy, he said nonchalantly to Laurin, "So, where'd your husband go?"

Smiling down at her son, Laurin replied, "He has business with some of the guests."

Hix raised his head and their gazes connected. *Oh hell*, he felt that spark of electricity like a jolt of lightning. Words flew out of his fried brain, he could only stand there and gawk.

Was he nuts? The girl was a violent immoral tramp, for cripe's sake. He told himself the attraction was purely physical, a totally normal reaction of a red-blooded male to a drop dead gorgeous female with a rocking body. When he realized he was leaning in to inhale her scent, he shook himself. All that crap about pheromones being a scent of attraction was apparently true.

"Mr. Man!" Benji shouted, waving his truck. "Mama says we gonna have cake! I love cake! Do you love cake?"

Hix and Laurin laughed at the joyful boy. He had become unfrozen the second his father left them, like a wooden puppet come to life.

"*Aiwa,* uh, that is yeah," Hix shared a grin with Laurin. "I do love me some cake." Although he'd worked hard to not slip, when he was distracted, like now, he tended to revert to his native language. And he had grinned again, the child was infectious.

Rolling his truck along the pew bench, Benji said, "You sound funny, you talk different than Mama."

Laurin went to apologize again, but Hix held up a hand with a smile. That very rare smile. "It's okay, Laurin," her name felt sensual on his lips, it rolled out differently on his accented tongue.

He lowered to his haunches to be closer to Benji's height. "That's because I'm from a land far far away from here."

The boy's eyes widened. "You mean like Never Never Land? Do you know Peter Pan? You got a beard like Cap'n Hook! Are you a pirate?"

Hix couldn't help but chuckle, he nodded. "Yeah, like Never Never Land, but I don't know Peter Pan, and no, I know I look like one, but I'm not a pirate." Peripherally he saw Laurin smile warmly at the child, and that set off butterflies in his gut. He found it hard to believe this sweet, soft, loving mother could be the cold-hearted bitch the media described.

She was clearly petrified of her husband, the boy was equally terrified of Ajanel, why would she subject them to that terror? Was she somehow being held prisoner? Rádolfo Ajanel was a suspected criminal doyen, Hix wouldn't put it past the bastard to ensnare a woman against her will.

"So, Laurin," his voice soft, he said, "how about since you're on your own for the moment, I buy you a drink?"

Her smile sobered, eyes lowered. "What about your date, won't she be um, displeased to have company? She's so pretty."

It appeared to Hix that Laurin compared herself to Carmella and found herself lacking. To Hix it was quite the opposite. Carmella was flamboyant and overtly sexy, trashy sexy, larger-boned, brash and loud. And, he suspected much of the narcissistic woman's body had been purchased. Plastic wasn't his thing.

Laurin was petite and delicate with delectable natural curves, spoke softly, and was sweet and kind, patient and loving with her son. Her characteristics so opposite to his own. Except for the violent part. He was having more and more a hard time believing that this beautiful girl that smelled like fresh wild flowers could kill anything, even an ant.

He'd forgotten all about what's-her-name. "Ah, she's not exactly my date, my mother kind of talked me into taking her. Carmella is my mother's friend's daughter. Carmella is relatively new in town. My brother is actually the one that's friends with the wedding couple. But my brother is occupied so my mother's friend asked my mother to ask me if I would escort the girl to the wedding. We've actually only met a couple of times before and I guess she asked her mother to talk to my, ah," *fuck, why was he rambling on like a teenager?*

Muttering, "Anyway," he could feel his neck heating in embarrassment.

Her expression was puzzled, yet Laurin was smiling at him, apparently shyly amused at his babbling.

He cleared his throat and asked, "So how about that drink? We'll get the little guy a soda or lemonade. They'll start the buffet soon, growing boys are always hungry."

Oh crap, was he actually using a child to hit on some guy's wife? Only a real prick would do that. He needed to back right the heck off, right now, he needed to head out…now. But she kept smiling at him. And he wanted more of it.

Unfortunately the smile left when she spoke. "Detective, you've met my husband. I can't have a drink with you." Her head swiveled around as if she anxiously searched for her husband to suddenly pounce on them. Her voice lowered to a whisper, "I shouldn't even be speaking to you."

"Even as friends? With the boy present?" He was such a jerkoff, why couldn't he just shut himself up? He stood in her way making it impossible for her to pass by. A gentleman would move. Hix had never pretended to be a gentleman except with his family whom he loved, and co-workers he had to get along with. His dress boots stayed glued to the rose-petal covered carpet.

Her eyes fell downcast, voice hushed, she said, "No, not with any man. Or any woman either if he or a family member isn't present." She blinked up at him and said firmly, "Besides, even though you're just offering a friendly drink, I certainly would not disrespect my husband by having a drink with another man."

"Yeah," Benji spoke up between vroom vrooms. He said absently, "Pa-Ray hit Mommy bad when she talkin' to mens. We not allowed to go out a lot." The wheels rumbling over the wood, he raced the truck down the pew and back up to where the adults were standing.

Laurin's face burst with red.

Hix felt like he got punched in the gut. "Laurin, you-"

Laurin grabbed her son's wrist and tugged him out of the pew. "We have to go, there'll be a car waiting for us." She sidled around Hix, he had to move or he'd be a pervy cad.

"Laurin," Hix called, starting after her, "wait!" *Let her go you creeper*, he admonished himself but his boots kept moving.

Moving down the aisle, clutching Benji, tears in her eyes, she said over her shoulder, "We're not going to the reception. Rádolfo will be attending due to business, Benji and I are to be taken home."

Benji bounced up and down. "Pa-Ray wonnta let us have cake. I forgot, Mama, he said that, right?"

Laurin smiled sadly at her son. "Right, sweetheart. That's why we're having our own cake at home, remember?" She said to Hix,

"We have to go, nice, um seeing you, Detective, um, Hixman." Pulling a bouncing Benji along, she hurried away from him.

"That's Penn, Laurin," Hix muttered after her. His phone buzzed in his pocket. His eyes on the beautiful blonde disappearing out the door, he slid it out of his pocket. "Hixman," he snapped irately into the cell.

"Whoa, pard," Thomas Princeton chuckled, "what burr got up your ass?"

"Nothing, never mind. What's up?" Hix raked his fingers in agitation through his thick black hair.

Princeton's tone turned somber. "We got another one, Penn."

Hix sucked in a breath. "You talking another girl in a box?"

"Yeah. Not too far from the other one. Bingham and Third."

"On my way." Hix clicked off then texted Carmella that he had to leave and he'd leave his credit card number with a car service for her for when she was ready to go. After making the call to the service, he shoved the phone in his pocket and strode quickly to the exit.

As he hopped in his truck and turned the ignition on, his cell buzzed. Swiping it he read the text. He had put the first dead girl through photo rec when her prints didn't come up in the system, the text stated he got a hit. Kimi Consuelo, 26, 5'4. Sarg was right on the money. Her address was included. They could match her prints now.

He dialed. A man answered, "Klaus."

"Kurt," Hix said. "I'm on my way to a fresh one. Grab Teague and some crime techs and go to the address I'm gonna text you. We ID'd the girl in the box. Check her place, you know the drill, neighbors, job, friends, boyfriends. I'll catch you later to go over what you come up with."

Clicking off, he steered from the curb and hurtled towards the new crime scene.

# Chapter Eight

**H**ix parked behind Thomas Princeton's SUV and jumped out. It was the same scene, but not an alley this time, but behind a small strip mall.

The three-walled, big wooden box with a roof and floor and a small barred window in the back, curlicues carved in the frame and a chain, everything basically the same, yet slightly different was there.

He noted gratefully the police had quickly put up a forensic tent to block the cameras including the news copters buzzing in circles above the site.

Last thing they needed was a picture all over the newspapers and web of a naked woman on her knees painted rose-gold, perched twelve inches outside of a huge box, hands bound behind her back.

Hix took photos of the scene with his phone, then moved close up to the victim.

Her head lolled to the side, gold painted hair draped in one solid mass over part of her face. Her body was held upright by the chain attached to a clamp around her neck that was strung up and tied to the top of the box.

Hix strode around to get a view of the front of her. Same wide-eyed frozen horror.

Detective Princeton noticed Hix arrive. Leaving an officer he was speaking with, Prince ambled over to join him. "Blonde, blue again, Penn, relatively petite, although this one was on the plump side. Close to the same age but a little older." Their heads lowered in unison.

"Identical cutting and burn pattern," Princeton stated the obvious.

"Yeah," Hix murmured, his eyes roving over the girl, the box, the perimeter of the scene.

Police and forensic techs milled around the area. Cars were pulling up and parking in the street behind the mall. Spectators climbed out and were gathering with curiosity at the activity.

Hix asked, "Anyone see anything?"

His arms crossed, Princeton glanced around the area. They were standing in the parking lot behind the strip mall, responder vehicles were parked close by, reporters and civilians were kept back by police. Even with all the people rambling about, conversations were hushed, the atmosphere felt eerie.

They were near the back doors, only trash dumpsters and beer bottles in sight. A brisk wind had picked up, it stirred and swept litter along the weathered blacktop.

Shrugging, Princeton replied, "Nope. She was found before the stores opened, not much traffic foot or car. No surveillance cameras either."

"Okay, Thomas, who's in charge?"

Princeton waved an officer over.

The man hoofed right to the men. "Sirs," he nodded with his greeting.

"Officer," Hix glanced at his nametag, said, "Rosemont."

"Sir."

"Sergeant Sinclair coming?" Hix asked him.

"Yessir, on his way."

"All right. Tell him to call me when he's finished up here and the canvass is completed. I'll be at the morgue."

"Yessir."

Prince commented, "The word 'please' still not in your vocabulary?" Hix's grunted response brought a chuckle from Prince.

The two detectives headed to the building where the medical examiner was located.

They called ahead, met Doctor Burke in his office. The burly man stood up behind his desk when the detectives entered. As he moved, the fluorescent light shone over his shaved pate and made the gold hoop earring glisten. "Boys," he greeted, his voice gruff, the long beard shifted with his jaw. "Have seats," he motioned to chairs and sat back down.

Hix and Princeton settled down in front of the desk in chairs with thick leather cushions.

"You said you completed your exam of Kimi Consuelo," Hix started.

Burke nodded. "I have. Tox just came in. Considering the circumstances, I set the other bodies aside to go right to work on her."

"Brevet Bay ain't that big, Doc, how many homicides you got?" Prince asked with a raised sandy brow.

Burke rested his big shoulders against the back of the large office chair, the leather squeaking from his bulk. His smile placid with a hint of condensation, he replied, "There's murder in every town, as you boys know, fuck's sake, it's your job. If it's at all suspicious, I have to do an autopsy. Some deaths are just accidents, or suicides, but I still have to work 'em. Anyhew," he tapped on the computer in front of him with stout fingers. "All right, Kimi Consuelo. She had been tortured. Horribly."

"Clearly," Prince mumbled.

Doc's lips pulled in as he read the screen. "She had some bruising on her knees and arms, those could have happened when she was abducted. The knees had abrasions, she was discovered kneeling on rough asphalt."

Hix said, "There was no paint anywhere except on the body, so the killer spray-painted her before he brought her to the site. Did the abrasions show through the gold?"

"Some of them. So the abrasions occurred while he took her and also when he was posing her. The twine around her wrists wasn't the one that originally bound her. There were several different loop markings around her arms and wrists by a slightly thicker rope. But those dug deep enough to cut into her wrists, so deep they would have bled pretty well.

"She struggled hard, fought for her life, desperate to get free. There was no blood on any part of her body when she was found." He tapped some more.

Hix muttered, "He cleaned her before painting her."

The Doc concurred with a brief head motion. "He did. So it would appear she was situated the way she was, bound with her arms behind her back for a deliberate reason, because she was already dead, he hadn't needed to restrain her. He had distinctly posed her. There were rope burns around her ankles, but they weren't bound when she was found. There are other marks I'm still investigating. Lividity indicates she died while she was upright."

"Like standing?" Hix asked. "Bind a woman then kill her while she was standing there? That sounds odd."

"Nothing not odd about this whole thing, Detective," Burke responded.

Prince inquired, "Was she killed with a knife? You know anything about the knife? The burns on her stomach? Were they from cigarettes? Or cigars, they would make bigger circles."

"No," his eyes on the screen, Burke replied, shaking his head. "Larger than a paring knife but he only used the tip to slice the X's in her stomach. I'm guessing so they'd hurt like a bitch and bleed like crazy, but she wouldn't die too quickly.

"The burns aren't from cigarettes or cigars, they aren't ragged markings, there's no ash or paper in the wounds. The circles are flat and actually perfect circles. Perhaps from some type of metal rod, or circles like quarters. Wasn't quarters though, there's no design burnt into her skin, the item was flat. Also, there was residue from electrical tape on her mouth."

"Uh huh," Hix grunted. "COD, Doc?"

Burke squinted an eye at him. "Patience, boy. As I was saying, the clamp was heavy and tight, if she'd been alive when it was put on her there would have been bruises on her neck, and it was clamped over the paint. So, she was dead when bound the way she was found, but she was alive when he cut and burned her belly. He cleaned her but there was still blood in the wounds."

Both detectives shifted in their seats, Princeton winced, Hix had zero expression.

Doc's eyes bolted back and forth as he read the screen, he said, "She had an intravenous injection of vecuronium bromide in her system. I found pinpricks on the back of one of her hands, that's how it was administered."

"What is that?" Princeton asked. Leaning forward, he clasped his hands and rested them on his thighs.

Hix sat back and set an ankle on a knee, crossed his arms, prepared to learn something new. Something that could hopefully help the investigation.

"Vecuronium bromide is like succinylcholine." At the detectives' blank stares, he explained, "Some call it a muscle relaxant. It's that and more. It's used in surgery to paralyze the body so it doesn't jerk around and the doctors can easily intubate the patient."

"Uh, layman's," Princeton requested, his forehead scrunched.

Burke folded his hands on the desk, his thick shoulders hunched. He turned his attention from the screen to the detectives. "The person is paralyzed so they can get the air tube down the patient's throat without them choking or gagging."

At the men's nodded heads, he went on, "In surgery, there's also a sedative given so the patient is unconscious and can't feel pain. In this victim's case, there is no evidence of sedation, but there were scraping inside her throat indicating a tube was used. He paralyzed her and issued her oxygen, but gave her nothing for the pain."

"For what reason?" Princeton asked, his mouth pursed as he considered the implications.

"Ah, Prince." Burke shifted his bulk uncomfortably. "I believe he wanted her to be fully conscious and aware of what he was doing. Fully feel every scintilla of excruciating pain of the cutting and burns, and be unable to move to fight him, or even scream.

"Unlike a fly pinned to a board, it can at least struggle, wriggle in its agony and fight to escape. This killer didn't want the victim to even have that, he wanted absolute omnipotent control, he played God. He made her watch and feel every single slice and burn he did to her, and made her helpless to even flinch or beg for mercy."

Prince turned a shade of green. He growled, "A fucking monster."

Hix's jaw worked, he'd seen horrors in his military days, he was never surprised at the unspeakable things one human being can do to another. He asked again, "COD?"

"Gettin' to that, son, chill." Burke smirked at the twitch of Hix's black brow.

"What happens is, the lack of sedation meant she felt everything, the lack of a breathing tube meant that eventually she died from lack of oxygen. He likely gave her a low dose of Vecuronium to keep her alive long enough to endure the torture before she succumbed. She also had minute traces of chloral hydrate. He gave her just enough to knock her out, probably when he originally abducted her."

His eyes flit from one detective to the other. "And, yeah, there was sexual assault, but I believe it was after she expired."

"Ew." Prince's lips twisted with repulsion.

"Exactly," Burke agreed, his mouth turned down hard. "There were extensive lacerations, horrible gouges, but no bleeding from the wounds, so it was after death. I'd say implements were use along with penile penetration. I discovered spermicide in her tissues. He cleaned her but due to the…damage he did, evidence was found in the ravaged tissues."

The three men sat stoically trying not to picture what torture the girl had gone through.

Doc told them, "I have training in forensic psychology, you see in some cases like this where he's enraged at someone, likely a female, and he's exerting his complete power and dominion over her with the torture and the final act of sexual penetration."

"Why screw her after she's dead? Makes no damned sense." Prince wiped his palm across his forehead that beaded with sweat.

There was a pair of glasses on the desk but Burke hadn't worn them to read the computer. He picked them up and tapped one end on the desk with the frames.

Answering Prince he said, "He's getting the last revengeful punch in, the last laugh. Or, sometimes the perp commits the assault because he really wants it to be someone else, so crazily he waits until his victim is dead so he's thinks technically he's not cheating, he's saving himself for the other female he really wants. Could be all sorts of deviant reasons."

His tongue hanging half out, Prince remarked with revulsion, "At least she was dead during that last assault, she didn't have to endure the final torment. You're right, I'm sure there's a ton of sick reasons for fornicating with a corpse."

"Yessir," Burke sighed, sitting back. "He could be just a sexual sadist and gets off on the victim's terror and pain. She may have even perished before he could rape her with her awareness that he was taking even her last dignity away but screwed her anyway as part of his ritual, or he was just plain horny."

"All boils down to control," Hix grunted.

The men were silent ruminating on the results of the exam and the doctor's words.

Hix muttered, "He ain't done. Already got another one."

"Yeah," Prince said, nodding glumly, "we got us a serial."

"No doubt," Burke agreed. "If he's done two, this symbolic kind of killer won't be satisfied with two kills. He'll do it until he's stopped."

# Chapter Nine

**T**wo days later, Hix and Prince rolled to the station. Driving past the wide driveway that arched a semi-circle at the front entrance with parking lots on either side of the station, they parked in back and entered through the back door.

Hix used his key card for the lock. They took the stairs up to the detective offices on the second floor of the half modern half rustic, red brick and white mortar building.

After checking in with their captain, the men headed for Princeton's office since Hix tended to just pile paperwork and shove it off to the side hoping someone would come along and either burn it or organize it and put it somewhere.

He didn't see why they were still using paper when everything can be entered, scanned and graphed in the computer. The stuff he wasn't proficient at could be handled by staff expert in computer science.

They had scheduled a meeting to take place in Prince's office and were right on time for it.

Inside Prince's pin-neat office awaited Sergeant Daron Sinclair and Officers Kurt Klaus and Emilee Rivera. They were sitting on chairs with wheels in front of a board one of them had brought in, a common murder board.

They had taped photos of both victims on the board, adding the locations of where they believe they were taken, and where they'd been discovered, their names, addresses, ages, physical descriptions, job information, family members, friends, boyfriends. Anything matching between the two had lines drawn connecting the information. So far the only connectors were the women's vague physical matches.

Penn Hixman and Thomas Princeton shrugged out of their suit coats and hung them on hangers then on hooks by the door and loosened their ties.

Hix crossed over to the board and stood intently studying it.

Prince dropped his notebook on his desk and pulled another chair over joining the others and sprawled on it.

"You've identified the second vic," Hix observed. He nodded a greeting to Sergeant Sinclair, "Sarg," to the officers, "Kurt, Officer Rivera."

Daron Sinclair stood up. He and the officers wore the brown uniforms with gold embossing of Brevet Bay. Daron replied, "Yep. Her prints were on file, had a DUI a few years back. I had officers jump right on her, went straight to her home, job, etc." Clasping his hands behind his back he said, "Reporters are already swarming her house."

Long legs bent at the knees, feet planted on the floor, Kurt Klaus revolved his chair back and forth on the wheels, his arms resting along the chair arms, he said, "Poop has hit the fan, the murders are all over the news. They posted the victims' personal photos and a loose rendition of how they were found.

"Fortunately, no pictures of the crime scenes have been released, but the media got a hold of descriptions of the box, chain, nudity, the gold paint, but not the COD or the cuts and burns. Those are being held under the lid until we have a suspect in custody."

His attention on the board, Hix murmured absently, "We need to speed shit up before another vic is taken, and the citizens start buying guns and shooting anyone who talks to them."

Reviewing the information recorded on the victims, Hix noted Kimi was 26, and the latest vic, Eden Lombardo was 28. He asked, "Anything more alike than their close ages, blonde hair, relative height?"

He peered at the notations, Eden was 5'3 and weighed 30 more pounds than Kimi Consuelo who was 5'4, "Their weight isn't that much off, Lombardo is a bit pudgy looks like."

Emilee Rivera noted, "They were both taken on the weekend. Possibly the perp works a regular day job."

"There were some differences in the MO of both women," Kurt supplied.

Everyone turned to him with expectancy.

He said, "Eden Lombardo had much more severe rope marks, burns from struggling according to the medical examiner. The marks were around her arms and ankles, and a length had crossed under her ribs. She," he paused, "was tied upright to…something. Don't have a clue what.

"According to Doc Burke she was bound off the ground, her shoulders had been dislocated from the gravity of her weight pulling on them. Kimi had some rope burns but nowhere near the damage Eden suffered. Kimi's shoulders weren't dislocated. Kind of solidifies Doc's theory that the killer mistakenly killed Kimi too soon."

The room was quiet as they pictured the additional torture and prolonged terror that Eden Lombardo had been subjected to. Kurt's head was down perusing his notes. He stood up to add the extra information to the boards with a black marker.

After he wrote down the bit about the rope burns and the dislocated shoulders, he turned to the team and said, "Eden was viciously raped, and sodomized before she died. Doc thinks she was assaulted before she died because spermicide was far up the vaginal channel, and there was blood inside from tearing.

"He also told me he thinks she was raped again after she was deceased. There are lacerations that hadn't bled. The perp used a condom." Kurt cleared his throat and added, "Doc says there is evidence that she had also been violated with…implements. Including, ah, in her mouth."

In the grim silence, Sinclair noted, "Kimi wasn't raped before she died, Doc had said she was afterwards. Why the difference?"

Sitting back down with a slight huff, Kurt answered him, "Like I said, Doc thinks the offender accidentally killed her too quickly. He said he thinks the killer didn't provide oxygen so Kimi perished before he could rape her while she was still alive. He remedied that with Eden. If he kept her hooked up to oxygen he could have tortured her all night."

Sinclair winced, then said, "Burke told me there were indications such as stages of petechial hemorrhaging in her eyes that the killer didn't keep the oxygen flowing steadily in Eden Lombardo, that he likely turned it on and off and on.

"Along with the torture of impaling her with his penis as well as various implements, and the slicing and burning, he let her just about suffocate, then he brought her back to life to endure it all over again, over and over."

The room stilled. Her skin pale, Emilee Rivera stared wide-eyed at the floor. Kurt gulped repeatedly, loudly. Prince's skin tinged with nauseous green, his lip curled.

Hix muttered, "Sick motherfucker." The others nodded in silent agreement.

Drawing in a rough breath, Sinclair said grimly, "We need to catch this bastard, put him away before he gets his hands on another woman."

"I'd like some time alone with him, first," Kurt murmured. The other males dipped their heads in accord.

Emilee left her seat, brushed against Hix then faced the board with a quick once-over scan. She had long lean legs, a trim build, short brunette hair curled behind tiny ears, and a sunny disposition. Color returned to her face.

Turning from the board, she told the group, "Both have blue eyes, fair skin. Kimi's heritage is part Hispanic, part Irish. Eden's is British, Dutch and Swiss. Kimi is a nurse's aide at Saint Aubins General Hospital and is basically single, but she sees a guy occasionally.

"We haven't been able to reach him, uh," she glanced at the board, "Troy Gardner. Her friends say their relationship is the on again off again kind, they weren't exclusive. The friends said Kimi was a bit of a barfly, she did the pickup one-night-stands kind of thing."

Smiling at Hix she went on, "We have questioned the people the second vic, Eden Lombardo, works with and her close friends and family. Um," she reviewed the board again.

"Eden is married and her husband is a stock broker who is loaded. She does lunches, not work. Neither of the vics have children. Both were born and raised around the Washington DC area."

"Anything in common like church, education, clubs? Cheating spouses and the like?" Hix asked, staring at the board. He had interviewed several people in Kimi Consuelo's orbit himself.

Sinclair answered him, "Nothing. Zilch. Found no connections between the women or their families. Their phones haven't been found, probably destroyed. We're still waiting on the phone records."

"What about possible abduction sites? I'm assuming someone would have mentioned earlier if any witnesses had been located?"

Scooting his chair closer to the board, Kurt fielded his question. "No, no witnesses found yet. We asked Kimi's friends what her itinerary was the day she went missing. They said she had worked all day and was excited about a date that night, not her regular fuck buddy.

"They had no information other than she was going to meet this great guy at a restaurant right after work, called, ah," he skimmed the information on the board. "Yeah, the Sailor's Knot. We checked with the staff and cameras nearby, she never made it to the restaurant. And, they confirmed that no male had come in and said he was waiting for someone that never showed."

"What about the hospital? The parking lot?" Hix still studied the board.

"Bingo." Kurt grinned and stood up with enthusiastic energy.

Hix turned to him. "Yeah?"

Kurt trod to a chair and picked up a laptop. He powered it on and set it on the desk and sat down. Everyone moved their chairs so they could view it.

Hix stood behind them, bent over and set his hands on his thighs.

Emilee remained standing, she inched close to Hix, bumping him lightly with her arm. He ignored her.

Nodding, Kurt gestured to the screen, a fuzzy video showed Kimi exiting the back of the hospital and crossing the parking lot.

He said, "Okay, watch. She was abducted from the parking lot. The actual abduction was obstructed by a black van. It was parked we think deliberately to obstruct the camera. The freak did recon, he's a careful planner. Makes him patient and his IQ is likely not low."

They viewed Kimi walking towards her car, a blue Toyota.

"But she doesn't make it there," Kurt said, as the group watched the video. "She looks surprised then moves behind the van which is parked strategically so the tag can't be seen, or the driver."

Moments after Kimi is behind the van, the vehicle speeds out of the lot, and Kimi is gone.

They replayed the tape several more times but learned nothing else.

Kurt told them, "We picked the black van up on a storefront camera on a few streets before the hospital but the tape is really grainy. But I think even if it was clear it hadn't caught anything worthwhile, the tag looks obscured, maybe with mud, the perp knew what he was doing.

"There were no surveillance cameras near the site of where she was found. You're up," he tapped a few keys and another video came up. He nodded to Sergeant Sinclair.

Sinclair carried on the account. "The second victim, Eden Lombardo, had told her husband she was having breakfast with her girlfriends. The girlfriends told us they had had no plans with her. One of them informed us Eden confided in her she was meeting a man for a secret rendezvous.

"Like Kimi, Eden didn't spill the name of the guy or anything relevant about him other than where she was going to meet him in front of the Galleria strip mall. He was supposedly taking her to his posh cabin outside Alexandria for their illicit tryst."

"Uh huh." Kurt tapped a key.

The group could see in the video, dawn clouds were still dissipating, a strip of orange sky was lighting in the east.

Kurt said, "We obtained this video from the mall's security cameras. Here she is early Saturday morning outside of Merck's Specialty Shop at the mall. And here, watch," he pointed at the screen.

They observed Eden Lombardo checking out her reflection in the store window. They looked where Kurt pointed. A few yards down the street they saw a black van parking along the curb. A moment passed then Eden suddenly turned towards the van, then her face registered concern.

"What is she doing?" Emilee asked. Eden had started towards the black van walking quickly.

"She's talking to someone," Princeton said, eyes narrowed at the computer. "He's hidden by the van. Come on mister, or miss, show yourself, come on."

Hix's cell buzzed, he pulled it out and glanced at the text, then resumed watching Eden moving closer to the van. They never see Eden again after she steps behind the van.

The next thing that happens is the van drives off down the street, same scenario as Kimi Consuelo's abduction.

"Tag is still obscured," Emilee pointed out, "like Kurt said, looks like mud or something."

The video ended, they sat back, exhaling the breaths they had been holding.

"Anything else?" Hix asked, looking first to Kurt then Emilee then Sinclair.

"No," Kurt replied. "Nothing on any other cameras near the locations for either vic. Same as Kimi, there were zero cameras behind the mall where Eden was found posed. Like I said, perp knows what he is doing, he sets up the meets where they would be deliberately covered, and there is nothing distinct about the van to go on other than it's black. No dents, no markings, no rust, no broken headlights.

"The guy was supposed to meet Kimi at the restaurant but surprised her in the parking lot. I think because he knew he could avoid the cameras better there. He didn't tell her to meet him in the lot in case any coworkers walked out with her just to check him out."

"Eden was found behind Merk's the day after she was taken," Sinclair mentioned. "No cameras out back."

Hix stood straight, his hands on his hips. "Okay, keep at it. Check traffic cams. Knock on doors around the strip mall."

"All the stores were closed where Eden was taken, Penn, it was very early Saturday morning," Prince remarked. "And when she was found on Sunday by someone that just happened to drive by, the stores were again closed. Brevet Bay still has the Blue Laws."

"I know," Hix responded to his colleague and friend, "but there is a neighborhood in the vicinity." He said to Sinclair, "Knock on doors. See if anyone saw the van or Eden." He turned to Emilee, "Officer Rivera."

She smiled at him, dark brows arched in question.

"Teague got a hit on the wood that made up the big box. Collier's Depot. You know, where you buy supplies to remodel homes and tools, appliances, paint, piping, that kind of stuff. Teague said the wood appeared unusual, he took pieces around furniture stores that dealt in mostly wooden furnishings to find out what kind it was. It's called Indian Rosewood. Comes from India and parts of Iran."

Heads swiveled to Hix, his face remained blank.

Prince joked, "That's around your Egyptian neck of the woods, Penn."

Ignoring him, Hix said, "Teague's still checking on the metal the chains were made out of and the twine. Officer Rivera, go down to Collier's Depot and speak with Jim Scott, he's the manager. Teague said Collier Depot is the only place around for hundreds of miles that sells the Indian wood. Find out who bought any.

"Then, check with hospitals to see if there's a way they can track who has access to the- uh, V paralyzing stuff and if any is missing. Again, grab any surveillance if they have it where the drugs are kept."

"Yessir." Emilee grinned and grabbed her jacket.

"Wait a sec," Sinclair said to Emilee. "Kimi Consuelo worked in a hospital. Maybe she stole her own death serum not realizing it was going to be used on her, you should start at that hospital first. I'll go back to the Eden Lombardo location with some uniforms and knock on doors."

There was a buzz. Sinclair unclicked his phone, swiped and answered, "Sinclair." He listened then, "Thanks," clicked the phone back on his belt. "They brought in Eden's husband, Dante Lombardo. He's down in Interview 3."

"Go to the Depot first," Hix told Emilee, "then the hospital. Start with the Kimi medical connection, check her access then anyone else's access to the drugs in question."

"Gotcha Boss. I'll call as soon as I have anything." She gave Hix a lingering touch on the back before she swept out of the room.

Kurt stood up. "I'll also do another search of the Consuelo site and ask around if anyone saw the black van. I already put a BOLO out for the van even though we have nothing other than it's a plain black van. Not seeing the back I have my guys looking at what make and model it might be, but it'll be tough."

He grabbed up his phone and clicked it on his belt but another tiny one remained on the table.

A brow arched, Hix asked, "Two phones?"

Kurt's lip tugged in. "Yeah. It was one of my informant's. But he's getting big for his britches, says he wants a fancier one. This one has no internet or frills, just calling and texting. It has a ton of hours left on it. It's great for undercover since it's so tiny. I was going to drop it off out front to go back into inventory."

Hix stared thoughtfully at the tiny flip phone. "It have a GPS tracker on it?"

"Sure, most do these days," Kurt told him.

"I might have a use for it, sign it back out in my name." Hix scooped up the cell and dropped it in his pocket.

"No prob, later," Kurt said, and he and Sinclair trotted out the door chatting together.

"What are you going to do?" Prince asked Hix as he rounded his desk to his office chair.

Hix tossed his keys up and down in his hand. "First I'm going to interview Lombardo, then I promised Ma I'd help my old man nail down a couple of loose shingles. She doesn't like him up on the roof alone, and he won't ask for help. My brothers are tied up but they're stopping by briefly for lunch. She's cooking macaroni béchamel. You liked it, Thomas, you wanna come with me?"

"Oh, hell, Penn, wish I could. I have a lunch date with Tracy, she's craving sushi. Your ma ever going to learn to cook a different Egyptian dish?"

A short crook of his lips, an almost grin, picking up his suit coat Hix shook his head. "Nope. She'll do the occasional meat pie or stuffed grape leaves, but she's really not too fond of Middle Eastern food. Thank God she's into meat and potatoes and less into vegetables. Tracy?"

Prince palmed his hands over his light hair and winked with a smirk. "Yeah. She spilled her chai tea on me at the coffee shop, and well, one thing led to another. You should try it sometime, you know, have a relationship with a girl?"

A flash of Laurin Ajanel popped into his mind. Hix turned his head away, hell, what is wrong with him, the woman is married.

"Not for me, Thomas. I tried it once, it didn't work out. I gotta go, catch you later."

The door to the interview room was open. Shrugging his suit coat on, Hix gave a couple of raps on the door to announce his presence.

Sitting inside, a harried man was mumbling and raking his fingers through his thick dark hair. His head jerked up at Hix's knock.

"Dante Lombardo?" Hix asked, as he came in and took a seat opposite him at the white plastic table. Tugging out a notebook from his inside coat pocket, he set it down and opened it to a blank page and took out a pen. Setting the pen on the notebook, one black brow arched at the man.

The man nodded, blew his Roman nose into a handkerchief and dabbed at tearful eyes. He wore a long-sleeved white shirt with a blue tie, beige slacks and brown loafers. A camelhair coat was draped over the back of his chair.

Hix said, "I'm Detective Hixman. Ah, sorry about your wife, your loss, but to catch the person that murdered her I need to ask you some questions."

Dante shoved his white plastic chair back and wrenched to his feet, slammed his palms on the table. Hix didn't flinch. He sat back and clicked the pen open.

Pounding the table with his fist, Dante shouted, "Why are you here questioning me when you need to be out there-" he waved his hand in an arc, "searching for the bastard that killed my wife?"

Ignoring the distraught husband's rant, Hix calmly asked him, "When was the last time you saw your wife, Mr. Lombardo?" He fixed hard blank eyes onto the man.

Lombardo's face screwed up at Hix's accent, his eyes slit at the detective in animosity. "You even legal here? I don't believe in that Islamic shit, you guys need to keep that crap over on your side of the world."

With a surly scowl, he bent over and splayed his fingers on the table. He stared down at his fingers spread on the white plastic. A gold ring circled the ring finger of his left hand; a Piaget glimmered at his wrist.

Hix's face remained a stony visage, he didn't blink, just gazed calmly under hooded lids at the man.

Feeling the detective's staunch glare, Dante's mouth opened and closed like a fish. He shoved the thick hair he'd raked furious fingers through out of his brown eyes, and plopped down on his chair. He peered up at the buff detective, blanched at the strength not only of Hix's strapping body but the cold, fierce steel in his dark eyes.

Forking his fingers through his hair again, Lombardo shrugged one shoulder. "I last saw Eden that morning before I left for work. I leave early, Eden normally doesn't rise until oh, ten or eleven. She may have gotten up earlier that day because one of our neighbors commented on how she'd never seen Eden out and about before noon and she'd noticed that an hour give or take after I left at five, Eden had dashed off in her car. I remembered later that she'd said something about breakfast or brunch with her friends, but hell, she still never leaves that early."

Hix jotted a few notes. He already knew this because all the neighbors had been interviewed. Lombardo was noticed by the next door nosy, insomniac neighbor leaving around five as usual, and Eden was seen leaving only an hour or so after him, which the neighbor said was unusual. Neither had returned home, until Dante came in around eight that night.

Their house had been searched and no sign of a disturbance or blood was found. So, if Lombardo killed his wife, it wasn't in the home. The police theorized that he could have killed Kimi Consuelo and staged the elaborate scenes to deflect suspicion that he murdered his wife.

Hix asked, "You always work on Saturdays?"

Rubbing his nose with the hanky, Dante nodded. "Pretty much. Stocks are closed but the research and client contact is unending. Sometimes we have staff meetings as it's quieter and calmer on the weekends when the market is closed."

"You didn't notice she didn't come home Saturday night?"

He squirmed, appearing suddenly uncomfortable. "Uh, well, actually we were supposed to meet at our club for dinner at 6:30. She didn't show. I…well…frankly, I was kind of relieved when she didn't because I was so tired, didn't feel much like talking. I hung out at the bar and waited until almost 8. I was exhausted and went home with take-out and hit the sack."

Dante's shoulders hunched, his head lowered slightly. "I figured she just got tied up with her friends or…whatever. When I woke Sunday morning and realized she'd never come home I started calling her friends. It wasn't until the police contacted me that…I…" His body sagged with grief. "I…I've been at the morgue." He glanced up at Hix, tears shone in his wretched eyes. "They wouldn't let me see her."

Hix paused, letting the man gather his composure then asked him, "Do you know exactly where she had planned on going Saturday?"

Dante shook his head, shoved strands of hair back off his forehead. "No. Eden did as Eden pleased, she didn't always keep me abreast of her comings and goings." He took a handkerchief from his pocket, blew his nose, wiped his eyes and tucked it back in his pants pocket.

"Did you care?"

Taken aback at the question, Dante blinked, then sat back in his chair with a wry smile. "No, frankly, not really. I do my thing, she does hers. I'm a stockbroker, my hours are...intense. You're never really off the clock, even when on vacation you do research, follow the market, business trends and shit. Long ago Eden found ways to entertain herself."

"Such as?"

With a shallow, "Ah," he crossed his arms, shrugged again a bit doleful. "I don't actually know her schedule. She gets her hair and nails and what-not done which seems like daily. She shops, she lunches, plays tennis at the club in good weather. Visits with her friends, I think she's on a few charity committees.

"I only know that because a couple times a year I'm dragged off to one black tie affair or another. Fundraisers. Hell," his grin crooked with slight sarcasm. "The bucks they spend on food, entertainment, renting the facility, they could give to the charity and save everyone time and bland food. You know?"

Having had to attend the fundraisers himself, Hix agreed with him. But he said, "How were you and your wife getting along?"

Another shrug. "Ah, well, as long as we stayed out of each other's way we did fine. I mean, we've been married for six years, known each other for ten, our parents were close. Shit gets old, stale, you know."

"Did she have someone on the side? Affairs?"

Lombardo's cheeks reddened in his olive-toned face. "I don't quite know. If she did, she was discreet." He moved his arms, clasped his hands and set them on the table, they shook slightly.

"And you, Mr. Lombardo? Did you stray from the marriage?"

Lombardo tugged at the tie under his Adam's apple, face turned redder. "Ah, well…"

"Honesty will help you in the long run, Mr. Lombardo. You may not be guilty of murder but you don't want an obstruction charge on your record, the brokerage won't like that."

Hix appeared to sit back relaxed in his chair, but his body was always coiled tight, like an aware animal on edge, ready for any kind of situation. He tapped the pen lightly on the table.

"Ah," Lombardo cleared his throat, tugged harder at the tie, then set his palms on the table. "I loved my wife, Detective. I swear, I've always loved Eden. It's just, a long time ago the…sexual interest waned, and, as I said, we each go off in our own directions."

"And," Hix prodded.

He cleared his throat again. "Well, yes. I've had a girlfriend for a few years."

"Her name? I need her address and phone number too." Hix tapped the pen on the notebook.

"Ahem." Lombardo cleared his throat and replied, "Her name is Lucia Renquist." He pulled his phone out and scrolled through it then rattled off her phone and address.

Hix jotted notes. "How long have you been seeing her exactly, where did you meet?"

Lombardo's eyes shifted around as he thought. "We met at work. Lucia was an assistant to the head boss. She was transferred to another office when the boss found out about the affair. We see each other about two or three times a month. I've known Lucia for about," he thought again, "I recollect about two give or take, maybe three years now?"

"Did your wife know about her? Does Lucia know you're married?"

His olive skin flushed, eyes lowered. Brushing a hand across the Roman nose that had turned red, he said with slight regret, "Eden probably knew, she never said though. She's egocentric but sharp as a tack. And, yes, Lucia knew I was married. She didn't care, she didn't want a man underfoot daily so it suited all of us, I suppose."

"Would Lucia have any reason to harm Eden?"

"What?" Lombardo shot forward, his forearms on the table. Shaking his head adamantly, he said with horror, "No, no of course not. Lucia didn't want to get married. She liked her independence too much." He sighed. "Just like my wife."

Hix didn't think the girlfriend was the killer, she would have had to do in Kimi Consuelo as well and that didn't seem likely. There was the rape that indicated a male, but the killer could have put a condom over something and used that to simulate the sexual assault thereby leaving no metal or wood trace.

But that wouldn't make any sense since Doctor Burke said there was evidence that foreign objects were also used to penetrate the victim. He'd found slivers of wood embedded inside her as well as traces of metal in some wounds.

Hix asked, "Do you or your wife know a Kimi Consuelo?"

"Kimberly? I know a couple."

"No, just Kimi. Kimi Consuelo."

Lombardo thought about it, shook his head. "No, doesn't sound familiar."

Jotting notes, looking at the notebook, Hix asked, "Can you think of anyone who would want to or have any reason to harm your wife?" He leaned back and gazed levelly at Lombardo.

Appearing ready to cry again, Dante shook his head. "God no, Detective. Eden was, ah, narcissistic to be sure, but harmless. She didn't work, had no interest in any kind of business, she could be flighty and flakey, but there would be no reason anyone would want to...harm her," Lombardo's head dropped as sobs shuddered his shoulders.

Hix closed his book. He wore a black tie and black trousers, he opened one side of his black suit coat and slipped the notebook and pen inside a pocket and stood up.

He studied Lombardo for several minutes. Lombardo appeared to be experiencing real grief. The man tugged the handkerchief back out and dabbed at his eyes then his nose.

"Okay, thank you for your time, Mr. Lombardo. If I have any more questions I'll be in touch. If you think of anything that can help us, give us a call. You're free to go whenever you're ready." He set a business card on the table in front of the devastated man.

Lombardo crossed his arms on the table and set his head on them and wept.

Hix left without another word.

# Chapter Ten

His mother as always was thrilled to see him.

As soon as Hix stepped through the door, Vageline Hixman hurried out of the kitchen and threw her arms around him, giving him a long hug. "I miss you, baby, so does your dad and siblings. You don't come around often enough." It was her usual refrain.

Hix patted her on her back. "I'm busy, Ma. Work you know."

She stepped back, frowned and brushed a lock of hair off his brow, chided him, "No one is ever too busy for family, honey. You're just afraid we'll break down that wall you have up. Listen, Marjorie Simmons has the most delightful niece. Julia is lovely, in her fourth year of college. I know you and Carmella didn't hit it off, but Julia is-"

"*Laa Mama*," he lapsed into his first language, "ah, no Ma, come on. Where's Pop?" Hix gently set his mother aside and went in search of his father.

Carmella had blown up his phone ever since the wedding. He'd had to block her number, and tell staff at the station not to let her in when she came by. Which she did, frequently. He'd barely dodged her twice. He didn't want to be rude, or get harsh with her, but it was heading in that direction if she didn't back off.

He made his way around the back of the large, two-story house. White with hunter green shutters, the house was surrounded by waves of thick green grass studded with tall trees just beginning to bud after the winter. Behind the house, he found his father on a ladder with a hammer sticking out of a tool belt slung low on his waist.

"Geeze, Dad, you were supposed to wait for me." Hix jogged over and grabbed a second hammer off a table on the patio. Sticking his hand in a can of nails, he filled a pocket with a handful.

He'd left his suit coat in the car, his tie knotted but loose around his neck, he rolled up his sleeves and followed his father up the ladder.

Two hours later, after washing up, they went into the living room and were greeted by his brothers Kullen, Clifford and Aven. Each held a beer and they were lounging on the sofas and the recliner.

"Sure, ya lazy bastards, show up for food and beer, way after the work is done," Hix pretended to reproach his brothers.

His sister, Suzetta Somerset went up to him and gave him a kiss on his bearded cheek. She whispered a smiling scold, "Language, Penn."

Twin squeals came from the doorway and two bodies hurled themselves at their uncle.

Laughing, a rusty sound, Hix let the eight-year-old boy, Michael hug his waist, and then lifted Michael's six-year-old sister, Holly to perch on his hip. She gave him a loud smack on his cheek then giggled. "You're fuzzy, Uncle Penn."

"Yeah, I am," he agreed then set her down with a swat on her butt and she and Michael darted back to the where they'd been playing their game and dropped down to the carpet to continue.

The living room was comfy and welcoming decorated in creams and pale blue cushions, rugs, curtains. The house was designed for comfort with large, open rooms, the Hixmans loved to entertain.

"It's nice to see you smile, Penn," his sister commented handing him a beer.

He accepted it and slugged down half the brew.

"We didn't think you were capable of smiling." Suzetta had her mother's fairer skin but her father's deep rich dark hair. Her eyes slightly almond shaped were lighter than her male siblings' and sparked like gold fire against that dark hair.

The smile disappeared to whence it came and Hix edged past her to flop on one of the couches beside Kullen. "Where's your old man?" he asked Suzetta.

Exhaling loudly in exasperation, she rolled her eyes. "Brett couldn't get away. Starting a big trial and they had to prepare their opening statements. He said to say hi, was sorry to miss you since you so seldom come around," she said with another slight scold.

Setting the bottom of the bottle on his leg, Hix slouched way down in the cushions to avoid further conversation. Not that it stopped anyone.

Lunch was tasty and boisterous, laughter bounced around the loud table. The children shouted louder and louder vying for attention. Hix sat back with another beer and regarded his niece and nephew.

He thought of the Ajanel boy, Benji. His mouth flattened. The child appeared desperately lonely, as did Laurin. He wished he could bring the boy here to play with Michael and Holly.

A picture of Laurin and her son sitting at the table blew right into his mind. Benji laughing and shrieking along with Michael and Holly, Laurin eating daintily, enjoying conversation with his family.

A partial smile curved one side of his mouth. He blinked away the picture, was never gonna happen, when was he going to drill it into his head that the woman was married?

"Wow, that's a first, Penn. You almost looked human," Suzetta teased.

Hix's features hardened back to their normal harsh, implacable blankness. He abruptly pushed his chair back and stood up. "I gotta go. Lunch was great, Ma." He nodded to his father, "Pop. Call me when the next project Ma has planned on her honey-do list for you comes up."

Kresskin Hixman, the last name changed long ago to be more Americanized, thanked his son for his help in their own language. He was a quiet man who had fought until near death in Egypt to keep the military from taking his young son so many tough years ago.

He'd had to physically lock the other children and their mother away to keep them safe as they fought tooth and nail as well to hold onto the young Penn. Even as young as they all were, they were aware of the harrowing vicious life Penn was fated to live as a covert soldier.

The family had had only brief and sparse meetings with Penn over the years. The military didn't want him softened, and they kept their time together under guard and fleeting to prevent the Hixmans from snatching Penn and running away with him.

Sometimes a year would pass before Penn visited his parents and siblings. It made them all feel like strangers. Now, in America, the Hixmans struggled to pull Penn into the familial fold, but he wasn't used to people, civilians like them anymore.

He spoke business with the people he worked with, but except for Prince and Kurt, he kept small talk to the barest minimum.

He'd been called it all, cold, hard, rude, arrogant, it went in one ear and out the other. The life he'd lived in the military, if insignificant things like name-calling bothered you, you would have nothing left over for the big stuff.

Penn had to mentally shut himself off to simply a killing machine to survive the brutal life he'd led. It wasn't so easy to open up. Towards the end of his time as a soldier, he met a girl he'd thought he'd spend the rest of his live with.

Now, the ugliness of his one serious relationship turned him off to any other entanglements with women. He became used to the types of females that were brought to the camps to relieve the soldiers. Coarse, hard, tough, like him. Hell, he'd been raised as more animal than human.

Hix's mother followed him to the kitchen archway watching Hix set his plate and beer bottle on the counter by the sink before he moved back to the dining room.

Kullen and Aven stood up together. Kullen mentioned, "Read about the girls in the boxes, Penn, they're calling the killer 'The Poser'."

Frowning at his brother's information, Hix sighed. "Damned media, they get in the damned way, and there are grieving families that don't want to see their loved ones' undignified horror plastered all over the news."

"Posed them naked like a sex slave, according to the reports," his brother Cliff said, joining them.

"Clifford!" their mother snapped. "Not in front of the children." She mouthed, "*No sex, no murder.*"

Gathering up empty plates, Suzetta sent her brothers a grimaced chiding of her own.

Michael and Holly bounded from the table and raced back to their game in the living room. Vageline had taken the teachers' work day as an excuse to have everyone come for lunch.

All four brothers looked chastised. More or less.

"Sorry, Ma," Cliff had the grace to apologize, but he winked at his brothers. "We gotta head out."

Vageline came over to them. Patting Cliff's cheek, she ordered him and Aven and Kullen, "Uh, huh, you guys go help your dad clean up the back before you leave."

She waved them off ignoring their half-hearted grumbles then she said to Hix, "Now, don't put so much time between coming here, honey. This is your home too. I expect you at next Sunday dinner unless you can come by sooner." She fixed his collar, neatened his tie then patted his cheek.

"Maybe," he avoided promising. "Got a murder case going on." He bent and kissed her cheek and rolling his sleeves back down started down the stone walk to his truck.

"Love you, baby," his mother called out.

Without turning around, Hix shot a wave then took off back to the station.

# Chapter Eleven

Laurin closed the door to the closet and whispered into the phone. "I'll be at Pulio's Bayside on River Street around six. My sister-in-law and some of her friends want to have drinks while planning a bridal shower for one of the girls. I can meet you out back.

"But we have to be quick. You know that my husband keeps a guard on me when he lets me out. I should be okay tonight though, because he thinks nothing will happen if I'm with Jewel and her friends."

Little did Rádolfo, or Jewel's husband, Chevalier know, Jewel set up these nights out really to meet with whomever was her most current lover. She has drinks with her girlfriends and then sneaks off to a hotel with her beaux de jour. Her girlfriends don't mind, half of them were doing the same thing.

Jewel brought Laurin along purely as a beard. She figured no one would be suspicious that Jewel was up to anything with her sister-in-law alongside. The two nannies took care of baby Channing while she was out.

Laurin didn't feel right about conspiring with Jewel, but Rádolfo kept such a tight leash on her, other than the charity ball and church, she hadn't been out of the house in six months.

Thank goodness Rádolfo was out of town on business this week. As an ambassador, one of his duties involves issuances of

VISA's. In addition to giving speeches at governmental events, he has meetings regarding political and economic, trade and commerce issues. He has 45 people that work with him, one or another is always calling or asking him to go to the office for his assistance on some matter. He also has to frequently travel out of the country.

Then there were his illegal enterprises. Those were what the cops were trying to get evidence on. It was those illegal activities, gun trafficking, blood diamond smuggling, that the CIA was after Laurin to produce the goods on him.

Laurin had no doubt at all that her husband would kill her if she was caught taking pictures of papers in his desk drawer they had taught her how to break into. The CIA also wanted photos of people coming and going from the mansion.

She heard a splash outside and hurriedly stashed the phone in the hiding place where she kept things she didn't dare let Rádolfo know about. The old phone was huge, there was no way to hide it on her person.

She went to the window and looked down at the backyard to the patio.

Rádolfo's sons, Blane and Chevalier were leaping off the diving board landing huge splashing cannonballs into the pool. It was heated against the chill of the air.

She saw Geraldine wrapped in a bulky sweater sitting in a lounge chair on the patio holding Channing, Jewel and Chevalier's baby.

Shona was stretched out on a lawn chair catching rays although it was still downright chilly. A space heater hummed beside her on the deck. Lying on her back, wearing sunglasses and a floppy straw hat, Shona untied the strings of her bikini and quite unselfconsciously pulled her top off and dropped it beside her chair.

Geraldine, covered primly from head to toe in the ugly sweater and loose slacks hiding her chubby thighs, quickly turned away with the baby.

Jewel ignored everyone, she was fixing her makeup in a mirror, she and Laurin were leaving shortly.

Blane, used to his wife's exhibitionism never stopped conversation with Chevalier. The men were still in the pool and had folded their arms and propped them on the rim of the pool. They both wore t-shirts and surf shorts.

Chevalier kept glancing over at Shona, his cheeks turned red. Blane went right on talking uncaring that his brother was staring at his wife's bare breasts.

Laurin gave Benji a quick kiss on the top of his head. He was in his room playing with the animals. Two of the servants who felt sorry for Benji secretly took care of the animals.

One walked the lame Poochie, and they took turns cleaning the kitty litter and sneaking in food for the pets. It all had to be done when Rádolfo was not home. Rádolfo knew about the dog but he said if he saw him he'd toss him off the roof.

"Laurin!" Jewel called up the stairs.

Time to go. "You be good now, for me, sweetheart," Laurin told Benji, kissing the top of his curly mop.

The boy nodded, one of the cats, Cobweb, had his attention. He had been named Cobweb because he'd been hit by a car and ever since moved around in a fog. In confusion, the orange tabby ran into walls, stepped in food dishes.

Laurin had rescued him from one of the church members who was going to have him euthanized. Cobweb was the first cat Laurin had snuck into the house. She noticed he was getting better and better every day. The more Benji played with him the less disoriented he seemed to be.

"Laurin!" Jewel shouted. "Let's go!"

"Coming," Laurin responded, slipping her jacket on. Shona and Geraldine did not often go with them. Geraldine couldn't keep a secret, and Shona had her own fish to fry. Tonight Raoul, Geraldine's husband had gone on the brief trip with Rádolfo.

With the two men out of the way, it was a perfect time for Jewel and Laurin to go out. Whenever he was around, the oldest son, Raoul tended to watch Laurin like a hawk tracking a field mouse he was lip-smacking his beak over. His infatuation with Laurin amused Rádolfo.

As they reached the front door, Chevy crossed the foyer with a smile, his bare feet making slapping sounds and leaving puddles behind him as he walked. "Hey, honey. You have a good time."

He slid his arm around Jewel's shoulders and gave her a peck on the lips. "I won't worry about you drinking since you have the driver, but be careful anyway, okay hon? Call me if you need me."

His bathing suit dripped pool water on the floor. He'd tossed off his shirt and now a fluffy towel was draped around his bare shoulders modestly covering most of his torso.

Chevy winked at Laurin. "You too, honey. You girls behave yourselves now, don't get into any trouble." He grinned like he didn't believe the two women were capable of getting into trouble.

Laurin felt a terrible twinge of guilt. Chevy was always so nice, bland, but nice. She felt horrible for being in cahoots with his wife cheating on him.

His geriatric business was booming and he spent a lot of time at the clinic. Perfect job for a softhearted intelligent man like Chevy. If only Laurin had been forced to marry him according to the plan instead of…well, that's water under the bridge.

The scheme had been concocted when the CIA learned that Rádolfo planned to purchase a mail-order-bride for his shy son who was too busy to date. CIA Agent Brewer's brilliant idea had been to have Laurin inserted right into the family as a spy.

He was ecstatic when Rádolfo claimed her for himself. Instead of periodically visiting with Chevy if she had married the youngest son, now she'd be living right in the house and could more easily spy on Rádolfo and gain information.

Jewel had even more reason to dislike Laurin as she was well aware Laurin was to have originally married her husband. And Chevy hadn't hidden his angst when his father stole his bride from him. Within weeks of Laurin and Rádolfo's wedding, Jewel and Chevy who had known each other through charity work married shortly after. Baby Channing popped out making up for everything and they were now a contented family.

Sadly, being the sociopath that Rádolfo was, he barely paid any more attention to his grandson Channing than he did to Benji. Of course he was less brutal to the infant and occasionally even held him. Laurin guiltily avoided Chevy's sweet smile and wink as they said goodbye.

A short twenty-minute drive, and the chauffer parked briefly in front of Pulio's Bayside, and five giggling women piled out onto the cobble stone sidewalk. The driver was also Laurin's guard and he would stay in the car until it was time to take the women home.

After the women disembarked he moved the car and parked a short ways down on the street, he could easily observe if Laurin slipped out the front entrance. He looked the other way when Jewel went on her 'jaunts.' Squealing on Jewel Ajanel was not his job.

Jewel's head spun around as she hoped her lover would be waiting outside for her. Her lips thinned when the walk proved empty. The evening air bit crisply with a hint of dampness lingering. Traffic whizzed by, a horn blared twice down by the traffic light at the intersection.

Shrugging with ill humor, Jewel held the door open for her friends and they all strolled into the restaurant. Their heels clacked on the blue tiled floor that matched the blue seat cushions.

The tables were covered with white mats, and small lamps with white lampshades adding personal light to each table. Windows took up much of the front, and the panoramic view of the blue bay was partially visible through the restaurant at the back.

They chose a round table they could all fit at and placed their drink orders right away. Laurin had no desire to drink. She was too nervous about what she had to do tonight.

Jewel tossed down her first martini and ordered a second. Her eyes revolved ceaselessly as she searched the place for her lover in case she had missed him coming in.

Laurin didn't know the other girls that well, so she sat on the peripheral of their conversation which was mainly about their jobs and children, how hot the new trainer at the gym was, and how terrible their husbands were. Aware of Laurin's past scandal, unless sneering in her direction, they acted as if she wasn't sitting with them.

After half an hour, Laurin glanced at her watch and cleared her throat. "Uh, I need to go to the ladies room, I'll, um be right back." She pushed to her feet and grabbed her purse, left her jacket hanging around the back of her chair to allay suspicion.

As she stood, one of the women, Cheryl, a Botoxed blonde asked her blithely, "You need company, Lorie?" The only reason to accompany Laurin would be for Cheryl to dig up more scandalous gossip. None of the women ever treated Laurin as a friend.

Laurin had given up on telling the women for the umpteenth time that her name was not Lorie or Laura or Lorraine. She shook her head with a mild smile. "No, I'm fine, I'll-"

"Oo! There he is, I gotta go, girls!" Jewel squealed with glee, her gaze arrowed across the crowded room. Grabbing her purse and jacket, as she twirled away from the table, she gloatingly cawed, "Ta ta, girls, I'll be back in a few! Alan has only a short break, he needs to get back to work. Don't be jealous now!" Her friends waved her off and carried on with their conversations.

Then Jewel hesitated and glared at Laurin. Through closed teeth, her finger pointing at her, she warned, "Not a word, Princess."

Laurin's mouth tugged in then pursed, she didn't need more threats. Her life was one big threat.

Not waiting for Laurin's response, Jewel danced away. At the door she stood on tiptoes and kissed a tall, stocky man with wavy auburn hair. His arm wound around her, and by the time they walked out the door his hand was cupping her narrow ass.

Laurin hurried off in the opposite direction. She moved down the hallway past the restrooms where she knew there was an exit to the back parking lot. Taking a quick glimpse behind to make sure no one followed her, she slipped out the back door.

It was almost dark, she hugged her body with a shiver, wishing she'd brought her jacket but that would have looked too suspicious. Staying out of sight of the huge back window, she peered around in the dim lot hoping she didn't have to wait long for-

"Laurin."

She recognized his voice. Laurin spun around and saw Agent John Brewer heading towards her. She held her breath, she hated these meetings. Not only was she taking the chance of someone seeing her and telling her husband, she was putting hers and Benji's lives on the line if she was caught, but the agent was never satisfied.

"Agent Brewer," she greeted. Opening her purse, she pulled out a folded file and handed it to him. "That's all I could get. Now, please," she hated begging, it made her feel all the more a victim. "My brother, Robbie, you must let him go. I've done everything you've asked. Please."

Agent Brewer opened the file and leafed through it. He grunted. "Not a hell of a lot here, Laurin. Not enough yet to seek prosecution. No," he shook his head while flipping photos and studying copies of the papers in Rádolfo's desk drawers. He closed the file and tucked it under his arm.

"No, Mrs. Ajanel," he always spoke formally to her when he wanted her to remember what he held over her head to control her. "I need more. We had Intel that Ajanel smuggled a shipment of guns from South Africa to the port of Baltimore. You find me something with his handwriting that shows he was in on it, or something equally as good. Then we'll talk about bringing your little brother home."

Anguish pushed tears from her eyes, Laurin's heart crushed. She folded her fingers together bringing them up in prayer. "You promised. You said if I brought you these photographs you'd get Benji and me out of the house and reunite me with my brother. Please," her voice strung taut, she struggled to keep it from going shrill. She turned slightly so the chilling wind would blow her hair off her face.

Brewer was on the gaunt side with a rangy body. He wore a tan overcoat that fell to his calves in true spy agent style, and a fedora covered his thinning hair. Evening dew was settling on his hat. Stuffing his hands in his pockets, his shoulders humped against the whipping wind that threatened to blow his hat off, the bottom of his coat flapped against his legs.

"I told you, Laurin, you bring me the goods and I bring young Robert home. He'll be relatively safe for a little while longer. So, get to work. Text me when you have what I want."

He turned to march off, Laurin grabbed his sleeve, pleading, "Please, Agent Brewer, at least take Benji from the house. It's too dangerous for him. Lately when Rádolfo's gotten angry he's threatened Benji again. You-"

"Oh come on, Laurin stop with the histrionics. Ajanel hasn't hit the boy in a while, you said the last time he belted him was a few months ago. The kid is safe enough. Just keep him out of Ajanel's sight." The smile was unpleasant in his plain face, small, round brown eyes glowered at her under a copiously creased brow. "The sooner you get me the goods, the sooner all of this is over and you're all home safe."

"But-"

Brewer cut her off, "Ajanel must have a computer."

Laurin nodded numbly. "I've seen a laptop in his office. He never leaves it out."

Tugging at his lips with a few fingers, Brewer said, "Find the laptop. You need to figure out his password. You can email me any information or documents, but then delete the email, make sure there's no trace of it. I don't want him to suspect you. I'll need you to stay there so you can possibly find something else we can use. Let me know as soon as you find the computer."

"No, but I don't know where he hides it! Even if I did I don't know the pass-"

"Text me, soon," the agent snapped. He stalked away and quickly disappeared into the dark.

Her head spinning with disappointment and dread, Laurin stumbled blindly to the wall of the restaurant and slid down to sit on the cold asphalt. Pulling her knees up, she gave vent to the tears of despair she'd been holding back.

She'd been a virgin when Brewer forced her to whore herself to Rádolfo to save her brother's life and it seemed like she would never be free of him.

She had to pull herself together before she rejoined the ladies. Picturing her brother Robbie being held somewhere, Laurin, the only family he has, he's undoubtedly frightened for himself and worried about both of them. Who knows if he's suffering horrific abuse?

Then poor Benji, the image of the last time Rádolfo took his anger out on the boy crashed into her mind, he'd twisted Benji's arm right out of the socket and hit him in the face with his belt. Her head fell into her hands as more tears flowed. It was going to be a while before she regrouped her composure.

Brief tinkles of music and voices floated on the breeze from the front door sporadically opening as customers came and went. Laurin could hear waves in the bay slapping against the seawall at the far end of the restaurant.

She breathed in the faint smell of salty brine noticing a few early bluebells flaunting their flared petals in the grass. Fuzzy brown cattails down by the bank poked up through tall grass, the stiff stalks bending and slapping in the brisk wind.

It seemed to take forever for the tears to wane. Laurin was feeling too sorry for herself. She needed to buck up, two young lives depended on her to keep her cool and find what Agent Brewer demanded.

The laborious sigh sounding loud in the night, Laurin slowly rose using the wall for support. "Goodness," she murmured to herself. "I don't know how long I've been gone, but it seems like it's been quite a while. The women will surely be suspicious of my lengthy absence."

Combing her hair with her fingers, Laurin made her way back inside. After stopping in the restroom, she trod down the side hall and to the dining area, and stopped abruptly. Her breath stalled.

The table the women had been sitting at was filled with new customers, and her jacket was gone. Anxiously, Laurin swung around in a circle searching for any of the women, but, they were gone!

"Wait, the car," she reassured herself, clamping down on the panic rising up her throat, "sure, they're in the car waiting for me."

Already hearing their complaints and insults in her head, she nimbly threaded her way quickly around the crowded tables and burst out the front doors. And stopped dead.

"No, no, no, no," her heart banged like a drum against her ribs. Where the driver, her guard, had been parked, now an SUV was in the space. They had gone. Left her there.

Clutching her purse in burgeoning agitation, she had no money, no phone. Rádolfo was going to find out that she had left the restaurant, and that she'd ducked her detail again.

"Oh God." Frantic breaths spiraled so rapidly she thought she was going to pass out. For sure Rádolfo was going to hurt Benji. She'd left him there unprotected.

The child would be utterly defenseless against the demon that she was married to.

She checked back inside to see if someone had turned in her jacket, but was told no. With no choice, Laurin gathered her nerve and started walking towards home. Miles away.

# Chapter Twelve

**H**ix answered his ringing phone. On the other end was Officer Emilee Rivera. He spoke brusquely, "Whatcha got, Officer Rivera?"

"Hey Penn," a throaty bit of a sultriness came through the line.

Emilee was another female Hix generally went out of his way to avoid when he was alone. She pestered him for a date, dinner, or just drinks, just sex, she told him anything he wanted she was game for.

When she totally ignored Hix telling her he wasn't interested, he'd tried to dissuade her politely by tossing out that fraternization between staff was not allowed.

She had laughed her throaty laugh and had told him that was BS. She'd looked up the OP orders, there was nothing in them that said employees couldn't date or even be married.

"That's Detective Hixman, Officer, I've told you that." Hix tried to keep their rank as a wall between them. His tone terse, he asked, "You have something on the wood?"

More throaty laughter. If she only knew that laugh was like fingernails grating on a blackboard. Apparently someone had told her it was sexy. "Uh huh, yeah baby. I wouldn't mind if you had wood for me, Penn," she purred. "You-"

"Fuck, Rivera, tell me about the goddamned Depot."

"Okay fine, spoilsport. The manager Jim Scott, Jimmie," her voice purred coyly.

Hix assumed the officer and the manager hit it off. "And?" he prompted.

Her sigh came out staticy through the cell. "Jimmie said the Indian Rosewood was expensive and a relatively rare wood. He checked his records and found three receipts. The same buyer made three bulk purchases. We then reviewed the surveillance tapes together," she paused with a smothered giggle.

It sounded like they had done more than just view the tapes. "How much bulk did he buy at each time?"

"Oh, uh, I wrote that down, hold on."

Hix heard ruffling around, papers sliding against each other.

"Here, considering the sizes of the boxes, the killer, or killers, bought enough to make at least six or seven boxes."

Great. The perp planned more victims, not that the police didn't figure that, but still, one hoped the sick bastard was done. "All right, tell me what you found out about the buyer."

"Jimmy was so helpful, Penn, what a doll."

Now she was trying to make him jealous. He was at the end of his tether. "Go on, Rivera," he ordered curtly, losing his patience, not that he had much to begin with.

"Okay, okay don't get your briefs in a twist." She paused again, then her tone flirtatious she asked, "Do you wear briefs, Penn? Or boxers, or…" she hesitated, "commando? Do you-"

"Fucking A, Officer. Knock it the hell off or I'll put you on report for inappropriate behavior. Now," he took a breath, geesh, what happened to professionalism? "Spit it out without the extra frills."

Emilee sniffed. Sounding piqued, she huffed, "Fine. We matched the receipts with the tapes of the man. Checked his name and face with his DMV pic. The buyer is a Howard Dennis Fernell. White, 39. Kurt and Sergeant Sinclair are out searching for him now. They-"

"What're the dates on the buys? How long ago?"

"Oh, I don't know, wait." It took her a minute to find the receipts where she'd put them. "Um, that's why Jimmie and I got on so well together. It took him some time to locate the first receipt.

The purchases were made over a period of time. If it wasn't such rare expensi-"

"When?" It was all Hix could do to keep from shouting into the phone.

Perhaps detecting the rising fury in his voice she said quickly, "The first purchase was March of last year, so around a year ago. The next in September, the latest purchase was one month ago. Anyway-"

"I want Fernell's info and the tapes and receipts on my desk." Hix clicked off without a goodbye. He'd had enough of the brazen officer. He phoned Sergeant Sinclair and forwarded the information.

Hix had missed lunch and it was well past dinnertime, his growling stomach told him to find a burger joint. Tossing his jacket on, he took off for his truck, Sinclair would call him when they picked up Fernell.

On the way to the center of town, Hix called his brother Kullen. A bunch of rings went on before Kullen finally picked up.

"Yeah, bro," he sounded slightly out of breath.

"Hey, K, on my way to grab a quick burger, wanna meet me?" Hix heard a female voice then a giggle, then a muffled, "Shh, wait, Kristi, gimmie a second," and Kullen's deep chuckle sounded.

Kullen coughed, then chuckled again, a muffled, "No, just a sec, honey." His voice firmer he said, "Uh, bro, listen, can't make it tonight. Rain check? Stop that, Kristi," his laughter reverberated through the phone.

"I see. Would that be Pinky from the ball?" Hix found himself smiling.

More muffled sounds, then, Kullen laughed. "Yeah, you got it. Later, bro."

Hix tucked his phone away and drove for fifteen minutes. There was a diner on 39th that made the best flame-grilled burgers. He turned down a relatively dark street, a few before the diner, and, he couldn't believe it.

A woman was walking alone along the side of the road, in the dark, on a long stretch of blacktop where houses and shops were few and far between. Shadowed fields blanketed to the woods on both sides of the road.

Cursing, he swerved over and slowed down behind her muttering, "Of all the stupid, reckless, the idiot female." She's gonna get a goddamned earful while he drives her to her destination. If she was his he'd blister her ass for being so foolhardy.

Nearing the woman, he pulled up beside her and came to a slow stop. He got out of the truck with his badge in his hand so she wouldn't be afraid of him.

"Miss," he called, stalking quickly to her. "I'm Detective Penn Hixman, I'm going to give you a ride, get in-" he blinked. And again. No one has that bright of hair, not that light flaxen, *no, no way-* Laurin Ajanel.

She didn't stop walking. Keeping her head down she strode faster away from him.

"*Damn*," he cursed more. She didn't hear his words, his accent so harsh, rough, had obscured them and frightened her.

"Laurin!"

She broke into a run.

"Aw fuck." Hix dashed after her.

Afraid that he was chasing her, Laurin ran into the grass off the side of the road towards a grove of trees like she thought she could hide in the woods.

"Laurin! Stop!" His legs twice as long as hers, he jogged across the grass cutting her off and snagged his arm around her waist, her feet flew up in the air and she screamed.

"No! No! Help me!" Laurin screamed, kicking her feet.

He held her back against his chest so she couldn't hit him, she still didn't realize it was Hix.

He set her on her feet but wrapped his arms around her and over her arms so she couldn't fight him, her back to his front. "Hush, Laurin, it's me, Detective Hixman, Penn, remember me? Calm down, I'm not going to hurt you. Calm down now."

They stood in the vast field, the wind slapping their skin, the night sky surrounding them made darker with heavy clouds.

Out of breath, her screams lessened to squeaks as his words registered. Chest pumping she huffed, gasped, "De- Detective Hixman?"

He held her firmly but not squeezing her too hard, he had to watch his strength, she was so delicate, fragile even. He'd bet dollars to donuts she was so petrified of her abusive husband she scarcely had an appetite.

"*Awai,*" damn language, "yeah, yeah," he switched quickly to English and softened his voice. "It's me, I won't hurt you, calm down so I can let go of you."

Her soft body squirmed in his hold, her backside flush against his pelvis, breasts heaving over his arms.

His stance planted wide to hold them steady, being a male with a gorgeous female in his arms, pressed against him, his arms tightened around her automatically. She fit into him like they were flesh and blood pieces of puzzles.

But what was happening to Hix down below was not good. "Uh, you okay, Laurin? I'm going to let you go now," he slowly released her and stepped back a few inches.

She spun around, her lips parted with rapid panting, eyes flapped with distress. Strands of light hair caught across her face into the corner of her mouth. "You- you," she huffed, "you scared the heck out of me. Why did you chase me?" A hedge of accusation mixed with the fear in her shaking voice.

Hix glowered his ire, words exploded with anger, "What the fuck are you doing out here on this road all alone in the middle of the goddamned night?"

Her face whitened, eyes stricken, she backed away from him. Her gaze darted around him as if she was planning to flee again. Her fingers wound tightly around the strap of her purse, strangling it.

He knew between his hard looks and harsh voice he was scaring her all over again.

Hix held his palms up, lowered his voice, "I'm sorry, I didn't mean to bark at you, curse like that. You...took me by surprise. When I saw you walking along the road all I could picture was a woman getting raped and beaten and left dead in the gulley. When I saw it was you, I-" he shook his head.

"Anyway, why are you out here?" He saw shivers grip her, she wrapped her arms around her body. The wind picked up and lashed her hair, fluttered the ruffles on her blouse.

He pulled off his jacket and went to drop it around her shoulders but she took another step back from him.

Frowning, he said quietly, "Laurin, please don't be afraid of me."

He waited a few beats, watched the fear in her big eyes diminish at the sincerity in his deep voice and he set his jacket on her shoulders. Their breaths were white puffs, her little nose was red, her teeth were chattering like chirping chipmunks.

"Come on, let's get in my truck where it's warmer." He held his hand out to her.

She regarded him with wary hesitation, then, nodded. She didn't take his hand but she walked with him to his truck.

He opened the passenger side and helped her up the high running board, closed the door and hustled around to climb in behind the wheel.

The truck was still running, he had gone after her in such a hurry he'd left it on. He turned the heat up, then sat back against the driver's door to give her as much space as possible for her to feel safer.

Hix watched her arch her neck, her head fell back slightly, a hard swallow indicated her distress. Her neck was long, soft looking. He urged to lean over and smell her, lick that skin, bite- he blinked those thoughts away. Again, here he was lusting after another man's wife.

Her husband was a criminal, and she was a cheating, murderous woman. What the hell was wrong with him? Unfortunately his dick and his brain were not on the same page when it involved this woman.

"Okay, Laurin, tell me what's going on. Why are you out here like this? Alone, no jacket." He rested an arm on the frame of the window, the other hand on his thigh while she salvaged her poise, caught her breath.

His eyes drifted to her chest still rising and falling rapidly with her fright and flight, he forced his gaze to move up to her stunning face. It was all soft curves and roses, just like her body. Her round cheeks were bright cardinal red from her running and the cold air.

Her chattering teeth lessened in the heated truck, she glanced shyly, briefly at him then stared down at her hands where she clutched her purse in her lap.

Her chest filled with air then she let out a tight sigh. "I, uh, I went with my sister-in-law and her friends to a restaurant. I, um," her eyes flicked back and forth. Hix was feeling a lie coming. "I had to go to the uh, restroom. When I came out they…were all gone. Including the car."

Thinking to himself, it must have been a helluva long restroom visit. Seeing her fidgeting with her purse strap, eyes flitting, breath quickening, skin blushing even brighter, he knew she was lying. And she really sucked at it. "So why didn't you call home for someone to come and pick you up? Or call a taxi?"

He waited but she didn't answer him. "Laurin, you are sitting here until you answer my questions." The terse tone of his voice told her he wasn't bluffing.

Her head turned, she looked to the door handle. Hix pushed the lock set, she jumped at the click. "Laurin."

"I…"

"Look at me please when you're talking to me, Laurin." His fingers gripped the edge of the window frame.

She paused, then turned slightly to face him. Her lashes fluttered uncomfortably, her chest rose with a taut inhalation, she sighed it out. Pink crept back into her cheeks. "It's…embarrassing." Her gaze flicked up to him then away.

"I'm a cop, Laurin, I've heard everything. It's not my place to judge you or anyone." Although he had judged her, said cruel words to her at the ball.

"Go on. Please, look at me." His gaze lowered to her plush lips then rose. Those large sapphire eyes lifted and his heart clinched. The utter sadness and helplessness in them overwhelmed him.

Her lashes fluttered again as if she knew her expression was telling, and was trying to hide her pain. "My...husband does not allow me to have a phone or...or money. No cash, no credit cards. I'm not allowed to...work. Even leave the house actually. He had sent us with a driver who was also my...guard. When I returned from the, uh, restroom, everyone was gone including the guard and car. My husband will be...very...angry with me." The terror flamed in those beautiful eyes.

"I'm sure at this point he would be much more concerned that you were out here alone and not safe at home."

With a small snort, her lips twitched in derision, she said softly, the fear evident in her voice, "No. He would think I had left him. He will be...enraged." She slipped out of his jacket and laid it on the seat between them.

Hix's stomach turned over. "Laurin, listen, there are shelters. You can press charges against him if he's...hurting you. Get an order of protection, a restraining order to keep him away from you. I'll help you-"

"No," she replied flatly, her head lowered, breaking their eye contact. "Please, Detective, please if you would, just take me home."

"Laurin, listen, let me-"

"No," she said with a bit of a snap. "I have a young boy at home I must get to. If I'm not there my husband will take his anger out on him-" she bit her tongue. "Please take me or I'll get out and walk."

Hix's teeth grit. "Listen, I can take you and your son-"

"He's not my son-" her hand slapped over her mouth too late to stop the words.

"What?"

"Never mind, Detective, please, I beg you to drive, or, I'll get out and walk. Even as a lawman, you can't hold me against my will." She put her hand on the door handle.

Hix scowled his loss, she wasn't going anywhere until he released the locks. But, with a grunt of frustration, he put the truck in drive and pulled back onto the dark road.

They didn't speak on the drive to the mansion. He had to stop at the gate, the guard bent down and saw her then waved them through.

Hix drove up the long winding drive to the house and parked out front. "Wait," he said as she tried to lift the handle.

She turned big sad eyes to him, but the plush lips were tight, preparing for another fight.

"Just, here." He fished the phone Kurt had from his informant. He handed it to her.

She stared blankly at the tiny phone in her hand.

"I want you to keep it. My number, a few other officers and the station's main numbers are in contacts. There's a ton of minutes on the phone. If you need help, or find yourself in the same situation as tonight, or, just anything Laurin, call me. Don't hesitate."

"If he finds it he'll be furious and take it from me. I have one at the house a- a friend gave me that I...hide. But it's really big and the minutes are almost out."

"This one is tiny, Laurin. Hide it in your sock or make a hidden liner in your purse to stash it, that way you can have it on you. I wouldn't be angry with you if he finds it and takes it from you, I just...don't want him to hurt you."

When she started to hand it back to him with a shake of her head, he curled his big hand over her small one closing it around the phone. "I insist. If you don't accept it I will be forced to take some kind of action." He removed his hand from hers. That was a bluff, his hands were tied to help her unless she asked for it.

Staring at the phone, she blinked then looked up at him with a frail smile. "Thank you, Detective. It's very kind of you. I uh, really must be going. His limo isn't here, Rádolfo isn't home yet. I may have time to convince the guard and my sister-in-law from telling on me. They'll be in almost as much trouble as I am if he finds out they left me at the restaurant."

The side of her mouth nicked in wryly. "The last thing Jewel would want would be for anyone to find out about her secret lover, so, hopefully she won't say anything. And the guard," a shiver rolled across her slender shoulders. "Last time I ducked out on my guard, the men were just as thrashed as I-" she shut her mouth. "I have to go," she pulled on the handle.

His lips bunched at what she had been about to say. But, seeing the determined rising of her chin, he unlatched the locks. "Okay, go on. Just, if you need help, call. I mean it."

She opened the door and slid a leg out. He said before she closed the door, "And it's Penn, Laurin, remember that, okay?"

She closed the door and smiled bleakly up at him then turned and quickly dashed up the walk and then the steps.

Opening one of the big double doors, she turned back, gave him a little wave then stepped inside and closed the door.

Hix backed down the driveway, apprehension wrinkled his forehead, chewed at his gut. This was the first time he'd felt apprehension since after that first year he was taken from his home.

After that, even as young as he was, he endured the wretched life, the beatings that turned him into that cold, ruthless killing machine. He learned to wrest control over any situation, be the beast on top. After his first few kills, anxiety became a foreign emotion to him.

Until now. He didn't know what the hell was truly going on in the Ajanel household. He had experienced Ajanel's manhandling of his young wife, the utter stillness of the boy Benji when in his father's presence. As if perhaps if he remained perfectly still, he would be invisible and therefore not draw his father's wrathful attention.

With no overt signs of abuse, or without anyone's complaint, Hix could not charge in and remove the woman and child. But then, he mused, maybe Ajanel was so outrageously possessive and restrictive of his wife because she was a whore.

It was hard to reconcile the sweet, loving, petite blonde of anything nefarious, but, he'd finally read the report of the incident. She had an affair with the Secretary and got pregnant. The lover wouldn't leave his wife for her, of course Laurin was also anchored by her own marriage, she grew enraged and tried to off St. Lawrence.

Ajanel had made some huge public statement of how he loved and forgave his very young wife for her foolish transgression and they would move on from the travesty and live happily ever after.

Hix stepped hard on the pedal, the truck fishtailed. Hadn't he learned his own lesson? He loved, had trusted Chantal, wanted her to be his wife.

They had met in a bar when he was home briefly for a holiday. Had a whirlwind romance and he put a ring on her finger before he headed back to the service. Later, he realized it hadn't been love. He was flying back to a war zone and had wanted something to hold onto, something good to hope for.

When he found out she was pregnant, he was barely alive in a hospital over-seas. But, he'd sent her word he was putting in for leave so they could marry immediately.

Before he was released from the hospital, Chantal had sent him a cold, brief note stating that she had terminated their child, and was going to marry Barnie Parker, one of Hix's best friends in the military.

Barnie had been discharged from the service. Apparently he had liked the pictures Hix had shown him of Chantal and went straight to her and swept her off her feet. Double betrayal.

She had no intentions, Chantal told him, of marrying a cripple and being a soldier's wife. It was beneath her. She was bound for better, richer, loftier things.

Hix knew she came from wealth, she had begged him to work for her father in Econ Enterprises. Instead, Barnie took his place at the job and with his fiancée.

Hix had been laid up for a long time, but thank God, through the blood and sweat of hard work and physical therapy, he wasn't permanently crippled as the doctors had first diagnosed.

He realized now he had dodged a bullet. Two bullets. Chantal turned out to be a nasty, cheating slut who had aborted their child, and Hix would have hated working an executive desk job.

Hix had known Chantal's upper-crust familial background, but the brassy girl was bold, tough, tall and strong like him, she cursed like a sailor, was as bawdy as the boys.

She didn't have quite the rough artic exterior as Hix, but he had thought they were much alike. And they were, she turned out to be as cold and callous as he. But he would have never have cheated on her, or killed their child.

His attraction to Laurin was inexplicable. She was everything opposite to what he usually went after in a female. He liked them tough enough to take his rough sex and boorish behavior. His cavalier conduct, have a quick one then get the hell out of his way.

But Laurin, so ladylike, sweet, dainty, the more he spent time with her the more he wanted to spend time with her. His protective urges were in full force over the small female. The bitch was bewitching him.

Well, he swore, not anymore, he would put the woman right out of his thoughts. It would be harder to get her out of his manhood's thoughts though…and out of his dreams.

"Women," Hix spat, whipping onto the highway heading for his apartment, "more trouble than they're worth." He shoved all thoughts of the beguiling Laurin from his mind, and concentrated on the murders he was supposed to be investigating.

Later, he would visit Isabella, she would take care of his physical needs without female chatter or wanting more, or drawing on the odd protective possessiveness that Laurin Ajanel provoked in him.

# Chapter Thirteen

**H**owie Fernell toddled into Mabel's Diner, his heavy face was flushed, eyes still bleary from the binge he's been on. "You can't just drink all that money away, Howie," he scolded himself. He needed to eat, think about what he can do with all the cash he was expecting.

Inside the bustling diner, Howie hefted his tonnage onto a red vinyl stool and waited for the waitress to come over. He was sweating buckets, snatching several napkins from the dispenser on the counter he blotted his damp forehead.

He didn't know what was making him sweat more, the hangover, or the deeds he's been paid a lot of bucks for. Well, he was *gonna* be paid big bucks.

He glanced at his watch. The crystal was badly cracked but the time still worked. He had an hour before meeting the guy and getting the rest of his payoff. It's not like *he* did anything illegal, it was the guy paying him that was the criminal.

Howie glanced around at the typical diner.

Customers dotted the stools at the white counter and lounged in the red booths along one wall, two cooks hustled behind a partial wall. The sizzling smell of bacon frying, and pastries baking filled the air. Howie took a long, loud, sniff.

"Hey, Howie, you look like shit." Frannie Belmer wiped the counter in front of Howie and set a steaming coffee mug down on it.

"You need the hair of the dog, honey, you know you ain't gettin' it here. You want the usual?" The waitress pulled several creamers from the pocket of her white apron tied over the yellow and white striped uniform, and set them beside the mug along with a paper place mat and cutlery rolled up in a napkin.

Brunette hair pinned up at the sides, the rest of it curled on her shoulders. A fluff of bangs curved over tawny eyes, she set her elbows on the gold-speckled stained counter and leaned over so Howie could get a good look down her front. She'd left several buttons open for his, and every other man's viewing pleasure.

"Yeah, same as always," Howie obliged, his gaze dropped to her cleavage. A fat tongue came out and slobbered around his thick lips. "Uh, the number 2, eggs over easy, hash browns, double toast, gravy and sausage and extra bacon. Say, listen Fran," he spoke to her without looking up at her face. "How's about you and me goin' to my car for, you know..."

Chuckling, Frannie wriggled her breasts to make his ogle that much more enjoyable. In her early forties, Frannie got off on teasing men. All men. She was as easy as spreading melted butter on toasted bread, but she only gave it to men that could pay.

Sadly, she was getting up there, so her interest was starting to turn towards a man that could either marry her, or set her up in a nice place.

Frannie's face was just shy of pretty, a bit too angled and sharp, she used her body to garner the attention she lived for. Voluptuous on top, she was a shade too flat in the derriere for most men's tastes, so she flaunted her breasts to keep the interest up there. She had an extensive sex life, and serious skills to beat the band, but again, she only gave it to those who could afford her.

She leaned over further watching Howie's eyes round and his pupils enlarge.

Just as it appeared he was about to dive into her blouse, she stood up straight. "I'd love too, Chubs," her nickname for the portly man in his late thirties, "but you know, you ain't got the scratch," she rubbed her fingers together indicating money.

Howie blinked hard to pull his heated gaze from her cleavage. "Yeah, but no, but," he stammered. "I do have it, money that is. Whatever you want, I'll pay it."

His pudgy fingers wrapped around the mug, the steam spiraled up to heat his already hot, flaccid face. Straight dirty blond hair swung over piggy eyes that still blinked lustfully at her.

"Oh come on Howie, everyone knows you put in so few hours at the distillery you can barely afford a six pack. Yer always beggin' for drinks down at the Cowabanga Pub every night. I'll go put your order in." She sashayed to the metal wheel on the low wall behind the counter to clip his order for the cook.

When his order was up, Frannie brought the egg platter over and set it down in front of him with a slight clatter and refilled his coffee. "Eat up, big boy," she said, smiling off-white teeth.

"No, but listen, Fran-" he picked up his fork and dug in, stuck a pile of runny eggs onto the side of a piece of toast then shoved half the toast in his mouth.

Talking while chewing, he waved his fork at her and said, "Babe, I'm comin' into some money today, big money. I'll buy ya dinner *before*," his lascivious gaze latched onto her bosom, "and then breakfast *after* we get together." He poured ketchup all over the hash browns then shuffled a huge forkful into his wide-open, thick-lipped mouth.

Frannie studied him warily, her eyes narrowed in suspicion. "Since when you got any dough, Chubs?" She sent a quick nod to a man down the counter calling for her with a raised coffee mug.

Chewing loudly with his mouth open, Howie wiped his flabby lips with the back of his hand and dug in for more eggs. "I got a job I done, and the fella's payin' me big. He gave me a deposit, see?"

He pulled a stack of bills out of his pocket and flashed them at her. "Guy said he might even have more work for me. So see? I can show you a good time. When you off shift?"

Thick false eyelashes lifted high, then tapered at the fistful of money he quickly stashed back in his pocket. Licking her own lips she smiled. "Uh, yeah, sure, Chubs." Leaning in to give him another view of her cleavage, she asked in a low voice, "What'd you do, rob a bank?"

Frannie's off-white grin flashed, she said quickly before he could answer, "Not that I care, hon, as long as it's green I'm not particular where it comes from. I get off at six. I been dying to have supper at that new place, Abe's Chuckhouse. You can take me there. And then," she leaned over further, tapped the side of his fleshy, chewing cheek with a few fingers, "I'll show you my thanks. Okay?" She wriggled her bosom at him.

Chewing heartily, Howie's eyes fastened onto her swinging breasts, he nodded greedily. "Six. I'll meet ya out front. You know my station-wagon."

About to roll her eyes at his mention of the ancient peeling and rusted vehicle, she caught herself and gave him her prettiest smile. "You bet, Chubs, uh, I mean Howie, six sharp."

She bent over and kissed him on his moving lips ignoring the whiff of eggs and stale booze and God knows what else then she stood back and grinned. "I can't wait. Make sure you have some extra to give me, you know what I mean, big boy?"

Scooping up a soupspoon full of biscuits and gravy, gobbling the greasy mess, Howie nodded eagerly, gravy dripped down the corner of his flabby mouth. "Yeah, babe, can't wait. I'll give ya a little some'im some'im tonight, then when I get the rest of the money I can give ya more. On our second date," he added.

He was letting her know this wasn't gonna be no one-and-done, he planned on getting himself plenty of tits and honey until his dollars ran out.

Hours later, at 6:30, a steaming Frannie still in her uniform slammed a hand on her bony hip and snarled, "Son of a bitch, stood me up."

Her face a furious mask, she stomped off to the back lot where her old VW was parked grumbling, "Fat bastard, I bet Colleen O'Hara got her claws into him. Dammit, wait until I see them, I'm gonna," her angry voice disappeared around the back of the diner.

A scream loud enough to wake the dead could be heard all the way inside the diner. Heads popped up, ears cocked.

At the station, Hix traipsed inside lifting his chin in greeting to those busy in the bullpen. He kept going past the pen and down the hall to an interview room.

The door was propped open and he strolled inside the small, windowless room. A square, white plastic table with four matching chairs around it were placed in the center on scuffed tan tiling. They weren't dirty but did show signs of long time use.

Thomas Princeton was seated at the table, he jerked his jaw to his partner, nodded to the man sitting with him. "Penn," he said and motioned to the man, "this is Troy Gardner, Kimi Consuelo's boyfriend."

The young man in his early thirties, leaned back in the plastic chair, his fingers curled around the edge of the table. He frowned at Prince, then glared at Hix. He announced with some defensiveness to Hix, "We're not dating, Officer."

"Detective," Hix corrected, taking a few steps inside but stopped and leaned his shoulder against the plastered wall. Casually tucking his hands in his pockets he crossed one booted toe over an ankle.

At the cruel coldness in Hix's Egyptian ebony eyes, and his harsh lips pressed in a dour scowl behind the short black beard, Gardner quailed and dropped his gaze. He peered up through his own light brown bangs at the safer appearing Princeton with his sandy hair and blue eyes.

"So you said," Prince remarked, turning to Gardner. "That's not what her girlfriends tell us. They said you took her to the movies a few days before she was killed. When was the last time you saw Kimi?"

Troy shifted uncomfortably in his seat, his head lowered, dark brown eyes rolled up briefly to look at one detective then the other. He shrugged one shoulder. "Uh, yeah, so we hooked up Sunday night a week ago. Had dinner at the Sea Chest then caught a flick. Last I saw her was like about one a.m. I split after, you know, and went home. I heard she was…uh…found, on, uh, the Saturday after," red crept up his neck.

He nervously shoved a wave of light brown hair off the side of his forehead. His neck was red, but his face had bled stark white. He looked about to toss his cookies.

"You and Kimi have a fight, Troy?" Prince set his forearms on the table and leaned into the man, broad shoulders humped, his words came out rapid fire, "Maybe she wouldn't put out, maybe she told you that you guys were through? Maybe she had a new guy?

"Maybe she said you just didn't measure up in the junk department, huh? You lost your temper and killed her. We can understand that, shit pisses us men off and we lose control. What happened, Troy, get it off your chest, man, you'll feel better."

There was still that theory that one of the women was killed to divert suspicion from the other's death. The box and spray paint and the rest of it could just be a flamboyant ploy to trick people into thinking it was a wacked out serial killer and not a husband or jealous boyfriend.

His skin leeching paler than snow, Troy pushed at the table, his arms rigid, his head flicked from Prince to Hix and back to Prince.

Prince was questioning him, but Hix was the dark, frightening shadow looming in the corner of the room.

"N- no, no, we had fun, sex was okay. When I left her, she- she was asleep. She was fine, I- I swear!" His lean chest billowed with panicking breaths.

Prince moved closer, leaned in further to him, into Troy's personal space. Troy pushed at the table, his back flush to the chair, he couldn't move away from Prince, he was afraid to move his chair back.

"Troy, we need to know your whereabouts the day before and the day that Kimi was found." Prince didn't tell Troy they verified Kimi had had dinner with her parents on the day before her death. He wanted to see if Troy would lie about when he'd seen her.

His eyeballs rounded, the white showing around brown irises, Troy appeared about to faint. He stuttered, "I- I, let me think, let me think." He closed his eyes, dragged his fingers down the front of his face, then clutched his forehead, shaking his head. Tears eked out and started down his handsome face.

Wiping at them with his hands, he lifted his head, swiped at his runny nose and said, "I...I was with Betsy Lou, Betsy Lou Whitten. From Friday night until, uh, the morning after Kimi was..." he trailed off, wiped at his nose. "You can call her, she'll tell you, I was with her."

"Uh huh." Prince settled back, folded his hands together on the table in a more benign position. "Maybe Kimi found out about you and Betsy Lou and she was jealous. Maybe she threatened to tell Betsy Lou that you and she had just had sex. You got mad, didn't want to lose Betsy Lou so you killed-"

Troy jumped to his feet, the plastic chair clattered to the floor. "No!" he yelled. "I- did- not- k- kill Kimi, for fuck's sake! I, yeah," he took several deep breaths, his hand splayed across his heaving flat stomach.

"Kimi had her own guys, we weren't exclusive. We were just," he bent and straightened the chair then flopped back down, the breath expelled. "We just fucked, man, whenever one of us was at loose ends. It was nothing serious, I swear. Nothing to- to- kill over. I swear." The air and distraught yelling seeped out of him, his body sagged.

Hix stood silently, not asking questions. It was his and Prince's method of making the person being interviewed nervous, letting them be afraid of the silent darkness lurking in the corner, hovering, watching, listening. Sometimes the suspect would open up to Prince thinking he'd protect them from Hix. Good cop, bad cop. Hix and Prince shared a glance.

Prince stared at Troy without saying anything. The only sound in the room was Troy's sniffing and panting breaths.

After a few minutes, when Troy didn't suddenly confess, Prince asked, "Can you think of anyone that would want to harm Kimi? A friend? A new boyfriend? One of the other men she's seeing, maybe someone got jealous? Co-worker with a grudge? Boss pissed she wouldn't put out? Anyone she may have angered at a bar or something? She complain about someone watching her? Following her?" He waited, his hands still calmly folded.

Troy blinked back the tears, swiped at his eyes and nose, shook his head. "No. Kimi was one of the most harmless girls I know. She liked to fuck around, but never anything serious, and she chooses the same kind of guys, men that didn't want to get involved in a relationship. Kimi was all about having fun.

"Though I think she was growing tired of the bar pickups, the one-night-stands. Still, there is no reason why anyone would want to kill her. She never mentioned anyone bothering her, stalking her." His head hung, tears splatted on the plastic table.

"Okay. Saturday the 22nd, where were you then?" Prince asked about the day Eden Lombardo was taken.

Troy scratched his head. "Uh," he sniffed, swallowed loudly. "I, uh, Betsy Lou's family. They had a barbeque, her old man's birthday. I was there all day. There's pics on social media." He exhaled his nerves harshly then the tears fell faster.

The detectives were quiet as the man wept.

Then Troy sat up straight, wiped his nose on his long sleeve, sucked in a calming deep breath and let it out slowly.

Prince said, "Okay. That's all for now. Write down Betsy Lou's name and number, and her folks' and you can leave." He shoved a notebook and pen at Troy.

Hastily, Troy grabbed it up. Then he raised his eyes warily, fearfully at Prince. "Hey, you don't gotta tell Betsy Lou or her folks about this. I mean, about Kimi and…uh…me?"

The detectives glanced at each other. Prince said, "Not unless it becomes necessary." He pointed at the notebook, ordered, "Write."

Troy pulled out his phone to find the information, then scrawled some words and numbers on the page. Slapping the pen on the notebook he shoved them back to Prince and climbed quickly, albeit unsteadily to his feet, his cell clutched in his hand. "I uh, can I go?"

Prince nodded. "Yeah, don't leave town." Troy fled the room.

Hix waited until he was gone then said, "You can't tell the guy he can't leave town, Thomas, we have no hold on him. You watch too many cop shows."

His lip quirked at Prince's grin. "Anyway, pretty unlikely he murdered Kimi. He would have had to do Eden too. I'm sure his alibis will hold up. This is the work of a sadistic serial, not some horny kid with a short fuse."

"Kid?" Prince laughed. "He's no younger than you and me, might even be older."

"Whatever." Compared to Hix's past, an 80-year-old man was a kid to him. His phone buzzed in his pocket. He lifted it out and glanced at the screen. "They got Howard Fernell. The guy that bought the Indian Rosewood from Collier's. Let's go."

The detectives grabbed their coats on the way out to the car.


When they drove down the street and neared Mabel's Diner, they saw a half dozen police cars, blue lights twirling in the looming darkness.

A fire truck was parked in front of the diner, its red lights mingling with the blue, the colors flashing around and around bouncing off buildings on the street. The diner's neon signs blinked like grotesque eyes behind the swirling lights.

With the weak setting sun's warmth, the evening air was sharply cold, sleet started falling with a knifing wind that smacked at the detectives' exposed skin.

Wearing coats over their suit jackets, pulling their collars up to cover their necks, they exited their cars and trolled around to the back of the building where a droning crowd was gathering.

Police swarmed the area, but stayed back from the yellow crime tape. An ambulance stood off to the side, paramedics moved towards the taped off area. Everyone was bundled in jackets with hoods or hats covering vulnerable heads.

Hix saw Sergeant Daron Sinclair's head above the crowd and made his way to him.

Sinclair was standing by the tape, sleet dotting his Stetson. He nodded to the detectives as they approached. He wore blue disposable gloves.

"Boys," Sinclair greeted them with his regular genial big-toothed smile. In the dimming evening, his milk-chocolate skin and bright white teeth gleamed. Two policewomen, one black, the other white, stood on either side of him, gazing adoringly up at the tall, muscular man.

The sergeant frowned at one then the other. With shrugging smiles, the two females moved off to make room for Hix and Princeton.

The detectives peered through the dim parking lot lights at the body lying prone on the ground.

Police were positioning a small tent to prevent the sleet from hitting the corpse. The detectives shared a grim glance with Sinclair before looking back at the hefty body.

"Howard Fernell?" Hix asked Sinclair.

The sergeant nodded, tucking the smile away. "Yep. We had officers out hunting him down when the call came in."

"Who called it in?" Hix asked, moving a tad closer to the tape.

Sinclair shifted slightly, nodded towards the woman two of his officers were questioning. She was huddled under a wool blanket someone had given her. It covered her head but didn't hide the gleam of eyes wide with horrified shock spooking out of the darkness.

"Frannie uh, actually," the sergeant paused and tugged out a small notebook from his jacket pocket and flipped it open.

He said, "Frances Jean Belmar found the body. She's a waitress here at Mabel's Diner. Said she had a date set with him for six when she got off work, she called him Howie. After waiting 30 minutes or so and he didn't show, she gave up and went around the back lot where she'd parked her car and found him."

"She touch anything?" Prince asked. Both detectives fetched their phones from their pockets and took pictures of the scene. They were careful to keep out of the way of the CSI taking her own photos with a camera.

"Naw," Sinclair replied, watching them move to take different angles of the site. "She saw him lying there, blood on his face, pooling around his head, she just ran screaming incoherently into the diner. The manager and other staff came out, but the manager was smart enough to keep everyone back. He had one of the staff put the 911 call in."

Setting one hand to hold the front of his coat from moving, Hix leaned over the tape, squinted at the body. "Bullet through the head?"

White particles of sleet littering his dark lashes, Sinclair nodded. "Yep. Two. Looks like someone came up behind him and popped him. Then gave him another one between the eyes to make sure. Looks like 9mm, coroner will get the bullets out of the skull for forensics. I found a wad of cash in his pocket along with his wallet, half a joint and an empty flask."

"Wits?" Hix asked. His hair growing damp from the sleet, he brushed a gloved hand over it.

"So far, no witnesses. Customers park in front and the staff park in the back but they were all already inside. A might coincidental, us looking for him to question in the murders and he's murdered?" Sinclair said without much certainty in his comment.

Stuffing his phone back in his pocket, Hix didn't respond.

Prince's mouth crooked a brief cynical smile, he responded drily, "No such thing, my man, as coincidences in murder, eh?" The wind swept his sandy hair up and around, he patted it down only for it to blow right around again.

Hix turned in a slow circle, he stated, "No cameras back here."

"Nope, none in front neither. There's one down at the grocery but one of the staff works there is here with the onlookers and he said he doubted it's functioning. I have officers canvassing," Sinclair told them.

The sergeant glanced about at the activity buzzing around them, then went on, "The waitress said Howie, who apparently was more the town drunk than anything, told her he was coming into some money. He'd gotten a bit of dough and was going to get paid big for a job he did, or was doing, or was going to do. She wasn't sure exactly what he said. She said the only reason why she was going to go out with Fernell was because he had money or she 'wouldn't have given the fat guy the time of day.' Her words."

"Huh," Hix grunted, "typical broad. I'm heading out, I want to see if we got anything back on the chains. Thomas?"

Prince told him, "I'm gonna stay here, see if anything comes up. Daron will give me a ride back, woncha Sarg?" He smirked at Sinclair.

The sergeant grinned at him from under the brim of the Stetson. "Mebbe. Mebbe I'll make you sit in back where Brutus hangs." Brutus was Sinclair's mastiff.

"Aw, hey now," Prince protested, "all that dog hair? Come on, man, I have an image to uphold with the ladies." Panning his suit with his hands he grinned at Sinclair.

"Yeah, right, the lady canines you mean," Sinclair joshed back at him.

"Later kids," Hix tossed over his shoulder hiking around the diner to his truck.

Back at the station he hunted down Teague McGuire.

The officer was in his cube, a phone caught between his ear and shoulder, he glanced up as Hix stopped by his office. He motioned to Hix with a finger, one minute.

Hix pulled over a chair and straddled it, resting his forearms along the back.

Teague ended his call. "Whattup, Hix?" He laid the phone on the desk. "Kurt called me and said your person of interest, Howard Fernell was found dead behind a diner."

He picked up a pen and lowered his head to a notebook, brushed a palm over the top of his Marine style hair as he reviewed his prior notes.

"Yeah." Hix waited while Teague made a notation then turned his attention back to the detective.

"Random or what?" Teague asked, setting his pen down.

"Or what. I doubt he's our suspect. I'm guessing the women's killer, or killers were snipping a loose end. We checked his financials. We believe that Fernell was paid to buy the lumber that the boxes were made of, and now he was killed so he couldn't tell who paid him to purchase the wood.

"A waitress at the diner said he was getting paid big to do a job, or did a job. The wood they say is quite expensive, way out of

Fernell's pay range, which I understand is minimum wage, that's when he's actually working. His rep in town is that he's a deadbeat drunk."

Nodding, Teague mentioned, "Heard the dude lives in a shithole apartment, not likely he has a secondary place to build the boxes and torture the vics."

Hix nodded while jotting down his own notes, questions he'd thought of to pursue later.

"So, you're thinking the killer had Fernell purchase the lumber so there would be no evidence the killer bought it. Therefore, he wouldn't be caught on surveillance or his credit card pointing to him. Then he hit Fernell so he couldn't tell on him. Why'd Fernell use his credit card instead of the likely untraceable cash the killer would have given him to buy the wood?"

Hix grunted. "It was a debit card. Fernell deposited the cash as far as his financials tell us then used the debit card to purchase the wood. Probably didn't want to be wandering around with that much money on him. He spent most his time intoxicated so he would have worried he'd either lose it or someone would rob him.

"He did have a pack of bills in his pocket. He lives on the cheap, he doesn't have a phone so we can't check his phone records. Besides, paying that huge amount of cash for the wood would have drawn attention at the time."

Tucking his notebook away, Hix informed the officer, "We have some uniforms out to the bars, the really dive ones, seeing if anyone can place someone with Fernell. Someone that doesn't quite fit into the dumps. Guy rich enough to afford the wood and pay Fernell would stand out like a sore thumb.

"Mike Maverick is checking his derelict apartment, canvassing the neighbors. Judging by the description of the place, he'll have a tough time questioning stoners and thugs."

Teague asked, "Why the hell did the killer choose such unusual, expensive, hard to get wood anyway? Why not just buy run-of-the-mill, easy to find cheap plywood that could have been bought anywhere, or cherry wood if he wanted pretty?"

"The guy is a narcissist," Hix replied. "He's dramatic, wants his material to be exotic with his carved wood and fancy chains. He's showing off. You get anything on the chains?"

A large smile curved above the officer's strong jaw. Teague kept his chestnut brown hair trimmed in a short crew-cut, clean facial hair, light brown eyes twinkled with intelligence and good humor. "Oh yeah, lab determined the material. It's, ah," he poked at his phone.

Finding the information, he said, "They were made of palladium. Reserves are basically from Russia and South Africa, there's a limited supply. They make catalytic converters and electronic circuits out of the metal. I must say, your killer has intriguing taste."

"Uh huh, and lots of money, and special knowledge of the unique materials he, or she, is using, and the ability to find and obtain them. Any way to track where the materials came from? If we even have this, ah…"

"Palladium," Teague filled in.

"Yeah. Can you find out if there is any of the stuff here locally?"

Teague shrugged one shoulder. "Dunno. Already on it though. I'll give you a heads up when I get anything."

"All right." Hix got up, put the chair back. Said, "Later," as he ambled out the door.

# Chapter Fourteen

**H**e stood at the back of his van, annoyed that he had to do it this way. He had enjoyed enticing Kimi and Eden with his good looks and their sexual gluttony.

Unfortunately, he hadn't been able to give Kimi what she'd wanted, he'd forgotten about the intubation and she'd died before he could show her that good time he'd promised when they'd made their date.

He'd had to have sex with her without her awareness, she didn't get to enjoy it. Because of course she was dead. Still, he'd gotten his rocks off. Several times. It was more fun when they were alive, aware and terrified, but he'd take what he could get.

Moving a step from behind the van, he carefully checked around. Nothing. Damned bitch, making him have to do it the hard way. He muttered, "Yeah, Kimi had died too quickly before I could show her who was boss. But," his crafty smile lengthened, recalling the memory of his time with Eden fizzled tingles in his nether parts, making him hard.

He'd had hours of fun time with Eden. He had learned the proper amount to keep her paralyzed yet aware, and alive. He had set up an old oxygen machine before he'd snatched Eden. Alternating air, knife cuts, curling iron burns, and fucking her motionless yet fully aware body had been like his own little Disneyland.

Everything he did, he'd lean in close, watch every expression in Eden's eyes. Sure, she was paralyzed, but her eyes were so expressive, it was hellacious titilating.

The only thing was, she wasn't able to tell him how great he was. How big, how hard. He sort of missed being able to hear the groans, whimpers, screams from his women, not of pleasure, no, but of the blinding, excruciating agony. Now that was orgasmic. For him.

He had let the dose wear off a few times so he could enjoy Eden's fighting, her screams, but she was worn out, could only groan and hang limp as an old sausage towards the end, wasn't as much fun. Maybe this time he'd hold off on the paralytic drug for a bit. He-

A sound lifted his head, he cocked an ear to it. He had spent a good amount of time learning his next quarry's schedule. She attended church then had brunch with her family every Sunday before she headed out for her playtime.

His only opportunity to grab her was now, when she stopped at the ATM on the way. She picked up her money for the week's spending on her way to play. Peeking around the van that he had strategically placed near the ATM where she'd have to park, his mood lifted.

He wore a black hooded sweatshirt, a beanie covering his head with the hood over it. The sweatshirt zipped up to the neck, he had on black gloves and black jeans. He blended nicely against the black van.

There were two other cars in the lot. The people must have gone off with others, because he'd checked and the cars were empty and the stores closed. But that was good because his van wouldn't stand out in the stark lot and make her wary.

A large, silver Honda sedan pulled into the empty lot. Due to the antiquated Blue Law, it was Sunday, the stores were closed. The ATM was in front of a children's clothing store. He heard her pull up, shut off the engine, but her door didn't open. He assumed she was a little put off by the van.

There was no sound for a moment, he figured she was peering out to see if anyone was in the van that might be waiting to rob her.

He heard a door open and close with no beep-beep lock engage, and smiled. Apparently she felt safe that she was alone.

Her footsteps were light over the blacktop as she trod quickly up to walk in front of the shops and then to the money machine.

He stayed behind the van until she reached the machine, not daring to get himself caught on the ATM's camera.

He'd already put the other surveillance cameras he could reach out of action, knocked them off with a crowbar, then ripped them out and took the memory cards and video feeds. Those would be left in her car. The other cameras were too high for him to reach but their film would be blurry from the being so far away.

While the woman was occupied with the machine, her back facing out, he crept around the van, and silently opened the back passenger door of her car that she had negligently not locked thinking she was alone in the vacant lot.

Crawling inside, with the faintest of clicks, he shut the door, and slid down to the floor until he was hidden behind the front seats. And waited. The tinted windows and dark night would hide him. He had to suppress the giggles of anticipatory glee that threatened to escape his throat that was tense with excitement.

It wasn't long before he heard the front driver's door open. He held his breath as she climbed in, the leather seats crinkling from her weight. As soon as she slid the key in the ignition, he popped up.

Before she even became completely aware he was there, the needle was in her neck. Her wide eyes slammed into his in the rearview mirror, a silent scream gagged in her throat. As she slumped in the seat, he grinned his success.

The hard part was getting her unconscious body out of her car and into his van. Every inch of him was covered, last thing he needed was to leave his DNA in her car. Of course he was going to ensure none was ever going to be found.

After he threw her into the van and tied her up, he tossed the video cams into the sedan then took out the can of gasoline he'd brought and poured it all over the front and backseat of her car. He stepped back and ripped a match out of a matchbook.

He paused, craned his neck around to ensure he was completely alone, no one had driven by, and he struck the match and tossed it inside the car. Flames erupted instantly, the fire roared to life.

By the time he climbed in the van, the Honda was engulfed.

"Hey, that was exciting, what'd you think, Annalisa?" He heard no response from the back of the van, he didn't expect any.

Whistling his favorite tune, he trucked off down the highway with his prize rolling back and forth on the floor of the van with the rocking and swerving movements of the vehicle.

# Chapter Fifteen

Lurching into the room, Laurin's breaths gasped in a frenzy, her heart beating like cymbals banging in her chest. "What if he catches me, I'm so dead. Benji's dead," she murmured in overwhelming anxiety to herself.

Closing the door behind her as quietly as she could, she leaned her back against the door while trying to slow her pulse.

Before moving, her eyes bounced around the room searching, she'd already looked everywhere for his computer. She'd almost gotten caught the other night when he came home unexpectedly. She'd barely gotten out before Rádolfo came in the front door.

Her head swiveling, looking back and forth, up and down, she slowly made her way across the beige carpeting. She had previously gone through his desk, his cabinets, the closet.

She'd checked behind the two paintings in the room and searched the bookcase, pulled out every individual book. The clock on his desk told her she had a little more time before he was due back.

"Where, where, where did you put it, Rádolfo?" If only she could get the information, the goods on him, the CIA would arrest him and she and Benji and Robbie would be free. This whole nightmare would be over and maybe she could have a life, the boys could have real lives.

She could go somewhere, where no one knew her, no more snide judgmental hatred, no brutal abuse from her husband, and start a new life with the boys.

Maybe she could ask that detective for guidance. No, she frowned, shaking her head. He had been kind the last time she saw him, but he had told her the night of the ball what he really thought of her.

A shiver tingled up her spine at the thought of the big, dark, scary looking detective. He frightened the death out of her, yet, she felt uncannily alive, as if touching a live wire whenever he was near.

"Let it go, Laurin," she told herself, forcing thoughts of the tough man out of her mind, she needed to get on with business. She had enough trouble with the man she was tied to. She didn't need to get involved with the cop, who was very…attractive…in a dangerous kind of way.

Shaking her head, she already had too much danger in her life. She wanted peace and safety for her and the boys, and no one was going to help her, everything depended on her.

Stalking around the room, running her fingers through her long hair as the anxiety built, Laurin's seeking gaze darted everywhere. The floor, the walls, the ceiling.

Her eyes drifted to the bottom of the bookcase, she blinked. She had searched behind every book last week, but, something was different.

Hurrying over, she dropped to her knees. "Oh yes, the books have been rearranged. Hemingway has been switched with a reference book."

Moving quickly, she anxiously tugged the books out setting them on the floor. On her hands and knees, she lowered to her stomach and peered into the case, and yes, something was there.

"Oh, my goodness!" Her heart trilled with relief. The paint on the wall was a slight shade different than a foot away.

Laurin pawed at the wall, scratching and rubbing, her finger caught on something sticking out of the wall. It had been hidden by the border of the bookcase.

A tiny lever, she pushed it down, and heard a click. Reaching in, she was able to stick her hand in and push a small door aside, a pocket-door. Eyes wide, Laurin pulled the computer out, and a heavy breath of relief gushed from her tight lungs.

Setting it in her lap, her hands shaking, she lifted the lid and powered it on. As she stared at the laptop lighting up, her heart clenched. "Even if I get it on, heaven knows what the password is."

While she waited, Laurin ran ideas through her head. His date of birth, the dates of birth of his sons, his grandson baby Channing's, their address.

After she got it up and running and worked on it, her stomach sank, none of the passwords she tried were fruitful. She could literally hear the clock on the desk ticking, her time ticking away. She glanced up at it, he would be home soon.

Quickly, she powered the laptop down and shoved it into its hiding place and carefully put the books back exactly as they were. Standing up, she brushed her hands on her jeans and hurried to the door.

Opening it carefully, she listened if anyone was nearby. Hearing not a sound, she poked her head out, the coast was clear. Laurin stepped out, closed and locked the door behind her and moved swiftly to the staircase.

When her foot hit the top step, she about jumped out of her skin.

"Laurin, there you are darling." Rádolfo was suddenly right in front of her.

Her breath caught.

"I looked for you in our bedroom, the kitchen, the library, the morning room, the boy's room, I, well," he grinned with a sigh at her. "I thought for a moment there that you had gone. Made a run for it. However," the grin curved to evil points on both ends, "I didn't think you'd leave the boy alone in the lion's den."

"Oh, um," she steadied her voice, tried to smile at him, kept her hands still so she wouldn't nervously fidget with her hair showing her guilt. "Of course I didn't go anywhere, I would never leave," she was about to say Benji and was smart enough to say, "you." That earned her a smile from her husband.

"How sweet, darling, come with me, let's see how I can reward you for that kind sentiment. It's been over a week since we've spent time alone together." Tall and fitting handsomely into black slacks and a cream-colored cashmere sweater, dark hair combed neatly to the side, his dark brown eyes wandered up and down Laurin's body, they narrowed on a bruise showing on her collar bone as she shifted.

"Oh." He smiled, said with false regret, "I need to be more careful where those bruises show, don't I, my little wife?"

A pang struck her heart, he wanted to have sex. Of course he did, he always did. Brutal sex. At least he wasn't mad, thank God for that, he was tortuously vicious when angry with her. "Sure, um, honey."

He took her hand. Smiling tenderly down at her, Rádolfo lifted her hand and kissed her knuckles then walked her down the corridor to their bedroom. As they entered, he said casually, "So, you were about to tell me where you were."

Her breath stunted, she almost tripped. Keeping her voice level, she said, "Oh, um, I was in the kitchen checking to see if we had confectioner sugar so I could bake your favorite cake."

He closed the door, locked it, stepped to her and plucked at the top button on her blouse. Sliding his hand around to cup the back of her head, he lifted it then bent and kissed her gently.

Laurin prepared herself, he was never gentle. She responded the way she knew he liked, rolling her hands around his waist with a soft hum.

"And was there enough?" he murmured against her lips.

"Enough?" Laurin was steeling herself for his attack.

"Sugar."

Letting him slide his tongue in her mouth and take possession of it, she nodded.

Rádolfo suddenly gripped the sides of her blouse and tore it open. Buttons flew through the room. Jerking the blouse off, he dropped it to the floor and put his hand around the front of her neck, and squeezed.

125

At her gasp, he said softly, "Thing is, darling, I checked the kitchen. You weren't there, and Cook said she hadn't seen you. Now, tell me where you were."

Laurin couldn't draw air through her crushed throat. She pulled slightly from his grasp, sucked in a huff and said calmly, "I was in the back pantry, Rádolfo, where the baking supplies are kept. Mrs. Lanfield was not in the kitchen when I went in or came out the side entrance so she couldn't have known I was there. You can check the outside surveillance monitors, you'll see I never left the house."

Laurin prayed he'd be appeased with that. He would think she would be too afraid to go into his office, and as far as he knew, she'd have no reason to be there, and no way to pick the lock. So he wouldn't have thought she'd been in there. His concern was that she'd been outside trying to get away.

His fingers still tight around her throat, Rádolfo stared hard into her blue eyes, trying to detect her lie. He was sure she was lying... "All right, darling, I'll believe you, for now."

Releasing his clutch on her throat, his strong hands skimmed down to the button on her jeans. "But, you will pay when we're done for making me have to look for you. You deserve it, don't you, my darling?" Popping the button, he reached around and cupped her bottom, his fingers like steel nails squeezed until she whimpered.

Her body slumped with resignation that after the brutal sex she would suffer a savage beating. "Yes, Rádolfo, I deserve it."

She held still as he ripped her clothes off her, destroying yet more of her meager wardrobe.

# Chapter Sixteen

**H**ix's team met early in the morning. He took a gulp of hot coffee, set the mug down then looked around at his team.

Thomas Princeton, Daron Sinclair, Emilee Rivera, Teague McGuire, Kurt Klaus and Mike Maverick were all present.

Hix asked, "Do we know the name of the vic?"

Sinclair nodded solemnly. "Yes. A Miss Annalisa Dominicci. Her car was found burned out in front of the Land O'Goshen Shopping Plaza. We ran the VIN and pulled it up on the DMV and matched the deceased with the picture." He motioned to the murder board. Another woman's photo was taped to the board, a list of words were written under it.

Hix reviewed the notations. Employees coming to work at the plaza Monday morning had discovered the latest victim behind the stores.

Originally, when a car on fire was reported, the firefighters and police cleared the burned car, but never checked behind the plaza. They assumed it had either been stolen and dumped, or set afire for insurance money. So the body wasn't discovered until the next day.

But, the perp had set the victim up behind the shops.

She was as the others, found nude in front of a wooden box, spray painted rose-gold, chain clamped around her neck, X's in a heart shape carved into her stomach, and round burn marks in the center of the heart. She was 23, blonde, blue-eyed, 5'3, 115 pounds.

And Hix knew who she was. Sort of.

He stood up with his mug in his hand, gestured to the board and said, "I know her."

"You know her?" Prince moved to stand beside Hix as he stepped closer to the board.

"Not exactly know. I attended a wedding, she was there."

"You went to a wedding? I thought that wasn't something the brooding detective would ever care to attend," Kurt joked.

His lips pulled in ruefully, Hix admitted, "My mother made me do it."

Chuckles wafted through the room. "The old 'my mother made me do it?'" Mike Maverick laughed. "And this from our fearless leader. Who knew you had a sense of humor?"

"Okay, enough of the joviality." Hix cleared his throat frowning at the grins. "Anyway, the couple that got married, the groom was a good friend of my brother Aven who was going to be out of town, so I was rounded up and forced to do the duty of escorting one of the bride's girlfriends that had fairly recently moved to town."

He left out the part about his mother trying to fix him up with Carmella, and also about Laurin Ajanel with little Benji being present.

"There was a young couple that sat next to me. As they were leaving, this girl," he nodded to the board, "Annalisa, joined them, she must have been sitting further back. I'll get a copy of the guest list so we can question, uh, I think it was her sister, Kelsey or Chelsea or something, that was sitting next to me.

"We'll question the bride and groom as well if we can get a hold of them, they're out of the country on their honeymoon. Okay," he tipped his chin to the board and asked, "witnesses? Video?"

"They're being brought in now," Sinclair told him. "This one was a bit different from the others. The outside cameras were pulled and destroyed and the vic's car was burned, it was deliberate, arson."

"Maybe he was in her car and was destroying any evidence, DNA," Prince said.

Nodding, Sinclair replied, "Remnants of the surveillance cameras were found in the car. Not enough to get anything off them."

For a moment the group silently explored the board looking for some correlation between the victims. Their jobs, friends, family, church, clubs, everything that could be found out about them was on the board.

So far, only their vague descriptions and that they were all killed on the weekend were the only things that matched between the three women, there were no other intersections. Then, a sound from the side had heads turning.

Emilee Rivera was blushing, she licked her lips then pinched them together.

"What is it, Officer Rivera?" Hix asked, his tone on the sharp side, the woman annoyed him.

"Uh." She stood up, pointed at the photos of the boxes, they were identical except for the carvings on the trim. "I thought they were somehow familiar in the beginning, now, now I recognize them for what they are," she swallowed hard as her face grew darker red.

"And?" Hix demanded. "What about them? What are they?"

All eyes on her, Emilee raised her shoulders and then her palms. "They resemble uh, boxes, cages you would find at a BDSM dungeon, or in, uh, a Dom's home."

Dead silence.

"Uh, a, ah, Dominant," she explained.

Mike Maverick laughed with disbelief. "And you know this how?"

Emilee's face glowed with embarrassment. "Uh, through personal experience. I've seen them...a few times."

"Whoa," Sinclair grunted.

"Yeah." Kurt and Mike grinned.

"You're positive?" Hix questioned her with a frown to the men.

She nodded, the short brown bob bobbed around her chin. "Yes. Positive. The chain collar, the slave position, their uh, the nudity, I'd swear it's all a takeoff on a slave box."

Hix waved his hand to settle down the sudden chatter in the room. He asked Emilee, "You recognize those in particular? I mean do you know whose they are?"

Shaking her head, Emilee patted her cheeks to dissipate the color. "No. I've never seen them before, or the chains. It's just the basic format that's recognizable. You can purchase the entire box over the net. The ones I've seen were at the, uh, clubs."

"This whole deal is handmade, Penn," Princeton offered. "It's a signature. The perp is familiar with the lifestyle. Since the things were handmade, someone might recognize the individual's particular design."

His hands on his hips, Hix asked Emilee, "How many of those…places, are there in the general area?"

The blush rose again. "Ah," Emilee replied, "I know of two clubs in Brevet Bay, there'd be another, three or four maybe in Alexandria? Washington?" Her shoulder bumped. "Who knows? They can be googled." With a sly wink, she said, "I'd be more than happy to take you to one."

Ignoring that comment and the snickers in the room, Hix said, "Rivera, you contact the ones here in Brevet. Kurt, you and Sinclair locate the ones in Alexandria, we'll start there. Brevet Bay is his killing field, it's more than likely he finds most of his…entertainment where he lives. Bring pictures of the boxes, the chains, and get a list of all…what are they called, uh, attendees?" Hix's brow arched at Emilee.

Her eyes flitting around the room, avoiding contact with the other men, she nodded. "They're called members. Most clubs you have to provide a lot of personal information, physical exams-"

"Exams?" Sinclair asked.

"Uh, yes, you have to provide proof you're clean, you know, no STD's and such, although condoms are mandatory. You can have no sexual or violent criminal histories. Most of the clubs are very expensive to join, background checks are run on everyone who submits an application. Sometimes you can attend as…uh, a guest." Her bright cheeks indicated that's how she afforded to attend the club on a police officer's pay.

"Mike," Hix said, directing his order to Officer Maverick. "You get back on finding out where someone could obtain the metal the chains were made out of. Teague, dig up some witnesses. I know we've searched and canvassed until the cows come home, but, there're enough locations, where the vics were picked up and where they were left that someone had to have seen something."

Both officers nodded their acquiescence to their orders.

Hix said, "Prince, we'll go through the surveillance tapes as they come in. Not all of the cameras were destroyed. Maybe there will be something that stands out about the scene in back, or the front of the store, the torched car or the damned van."

Everyone disbursed to attend to their directives.

Hours later, Prince was rubbing his blue eyes, he yawned big and shook his head. "Hell, I'm going cross-eyed, Penn. This is the tenth time we've watched the tapes. Same black van, same no wits."

Hix replied with his eyes on the film still running, "We need to keep studying this camera video that was up too high for him to destroy. This time we got lucky, we see the abduction, watch him in action. We can see the perp remove Annalisa from his van and carry her to the box."

They had sat silently watching the van pull up behind Land O'Goshen Plaza. A hooded figure all in black got out and proceeded to haul out the large pieces of wood.

The video was fuzzy and staticy like the others had been, things jumped and jittered around on the film, the suspect's blurry body wavered as he moved.

Dawn breaking in the background lent just enough light to observe the activity. It was the perfect time for him to do his thing. Light enough to see what he was doing, but too early for employees to start arriving and catch him, and dim enough if someone drove by way out in the street it would be difficult to detect what he was doing.

With rapt interest, the detectives observed the person work on the box. They thought the person was male by his size and the way he was strong enough to carry the wooden walls, but they couldn't be positive. He was careful to keep his face from the camera. His clothes too bulky and loose to detect a figure.

131

After he put the box together, he went back to the van and stepped from the truck with Annalisa in his arms.

"Could be a very strong female but ten to one that's a male," Prince said.

The suspect carried the woman to the box and set her down in front of it. She was already painted the rose gold.

She was lying on her side at first, then he clamped the chain around her neck and lifted her up by pulling on the chain until he maneuvered her to slump on her knees. Then he positioned her to sit back on her heels.

He drew the chain harder, until it was taut and her torso was straight, then he hooked the chain to the top of the box securing her in position. Her head lolled to the side, the clump of painted hair draped over half her face.

Then he squatted behind her, pulled her arms back and wrapped the twine around her wrists. He tightened her bindings, winding the twine a few inches up her wrists to force her back to arch hard and that pushed her bare breasts up and out, posing her as a sex slave.

"Perv," Prince muttered, "sick bastard."

"When rigor is full on she'll be like a perfect statue," Hix commented. "She's freshly deceased right there. He's definitely posing her not just as a nude slave, but as a lewd exhibition."

"I think he's showing his total disrespect and callous uncaring of females," Prince said, his voice laden with disgust.

The perp wore gloves as he trotted back and forth bringing items from the van then returning tools to the van. He made one more trip to stand and view his work. The detectives could even observe an imperceptible nod of satisfaction from the back of him. He was pleased with his work.

Slipping his cell from his pocket, the perp took a few pictures, then stuffed it back in. Nodding to the woman, he blew a kiss off his fingers and wiggled them at her like a lover before he turned away.

The person started back to the van peeling off his gloves. Twisting his neck to take a last look at the girl and keeping his face from camera view, not watching where he was going, he ran into a small post that marked off medians in the lot.

When he hit the post, he dropped a glove. In one swift fluid move, he placed his hand on the post for balance, bent to one knee and picked up the glove. Tucking them both in his back pocket, he went on to the van, within a minute he drove off.

"That's it," Hix announced, rewinding the tape.

"What? What's it?" Prince's brow furrowed as he stared at the screen trying to see what Hix did.

They watched the tape again, and when it reached the end, Hix said, "See it?"

"Oh my God, how did the techs who watched this first then us the last nine freakin' times we saw it, miss it?"

Hix slid his phone from his pocket and swiped it on, hit some buttons. "We were all so intently focused on the perp trying to catch a shot of his face, and the van, and the victim, how he built the box, placed her, the chain, scanning the area for anything of value. It's dark enough it's hard to even catch that he dropped the glove.

"The camera was up high and aimed more towards the stores than where he had parked, he was at that point a tiny image. And, as bad as the fuzzy wavering film was, when he dropped the glove and picked it up so fast it's mostly a blur."

Hix held the phone to his ear and without a greeting ordered, "Grab a couple of CSI's and go to the last vic, Dominicci's location," he said to whoever answered. "The perp touched the top of a post with his bare hand."

He raised his eyes to the ceiling at the question from the person on the phone, with a duh sound in his voice, he told them, "The one closest to the vic. Print it and do all the others just for fun. Print the rocks on the ground, the sides of the posts, check for any clothing being snagged, buttons popped off.

"Look for nails or anything that could have fallen from the box or the van, or the perp's pockets. I want the minutest search you and your people can achieve. Go over the entire lot with a toothbrush."

He listened for a second then said, "I know you did it already, do it again." Hix rolled his eyes and said with diminishing patience, "I didn't say you were incompetent. Call me when you're done."

Shoving the phone in his pocket, Hix said to Prince, "Let's see if they have anything on the clubs yet."

Prince pushed his chair back with a grunt, and the two men rose and trod down the hall through the bullpen and further on to a room crammed with cubicles.

Kurt was there, he was hanging up a landline. "Hey, Penn, they were reluctant at first, confidentiality and all that shit. Then we threatened with sending all this to the press and see how much business they lose when it gets out the murdered girls may have had something to do with the clubs. They decided to cooperate and are emailing their member lists."

"All right," Hix nodded. "I'll check back in a while and review them with you all." He had an itch. The itch was to see Laurin Ajanel.

Hix despised cheaters, but married or not, his stomach clinched, whether she did her husband wrong or not, the bastard was abusing her. The itch was in his gut burning like agita, he rubbed his belly.

It wasn't far-fetched of his alarm to rise when he had also realized Laurin matched the descriptions of the victims.

She was younger, but she was blonde with blue eyes and petite, much more delicate than the other females, but she matched close enough. She was assuredly safe, she had told Hix she always had a guard on her, but he recalled she'd mentioned she'd previously gotten in trouble for ditching them.

He tried to call her on the cell he'd given her, but it only rang and rang, no voice mail picked up. He called the Ajanel household.

"Ajanel residence, Rogèt speaking," a snooty male voice responded.

"Ah, hello, this is Detective Hixman with the Brevet Bay Police. I would like to speak with Mrs. Ajanel."

"In reference to?" the haughty voice inquired.

Hix barked, "None of your damned business. Put Mrs. Ajanel on the line before I come out there and find some reason to haul you down to the station."

It was quiet, then Rogèt said with a sniff, "Mrs. Ajanel is out purchasing a gown for the Embassy Banquet fundraising event."

"What store is she at?"

"Now see here, Detective, I am not telling you another thing. You can come here with a- a warrant or whatever before I tell you anything else," his affronted sniff rife with arrogance.

"Mr. Ajanel, where is he?"

"He is at the Embassy in Mozambique."

"The boy, Benji? Is he home?"

"That's it, not another word from me, sir. You want more you can-"

Hix stuffed his phone in his pocket and started for his car. Grabbing his jacket from the hook by the door, he shrugged it on and went to his truck. He just needed to see her, ease that feeling that she was in danger.

Starting the car, he initiated the GPS on the phone he had given her, and followed the directions.

# Chapter Seventeen

In the back of the coffee shop, Laurin was in a heated whispered argument with CIA Agent Brewer. She wore a pale butter-colored sweater under a jacket, jeans and ankle boots.

Shoving a hand under her bangs, she rubbed her forehead. "Agent Brewer, I did the best I could. I couldn't get into the computer. I don't know the password."

The tan trench coat he wore on his rangy body wafted around his calves as the agent moved. One hand tucked in his trouser pocket, he scratched his gaunt chin with the other then motioned his hand signaling Laurin to calm down.

He wasn't wearing the fedora or sunglasses so he looked a little less like a CIA agent today. The wind had mussed his thinning brown hair, he spoke in a low voice, "You found it. If you couldn't crack it you should have taken it and brought it to me."

"To you? Are you kidding?"

At his waving hand, she lessened the shrill in her voice and said in an angry whisper, "First of all I'd never get it out of the house. There are monitors surrounding the mansion and the perimeter, I wouldn't have gotten one step out the door before I'd get caught. There's no way I could get down the long drive and out the locked, guarded gate.

"And second, I have no vehicle and no way to leave the premises. And, thirdly, if I did manage to get it to you, and your agents didn't find anything on it, Benji and I would be in deadly trouble. Rádolfo would know it was me that took it. You know I can't get Benji out, and I can't leave him there."

Brewer nodded stiffly. "Yeah, yeah, I know. Okay, listen, I want you to give it another try. Just brainstorm some passwords, search his desk, maybe he wrote it down somewhere, maybe in a notebook or something."

Sifting her fingers in agitation through the sides of her hair, Laurin said desperately, "No, I can't. He- he'll catch me, he'll-"

Brewer stuck his palm up in her face.

When she shut up, he pointed a knobby finger at her, thin lips threatened, "You will do as I say if you ever want to get out of that house. You and Benji, and don't forget your brother. You do what I say. You are all stuck until you come through with the goods. I told you what the score was when I planted you in that house."

His head swiveled, he asked, "How'd you ditch your guard?"

Laurin glanced over her shoulder. "I told him to wait in the car that I was just running in for coffee before dress shopping. He isn't watching me like a hawk like he was. He got beaten pretty badly the last time I ditched him and he's furious with me. He has another job lined up, he's leaving next week, so he doesn't really care what I do."

She was still fretting over the night out with Jewel when she'd almost gotten caught. Jewel's lover had wanted her to give him money. Infuriated, she dumped him and that's why everyone had left the restaurant so quickly. As Laurin had hoped, no one had blabbed about her disappearing for so long, or how she'd gotten home that night.

They'd all had secrets to hide. Jewel's adultery, the driver leaving without Laurin, and of course Laurin herself. If her husband knew she'd been left behind because she hadn't stayed with the group- a shiver roiled through her at the thought.

Brewer mumbled, "Uh huh. Yeah, well, okay. You do as I say, text me. Soon." He nodded sharply to her, spun on his heel and ambled through the coffee shop.

At the door, he peered left and right out the picture window, then quickly exited.

Trying to hold back her frustrated tears, Laurin sucked in a deep breath before squaring her shoulders and walking out of the shop.

She didn't even bother pretending to go for a coffee, she didn't have her purse with her. Not that she had any money anyway, she would have had to go back to the guard and ask him for the money.

Her mind on the meeting with Brewer, she hadn't thought to get cash from the guard before she went in. Her husband never gave her cash, he feared she'd use it to get a taxi and flee.

Laurin was halfway down the cobbled walk to the car when she passed an opening between two buildings at the same time that a group of people did.

"Hey, there's that murdering slut!" someone called out.

Cringing, Laurin ducked her head and moved faster but something hit her in the back of the head and she stumbled into the alleyway.

Catching her balance she turned around aghast and saw a woman swinging a large purse at her head. Laurin threw her arm up and blocked the blow but the hit was hard, it knocked her to the side.

"Yeah, bitch! Let's show her what we think of whoring killers!" a male shouted.

More angry voices rang out, and suddenly Laurin was being pummeled from all sides, each hit knocking her deeper into the alley. Trying to get away, she pushed at people, tried to run, someone grabbed her jacket.

Leaving the jacket in the man's hand, Laurin screamed and attempted to run back to the front of the alley when one person grasped her sweater, another slammed his hand into her hair and snatched a handful, preventing her from fleeing.

The man held her arms behind her back and a woman slapped her, then another, she dropped to her knees on the hard cobblestone and they started kicking her, punching her.

**Hix** knew when he saw the Lincoln SUV parked along the curb he was in the right place. Parking his truck, he strode up to the Lincoln and rapped his knuckles on the window.

The window rolled down, a bored looking man drawled, "Yeah? What do you want?"

"You work for Rádolfo Ajanel?" Hix flashed his badge.

The man's eyes dropped to the badge then shrugged. "Yeah, so what?

"Where is Mrs. Ajanel?"

Another negligent shrug. "Don't know, don't care."

"Isn't it your job to be watching her?"

The guard blinked bloodshot eyes at him, repeated, "Yeah, so what?"

"Well, how can you be watching her and not know where she is?"

His voice turning belligerent, the man snarked gruffly, "Listen, that little bitch caused me a badass beating a few weeks ago. Only good thing is she got a hell of a whuppin' as well. She ditched me and my partner, and Ajanel found out and I got a beat-down I'll never forget. My partner is still in the hospital. I got another job lined up. I don't need this shit. Pay is great, but the broken bones ain't worth it. So I-"

Shouts sounded from up the street. Hix's head turned, the uninterested guard remained placid.

"Where did Laurin say she was going?" Hix asked the guard with urgency.

When he didn't answer, Hix reached inside the car, grabbed his collar in his fist and jerked his head out the window. In his face, Hix ground out, "Where the fuck is she? Tell me or your last beat-down will feel like a kindergarten playground fight."

Hix's ferociously lethal face inches from the now frightened man, the guard opened his mouth stuttering, before he could get a word out screams ripped up the street with numerous shrieks and yelling.

"Fuck," Hix swore, let the guard's collar go and he sprinted up the street towards the noise.

The screams grew more agonized and frightened as he reached a wide passageway between buildings.

There were several people whooping and hollering at whatever was going on between the stores.

Hix pushed through the voyeurs and blanched.

A group of people were cursing and hitting, kicking Laurin. No longer screaming, she was on the ground rolled in a ball trying to protect her head.

"Goddammit!" Barking a string of curses in two languages, Hix shoved people out of the way, then grabbed the back of the man's collar that was crouching and punching at Laurin.

He wrenched him up and bashed him in the jaw so hard the man staggered backwards and banged into a wall smashing his head against the bricks, he landed on his ass with a thump and a groan.

Clutching his face, the man wailed, "You broke my jaw you bastard! Owww."

Hix socked a second man that was kicking Laurin, then slammed his fist into the man's nose. The sound of bones cracking came before the man screamed, clasped his face and fell to his knees screeching in pain.

"Police, get the fuck back," Hix shouted, pulling and shoving people until he reached Laurin.

Her clothes were torn, blood splattered her sweater, her jeans, the arms that shielded her head that weren't covered by ripped material were scratched and gouged.

"Damn, Laurin." Hix dropped to his knees and went to help her.

When she felt his hands on her she screamed hoarsely and flailed her hands at him.

"Shit, girl, it's me, Penn, Detective Hixman, let me help you."

He slid an arm around her, held her against his chest to secure her from hitting out, and fished his phone out. He pushed a number, barked into the phone, the address and to send police and ambulances.

People stood gawking. The two men Hix had punched were sobbing, a couple of women were trying to help them.

His arms around her, Hix lifted Laurin to her feet, but her legs crumpled. He slid his arm under hers and maneuvered her to lean against a wall.

He brushed the hair off her battered, tear-streaked face, blood poured from everywhere, bruises were already forming on her skin, her face, arms, her neck. "Damn, Laurin, what the hell happened here?"

Gasping, choking on sobs, Laurin bent over, clutched her belly and shook her head. "They- nothing, they called me names then- they just-" she coughed, cried, "they started hi- hitting me," her voice broke into choking sobs.

"Damned right, little slut," a boxy woman pronounced. "I hit the bitch with my purse, she deserves a lot worse for cheating on that handsome ambassador. She's lucky he publicly forgave her and didn't throw her out on her cheating ass! She should be in jail!"

Looking around, Hix commanded the vicious mob, "No one leaves, no one moves or I'll have everyone arrested." He glared at the people who were now appearing chastened, yet still threw angry, resentful glowers at Laurin.

He turned back to her and muttered, "You're still paying for what you did, Laurin. Your lessons are hard bought." He didn't notice her chest hitch with a pained gasp at his harsh words, sirens could be heard in the distance.

"Stay here," he told her. Making sure she was able to stand on her own with the support of the wall, he flinched at the damage done to her beautiful face. Then he jogged out of the alley to direct the police approaching.

The first car that pulled up, Hix held a hand out, flagging them, then walked up to the car as it stopped. Two officers climbed out.

"Detective Penn Hixman," Hix showed his badge, then told them the people gathered there were attacking a woman in the alley. He wanted all of them held.

"There are two injured males, I want them restrained at the hospital then brought down to the station, and arrested for aggravated battery. That female," he pointed to the pugnacious woman who had struck Laurin with her purse and said, "I want her arrested right now for battery. Question them all, anyone else that appears to have hit or restrained the victim, take them in and charge them. I'll fill out the probable cause reports later."

"Yes sir, right away, sir," one of the officers said, and they both rushed to follow his orders.

Another car rolled up. Cops burst from it and immediately started corralling the crowd so no one could leave the scene. Officers and civilians shouted at each other as people were hustled to line up against a storefront.

Seeing everything was under control, Hix jogged back to see to Laurin. He shouldn't have said anything to her, he was sure she was well aware that she brought most of this trouble on herself. Still, he couldn't deny her irresistible draw, and the ruthless beating she'd just taken was senseless, vigilante insanity.

He still found it hard to believe she was guilty of what she'd been accused. But from everything he'd read, Laurin had never denied any of the accusations, not the affair, the pregnancy, or the attempted murder. If she had been innocent wouldn't she have put up a fight to clear her name?

Hix stopped dead. Laurin wasn't where he left her. "*What the hell,*" he mumbled, where could she have gone? She was seriously injured, she couldn't have gotten far.

Looking down, he saw a jacket, he grabbed it thinking it might be hers. He felt something in a pocket and pulled it out, it was the tiny cell phone. Clutching the jacket in his hand, he saw a blood trail splotching the cracked cobblestones.

Dashing down the corridor, his boots pounding the red and brown stones, he saw a little ways down, a small road crossed the alley. Tracing the blood, he rounded the wall and found her.

Laurin was barely standing, her cheek pressed against the bricks, her head was down, her body collapsed into the wall. If it weren't for the bricks she would be flat on the ground.

"Dammit, Laurin, what the hell-" he hurried to her.

When he reached his hand to her, she let out a cry and turned from him. Pressing bloodied hands along the bricks, she used the wall to prop her up as she moved away from him.

"Laurin, stop," he commanded and put his palm on the wall, his arm fencing her, halting her movement. He gently cupped her damaged chin and lifted her face to peer at her.

Her eyes were wet and swollen purple, split lips trembled, bruised jaw shook. "Laurin, why did you move from where I left you? I called an ambulance for you."

"Leave me a- alone," she sobbed, futilely trying to free her jaw from his grip. Her chest hitched with choking sobs.

Hix looked down at the small hands urgently pressing at his chest trying to push him away. She was leaving bloody prints all over his shirt under his open jacket. "Hey, hey, Laurin, calm down, I'm just helping you."

"No," she choked, "you hate me just as much as- as all those other p- people. Just," the sobs shook her slender shoulders, "leave me alone." Her body was slowly sinking under her battered weakened legs.

Perturbed, Hix's palm was on the bricks next to her, he moved it to under her arm to hold her up. "I don't hate you, Laurin. Just what you did."

"Yes you do, you all hate me, just, leave me, I'll...I have to g- get home. My driver is waiting out front."

Actually he wasn't. As soon as Hix had moved away from the Lincoln the car sped off.

"He's gone, Laurin, come on, I'll help you to my truck and take you to the hospital." He slipped her jacket on her and slid his hand around to support her back.

"No." Shaking her head, tears spilled blending with the blood on her broken face. "I don't need to go to- to the hospital. I'll walk home," she sounded so weary, so sad, so hurt. "Please leave me alone," she gave him a weak push. "I don't want your help." She took a wobbled step and her body crumpled towards the cobblestones.

Muttering, "Stubborn woman," before she hit the ground, Hix bent his knees, slid his arms under her legs and back, and carefully lifted her up in his arms. Tucking her tightly against his chest, he strode back up the alley and out to the street.

The police were doing as he'd told them. They were getting ID's, taking statements, the two men he'd hit were being loaded into ambulances.

Hix nodded to the officer he'd spoken with as he passed by with Laurin. She was struggling for him to put her down. Her feeble attempts didn't slow him a bit.

Laurin cried against his shoulder, "Put me down, I have to go home, I'm fine, I'll...just...walk," her head fell into his shoulder, then it fell back. Her body went limp as she passed out. Her upper back arched over his arm, her head draped down, long hair a flowing yellow curtain.

Hix glanced down at her as he walked to his truck. Her entire face was bruised and swelling, her lips were cut, looked like fingernails had scraped across her cheeks and neck.

His stomach turned over, how could anyone beat this tiny female? She wasn't just a magnet to lusting men, she was a magnet to drawing abuse. Hadn't she paid for her crimes by now?

He carried her to his truck, propped her inside, buckled her belt then carefully lowered her to lie on her side.

She didn't wake on the way to the Imperial Summit Hospital. He lifted her out and carried her inside. A hospital staff member saw him and hurried right over.

"Sir, what happened?" She directed him to the emergency room, and when they entered it, she pointed to a gurney to set Laurin on.

His eyes on Laurin, Hix told the helpful woman gruffly, "She's been...beaten. Get a doctor."

"Oh," the woman paused. "I'm...sorry, if she's been assaulted we have to call the police." She nodded to a counter and said, "Let me get you started on the paperwork."

His head bent low to Laurin, Hix glared up at the nurse. "I am the police. Get the fucking doctor, she's bleeding, she may have internal injuries. *Go.*"

The woman's mouth opened, she slapped it shut and took off.

Hix was shuffled out of the emergency room and moved into a waiting area. While the doctor examined Laurin, Hix filled out paperwork. He didn't know about insurance and he wasn't about to contact her husband, or even tell the hospital who she was. He called the officer he'd given instructions to at the crime site.

When the officer answered, Hix said, "Look for a purse, I have the victim at Imperial Summit. If you find it have someone bring it here."

He waited for the officer's response then said, "Thanks," and shoved his cell in his pocket. Then he found a chair and settled back to wait for the doctor. He had pushed to stay with Laurin, but the doctor had adamantly ordered him out. Said he'd have security haul him out of he kept resisting.

It was taking so long, Hix started pacing, and was about to go to the desk and demand to see Laurin, when the doctor passed through doors that swooshed open automatically in front of him, and closed behind him. A file tucked under his arm, he strode up to Hix who was moving towards him.

"Detective?" the doctor held his hand out to shake.

Hix impatiently shook his hand, didn't wait for the doctor to introduce himself, he spoke tersely, "How is she? I want to see her."

"Ah, you aren't her...relative? Spouse? I'm not sure I can tell you-"

Through grit teeth Hix snarled, "I'm a goddamned cop, she's been beaten. Now, talk to me, I want to know the extent of her injuries."

The doctor, in his late fifties was fit and had only a feathering of grey in his dark brown hair. The file in his hand, he crossed his arms under the scope hanging around his neck, it jostled over the pens in the pocket of his white lab coat. "I think I should speak first to her family. I-"

"She has no family, she's an orphan. Doctor," Hix leaned towards him, his already fierce anger burning, he demanded, "fucking talk to me."

Somewhat taken aback, the flustered doctor, his hair combed neatly to the side nodded abruptly. "Fine, come with me." He turned back to the emergency room.

Hix followed him down a beige and yellow tiled floor lined with yellow walls to an office.

"Have a seat." The doctor gestured to a pair of chairs in front of a large, messy desk. The doctor set the file on his desk then sat in the leather chair behind it.

Hix settled in one of the chairs and stared at the doctor waiting for him to talk.

With a heavy sigh, the man said, "I am Doctor Ryan Rothschild." He waited for Hix to acknowledge his introduction. He knew the detective's name because he'd put it on the paperwork.

When Hix only glared back at him with his impatient steely gaze, the doctor sighed again. Rothschild took a long look at Hix's hands, they were rolled in tight fists resting on his thighs. There were slight abrasions and redness on his knuckles. His eyes rose to Hix in accusation.

Hix scowled at him, then flexed his fingers on both hands. "I did not hit her, for fuck's sake doctor. She was attacked by a small mob right out on the street between some stores. I had to knock a few heads to get to her."

Rothschild's brows arched in surprise. "Why on earth would a group of people assault that child?"

Dragging his palms down his thighs, his irritation making him brusque and rude, Hix snapped, "Why it happened doesn't matter." Realizing he was only hindering their conversation with his belligerence, Hix drew in a deep breath, exhaled, and said a shade more calmly, "Please, Doctor, can we talk about Laurin, I need to know her...situation to see how to proceed."

Rothschild brushed his back against his chair then leaned forward, his face grim. "She took quite a beating, detective, which of course you know. Head to toe bruising. Fortunately there are no fully broken bones and I didn't find any devastating damage to her organs yet. However, I believe her kidneys are bruised, she has two cracked ribs.

"The lacerations and heavy bruising on her body are going to cause her considerable pain for some time, she definitely should have complete rest for several weeks. She may have a concussion that needs watching. She shouldn't be left alone to care for herself. I want to keep her under observation for a week, after she's released someone will need to monitor her for any adverse reactions."

Hix's lids lowered shrouding eyes that flared with explosive rage.

"Ah," Rothschild hemmed and tugged at his chin, then drummed his fingers on his desk.

"What? What is it? Spit it out." Hix leaned forward, palms on his thighs, shoulders bunched as he tried to rein in his fury.

Rothschild opened the file. "Normally I wouldn't tell anyone this without first speaking with the patient and obtaining her permission, but," he took a breath that Hix's hard face, expression so on edge he appeared about to do something violent.

"Since you are law enforcement, and, some really bad shit, pardon my language, has been going down with that poor girl, I suppose it would be prudent to fill you in."

Hix forced himself to stay seated. Gripping the ends of the chair arms, he snapped his head with a nod, said tersely, "Go on."

The doctor studied him for a second, then said, "She had a lot of other wounds that are older than today, partially healed. She uh, is being horribly whipped. Not just on her back, but all over her body. It looks like besides using their fists, someone is hitting her with a belt, I believe there are markings from the buckle."

Rothschild picked up a few photos and stretched across the desk to hand them to Hix.

"There's old, but massive bruising on her thighs, fingernails were dug deeply into her skin like tiny blades. Considering the damage inflicted around the…insides of her thighs I wanted to do an internal exam, and a rape kit, but she refused. She is being abused on a regular basis, Detective. This girl is obviously not safe on the streets, and she is clearly not safe at home either."

Hix's stomach twisted. Holding up a picture, he pointed at faded fingerprints on her upper left arm. "How ah, how old do you think they are?"

The doctor studied the image, he shrugged. "I'd say a few weeks. Some are more recent." He pointed at the photo Hix held, and said, "I'd say those," he pointed to another photo, "and those," the pictures were of bruises on the insides of her thighs so extensive they almost completely covered her thighs, "were caused at the same time as the prints on her arm.

"The new bruises from today, there and there," he motioned at different photographs, "they overlap those long ones that are more recent than the marks on her arms and thighs."

His eyes narrowed with anger at Hix, he voice rough with emotion, he said, "The abuse is ongoing."

Hix blanched, the pictures he was looking at were from that day at the charity ball. When he'd watched Ajanel wrap his fingers so tightly around Laurin's arm he had lifted her off her feet.

His grip so brutal, he'd left his fingerprints gouged and bruised on her skin, and when he got her home, he beat the living shit out of her. Because Hix had been speaking to her. *And I let him leave with her.*

The doctor watched Hix's face ripple with emotions; rage, despair that Laurin has been a continuous victim of domestic violence and she kept her mouth shut and didn't seek help, she just endured the savage beatings, and obvious brutal sexual assaults. And now she suffered further brutality from strangers that had recognized her from the Woodrow St. Lawrence scandal. Helplessness followed the despair. How was he to help her when she wouldn't ask for or accept it?

"Do you know who is abusing her, Detective?" Rothschild sat back, steepled his fingertips, he tapped a few fingers together. "She's wearing wedding rings. Is it her husband?"

"Pretty sure, but unless she speaks up, or a witness talks, my hands are tied." Hix handed the photos back to the doctor, he couldn't stomach viewing the rest of them. He had seen the worst of the worst in battle, but this was…Laurin. Hell.

The men sat in contemplative silence. After a few minutes, Rothschild cleared his throat.

He scooped up the photos, slid them into the file and closed it. Setting a palm on top of the file, he said, "I discussed with her about women's shelters, and victim advocates she can speak with. Filing charges, getting an order of protection, she just shook her head and closed her eyes, shut me down."

"Yeah, been there done that."

"Well, we'll keep her a couple of days, likely a week, to keep an eye on the concussion and make sure her kidneys aren't bleeding. If nothing life threatening pops up with her organs she'll be discharged. We'll need a follow up in two weeks. If anything isn't right with her, nausea, dizziness, fainting, she will need to come back immediately. We'll give her paperwork on all this. There're a couple of prescriptions she'll need to get filled for after her release."

At Hix's nod, the doctor's eyes lowered then rose to look equably at Hix. "Hell, Detective. She needs total rest. I fear if she goes home, if she's beaten again while in this fragile condition, we may be looking at very serious injuries, or a corpse.

"You as a cop know how these domestic violence situations can go. My professional, and personal recommendation is that she does not go to her home, that she stays elsewhere. At least until she heals enough she can make a rational decision about her life."

Hix nodded wordlessly. He stood up. "Thank you Doctor, for being so forthcoming with me," they shook hands. "I can't tell you more about her, Doctor, but rest assured, her medical bill will be paid, but not right away. I think it's best for right now no one knows she's here."

"I understand." Rothschild's voice held great concern. "Maybe you can talk some sense into her once she leaves here? She has no relatives she can go to, but maybe a friend, a hotel? Except she'll need someone to stay with her. A woman's shelter would be best."

"Yeah, I'll see what I can do. Give me her prescriptions and I'll get them filled while I'm here. When can I see her?"

Rothschild hesitated. "We don't know her last name, only her first is Laurin. I can't write the prescriptions only to-"

Hix leaned towards the doctor, his palm on the desk, he said soberly, "I think, as a law enforcement officer, that for right now, for her safety, Laurin's last name be kept a secret. Write them out to me and I'll get them filled."

Rothschild sat still as he considered Hix's request. Then, his lips pursed, he bent and scribbled several prescriptions for pain and antibiotics. He handed them over to Hix.

"This is highly unethical, however," he sighed as Hix took them from him. "Extreme circumstances require extreme actions. I'd hate to see that little girl go through any more abuse."

Tucking the prescriptions in his shirt pocket, Hix said, "I'd like to see her now, Doc." His tone edged with frustration and anger.

"Of course, come with me." Rothschild came out from behind his desk and walked with Hix to the door. "It'll take a little time until Laurin is placed in a room."

Down the hall the doctor showed Hix a waiting area. "I'll have a nurse advise you when you can see her."

Hix thanked Rothschild, the two men shook hands and the doctor ambled off down the hall.

# Chapter Eighteen

Instead of staying in the waiting room, Hix located the pharmacy in the hospital.

He waited while they filled the prescriptions then went back up to the waiting room where he sank onto a chair and pulled out his cell. He called his team working on the murder cases for progress reports while he waited.

Over an hour later, a nurse entered the waiting area, glanced around, and grinned when her gaze landed on him. "Detective Hixman?" Her question was hopeful. Curly red hair was pinned on top of her head, whiskey light eyes traveled up and down his body.

"That's me." Hix moved to stand.

Her appreciative assessment of his body showed in the sultry broad-lipped smile. "Well, you don't look like a detective." Wearing a super tight, green smock uniform and spongy shoes, she was tall with a slender upper body and a huge booty that she appeared quite proud of considering she stood in a partial side pose.

Annoyed with her delay, Hix snapped, "Take me to Miss Laurin." He didn't care how harsh he sounded, his patience was hanging by a thread.

"Oh my," the smile lengthened, "an alpha. I love-"

"Take me to her now, Nurse, or I will call the doctor to take me."

The smile didn't fail, got bigger if anything. "Okay, gee, a grouchy alpha. Come with me," she motioned with her finger for him to follow her. She strutted, making sure the large hips swung wide.

They walked down the hall, the nurse attempted to make small talk, Hix merely grunted at her questions. His name and open calendar were none of her business.

Finally, she led him to a patient's room.

The door stood open, inside there were two beds. Laurin, looking tiny and frail, and badly injured, sat propped up in the one closest to the door. The other bed was empty.

Bandages covered parts of her face and body, he could see stiches near her hairline by one temple. Both eyes were swollen and bruised, she held an ice pack in her hand but appeared too weary, or in too much pain to hold it to her eyes.

Although heavily swollen, the blue eyes still rounded when she saw him standing there.

The nurse hurried to place herself between him and the bed. She didn't hide her hungry gaze eating down Hix's strapping body and back up to his dangerous face. She wasn't afraid of him like many were, on the contrary, she was avidly interested.

She practically cooed, "There, Detective, you see she's fine. Now, let's you and me-"

Hix stepped around the nurse and trod straight to Laurin's bed. "You look like shit," he told Laurin.

She blinked in confusion at him.

"Detective," the nurse vied for his attention.

Hix growled crudely at her, "We don't need you, leave us."

The nurse frowned at his cold rudeness. Nevertheless, she was an aggressive tenacious woman not willing to give up when she saw something she wanted. "Well, I think-"

Hix turned his back on her, muttered, "Don't give a fuck what you think." Louder, he snapped, "Leave us." He moved up to the side of the bed.

The nurse's peeved glare pinched her pretty face. Not used to men ignoring her, her gaze hopped from Hix to Laurin, the corner of her lip curled. With a huff, she flounced from the room.

"Ah," Laurin whispered, her voice slurred from her cut lip and other wounds, "although obnoxiously boorish, you still capture all of the females' attention."

Hix moved to stand directly in front of her. She tried to smile but couldn't, she spoke in breaking, short raspy huffs, "You must have a line waiting for dates."

His brows arched at her unexpected words, he didn't respond. He was relieved. She must not be on her deathbed if she can wittily criticize him.

Laurin's head drooped, the strain of holding it up was too much. Her voice small, shaking, with a moan of pain she said quietly, "I don't understand why you're here. I really have nothing to say to you. I am not filing any charges. I just want to go…home. I'm sure Rádolfo has sent a car for me." A shiver rolled over her advertising that the thought of going home clearly terrified her.

"You are not going home."

Her lashes flipped up exposing eyes beaten bloody. "Am I under arrest? I swear I didn't hit anyone back, sir."

His head twitched at that. "No, of course not. But, you aren't going to be released for a few days, and, I won't allow you to go to that…monster. So, call a friend. The doctor said you'll require complete bed rest and around the clock supervision. When you're discharged I'll take you to your friend's house."

It took a moment for her to comprehend what he was saying, then she shook her head. A mistake, she blinked to clear the dizziness and the pain the movement caused. She carefully inhaled, spoke in a rough hush, "No. If I don't go home, my husband will be…mad." An understatement.

"He allows me no…friends. Besides, he will find me, whether it's a hotel or a shelter or the police station," her breath sucked in a wheeze, "and then he'll make me pay." Her lips shut like a clamp before she let any more words out.

Crossing his arms, Hix stared down at her. She was in pain, and tired, and scared. He tried to speak gently but the anger at the situation was bubbling and burning in his chest. He figured as much. He had a Plan B he preferred anyway.

"Fine then. I have a place where you'll be safe and someone will be with you 24/7 to see to your safety and wellbeing." He glanced up at the nurse's return, ignoring her salacious wink he turned back to Laurin.

"No! No, Detective, my God, I have to go home, you have to understand, please!" Laurin's face a brutal mess, her voice rasping from screaming and crying hard at length earlier. Tears blurred in her eyes, her face twisted in agonizing pain from her injuries.

The nurse said, "She needs to be alone. Come with me, I'll show you where you can get something to eat." She trailed her fingers down his sleeve, smiled invitingly. "I have a break soon, I can join you and we can-"

Hix swung around spouted furiously, "Are you stupid? Deaf? You don't understand a command? Get the fuck out of here."

At the nurse's affronted mouth hanging open, Hix said, "Wait."

The nurse looked hopeful, her grin lurid. "Okay, handsome, what can I-"

"Can't you see the distress of her pain for fuck's sake? Get her more pain medication. Right now. Go." He waved a hand at her like she was an annoying insect. His glower would have scared the fiercest of warriors. She wasn't that stupid to disregard the threat of his wrath.

With a huff, the nurse cursed under her breath and stalked out the door.

Hix turned back to Laurin. He couldn't believe the nurse's utter unprofessionalism. Yet, he knew that's the kind of female he attracted. Tough, aggressive, overtly promiscuous, bawdy, brazen. The total opposite of the soft, ladylike bashed-up beauty lying in the bed.

He calmed the anger from his tone and said quietly, "Laurin, I do understand the pattern of domestic violence, you love him, you forgive him, he does it again, it's a vicious circle. You like the lifestyle Ajanel provides for you, you don't want to give it up. But I don't give a shit why you want to stay with this guy, you are not going home to him. He will kill you. You are coming with me-"

"No!" the scream rasped out, she gulped and winced, it hurt. "I have to go home," her voice rose in hushed anguish. "If I don't return home he'll hurt Benji."

That gave Hix pause, then he said matter-of-fact, "I'll send Child Protective Services to pick up the boy. They will keep him safe until you are well enough and on your independent feet to care for him."

Tears spilled, her jaw trembled. "You can't do that. There is no proof he is in danger, the servants won't talk, and Benji will be terrified. Even if he's removed, Rádolfo will get to him, trust me he can do anything, he has money and power, the right connections. He will hurt him to force me to come home, please, you can't do this."

Hix spewed angrily, "He would hurt his own son?"

"He's not his son." Laurin blinked the tears and turned her head from Hix.

That made sense to Hix, he'd seen how coldly Ajanel treated the boy, and how scared the boy seemed of Ajanel. "Oh. Okay. What about taking him to his biological father?"

"That is not possible, you must let me go home." She turned her head to face him. Glancing briefly up at Hix, her gaze dropped to his midsection and stayed there.

"I know you're worried about your son-"

"He's not my son-" this time she clapped a hand over her mouth.

At his confused consternation, Laurin pleaded, "He has to stay with me or- or my h- husband will..." she sobbed, "I can't tell you, you have to let me go."

Recalling she'd said once before Benji was not her child, Hix pondered what she was telling him.

Arms still crossed, he shrugged his big shoulders. "Fine. I will have him brought to the house as well." He needed to dig into the Ajanels and find out what was up with them. There was something off about the whole situation. The boy was neither of theirs' son? What was he doing there? The boy had called Laurin, Mommy.

155

Laurin cried, "You don't understand, there's so much more," the tears fell. Her breathing was shallow, rapid, the pain was causing her to wince and flinch. "A shelter would never allow them."

"Allow who?"

She mumbled, "The animals."

"Animals?"

Her eyes closed. "Yes. Our pets. If I'm not there, Rádolfo will hurt Benji. If he goes after Benji he'll find out about the animals and…will…kill them."

*Geeze*, Hix raked a hand through his hair. Ajanel outdoes a damned fire-breathing, bloodletting dragon. "What do you mean find out about them? You have pets in the house and he doesn't know about them?"

Her shoulders pitched then slumped. "He knows about Poochie, the black lab. Poochie is lame. Rádolfo forgets about him as long as he doesn't hear him or see him. We, um, slowly brought in a few more injured animals but we keep them hidden.

"The staff helps us. My husband made it clear that he hates animals; he said he'd just as soon wring a kitten's neck as look at it. But Benji is so lonely, and the poor animals, I couldn't just let them, well…"

Sighing wearily, Hix asked, "Is there anything else at the mansion I need to be concerned about? Like a clown hiding in the closet, or a one-legged dwarf in the basement?"

A tiny smile tugged at the edge of her cut lip, she shook her head. Someone had washed the blood out of her blonde hair and combed it. "No, that's all. But," her sigh mournful, "you see now, I must go home."

Hix stood staring at the fragile young woman all banged up, yet still so beautiful his heart ached. "Laurin, if he's such a monster, why don't you take the boy and leave? There are places, people that will help you."

The tears welled again, her head drooped. "It's…complicated. I can't tell you. It's, just the way it is."

"It's clear to me, Laurin, you don't love him. You and the boy are visibly in terror of him."

Her nonresponse was the answer to his statement.

Studying her for a second, Hix said, "He has something on you? Blackmail? What is he doing to you that you feel forced to stay in such a horribly dangerous situation, and keep the boy in danger as well?"

He watched her swollen eyes shift back and forth, she squirmed slightly then moaned from the pain. But she kept her mouth shut tight.

"All right," he sighed. "I have to go, I'll be in touch." He started for the door when she called out.

"Wait, Detective, Rádolfo will have sent a car. He may even be here himself raising hell. If he sees you anywhere near here he'll-"

"He's not here, Laurin. He wasn't called so he doesn't know you're here. I didn't give his information to the charging nurse. They don't even know your last name." He spun around and left before she could offer any more objections.

But he heard her cry out, "Benji-" as he headed down the hall.

Hix ordered the phone in her room be disconnected, and he wasn't worried about her sneaking out of the hospital, she could barely sit up and that was with the aid of pillows and the angled bed, and she certainly couldn't see out of the badly swollen eyes.

She didn't catch his last look back at her now that she thought she was alone, her body writhed in agony on the mattress, her face a wretched bruised mask of tremendous pain. The whimpers chugged out of her damaged body with painful helpless sobs.

Before he left the hospital, Hix stopped off and asked to see Dr. Rothschild.

"Detective?" Rothschild inclined his head in greeting when Hix stepped into his office.

"Yeah, Doctor. I want a different nurse to be assigned to Laurin, and her pain medication needs to be increased immediately."

He hesitated before saying, "Listen, Doc, she will try to leave regardless of her condition, perhaps you can keep her...slightly sedated so she doesn't attempt to go? Prevent her from returning to her deadly situation?"

Rothschild nodded, he had seen her stubborn determination. "As you wish, Detective, we need to keep her from further injuring herself. May I ask why the change in nurses?"

"I'll get with you later, Doc, I gotta go now." Hix saluted two fingers off his forehead and strode out.

# Chapter Nineteen

At the station, Hix needed to write up some reports before he could attend to personal business. Like getting the kid out of the mansion before Ajanel discovers Laurin is gone and not coming back.

He was finishing up when Kurt Klaus knocked on the frame of his office door. Hix was just getting to his feet, he looked up. "Hey Kurt," he greeted him.

"Hey." The officer walked into the office, he had sheaves of papers in his hand.

"You got something?"

"Oh yeah." The dashing officer grinned. Shiny black hair waved across his head, dark brown eyes glinted with elation. He handed the papers to Hix.

As Hix rifled through them, Kurt said, "Those are partial lists of memberships to the BDSM clubs in Brevet Bay and Alexandria. See if you recognize any names. Particularly the name of a woman you called in about earlier. Something about an attack on the street."

Hix's eyes jumped to Kurt then back to the papers he held. Scanning each name, it was the seventh paper he reached when he understood what Kurt was referring to. "Ajanel," he muttered.

"Yup." Kurt grinned with satisfaction. "All of the male Ajanels. The patriarch Rádolfo and his sons, Raoul, Blane and Chevalier. I didn't see their wives' names anywhere, just the men.

"The father, Rádolfo, he is an ambassador from Mozambique, he hasn't gone to a club for a couple of years, but the sons regularly attend several clubs in Alexandria. After members are vetted and pay an enormous fee to belong, they are given cards that get swiped so there is a record of which clubs and how often they attend."

"Uh huh." Hix continued scanning the sheets.

"Could be a coincidence, but, hell Hix, the FBI and CIA have been stalking Rádolfo Ajanel for years trying to get him on arms trafficking and diamond smuggling, and a bunch of other nefarious crap. Your call this morning for assistance was regarding his wife, Laurin. A few clubs offered reports that the sons, and the father when he attended, tended to have complaints issued against them for excessive brutality.

"Apparently the fun of the clubs is all about light paddling and whipping, not damaging hospital visits and permanent scarring. That's a lot of news about one family when we're searching for a serial killer."

"You're right about that, Kurt. Plus, that unusual metal the chain was made of originates from Russia, and also South Africa where Ajanel comes from."

Hix handed the paperwork back to Kurt. He said, "Apparently the Ajanel apples don't fall far from their father's tree. Have them all brought in for questioning. The one with the absurd name is a doctor, he could have had access to the serum Vica…ah, the V shit. Check their alibis."

"Already in the works. Can't get Rádolfo Ajanel, he's out of the country on business. As soon as he lands, private jet of course, I'll have him brought to the station."

That was fine with Hix, he wanted words with the bastard. He had planned on talking to him about Laurin and the young boy when he went to the mansion.

But that talk with Rádolfo would have to wait. He didn't give a shit about any illegal activity Ajanel was involved in, other than if Hix could use it to get the man taken away and out of Laurin and Benji's lives. Getting him arrested or deported would work for him.

He told Kurt, "When you bring Rádolfo Ajanel in, I want extra security on him. He may be dangerous, and I want him checked for weapons. Search them all."

When Ajanel discovers not only is he being dragged to the police station for questioning in a triple murder, but that his wife and son were gone, the shit will hit the explosive, political diplomatic fan.

"The wives too, bring them all in. Except for Laurin Ajanel. She's in the hospital, I'll see to her." He didn't miss Kurt's raised brows at Hix's lowered and tempered tone of voice when mentioning Laurin Ajanel.

"Sure thing, Penn." Kurt shuffled the papers then curled them in his hand. "So," he said slyly, "what's up with Mrs. Ajanel? You're a detective, not a cop, how did you get called to the scene of her assault?"

Hix powered down his computer then shut it off. Not answering the officer's question he asked, "Any word on those prints found on the post?"

Kurt shook his head with a puzzled smile at Hix's evading his question. "There was only a partial. The little they could enter into AFIS came back without a hit. If we get a suspect in, if they agree to be printed, we might be able to match it. But because of the lack of points to match, it'll be useless in court. Unless we have other evidence, the partial won't be enough for us to obtain warrants to induce the prints or search houses."

"Nothing from witnesses? The palladium chains? What about Howie Fernell? Have we found a connection between him and the vics or anyone else? Maybe he did time and had a friend in the pen that could tell us about him? Were Fernell's prints matched against the ones from the post?"

Kurt replied, "No to everything except the prints. Fernell's were not even close to a match. He was too fat to be the figure in any of the videos. He only spent small time in the county lockup for drunk and disorderly, trespassing, petit theft, misdemeanor pot charges, minor crap like that. Prince, Emilee, Mike, Teague and Sinclair have checked in, they got nada. The phone dumps on the vics' led to nothing. Too many burner numbers that were untraceable, and none matched all the victims. We've hit a brick wall."

Hix's mouth bunched in dissatisfaction. "Yeah. Okay, everyone stays on it, call them and tell them I want periodic updates. Every hour, two hours max. I want those burner numbers searched as in-depth as possible. Sometimes they can be tracked back to where they were purchased. I'm gonna have to institute shift work so people get rest. Organize that shit, Kurt, and fill them in on their hours."

"You got it, Boss."

Hix made a few calls including having backup meet him at the Ajanel house. Although the patriarch wasn't home, Hix still expected trouble.

While waiting on the phone, he sifted through notes. He wasn't surprised to discover Laurin didn't have a DL under her married name. Ajanel apparently felt as he refused to allow her to leave the residence alone it wasn't necessary for her to update it. She did have one under her maiden name, Laurin Cristine Cerridwen. Kullen was right, she was Welsh.

She obtained her license at 16 but it has since expired. Hix assumed that prick never let her drive anyway. And, the records show she never owned a car. She was too destitute.

Before her marriage, the report indicated she worked several jobs to support herself and a younger brother. Hix had Teague McGuire trying to locate the boy and more information on her family. It sounded like Laurin and her brother were orphans. Maybe the boy was in foster care somewhere.

Finishing his calls, he drove to the Ajanel mansion. He knew the way from bringing Laurin home that night he found her walking alone on that dark road.

It still brought on a blaze of anger, his jaw clenched. That she was so afraid of her own damned husband she was traipsing along for miles in the dangerous night without calling for someone to come and retrieve her.

A husband's job was to protect and cherish his wife, take care of her. Not terrorize, bully and abuse her. Hix couldn't wait until he and Rádolfo Ajanel came face-to-face again. His hands fisted in anticipation.

He was stopped at the gate. The entire perimeter was enclosed by what Hix presumed was an electrified fence.

A man in a grey and red uniform stepped out of the guard booth.

The guard bowed politely and asked, "Your business here, sir? Do you have an appointment?" He held a clipboard and reviewed the acceptable names on it while he waited for Hix to tell him his name.

Instead, Hix held up his badge. "Police business." He glanced behind him as he heard a car approaching, Thomas Princeton was right on his heels. "He's with me," Hix motioned to Prince, saw other cruisers behind him, "and the two police cars. Let them all in."

The guard stood unmoving in shock at the orders, his eyes widened as each car pulled up one after the other.

"Open the gate, now," Hix commanded.

The guard slapped his lips shut, reached inside the booth and pushed a button. He was on the phone before the gate opened slowly and Hix drove through, Prince right behind him.

The driveway was wide and curved from the gate for several hundred feet before the house came into view.

They parked side-by-side and got out. The two police vehicles stopped behind them.

Prince strode over to Hix. "What's going on, you have a lead here?" Both men wore suits and ties.

"No, not exactly," Hix replied, his attention roving over the three-tiered mansion. His face hardened along with his dark eyes under black brows. He was infatuated with a married woman that was so way out of his league he couldn't believe what a fool he was. Nonetheless, his mind and body dwelled on the young woman. Talk about obsession. He coveted his neighbor's wife. Great.

One of the big commandments, and he still couldn't stop himself from desiring her. And not just sexually. That's the part that scared him. If it were just sexual, he'd get over it and find another woman to bang. But, there was just something about Laurin, the light inside her even after the hell she's been through just shines so brightly, and Hix wanted that warmth, that light shining on him.

And, he'd seen her eyes flare when she looked at him, she felt it too. Although as young as she was, and under the tutelage of a violent abusive husband more than twice her age, she likely didn't recognize what she was feeling.

"Penn?" Prince pulled him back from his thoughts.

"Yeah, we're here to take a kid."

Totally confused, Prince's forehead creased with question.

Hix gave the detective a quick rundown of the situation, leaving out the part about his obsession with Ajanel's wife.

But, Thomas Princeton wasn't obtuse, he could read between the lines.

Hix's tone of voice changed whenever he spoke about Laurin. The barely suppressed rage at Ajanel, and what had happened to her in the street was expressed in the working of his jaw, the clenching of his fists. The soft sound of his voice when talking about Laurin became hard and abrasive when he told Prince about the attack, and Ajanel's alleged abuse.

"Uh, you sure about this, Penn? This guy is a wealthy ambassador for heck's sake. You plan on barging in and taking his son and putting the boy and Ajanel's wife in hiding? This is a police matter, a political wormhole, not a detective's business."

At the sounds of car doors opening, Hix turned towards the officers exiting their vehicles. "The bastard is beating his wife, Thomas, viciously, horribly, and I think he's harmed the child as well. If she goes home, Ajanel will whip her. Literally. If she doesn't go home, he'll beat the boy until she does return.

"Without a proper complaint from a victim or a witness, the cops won't do a thing, can't do anything to help them. I believe the monster has some kind of hold over her. Mrs. Ajanel and the boy are literally being held prisoner and abused and can't extricate themselves. She's too terrified for their lives to ask for help. What do you think we should do?"

Forking his fingers through strands of sandy hair in consternation, Prince let out a heavy breath, he grimaced at the big house. "All right, let's do it."

Hix met with the four officers. He told them, "I'm removing a young child from the home. I don't have a warrant and I don't know if there will be interference or not. You all are backup. One of you stays outside, another in the doorway, the other two go with us. Expect trouble. Got it?"

The officers acknowledged his instructions and the three men and one female officer marched up the steps to the big house. Hix didn't have to knock, the door swung open.

A man in a black suit, sneered down his long nose at them. He indignantly demanded in a tight French accent, "What is the meaning of this?"

"Huh," Hix grunted. "Rogèt, I presume?"

A female wearing a black uniform dress with white collar, and another male also in black peered at them from behind the man.

Rogèt's head jerked back in surprise, then his eyes narrowed at Hix. "Who the hell are you?" The French accent went from formally lofty to lowbrow, coarse English cockney.

Hix announced, "Detective Penn Hixman," and he moved forward muscling his way inside, Rogèt had to move or he'd get bulldozed.

"Hey! Sir! What is the meaning of this- this intrusion!" Rogèt stepped behind Hix and Prince as the rest of the officers except the one that would remain outside, entered the house and fanned out.

The servants moved far back from the police, they didn't want any trouble. Several more poked their heads in from doorways.

"The boy," Hix said to Rogèt. "Benji. Where is he?"

"You- you-" Rogèt was a tall, narrow man, with slicked-back dark hair, he had a weak chin and thin dark eyes.

Hix glared at the man. "Who exactly are you, what is your position here?"

Rogèt took a step back, blinking rapidly, he was starting to become unnerved. "I, ah, I am Pieter Rogèt, Mr. Ajanel's major domo. I am in charge of the household when Mr. Ajanel is not home.

As I told you over the phone, Mr. Ajanel is not presently at the residence. So, you may take your," he waved his hand at the officers, "posse, and leave.

"I will advise Mr. Ajanel upon his return of your desire to speak with him. I-" he broke off as Hix stepped so close the toes of their shoes touched. Hix's dress boots met Rogèt's gleaming wingtips.

"I said," Hix's voice dropped dangerously low, "tell me where the boy is. You interfere and I will arrest you for obstruction. Now, take me to the child."

The major domo continued blinking in agitation at Hix, his eyes traveled around to the other officers and met uncompromising sober faces. He exhaled loudly then twirled around in the foyer and crossed over the cream marble with gold veining to a staircase, the wingtips tacking the glossy tile in perturbation.

The staircase was doublewide and boldly carpeted in bright ruby, with a polished bannister that flowed up the stairs with the steps, a parade of gilded ancestral paintings ascended up the wall with them.

Rogèt started up the steps and Hix, Prince and the two male officers followed right behind him, the female remained inside the doorway.

They reached the top and followed the lush carpet down a broad hallway passing numerous doors, then they reached another staircase. Rogèt moved up the steps and everyone, including several curious servants trekked after him like the Pied Piper.

Another long corridor and many doors, and he stopped at one. Sucking in a deep breath, Rogèt let it out and opened the door. He stepped aside so Hix could enter the room.

Inside, Hix recognized the dark-haired imp. Benji was sitting at a small desk, an older woman was speaking to him, they both looked up at the interruption.

Hix stepped forward, fashioned a smile onto his hard face. Working to keep his guttural accent to a minimum, he said, "Hey there, Benji, you remember me, doncha, from the church? Remember the wedding you and your mommy went to?"

The boy stared round-eyed at him for a split second, then the cherub cheeks plumped with his grin. "Mr. Nice Man! The pirate!" he shouted and jumped up. "Penn! Penn! Penn! You here, mommy not home."

The woman sitting with him got up as well, and smoothed the full, long-skirted flowered dress. She asked politely, "What is going on?" Her worried eyes bounced from Hix to the officers back to Hix.

"You are?" His voice abrasive, Hix spoke to the woman so harshly she took a step back from him.

"Well, I," she peered around Hix at Rogèt hovering in the doorway flanked by the two police officers and Princeton.

Rogèt just stared at her, then glared at Hix.

Showing his badge, Hix asked again, "Your name, what is your duty here?"

Taken aback, her hand splayed over her heart, mouth dropping open, eyes wide, she glanced at the major domo again who was now staring at the floor. Apparently he wasn't going to act in charge like he normally did when Mr. Ajanel wasn't around. "I- I am Winifred Wickens. I am Benji's tutor."

"Tutor? I understand the boy isn't even four yet."

"Four! Four! Four!" Benji shouted. The officers grinned at him. Rogèt's austere eyes tapered to annoyed slits at the boy, but Benji's joyful attention was fixed on Hix.

Nervous fingers poked at the grey curls around Wickens' lined face. "Um, well, Mr. Ajanel wants his son to learn his letters, numbers, simple math, reading, as he uh, won't be attending formal school. Mr. Ajanel's main focus at the moment is he wants the child fluent in several languages. We are currently learning Portuguese."

Her English was perfect, unaccented, his brow arched, Hix repeated, "Portuguese?"

The grey curls bounced with her nod. "Yes, his father's native language. I am fluent in six languages. Why are-"

Ignoring her, Hix moved to Benji and lowered to one knee to be closer to the boy's level. "Hey, little man, I'm going to take you to see your mama. Is that okay with you?"

Benji looked to Mrs. Wickens then to Rogèt who shrugged and looked away. A quaver entering his child's voice, Benji asked Hix, "Is Pa-Ray going too?"

Hix's heart clenched at the sudden fear in the boy's tone. Shaking his head, he said gently, "No, just you and your mommy."

Standing up, he spoke to a maid looming behind everyone, "Miss, I need you to go to Mrs. Ajanel's room and pack a suitcase for her. Enough for a few days, we'll come back for more later. And you-" he was addressing Mrs. Wickens when Rogèt cut him off.

"What the hell, man. Are you saying Mrs. Ajanel is staying away for a few days and you're bringing the boy to stay with her? I don't think-"

"I don't need you to think, Rogèt." Hix said to Mrs. Wickens, "Can you pack a bag for the child, again, enough for a week? Make sure you include," he glanced around at the stark room. "Where does he keep his toys?"

Mrs. Wickens flushed uncomfortably. "He isn't allowed, um, toys." Her gaze flipped to Rogèt and the maid, their eyes lowered to the floor.

"Ah," Hix drew in an angry breath. As a child of combat, he knew what it was like to not have things to play with, other than knives and guns. "Just get the cases packed and have the officers bring them downstairs."

To one of the officers he said, "See that the cases are loaded into my truck, it's unlocked. Okay," bending to talk to the boy, he said, "is there anything special you want to bring with you, Benji, son?"

The child was perplexed, then became gleeful that he was being freed from the painful, lonely, frightening crypt. He ran to his bed and stuck his hand under the pillow and pulled out the tiny truck he'd had with him at church.

"What is that?" Rogèt barked. "You know you aren't allowed anything to play with. How did you get that? Give it to me right now," he snapped his open palm out for the truck. Benji shrank back from him.

Hix about punched the man in the jaw. Placing himself in front of Rogèt, he snarled at the major domo, "How about you help the maid with Mrs. Ajanel's things." It wasn't a request, his tone said 'get the hell out of here before I damage you.'

Rogèt sputtered, then shut his severe lips and stormed out of the room.

Hix addressed Benji, "Okay, son, no one is going to take your truck. Is there anything else you want to bring with you?"

Benji stood motionless, his truck clutched in his hand pressed tightly against his small chest terrified the major domo was coming back to take it from him.

Tipping his head back he looked way up at Hix, the determination and strength carved into Hix's tough face reassured the boy. A tiny sigh of relief, he was shaking his head, then he shouted, "Pets! Pets!"

Prince gave Hix a puzzled look. Hix smiled at him and said to Benji, "Your mommy told me about them. Show me where they are."

"K!" Benji shouted and bounced across the room and opened a connecting door. Hix went after him and Prince followed.

Hix wasn't surprised, but Prince gawked at the sight inside the room. There was a black lab, three cats, in the corner a cage held a bird, edging slowly across a wall they saw a tortoise inching along.

"*Holee* shit," Prince gushed, his eyeballs hopping everywhere.

Hix turned to the two police officers. "The animals go too. I think they are…special needs pets, they probably will require help. There won't be any cages. Prince," he said to the detective, "perhaps you can see if the household has any boxes, or even a laundry basket to carry them in."

"I can help." A young woman in a black uniform moved cautiously into the room. "We've been caring for the animals, litter boxes and what not. I'll show you where everything is." Her gaze travelled gloomily back to the house. "Of course now that Monsieur Rogèt has seen the animals, the cat, so to speak, is out of the bag. When Mr. Ajanel comes home-"

Hix interrupted her with a curt yet kind, "That will no longer be a concern for Mrs. Ajanel or the child." He turned from her stunned, confused, yet grateful smile and went to assist with getting everything moving

It took thirty minutes for them to carry the animals and their meager supplies downstairs and outside.

Holding Benji's tiny hand, Hix said, "Thomas, the animals have to go with you, I don't have the room." Laurin and Benji's suitcases were in the backseat of his extended pickup.

Shrugging that he didn't mind, Prince strode to his SUV and opened the doors and waved to the servants and officers carrying the animals and their food and other items apparently Laurin had managed to smuggle in.

Hix asked one of the maids carrying a cat, "How did Mrs. Ajanel obtain these items, the food and kitty litter? I understand she wasn't allowed to have any money."

Setting the birdcage with a green parakeet in it that had a warped wing into Prince's car, another maid told him, "Mrs. Ajanel appeals to the church members when her husband allows her to attend. It's all done in secret of course, if Mr. Ajanel knew," a shiver wriggled her shoulders.

"Well, anyway," the maid holding the cat said, "Mrs. Ajanel tries to pay them by helping with banquets and cleaning, cooking, painting rooms, again, when her husband lets her. When he doesn't, which is often, she crochets blankets and sweaters for the poor and gives them to the church to disburse. Unfortunately, she again needs the yarn donated for her to do so."

Benji stood wide-eyed at all the activity. The servants bustling, putting his pets into a big car. He grinned every time the major-domo tried to interfere and the detective glowered at him and said bad words. Mr. Rogèt would look frightened, shut his mouth and move back.

Prince took the cat from the maid and set it inside a box that had been placed in the SUV. He reached in and petted the cat that was meowing pitifully as if it was going off to the gallows. "There now, kitty, from now on, everything will be wonderful for all of you."

The lame dog was settled in the front passenger seat. Poochie observed the activity, his gaze returning always to the boy, assuring himself that Benji was going with them.

One of the officers retrieved a child's seat from one of the police cruisers Hix had requested they bring. The officer hooked the seat beside the suitcases in the back passenger side of Hix's truck.

Hix helped Benji into the pickup, fastened him in the child's seat. Hix found himself chuckling at the boy's jumping and yipping, excited to be leaving the house and going for a ride in Hix's big truck.

Closing the door, watching the boy gleefully studying the truck he was sitting in, Hix commented to the maid, "The boy is pretty happy to be in my truck."

The maid's face saddened. "Yes, Mr. Ajanel does not let the child out. Not to go to the store, or pre-school, once in a rare blue moon when Mr. Ajanel needs to, um, pose a family scene, he brings the boy to certain events." She smiled brightly waving at the child who now had his face plastered against the glass and was grinning at them.

Her voice somber she looked up at Hix. "Please, take care of them. You have no idea what goes on inside."

Hix erased the frown her words brought, he didn't want the boy to be afraid of his harsh looks. "I do have a perception of what Mrs. Ajanel and Benji have endured. Miss, ah," he waited.

"Janine, Janine Kennedy."

"Miss Kennedy," he handed her his card, "if you, or anyone here is abused, harmed in any way, even if you are illegal, call me. Okay?"

Taking the card, she looked down at it and nodded. Smiled up at him. "Yes, thank you. It's just his guards and Mrs. Ajanel that he-" she stopped and waved at Benji.

"Just see that they're safe, Detective, when Mr. Ajanel finds out his wife is gone, uh," she swallowed hard. "He will come after her with all guns blasting. And I mean that literally, sir. Literally."

He got her warning. When they were all packed up, he thanked the officers for their help and he headed to the highway with Prince behind him.

# Chapter Twenty

The entire way, although he was belted into the child's seat, Benji wiggled and talked nonstop, asking Hix question after question his head hopping and twisting as he looked out every window. "My truck the same as your, Mr. Nice Man," he announced loudly, holding up his tiny truck for Hix to see.

Hix chuckled. "Yup, sure is. When you get older maybe you can get a big one too."

"Big! Big! Big!" Benji shouted.

Hix stopped on the way for a bathroom and ice cream cone break.

While Prince stayed with Benji laughing at the child's face and hands dripping with chocolate, Hix called his mother.

"Honey," Vageline Hixman answered, thrilled whenever her son called. Her other children were always around and about, but Hix held himself back, kept his distance even when present. His time in the military had scarred him gravely, body and soul.

When the family pushed too hard for him to open up, find the joy in their lives, he shut down and stayed away. They'd learned to tread carefully with him, but didn't love him any less.

He'd gotten slightly better when Michael and Holly were born. But he still seemed afraid of letting his walls down. He'd lost a lot while in the military and was wary to let anyone close. His world had been nothing but fighting, hating, violence, and bereft of human comforts.

173

Any friends he'd made invariably were killed, so he stopped getting close to anyone. His best friend's and his fiancée's betrayals were just more stab wounds in his blackened soul, teaching him getting close to people was a fool's game.

"Are you coming by for dinner? I'll set another plate."

"Uh, sort of. You're going to need more than one extra plate." He broadly explained Laurin and Benji's situation. When he finished, he was met with silence. "Ma?"

"Um, honey, you know we're always willing to help someone in need, but, uh, I recall reading that this woman had been accused of...attempted murder. I mean, the children, Michael and Holly, their safety is paramount."

He agreed, "Of course. But, I seriously doubt what the press reported was true. I've spent some time with Laurin Ajanel, I honestly don't think she's capable of stepping on an ant much less harming another human being. You'll see, when you observe how she is with her child," he didn't bring up that Laurin had said Benji wasn't hers or Ajanel's son.

Hix needed to get to the bottom of all that. For now, he had their wellbeing to see to. When he had the time, he would to do a thorough investigation of Laurin Ajanel, find out how she ended up where she was. There was something too fishy about the entire set-up, including the adulterous attempted murder claim.

"But Penn," the uncertainty clear in his mother's hesitation came through.

"Right now, Ma, Mrs. Ajanel is in such a debilitating physical condition she couldn't fight off a butterfly. She needs round the clock care, and both she and the boy need to be safe. She has no one to take care of her while she recovers, and the boy is too young to help. They are in dire danger of her husband's wrath if he gets his hands on them.

"The security Dad installed will keep out an army. With my brothers on revolving security duty, everyone will be safe."

Hix rubbed the back of his head; he watched Benji and Prince laughing. "If you don't want to, I'll take them to my place. But hell,

Laurin needs care and the child can't be left alone, and I have to work. There's nowhere else safe for them to go."

Prince was ineffectively trying to show the boy how to lick the cone before the ice cream melted all over his hands. There was more chocolate on the kid's face than in his belly, but he was laughing with such unbridled glee Hix felt the iron wall structured around his heart fracturing.

The boy was the polar opposite of the frozen terrified statue that Hix had witnessed at the church when Ajanel had joined his wife and the kid.

"Oh, dear, well," his mother sighed. "Of course bring them here. Your place is tiny, there's no food there, and of course you can't nurse her. It'll be fine, son, bring them."

"Thanks, Ma, you'll see. We should arrive in thirty or forty minutes." The Ajanel mansion was located in Alexandria's wealthiest district, it was a long stretch from Brevet Bay where Hix's family resided. He hung up and joined Prince and Benji as the pair was finishing the last of their cones.

"Ah, I think we need to make another trip to the restroom, don't you think, Thomas?"

Prince grinned. They both watched Benji lick his fingers, his hands, his arms. "Yeah. This ought to be interesting." Fortunately they had tucked mass amounts of napkins over the boy's clothes or there would be a mess in Hix's truck.

"I'll take him, I don't want him overwhelmed with the two of us men in the bathroom with him. I don't think he's even used to one male being with him. Why don't you check up with the team, see if anything new has hit."

"Gotcha." Prince pulled out his phone. "I'll keep an eye on the pets."

"Okay, little man," Hix said, smiling down at the boy, "what do you say we go get cleaned up?" He held out his hand to the child.

Benji looked up at him, his face covered with ice cream. "How comes you call Mr. Prince Thomas?" he asked after slipping his hand into Hix's.

Hix grimaced at the wet, sticky little hand tucked into his. "Well," they started for the restroom, he explained, "his whole name is Thomas Princeton. Some people shorten his last name to Prince like a nickname. You know what that is?"

"Uhn huh." Benji shook his head.

"That would be like your name is Benji Ajanel, but someone might shorten it and call you Ben, or Benj or Aji or something like that, you know?"

The child thought about it. "But why?"

Hix didn't really know how to answer that. But that was okay because the boy plied him with more questions. Why do they call the bathroom a restroom? How does the paper towel know how to come out? How come yours is bigger than mine? Does everyone have one?

Hix realized at their first visit to the bathrooms that Benji had never been to a public toilet before, and he had never seen a grown man's penis. Apparently Ajanel did not introduce any fatherly teachings or spend personal time with the boy. He pictured Laurin trying to teach the little boy how to pee.

Hix helped the child clean up in the sink first, then he taught him about the urinal. Benji did better on this second attempt than he had when they had first arrived.

The whole episode had chuckles bubbling inside Hix's chest. He found he actually enjoyed teaching the child how to be a little man, hanging with him, answering his thousands of questions. Benji's childlike joy was engaging, and Hix felt his heart defrosting.

When they finished and returned to the truck, they saw Prince had the chore of walking the lame lab.

Poochie moved slowly, but Prince stayed patiently with him, speaking calmly and quietly as they moved about because the dog was skittish at being around so many people and the great, unfamiliar outdoors.

Benji and Hix let the cats out one at a time to stretch so they didn't scamper off. Hix learned the dog's name was Poochie. The orange tabby was Cobweb due to his brain fog. A white Persian named Toots because although her body had been badly burned she still strutted like she was walking the red carpet.

Spock was the black cat with the overly large pointed ears. He had been starved and beaten to the point he was a very weak and sick cat. The bird, Mortimer, with the warped wing had escaped from a pet store and gotten tangled in fishing wire, he stayed in his cage in the car.

Squeak was the tortoise. Benji explained because the turtle liked to crawl along walls, his shell would bump and scrap the plaster and sometimes make a squeaking sound.

Benji said one of the servants had found him outside in the grass, his shell so mutilated by perhaps a lawn mower that it was touch and go for a while to see if he'd live. Of course that wasn't how Benji explained it, but Hix got the gist. Laurin had picked up all of the animals at the church except for the tortoise.

After everyone had a short walk, except for Squeak and Mortimer the bird, the animals were given water and a snack then the humans and the pets were bundled back up in the vehicles and they took off.

A half an hour later, Hix and Prince parked in the Hixman driveway.

The front door opened wide, Hix's mother, Vageline, stood on the threshold watching as Hix climbed out of his truck and then lifted the boy out of the backseat.

As soon as his feet hit the ground, Benji's demeanor changed back to the frozen frightened child Ajanel had created.

Vageline, Hix's father Kresskin, and Hix's brother Kullen traipsed out of the house one after the other. They slowed their approach at the shake of Hix's head. The closer they came the more Benji's little body started trembling.

"Hey, Dad, Kullen, why don't you help Thomas with the animals and their stuff?" Hix suggested gently.

The family hid their surprise and perplexity at the entire situation but they smiled and went to help Prince unload his SUV.

177

Hix crouched down to Benji's height and set his hand on the boy's tiny shoulder. "Hey, little man, there is no need to be afraid. That is my mom," he pointed to Vageline who was holding the box they'd put Squeak the turtle in.

She smiled kindly at the child. Soft blonde hair curled around her pretty face.

"And that's my brother, Kullen," he motioned to Kullen who was carrying the big box the cats were huddled in.

Kullen grinned at Benji and said, "Hey, little bro."

But, other than from television, Benji had little understanding of what a brother was.

"And," Hix said, gesturing to his father that had the dog's leash in one hand and the birdcage in the other, "that's my dad."

At that, with a whimper Benji skittered behind Hix and hid behind his legs. His little fingers clutched at Hix's slacks.

"Hey, buddy," Hix said softly, "he's nice. He's not like your," Hix didn't want to badmouth Benji's father, stepfather, whatever he was. But the kid was shaking so badly Hix could feel him. Benji's tears were making Hix's pants wet.

Hix turned, bent, and lifted the child in his arms. Cradling his butt on his strong forearm, Hix patted Benji's thin back. Benji stuffed his face into Hix's shoulder.

"Hey, Benj, I won't let anyone hurt you, I promise. My dad is a really nice man, like you called me, you'll see." Benji rubbed his wet eyes and snotty nose on Hix's jacket.

"Okay? You'll be safe here, Benji. You can have toys to play with, and I have a niece and nephew around your age, they'll love to teach you how to play games."

"Hi there, honey," Vageline said softly. She had taken the turtle into the house and she was back outside. She moved slowly until she was a few feet from Hix and Benji.

She smiled kindly, and said with a warm gentle tone, "My name is Vageline, Benji, but it's a difficult name to say, you can call me anything you want, okay?"

The boy snuffled his face into Hix's shoulder but didn't turn around.

"Hmm, well, maybe you'd like to see the big back yard we have that you and Poochie can play in. There are swings and a jungle gym, Michael and Holly can show you how to climb on. Later, we're having hot dogs for dinner. You like hot dogs don't you, sweetheart?"

At that, Benji turned his head slightly and blinked big dark wet eyes at her. His lashes seemed miles long. "Can I have mustard on mine, Leenie?"

Vageline laughed at his nickname for her. She'd had so many different ones growing up because people had a hard time remembering what her name was. "Of course you can. Do you like tater tots? I might have them on the table too, with lots of ketchup for dipping. What do you think?"

Benji twisted fully around in Hix's arms.

Hix smiled at his mother then down at Benji. He told the boy, "I like my tots with ketchup on them."

"Really? I seen 'em on TV once an they sound funny so I wan 'em but Miz Clepper our cook said no, we cannit have 'em."

"Well, honey, this is my house, and anything you want, you can have." Vageline had surreptitiously moved closer. She stroked his arm then combed her fingers gently through his hair. His eyes half-closed at her soft touch. He nodded his head against Hix's shoulder.

Vageline said quietly, "I think he's getting sleepy, Son. How about I show him where he's going to sleep. One of the bedrooms has a small connecting room that I think he and Laurin can share. He'll feel safer close to her."

"You know my mommy?" Benji asked with a yawn. The sugar and excitement were taking their toll.

"Hmm, not yet. But I'm looking forward to meeting her. How about I take you inside and you can have a little nap. Would you like that?"

He nodded, "K." Then with a little urgency he said, "But what about Poochie and the pets?" He craned his neck suddenly worried about them.

"Hix's daddy and his brother Kullen will make sure they are fed. We have a playroom they can stay in until we get everyone settled. Here, can I take you to your bed?" She held her arms out to take the child from Hix. Benji shrank back against Hix, his head lowered.

"Benj, little man," Hix said softly. "She's my mom like Laurin is yours. She won't hurt you. You're safe with her."

"I might have a freshly baked cookie you can bring upstairs with you, honey, what do you say?" Her arms still out she made no move to grab the child.

Benji looked up at Hix who nodded affirmatively at him. "It's okay, Benj. She's got cookies." That was the clincher. The boy shifted in his hold and held his arms out for Vageline to take him.

Vageline cuddled him, kissed the top of his head. "There we go, baby, let's get you a cookie and see your room." She dabbed at his face with a tissue.

Poochie let out a woof.

Benji cried out, "Wait! Poochie needs me, Mama Leenie, please."

Hix's father brought the black lab slowly to the boy, he could tell Benji was terrified of him. "Here, son, here's your pup, you take him with you so you can watch out for him, all right?" Kresskin slowly lifted his hand with the dog's leash to give it to Benji.

Benji cowered from Kresskin and burrowed his face against Vageline's bosom. She petted his curls. "You don't need to be afraid, honey, Mr. Hixman won't hurt you, he just wants you to take Poochie with you."

Hix wrapped an arm around his father's shoulders and smiled at Benji. "See, Benj, not all fathers are, uh, not so nice. Some are really good and fun. My dad is fun and he likes you. He'll teach you how to catch a ball, what do you think about that?"

Kresskin still held the leash out to the boy with a kind smile. People initially were as wary of Kresskin as they were of his son Penn because of their dangerous looks. Benji's sleepy eyes darted back and forth between the two men, then he cautiously reached out for the leash.

When he closed his little hand around the handle, Vageline turned and she and the boy and the dog disappeared into the house.

Kullen grinned at Hix. "Heck brother, life is gonna get real interesting. Now, about the boy's mum..."

The men made sure the cars were emptied and the animals settled in the playroom. The cats were let out of the boxes and allowed to roam.

Kresskin gathered up some old towels to make bedding for the felines, water dishes and kitty litter boxes were set in the adjoining powder room.

The tortoise stayed in his box with a bowl of water and some lettuce leaves, the bird's cage was hung up by the window so he could look outside and get sunlight.

Mortimer immediately chirped and sang, he was happy with his new home.

# Chapter Twenty-One

**H**ix stayed the night sleeping on the bed in the room that was designated for Laurin if and when she arrived. Benji had become afraid when Hix said he had to leave and cried clinging to him like a monkey.

So, Hix climbed into the bed wearing sweatpants and a t-shirt. Benji curled up next to him in his pajamas while Hix read from one of Holly's picture books. The child fell asleep within minutes, the tiny truck clutched in his hand.

The next several mornings Hix got up and went to work but came back home, played with Benji until the boy went to bed begging Hix to stay with him. So he did until the child fell asleep, then Hix crashed in the bed in the adjoining room so he'd be there if Benji called out in fear. He set the alarm for an hour earlier so he could go home and shower and change there.

Aven told Hix he was spoiling the boy.

Vageline scolded her eldest son, "Boy that young, that deprived and traumatized can't be spoiled enough." She showered Benji with love and attention and sweets, and the child was thriving.

Between Hix, and his brothers and his parents, every day a new toy for Benji or for the pets showed up. With her own children all grown up and only seeing her grandchildren here and there, Vageline was in seventh heaven having the child there to care for.

Hix had it in the back of his mind to buy the kid a bike. He pictured himself teaching Benji how to ride it. He'd have to check with Laurin, get her approval first.

Two days later, in the morning, Hix ate breakfast with an excited Benji, the boy's eyes as big as the pancakes Vageline plopped on his plate. She added a dollop of butter, a bunch of blueberries and poured syrup over the whole thing. Then Vageline set a glass of orange juice and one of milk in front of Benji.

When Hix left, Benji was sneaking pieces of bacon to Poochie who sat begging beside him on the floor. Apparently, traumatized animals couldn't get spoiled enough either.

After stopping at his apartment for a shower and change of clothes, Hix drove to the station. Greeting the first shift crew, he trod down the beige tiled floor to his untidy office.

Before he could sit down, a man in a white button-down and black trousers poked his head in. When Hix waved him to enter, the red-haired man stepped inside.

"Have a seat, Mack." Hix motioned to one of the chairs in front of his desk as he circled the desk to stand behind it.

Mack continued to stand. "I'll only be a minute, Hix, I have a meeting to get to. I just wanted to give you our brief profile of the killer. Delton, Tammy and I worked on it, it's real slim, not much."

"Okay, go ahead." Hix spoke coolly yet politely, he doubted the BAU could profile the killer any better than Hix and his team had.

"Ah, all right." Mack McGregor glanced at his phone, he already knew the small amount of info that was there. "Since sexual sadist, serial killers tend to be males and they mostly offend within their own race, we believe we're looking for a Caucasian male. We think he has a white-collar job because he's intelligent, and is between mid-twenties and mid-fifties. He has to be young and strong enough to haul around the wood and the victims."

At Hix's brow lift, Mack bumped one shoulder. "Yeah, broad sketch, doesn't help much but we don't have enough to pinpoint more closely. He's likely a loner, but he could be married.

Judging by the videos he's tall and strong. He may have had some training in woodwork and metalwork which conflicts with the white-collar idea. The carvings on the wooden boxes were quite intricate and artistic, would take an accomplished hand. The chain links as well, but they weren't quite as expertly done. Could even be more than one accomplice."

When he paused, Hix said, "Anything else? We already profiled him to that point. We know he's quite bright because he snatches these women without being clearly observed or leaving clues." His frown expressed his disappointment.

"That's a shit profile, Mack. Serial killers as well as sexual sadists do go outside their race. Even the sex offenders we interviewed know more than you do for fuck's sake." Hix traipsed around the desk to stand in front of the officer.

Mack's forehead furrowed with indignation. Tossing his head in annoyance, red locks flopped over his daggered down red brows, he said, "Listen, Hixman, we can only work with what you cops bring us. Maybe it's you who is doing a shit job."

He had the presence of self-preservation to take a step back from the suddenly livid detective. He held his hands up when Hix leaned towards him with a growl.

Hix muttered gruffly, "You got anything else of use, Mack?"

His hands turning palms up, with a crooked weak grin, Mack offered, "Uh, he probably lives in Brevet Bay or nearby since he's so familiar with the area's cameras, and he's taken the girls and dumped them within the city's circumference."

Hix rolled his eyes in disgust. "No shit. Thanks, Mack. Come back when you have something to really give us." He turned his back to the hapless behavioral analysis and trod back to his desk.

Again, before he could sit, he heard a swift rap at his door. Swinging around in aggravated impatience he barked, "Enough, Mack, we're done. Take off." The chuckle drew his head up.

Kurt was grinning at him.

"Oh," Hix mumbled. Spreading his feet he set his hands on his hips. "What's up?"

Kurt chuckled again. "Hey, I'm just glad I'm not Mack MacGregor."

Holding several files in his hand, he moved further into the office. "They brought the Ajanels in early this morning." He scowled in repugnance, then smirked. "Was not easy, my man. They are a querulous, pompous bunch.

"The wives are just as bad as the men, well, two of them are rude, demanding, whiny, total fucking pains in the ass, the third is petrified to be in a police station and just blubbers. Every other word out of their mouths are threats of a lawsuit, vile curses, and 'Do you know who we are?'" Kurt laughed at the privileged family trying to run the police station.

"After meeting the father, I can imagine. So what's happened so far?" Hix asked. He picked up messages someone had set on his desk. Leafing through them, he dropped them back down.

Kurt told him, "Emilee and Sergeant Sinclair interviewed the wives and are now checking out their alibis for the murders. Mike Maverick is covering Blane Ajanel. Teague has the oldest son Raoul, and shit, Hix, guy is a tough son of a bitch. Like a hunk of cursing, threatening beef jerky." He chuckled shaking his head.

"No surprise there."

Nodding and still shaking his head at the same time, Kurt went on, "The last one, Prince beat you here, he's in with the youngest son, ah," he opened one of the files he was holding, said with a laugh, "Chevalier. Seriously, who names their child Chevalier? Musta gotten bullied like hell in school.

"When I called him Chevalier, boy did he pop off. Told me, it's Chevy, or Doctor Ajanel actually. Then he got all huffy and red faced and stammering. Could be our killer, Hix, with all the bullying, probably has mommy issues, wants to strike back, be in charge, right?"

"Uh huh. They are all on our persons of interest list. None of them hit on the NCIC for criminal histories, but we still need to check Interpol for overseas searches." Hix straightened the knot of his tie, ran his fingers down it so it lay neatly. "The others are done?" He started for the doorway to head to the interview rooms.

Kurt walked beside Hix down the hall and handed the file to him. "Yes, just about. Mike and Teague are working on the males' alibis now. You can review the tapes of their interviews whenever you want. Didn't get anything substantial out of the gang. They are thugs in suits, but it's really highly unlikely any of them is our Poser."

"Did we attempt to get their prints? Offer them coffee or soda or see if they touched anything?"

"Um, Raoul is wearing gloves, so far Blane has kept his hands in his pockets, both refused a beverage. They are obnoxious but not stupid. Except for Chevalier, he asked for a Cola. And he's the doctor, supposed to be the smart one. Anyway, Mike and Teague will keep vigilant for them to touch anything, or watch if Raoul chews gum, smokes a cigarette, whatever.

"The wives all requested drinks. We have no DNA to match with, and only that fragment of a print. But when we get something, we can clear them, or move them up the list. Where are you going now?"

"I want to see at least one of the interviews in action. Since he's still in process, which room is the doctor in?"

"Room three. He's not as aggressive and loud as the two oldest Ajanels, but he's just as pissed off, and embarrassed to have been dragged down here."

"Okay, we'll have a meet at noon, after I've reviewed the tapes. Tell the others." Hix went to the right, Kurt veered to the left.

Along the way Hix got a call. He answered his cell. It was Sinclair.

"Penn," the sergeant said, "found where the spray-paint machine and the rose gold paint were purchased."

"*Awai*? Ah, yeah?" A hint of excitement in his tone, Hix perked up.

"Yeah, don't get excited. They were two separate purchases also at the Collier Depot and made by Howard Fernell."

Hix's exhale was disappointment. "Great. When did the big Howie boy buy them?"

"Ah," Daron took a second to review his notes. "Was six months ago."

Hix pondered for a second. "He bought the first stock of the rosewood almost a year ago, then in September, then the third was purchased last month. He bought the paint stuff six months ago. He started planning at least a year ago and has been working right along on his plan. He's methodical, patient, and smart."

"And skillful, the carvings on the boxes are works of art. But yeah, sounds like he has planned this for quite some time. Of course we don't know what other things he might have been doing, or other victims that we don't know about."

Hix grunted. "Mike is cross-referencing copy crimes over the country looking for matches. Anything else?"

"Nope. That's all for now. Got the receipts and tapes, but I'm told there's no one with Fernell inside or outside of the store, so it's a no go. We can review them as a group at our next team meeting."

"At noon. We're having a working lunch. Sally Ann is sending an email to everyone getting their choices for food. See you then."

A minute later, through a one-way mirror, Hix watched Prince talking to Chevalier Ajanel. Not turning the sound on, he stood and observed their body language. Hix could tell more by their behavior and expressions than their words. He flipped through the file while studying the youngest Ajanel son.

After watching for a bit, he opened the door and stepped inside, closing the door behind him.

Dr. Ajanel was wearing a white lab coat, apparently he had been brought straight from his practice to the station. He wore a tie and pressed slacks and he did not look happy.

The photos in the file of his brothers, Raoul and Blane revealed the two eldest had darker skin like their father, they were swarthier than the doctor.

The table and chairs were different than in the other interview rooms of white plastic, this room contained four wooden chairs and a small square wooden table. The doctor sat on a chair, and Prince sat to his left instead of opposite him. They looked up as Hix entered. Ajanel frowned at him.

Prince made introductions. "Detective Penn Hixman, Dr. Chevalier Ajanel."

Neither man said anything or moved to shake hands. Chevalier grimaced at Hix then looked away.

Hix's iron angled face remained implacable; he pulled out a chair and sat down across the table from the doctor.

Exhaling his aggravation, Dr. Ajanel glared at Prince. "I have told you I do not know those…murdered women. I do not know who might have killed them. So what if we occasionally frequented the same clubs, not everyone knows everyone. My brothers may know more than me, they go to the clubs more often than I do. Now, I have given you my whereabouts on the days you asked about. I think I've been patient enough. I-"

As if the doctor wasn't speaking, Hix twined his fingers and set his hands on the table, and said, "I understand you have a geriatric practice?"

Chevalier's bluster dried right up at the question. His brows twitched at Hix's accent, but his chin rose proudly. He cleared his throat. "Um, yes. Right out of residency I took over a doctor's practice that was retiring." The defensive hardness of his features smoothed slightly in the handsome face.

"Gotta be tough dealing with aged people, all those aches and diseases, help me I've fallen and can't get up and shit like that," Hix commented.

Chevalier blinked at him then sat back in his chair. "Oh, sure. Like any practice, pediatrics, gynecology, there's good and bad moments. It's long, long days, you know? I barely get to see my wife and child." He relaxed into his more normal genial self and gave the detective a mild smile.

"Yes, as a homicide detective I can feel those long days with you, Doctor." Hix didn't smile but he un-grit his teeth, the most pleasant expression he normally showed.

Chevalier nodded his head in commiserating accord. "Yes, of course, you understand the emergencies that, well," he smiled, "you just can't get up and go home at five when you have a heart attack on the exam table, right? Or, in your case, a murderer to catch before he takes another life."

"Hmm." Hix cocked his head, took in the doctor's body language as he grew friendlier in their sharing of occupational hazards.

Chevalier's shoulders relaxed, he loosely clasped his hands together setting them in his lap. His anxious breathing slowed, he looked Hix straight in the eye and sustained a soft smile.

The doctor, close to Hix's own age albeit a few years older, was attractive in a quiet sort of way. His hair, eyes and skin were lighter than his brothers, as was his attitude

Hix had read that the Ajanel brothers were uncooperative and downright nasty. He could see the arrogance in the youngest brother, yet he didn't have the sharper air of superiority and egotism as his brothers.

Not only the teasing from classmates at his unusual name, the good doctor likely suffered much bullying from his older brothers. And their father was the toughest, meanest, most brutal example. They were a rough bunch.

Chevalier Ajanel fit much of the criteria of the profile of the killer. From what Hix heard, his brothers were cold and mean enough to torture and butcher hapless women. And the father, Rádolfo the crooked beast, hell, the bunch of them could all be candidates for The Poser.

"So," Hix asked, "as a physician, I guess you would be in contact with all kinds of medicines, drugs, right?"

Chevalier's smile faltered, his eyes narrowed wary at the question, then he bolstered with the importance of his job. "Of course. I write prescriptions all day long for mostly high blood pressure, cholesterol, bone density, arthritis, things that plague the elderly."

"Hmm." Hix nodded. "You ever have occasion to use a product called vecuronium bromide?" He had studied the drug to be proficient in its use and pronunciation. He carefully watched Chevalier's expression, looking for any sign of guilt or nervousness.

Chevalier's lips pushed out, he shrugged. "I know what it is, but it's used in surgery. I run a private practice, I don't do surgery."

"But you could access it, right?" Hix didn't change his position. His hands were folded on the table, he leaned forward slightly, his broad shoulders hunched. His long legs were tucked back, his feet each hooked around a chair leg.

Chevalier's curious gaze moved to Prince who sat quietly observing, his blue eyes returned his gaze calmly, non-accusing or threatening, then Chevalier shifted his regard back to Hix and his shoulders rounded slightly in self-protection. Hix was scary night to Princeton's bright day.

Under Hix's dark stare, Chevalier struggled to not squirm and drop his eyes. "Well, uh, sure, I suppose. Any doctor can write a script, but, I would have no use for it. There are records kept on certain medications and the doctors that order them. Feel free to check them out, you'll find I've never written a prescription for vecuronium."

"What about your brothers or their wives, your wife or your father?"

"Huh?" Chevalier blinked several times and looked back and forth between the two detectives. He set his palms flat on the table and pushed back slightly. "Why on earth would they? None of them are involved in the medical field whatsoever. Far from it, in fact. Detective, what are you imp-"

"How about a physician friend or other relative, could any of your relatives have gotten a prescription from someone else? Maybe someone accessed your prescription pad?"

Chevalier's brows drew down carving a line between his eyes. "No, of course not. Again, why would they? I don't understand what you're-"

Hix cut him off again, "Do you work on the weekends?"

The doctor blinked rapidly again at the sudden switch in questions. "Huh? Ah, no, not normally, sometimes in emergencies. Sadly there's been quite a few of them lately. Why-"

"What about your brothers, your father, do they work on the weekends?" The victims were all killed on the weekend.

Chevalier's brown eyes narrowed in confusion, he raked a hand through his hair conveying his bewilderment. "Yes, the business they're in frequently has them working weekends." Giving up trying to ask Hix questions, he settled back in his chair.

"You wrote down where you were on the days and times Detective Princeton told you?" Hix noted the soda can sitting next to Chevalier's right hand on the table.

"Sure, sure, I was as usual, at work most of the times indicated." Chevalier nodded cordially, inclining his head towards the notebook and pen in front of Prince wanting to be cooperative, helpful. He was a revered doctor, if it got out that he had been hauled down to the police station and interrogated like a common criminal, he could kiss his practice goodbye.

"All right." Hix stood up so abruptly Chevalier's head snapped up at him. "I think that's all for now. If you think of anything that can be of help, please call us."

Prince pushed his chair back, the chair legs scraping across the linoleum floor, and rose to his feet.

"Uh, uh, sure." Chevalier climbed awkwardly to his feet surprised that the interview abruptly ended. "I'll do anything I can to help. If I knew anything, or thought anyone guilty of the murders, hell, I'd speak right up. I already would have. I mean," he palmed the hair at the sides of his head, "I'm a doctor, I took an oath for heaven's sake to heal, never harm."

Smoothing his already neat hair, the doctor went on with angry compassion, "Those poor women, it's all over the news. They're calling him The Poser. Apparently he rapes them then kills them, paints them gold then poses them naked on their knees in front of a big wooden box." His skin paled, the quiver pecking his shoulders noticeable, he said, "It's sick, who would do something like that?"

The police hadn't released information about the chains, or the knife marks or the circular burnings hoping to trap the suspect with those facts. They also wanted to avoid copycat killers.

The rapes weren't mentioned in reports to the media, but, due to the population's fascination with salacious horror, and the nudity of the victims, the reporters tossed that *assumption* in there to heat up viewers, keep their attention glued to the net and the newspapers for more spicy details. Everyone knows, sex sells.

Hix standing by the door as if to say they were done and the doctor can leave, muttered only, "Uh huh."

Cheeks pink with humiliation of being so curtly dismissed, Chevalier sidled to the door.

"Thanks for coming in, Doctor," Prince said equably, "we appreciate your cooperation." He handed him a business card. "Any little thing, thought, give us a call."

"Uh, yeah, sure, no problem." The card in his hand, Chevalier slipped out the door and hurried away down the hall, his head swiveling back and forth as he sought the right direction to go in.

"Think he'll find his way out?" Prince laughed.

"Doubtful." Using a hanky, Hix picked up the soda can. "I'll take this to the lab. Then you and I can get with Sinclair and some uniforms and divvy up the clubs' personnel and members, and start the interviews. Find out who might have known our victims and nail down alibis."

"Gonna be a big job," Prince pointed out as the two started down the hall.

"True that."

Hours later, Kurt called Hix.

When Hix answered Kurt said, "Penn, Rádolfo Ajanel's personal assistant is burning up the wires. Ajanel has heard about his sons being called in for questioning, and he's asking about his wife, says she's missing and heard the police brought her in as well.

"His butler had called Ajanel and advised that you came and took his young son without cause or a warrant. And also gathered clothes for his wife and told the butler she wasn't returning home. He's…angry." Understatement.

"Major Domo," Hix muttered.

"Huh?"

"Not butler, he's a major domo."

"Okay, whatever. Mrs. Ajanel's doctor called as well and said her husband's people have been inquiring if she's at the hospital.

They said she hasn't returned home, they checked the police stations and all the local hospitals and believe she is at Imperial Summit. Mrs. Ajanel's doctor said he wanted to speak with you right away."

"Call Doctor Rothschild, I'll text you the number. Tell him I'm on my way and to stall Ajanel. At the moment Mrs. Ajanel is at the hospital only under her first name. It'll take a bit before they confirm she's there."

# Chapter Twenty-Two

**H**ix parked illegally near the front of the hospital, slapped his police blue light on the dashboard of his truck and hopped out. A security guard came right over.

"Sir, you can't park-"

Showing his badge, Hix said, "Official business," and shouldered past the officer. He called Dr. Rothschild when he got inside. The doctor directed him to room 203 and said he'd meet him there.

Ignoring the elevator, Hix took the stairs two at a time and strolled past door after door until he reached 203, Rothschild was there waiting. They shook hands.

Rothschild looked worried. "Laurin's husband has been calling searching for her. We haven't confirmed she is here, but it will only be a matter of time."

"I know. Sign off on the discharge papers, give me the information she needs to take care of her recuperation. I'm taking her out of here."

"All right," Rothschild said. "I'll order the wheelchair. What do we tell her husband when he calls back demanding to know if she's here? He's a government official, he can bring trouble down on our heads."

"It's okay, you can tell them that the police came and retrieved her and took her to a confidential women's shelter."

One brow arched. "Is that where you're taking her?"

Hix just stared at the doctor. Rothschild smiled. "Okay, what I don't know I can't tell."

"Here," Hix said, handing him a bag, "her clothes."

The smile broadened. "Good, good, can't have her going out in a paper gown, right?" He took the bag and motioned to the nurse waiting inside the door.

He handed her the bag then said to Hix, "Give her a few minutes to change, it'll be rough for her. Yesterday evening, her nurse caught her crawling on the floor trying to leave. Was not too happy when we literally forced her back into the bed. She's in great pain, she's scared and asking about her son. And," he grinned, "she is as mad as a hornet at you."

Hix's laugh was short. "No doubt."

"I have the discharge papers already prepared, I'll call someone to bring them. As soon as they're signed you can whisk her out of here." His pleasant face grew grim. "She's still in bad shape. I had hoped to keep her here a little longer for her to heal properly under our care."

Hix said nothing. If he left her to stay in the hospital, her husband would swoop in and haul her out and home. Once that happened, Hix couldn't protect her. He wanted to get her in a safe place with her son, give her a chance to get on her own feet.

He needed to find out what the hold was that Ajanel had on her, and help her get out from under his violent fist. First things first, get her to his folks' home.

"You're a detective, son, there's no way you can give her the round-the-clock care she needs."

"No worries, got it covered. Best I don't tell you, Doc."

His hand in his pocket, Rothschild grinned. "Understood." He turned at the nurse's voice. "Ah, she's ready, I'll wait out here for the paperwork."

"Coward," Hix muttered as he passed through the doorway, the doctor chuckled behind him.

Laurin looked almost as bad as she had a week ago. Small and frail, bandaged, cut and bruised, her eyes were less swollen and her lip looked better.

Hix hadn't considered what the boy would think when he saw his mom all torn up. But then again, he likely saw worse after Ajanel was done with her. The thought made him sick to his stomach and he had to tamper down the rage that instantly started to boil.

Her blue eyes tracked him as he entered the room. "Detective, my Benji, you've only sent brief reports to me, please, where is he? Is he all right? Is he scared?" Her voice trembled, her jaw shook, tears flooded her eyes. She was dressed in jeans and a blouse and was reclining in the bed. It appeared she was garnering the energy to get to her feet.

Hix moved quickly to her. "Hey, Laurin, it's all okay. I told you I have Benji, he's safe at my mom's house. My parents are taking care of him and the animals."

His lip quirked at the sight that he'd left this morning. Benji as always, asking Cliff and Kullen a million questions while slipping bites of bacon to Poochie. Hix had enlisted his brothers to rotate protection duty.

While Benji chattered, and the brothers chuckled, Squeak the turtle, had bumped along the kitchen wall. Kresskin laughed while watching him with a cat on each knee, Spock and Cobweb. The third feline, Toots, perched on top of the fridge looking down on all she reigned with the occasional meow of order.

Mortimer the bird chirped and sang gaily from the living room. It was noisy, but pleasant noise. Cheerful noise. Noise Hix could get used to.

"C- can I see him? Please?" Laurin sounded so small and afraid.

"Of course, I'm taking you to him right now."

The tears spilled over. "Detective, when my husband finds out about all this, he- my God, you don't know how he will punish us. He- might come after you. Oh, what have you done? You've put everyone in danger!" she wailed, her body crumpled into the pillows.

Hix sat on the edge of the bed and pulled her into his arms. He held her head to his shoulder, the same one little Benji had cried on.

"It's all going to be okay, Laurin. I promise. Benji is safe, you both will stay at my folks' until you're completely healed and on your own feet. Maybe get you a job, and yours and Benji's own place?"

Hix was actually picturing them in his apartment, the animals frolicking happily about. Or maybe a house like his parents', cozy and welcoming, pet and child friendly. With a pool. He could teach the children to swim. They'd have pool parties and barbeques, they would-

He squeezed the images out of his head, why did his ridiculous brain keep going there? He needed to check himself and make sure he was helping Laurin solely for her and Benji's safety, and not because he coveted her, and wanted to take her from her husband for his own pleasure.

"You don't understand," she said. Pushing from him, she swiped at her eyes with the heels of her palms. "Your family isn't safe. He'll come for me and he will destroy anything in his path. He has diplomatic immunity, you can do nothing to stop him." A sob of despair caught in her throat.

Hix grasped her shoulders and held her still, looked into her eyes. "Laurin, I'm a cop. My father has the house wrapped in security you wouldn't believe, nothing and nobody is getting in without us letting them. My sister's house is just as secure.

"My brothers are trained soldiers, they were American Marines, Special Ops." He didn't mention Hix himself was lethal as a rattler even if he had both hands tied behind his back and no weapon.

"Now, calm yourself down, wipe those tears." He leaned to the table beside the bed and snatched two tissues and handed them to her. "Trust me. You are no longer alone. You have protection now. No one is ever going to hurt you again. You hear me?"

"B-but, it's imperative I go home!"

"Why? Tell me, Laurin, let me help you."

"I...can't," she suddenly sounded defeated, her chest emptied like a punctured balloon.

He cradled her chin and lifted it. "Listen, you can trust me. Whatever else is going on, whatever it is that has a grip on you, I can help you," he repeated.

Her head lowered, she shook it, wiped at a tear. Clearing her throat, her voice husky with tears and emotion she said, "I- I have to get well as quickly as I can. I have someone I need to…to meet. I can't make any decisions until…then."

Hix waited, but she said nothing else. "Who-"

She shook her head again. "I can't. Please. I need to see that Benji is safe. I have only two priorities, and he's the immediate one right now. I just don't know what to do…" she closed her eyes, scrunched them tight.

Knowing she wasn't giving him anything else, not even who she planned to meet, much less what the second priority was, he said, "Okay," *for now*. "I'll take you to Benji."

Laurin gulped down her tears and strangling fright, and nodded weakly. Fighting Hix was like wrestling a relentless battering ram without ears.

He bent and scooped her ankle boots up off the floor and got a tiny giggle out of her when he struggled to put them on her feet.

"Stop laughing at me," he grinned, "I've never put shoes on another person before. It's not easy." He zipped up the side of one of the boots.

"I appreciate your efforts, Detective, in my condition I know it would take me an hour to get them on, the socks were hard enough." Her sadness brightened with a smile of gratitude.

His awkwardness with her shoes chased away her feeling sorry for herself, and the anxiety of not knowing what to do next. At least for a little while she could lay her worries on his broad shoulders, and that made her sigh with relief.

The nurse came in with the wheelchair. Hix got up and lifted Laurin off the bed and set her on the chair. He said to the nurse, "Dr. Rothschild is bringing her discharge paperwork, I'm going to get my truck and pull up to the main exit and wait for you there. All right?"

"No problem," the nurse assured him with a smile. This one was helpful and pleasant, not sex on rubber heels like the first one. "I'll bring her down to you."

Hix parked his truck in front of the main entrance door, got out and waited as the nurse wheeled Laurin out of the exit. Laurin wore a jacket, but Hix had brought a blanket to wrap around her lest she catch a chill in her weakened condition.

When the nurse pushed the wheelchair to his truck, he lifted Laurin from the chair and carefully settled her in the passenger seat of his truck. He locked the seatbelt, she didn't have the strength or agility to do it herself, and he arranged the blanket around her.

Hix closed her door and took the discharge information from the nurse. It contained aftercare instructions.

He jumped in behind the wheel, turned the truck on, then twisted to face Laurin.

Seeing her trembling jaw, he patted her leg. "It's all good now, Laurin, you no longer have to look over your shoulder, walk on eggshells, suffer beatings."

He went on over her gasp, her secret was no secret, "It's time someone else took care of you instead of you. Okay?" He gently cupped her jaw, smiled at her watery weak nod and pressed his lips on hers. Her mouth was soft, plush, immediately he pulled back.

"Ah, Laurin, I didn't mean to do that, it was...I...it won't happen again." He tensed waiting for her outcry. Instead, a tiny, almost imperceptible shy smile was there and gone so fast Hix may have imagined it. Wanted it to be real.

She said nothing so he took that as a 'let's not talk about it let it go' thing, and he drove towards his parents' home.

# Chapter Twenty-Three

Laurin stared straight out the window, she didn't dare glance over at the dangerous looking cop beside her. Detective. Every time she'd seen him a frisson of fear roiled through her, tightening her stomach, her shoulders shuddered. She wanted to hide from him, but he won't allow it.

His growly accent and swarthy appearance made her think of pirates, or ancient Egyptian warriors with his fierce dark looks, hard features. His face narrowed down to an unyielding strong jaw covered in a short black beard. The suit he wore did nothing to take the edge off his powerful warrior image.

Even in a suit, his shoulders stretched the seams, his chest was thick, she'd felt it when he'd held her. Every piece of him, his face, body, behavior, enigmatic dark eyes made her think of jaggedly carved iron. He was so big, tough, he could snap her like a twig. Just like Rádolfo.

At the thought of her abusive husband terror ricocheted through her brain, when he got his hands on her, she was so dead. After he tortured her, raped her, whipped, beat her, then he would kill her for running out on him and taking Benji.

Not that she was the one who took Benji away. But she would be blamed. Laurin wanted to spare a glance at the fearsome man beside her, but she was too afraid. Afraid he'd see inside her and learn the rest of her secrets and expose them, and she'd never see her brother again. Afraid he'd arrest her or worse, take her back to

Rádolfo, even though she knew she needed to return to him. She was afraid the detective would keep Benji from her. Afraid he'd kiss her again.

The frisson of fear spiraled again, but the feeling of his mouth on hers had threaded...heat...with the fear. Why had he kissed her? Was she to suffer rape and torment at this brutish man's hands too? Laurin peered at him under long lashes. His profile was as strong as the rest of him, the aura of danger viscerally present.

Yet, she'd felt something...something she'd never experienced with her husband. Was the tingling on her lips, the prickling between her legs, was that...arousal? She'd never felt this way before, as if she wanted him to do it again, but, longer, firmer, put his hands on her. On all of her.

Her cheeks suddenly flamed red at her indecent thoughts. He had all but said it was an accident, that it hadn't meant anything to him at all.

Her rigid body, rapid breaths transmitted to him, Hix said, "Laurin, please." His head turned briefly towards her, his gaze raked down her body and up to her flushed face then he turned back to the road.

"Calm down. I swear I am not going to hurt you. I'm only trying to help you, you and Benji. Please," his thumb tapped the steering wheel, "trust me."

Laurin twined her fingers so tightly in her lap she feared she'd break them. But she had nothing else to hold onto. No safety net. There's never been anyone to trust before, she didn't- The detective's large hand settled down over hers, he gave them a gentle squeeze.

"Stop thinking, just, try to feel safe for once in your life."

After a time, he drove down a street where the houses were set far apart, a lot of acreage separated them.

Then he turned onto a two-lane road and followed it until farmland and ribbons of green fields carpeted both sides of the road. The crisp air sprinkled dew on stiff leaves and early crops springing in neat rows.

Eventually, forested land came into view, and Hix turned onto a single lane, no, it was a driveway.

They passed an extensive fence somewhat like Rádolfo's then further up the lane there was an unmanned gate. But security cameras had lined the driveway and were perched in trees and at the gate. Hix rolled down his window and plugged in a code.

The gate opened and they drove through. Another couple hundred yards and another fence and another gate that Hix coded, waited for the gate to swing open and he drove on.

"Are," she coughed to clear her tight throat. "Are, your parents, um, criminals or- or celebrities?"

Hix laughed and pulled up to a huge white house with hunter green shutters and parked in the driveway. "No. It's just," he turned in his seat to face her, his left arm resting on the wheel.

"Where we came from, it was…dangerous. My family lived in peril because the military forced me to fight and the leaders were afraid my family would try to steal me back and flee the country. So, they were watched, and followed, and sometimes harshly harassed by the military as well as neighbors. So, my dad took measures in Egypt and then here in America to keep his family safe."

"But, what do they have to fear here?" Laurin studied the two-story, white brick building. Several chimneys and large windows made it appear more homey than austere.

"Nothing really, just old habits die hard. And right now, it's a good thing because you and Benji will be safe and protected for as long as you want."

Her head swiveled to him, then she quickly turned away. Could she believe him? Trust him? Her blue eyes darkened, of course not. She should have learned by now no one can be trusted. Especially men.

Not Secretaries of the State, not ambassadors, not CIA agents. Laurin forced herself not to look at him again, and certainly not handsome detectives with strange guttural accents and cold dark eyes.

Everyone was corrupt, evil, buyable. Laurin felt him staring at her, but she kept her eyes forward. She heard his sigh. Then he got out, closed his door and came around to her side.

He opened the passenger door and said quietly, "Here, let me help you down, it's a big step and you're kinda tiny. Put your hand on my shoulder." He unhooked her seatbelt, let it slide back inside the door, and moved the blanket.

Laurin blinked back sudden tears of fright. Feeling trapped again, she froze.

His tough eyes gentled. "Trust me, please Laurin, you can't stay in the truck. Benji is inside, he's dying to see you." He tried to coax her.

But was Benji really inside? Maybe this was all a trick to…to what? If he wanted to harm her he could have already done so. Maybe he was kidnapping her to get ransom from Rádolfo. But, the hospital knew she had gone with him.

Well, the detective will certainly not allow her to stay here in the truck. Letting out her held breath, Laurin turned to him and tried to shift her legs out the door but she flinched and stopped with a cry of pain.

"Ah shit, okay, wait, I've got you." He slid his hands in the truck and under her and lifted her out.

"Oh!" she gasped. Expecting to be set down on her feet, she steeled herself for the additional pain and unsteadiness. She had only gone from the bed to the restroom the past few days, and that wasn't without a lot of laborious work and considerable pain.

Her aborted attempt to leave the hospital only gave her a relapse, she re-injured wounds that had yet to heal. Looking up at the big house although it wasn't but a few yards it seemed thousands of feet away, she'd never make it.

But Hix held her in his arms, closing the door with his knee and started to the house.

"No, please put me down, I can- can walk." Even speaking those anxious words she was out of breath, her head wobbled faintly.

"Shh," his deep voice gruff yet softened, "just hold still, let me help you, walk for you."

The front door opened and a woman stepped out, her expression curious, interested, wary.

Laurin stiffened. The woman did not look like the detective at all. She had light hair and fair skin, not plump but she had a soft figure. In a blue dress, she clasped her hands in front of her stomach, and unlike the detective, she had an easy smile.

He told her, "Don't be afraid Laurin, no one here is going to hurt you, only help you. That's my mother, she's been taking care of Benji."

Laurin's eyes widened at the woman who had been tending to her son. How embarrassing, Laurin was such a loser some stranger had to take care of her child. She hadn't the means or ability to see to the welfare of her own son. Laurin shrunk in dejection against Hix's chest.

Hix shifted her so he could see her face. Seeing her downturned mouth, eyes full of guilt and grief, he said, "Hey, come on, we all need a leg up once in a while. Just," he stopped, glanced at his mother. She got the hint and paused as well. Laurin's lids covered her shame.

"Laurin," his voice was gentle yet commanding, "look at me." He waited, he could stand there all day if he had to.

Her mouth trembled, eyes turned up slowly to face his wrath. But he didn't look mad. In fact, his features were the softest she'd ever seen them.

"There, good girl. Now, this is the way it's going to be. You are going to reunite with your son. The two of you are going to stay here and accept care and kindness and protection. There will be no arguing on your part about any of it. You do not owe us anything except to get well." He almost tacked on the part about she wasn't leaving until he felt it was in her best interest, but she'd find that out herself if she tried to leave. She'd never get out the first gate.

Her eyes flashed around his face, the determined set to his jaw, unwavering gaze, gentleness in his dark eyes that stared honestly, levelly back at her.

He gave her a little shake. "Okay? We on the same page, Laurin?"

Laurin scrutinized him for a few minutes, then nodded. She felt his shoulders slacken with her acquiescence.

"Good. Come on, come meet my mom." He actually almost smiled at her, clearly his mouth was rusty with that kind of action, but time spent with Benji had brought laughter more easily to the hardened guy.

He moved towards his mother again, and his mother stepped aside as Hix carried Laurin inside, then closed the door after she followed them in.

Laurin whispered, "Please, Detective, please put me down." Gosh it was so embarrassing meeting his mother, and Laurin was so weak her son had to carry her.

Hix trod across a small tiled foyer and turned into a doorway. They entered a large room decorated in warm welcoming blues.

Thick sapphire carpet, powder blue sofa and chairs, a white brick fireplace took up half of one wall. Along the mantel Laurin could see framed photographs of what appeared to be their family.

In the center of the room, sitting on the carpet, were Benji who was surrounded by the animals and two young children sprawled on either side of him. The three children were jabbering all at the same time.

When Hix entered the living room, Benji glanced over, then, his mouth gaped into a giant grin and he leaped up.

"Mommy!" he shrieked and ran to her.

Hix carefully set Laurin on her feet but held onto her waist, helping her stay standing. Which was a good thing because Benji raced over and threw himself at her. He would have knocked her over in the frail state she was in.

Laurin lowered to her knees and the pair hugged each other, She sobbed silently against the top of Benji's head.

The other two children shyly approached. The girl held Spock, and the boy was cradling Cobweb. Poochie offered several woofs, and with Mortimer's vigorous chirping in the background, the room was alive with cheerful boisterous noise.

Laurin felt something nudge into her hand. It was a hanky. Hix was sneaking it to her, a smile helped diminish her weeping. He figured she wouldn't want Benji to see her crying.

Subtly wiping her eyes and nose, she sniffed back the rest of her tears and held Benji back at arms' length so she could get a look at him.

Her heart warmed, he was grinning. And he was…relaxed. Not afraid, not looking over his shoulder. A few days in this household had undone so much of Rádolfo's merciless reign of terror.

"I miss you, Mommy," Benji said, for once not in a shout. He looked oddly sad and happy at the same time.

"I missed you too, peanut."

"Are we stayin' here? Mr. Penn said Pa-Ray not coming, he isnna allowed here. Mr. Penn said we safe, Mommy. Is that right?" His little face was all screwed up with fearful hopefulness.

Laurin tilted her head up to Hix, the uncertainty brilliant in her eyes.

Hix crouched down and ruffled the top of Benji's hair. "That's right, little man. You and Mommy are staying for a long time. You okay with that?"

Benji arched his head back and let out a shouted whoop. He high-fived with Hix. "Mr. Penn said you had a accident. Mama Leenie say you gotta be careful drivin' in a car. Mr. Penn say you better now. You better?" he asked with concern.

"Yes, baby, I'm much better now that I'm here with you." Laurin hugged him to her again.

Pulling back from her, "Mommy," he said proudly, gesturing to the other children. "These my friends. Mikey and Holly. Mr. Penn say they are his," his lips pursed out, he couldn't remember what he'd called them.

Hix stood and clasped Laurin's arm helping her to her feet. He grinned at Benji then the other kids. "This is my nephew Michael and his sister Holly. They are my sister's brats. She'll be here soon and you can meet her," he inclined his head to the children with a nod.

The two kids grinned and said, "Hi, pleased to meet you," in unison. Well trained. Hix must have prepared them for Laurin's battered appearance because they just smiled cheerfully, albeit somewhat shyly. Laurin smiled at them.

Vageline quickly moved close to Hix. Hix said, "This is my mother Vageline, and this is Laurin Ajanel, Ma."

Laurin was overwhelmed, she didn't know what to say. Hix held onto her, if not for him, she would topple from her injuries and weak state.

Vageline held out a hand with a kind smile. "Hi Laurin, I'm so pleased to meet you. You and Benji are welcome in our house for as long as you need. Please treat it as your own home. We already love Benji, he's such a wonderful little boy."

At a loss as to what to say, what to think, Laurin was still confused as to why she was there at all. She just nodded.

A man stepped from another room, he approached slowly. He looked like an older version of Hix.

"Laurin," Hix said, turning towards him, "this is my dad, Kresskin. We didn't want to overwhelm you all at once, so after him, two of my brothers are waiting in the kitchen for their turn to meet you."

Kresskin bowed regally to Laurin. In the same accent as Hix's, his tone polite and heavily accented, unsmiling, again reminiscent of his son's dark mien, he said, "Very happy to have you in our home, Mrs. Ajanel. Please make yourself at home here. Ask for anything you need. As my wife said, we love your boy and I am sure we will love you as well." He took a deep breath. A man of few words, he'd said more than he had in days.

Still bewildered, Laurin just nodded. Then she said quietly, "Please call me Laurin, Mr., um, Hixman."

Kresskin nodded. "And I am Kresskin." A glimmer of a smile broke his stern face.

Another man entered the room. Again, he looked so much like Hix he had to be a brother.

"Hi there," the man said softly, his accent not as thick as Hix and his father's. "I'm Kullen. Glad you're here, Laurin. You have a great boy there, and your pets are a joy to have around." He grinned and Laurin saw the difference between the brothers.

A light flickered in Kullen's eyes, his smile was deep and peaceful and easy. It showed because he smiled a lot. Completely opposite to the darkly brooding Hix.

After another copycat brother, Clifford, introduced himself, Vageline seeing Laurin suppressing a yawn said, "Let me show Laurin to her room. Maybe you'd like a little nap, dear, this has to be so stressful on you."

Laurin's eyes shot in a panic to Hix. *No! She didn't want to be alone with any of these strangers.* She edged closer to his big body.

Hix's face melted, his eyes softened, a small smile lifted the corners of his full mouth. "It's okay, Ma, I'll show Laurin upstairs."

His gaze had never left Laurin since they'd entered the room. "If you want Benji to come too, we can do that," he knew she'd be afraid to leave him now that he was safely in her sight. But...

Laurin looked over and Benji was already immersed in whatever game the children had been playing when she came in.

They were laughing and screeching, Poochie hobbled around them with periodic woofs as they sprawled on the floor. Two cats lounged nearby, Kresskin was now cradling the Persian.

Laurin didn't want to expose Benji to her nerves. He finally had kids his own age to play with, and he didn't have a sadistic, savage father glowering at him with deprivation and endless threats of violence.

She didn't even realize Hix had slid a supporting arm around her shoulders and she had leaned into him. All this time frightened of him, and it was to him she'd gone for protection when she'd felt new fear.

"I, um, if you could escort me, Detective, that would be uh, okay...if, I mean, I don't want to be a burden." The last thing she wanted to do was be trouble for these people that had embraced Benji and accepted them both into their home.

Hix's face lifted in a rare smile down at her, he chucked her under her chin. "Never a burden, Laurin."

Her head lowered, Laurin peeked up at Hix through thick lashes and watched him glance at his family, they were standing quietly with bemused expressions.

To her, their expressions read, *why was their son, brother, being so kind to this sordid, married, adulteress, murderer? What was in it for him?*

Laurin was too weary and in too much pain to think about it. At the moment, Benji was safe, her lips curved in a gentle smile at the children playing. She peeked back at Hix's family, they also watched the children with fond, caring smiles. The boy couldn't be in better care.

Her husband wasn't there, and for the moment he didn't know where she was. For once in a long, long time, Laurin could let go of the panicked terror that relentlessly claimed her mind and body, and take a breath. If only Robbie was there too, life would be perfect.

Hix felt her tired legs start to shake, she grew heavier under his arm as her strength waned. Lines of pain pinched her eyes and mouth as she tried to hold it back.

"Okay, Laurin, let's get you to that bed." He bent at the knees and scooped her up into his arms. A breath of surprise left her, his family swallowed their gasps.

Heading towards the stairs, Hix told his family, "She's still recovering, she needs assistance."

Mortified, Laurin's face pinked, she cried out, "No, no, I'm fine, please, Detective, put me down." But her rasping, weak, trembling voice betrayed her lack of strength.

Vageline moved to the couple, she carefully reached out and gently patted Laurin's arm.

Laurin tried to sustain a raised posture, but her body gave out, and she slumped against Hix's chest. He held her closer.

"Honey," Vageline said softly, "you do not have to worry about a thing. We are taking care of Benji, and we are taking care of you too. Yes we are," she patted Laurin's arm as the girl opened her mouth to object.

Her smile kind and motherly, Vageline told her, "One reason you are here is because Penn said you need round the clock care and observation. And that is what you will have. No," she said as Laurin started to speak, "There is nothing to talk about. You are weaker than a newborn kitten, and kittens need care, and that's what you're going to get."

She smiled at Hix and told him, "Go on now before she works herself into a tizzy of protest, get her upstairs and comfortable."

# Chapter Twenty-Four

"You got it, Ma." Hix turned and made for the stairs before Laurin could get a word out and before Benji noticed she was leaving the room.

The child had expressed his worry for her, and though he was so young he was quite protective of her and would want to go with them. It would only keep Laurin stirred up when she clearly needed her rest.

At the top of the stairs, Hix turned to the right and his boots scuffed softly on the thick carpet down the hall. He passed several doors then went into one. Laurin's head lolled on his shoulder, she had lost the energy to protest his carrying her.

He strode right into the room and to the pretty queen sized bed that sat by a broad window. The room was frilly white and soft yellow, perfect for the beauty in his arms.

He brought her to the bed and gently set her down. Laurin wavered for a second then lay down on her side with her feet hanging off the side of the bed.

Hix studied her for a moment. She was fully clothed, she needed to be more comfortable. Damn. He was going to have to ask his mother to help her undress.

But, for now, he bent and lifted one of her tiny feet and slid off the ankle boot, then did the other and set the shoes beside the bed.

Then he pushed several pillows against the headboard, and sifted his hands under her and lifted her to sit, half lay against the pillows.

Lashes like blonde feathers fluttered, her tired blue eyes turned up to him. "Detective, I hate to be such a bother, please-"

Hix plunked down on the side of the bed and faced her. One leg bent, the other with his foot on the floor.

"Enough of that, Laurin. I don't want to hear another protest out of your mouth. You and the boy are here, you both are safe under a friendly roof. You have to have noticed that Benji's cheeks have rounded and are flush with healthy color. His eyes light up with vitality and vibrancy, he's put on a healthy pound. My family dotes on him, they love him. You think we can take care of him and let you go back home to hell?" He shook his head.

"But, Detective, the trouble, the expense-"

Hix set two fingers over her mouth to silence her. "I said enough. My family wants to do this, just be gracious and accept the help. Please." His family's wariness to take in the tainted woman vanished the second they met her.

The pads of his fingers tingled from the touch of her soft full lips. He ran the pad of his thumb over her lower lip admiring the lushness of it.

"I can't-"

"Hush now. You can and you will. It's a done deal. I don't want to hear another word out of your mouth about it. You want my ma to feel bad that you reject her help? I didn't think you were that kind of woman, Miss Boutique."

She frowned at the name. "Boutique? Why do you call me that?"

Hix had lowered his hand, but he stroked it down her shoulder, down her arm where he left it near her wrist. With a small chuckle he told her, "Because when I first saw you I thought you were one of those rich bitches that are high maintenance." Not his type, but his attraction to her had hit him like a charging locomotive.

At the sight of the sadness tugging her mouth down, he said quickly, "But I know you aren't like that at all. I'm just teasing you now. I'm trying to get you to smile. Could you give a guy a little smile?" His fingers stroked the soft skin of her arm, she didn't seem to notice.

"I..." she appeared to be about to object again, then the air deflated her lungs with a sigh. "I guess I should be thanking you instead of making things so awkward." A tiny smile hovered at the edges of her lips.

"*Aiwa*, yeah, there, that's what I'm talking about." Hix lifted his hand to cup the side of her face and his thumb brushed her mouth again. "You have a stunning smile, Laurin. I've only seen it briefly, and that's when you direct it to Benji. I like it now when you direct it to me."

His compliment made her cheeks rosy, she shyly ducked her head but the smile broadened.

The magnet attacked him again, and before he knew it, Hix cupped her chin and lifted it then leaned in and pressed his lips on hers. Laurin's mouth pulsed against his, her lips so lush and soft, he had to taste them.

Tilting his head, he licked the seam then pushed her lips apart to deepen the kiss. She was stiff, then a tiny erotic moan slipped out, and Hix's brain started burning. He angled his head further for a tighter fit then plunged his tongue inside and plundered her sweetness.

His hand moved to cradle the back of her head and their open mouths sealed together. Tongues embracing, his body on fire and his brain a bowl of buzzing lust, Hix went wild. So wild he didn't realize Laurin was suddenly trying to turn her head from his rampaging pillaging, her fists were pressed against his chest, she was struggling to push him away.

When he did become aware of her distress, he forced himself to release her and sit back with a harsh exhale. His chest heaving, raking his fingers through his hair, Hix worked to catch his runaway breath.

Laurin sank back against the pillows, her chest heaved with gasping pants for air to calm her reaction to his kiss, the big eyes hazed with passion rounded wide in confusion. Her hand splayed across her pitching bosom, she gulped and licked her lips.

Her tongue slicking over those bountiful lips didn't do anything to calm Hix's arousal. "Ah, um, Laurin, that was…I don't know what I was thinking. I…wanted to…comfort…" he trailed off. What the hell was he saying? He'd just thrust himself at a defenseless, injured female that he'd trapped on a strange bed in a strange room in a strange house. A woman who had been beaten and raped regularly. Dammit.

He quickly stood up then recoiled at Laurin's flinch. Great, she was afraid of him again.

Crossing her arms protectively over her chest, voice a breathy tremble of despair, Laurin cried, "Is that it? That's why I'm here, for sex?"

"God no, Laurin, no, no." His hands up in a surrender position, he said quietly, "I'm so sorry. I promise, you have nothing to fear from me. I would never hurt you, force you to- to do anything. I just," how does he explain he loses his mind when near her?

"I shouldn't have done it. I have to admit, I find you devastatingly attractive. But-" he turned his palms out. "I did not bring you here to take advantage of you. You are here purely, 100% for you and Benji to be safe. I swear to God, baby- ah, Laurin."

Shit, he's making things worse. Yet, his eyes slanted at her flushed face, she kept touching her lips. She had responded, no way did he imagine it.

Still, she was so vulnerable he was an ass for even touching her so boldly. Now she'd be uncomfortable around him. He caught the pinch of pain she tried to squelch and he stepped back several feet from the bed.

"Listen, Laurin, I'm going to get my mother. She'll bring your pain medication, and she'll help you to…settle in. I'm gonna clear out of here now, leave you alone."

He stood there hating himself for his lack of restraint. Who knew he was a marauding beast? She was nothing like the camp women that had been brought to him and the other soldiers. And here he had treated her like one. Pouncing on her while she lay helpless. How can he tell her she's safe in his parents' house if he assaults her himself?

"Detective, you…" she trailed off, started again. The fear in her gaze had mellowed to confusion, as if she was becoming aware of her own response to the kiss. "I'm a married woman. Obviously, things aren't um, copasetic in…at home. But, I have boundaries I can't cross. Please," she blinked back tears that sparkled in the low light of the lamp by the bed.

Hix didn't move, he was sifting her words through his fevered brain. The frenzy of arousal was clearing, he realized she hadn't chastised him for kissing her. She hadn't said she hated that he'd touched her. She had even been receptive for a moment. She only said she had boundaries, the boundaries of a heinous marriage.

After she recovers down the road, becomes comfortable around him again, he was going to start a conversation about possible divorce.

He'd never heard her say anything positive about Rádolfo. There was no inkling that she actually loves him, in fact her dreaded terror of him was blatant.

Somehow Hix got the idea Laurin had been forced to marry the ambassador. She had to want to be out of it, but hadn't seen a way out before now.

Hix would be her guide dog.

# Chapter Twenty-Five

**H**ix didn't return to his parents' home last night, he flopped at his own place.

Setting his empty bowl of oatmeal in the sink, he turned the faucet on to let the bowl soak and tossed back the last dregs of coffee and put the mug in the sink with the bowl.

Shrugging his jacket on, he glanced around at the dimly lit kitchen and felt gloom sludge through his veins.

The apartment was plain, basic furniture, neutral colored walls and carpet. Hix had never noticed how dismal it was before. And quiet. Lonely. It had never bothered him before, he liked being on his own.

But, his mind kept sliding back to his parents' home where everyone was happily interacting in a homey environment, the scent of something savory cooking in the background.

The corner of his mouth nicked in as a picture of his parents' cheerful cozy house floated in along with the remembered scent of garlic-tinted pasta cooking, or cookies baking, emerald and jade plants flourishing in the windows, frames of family photos scattered everywhere.

The nick lifted to a crooked smile as he recalled the little boy Benji, and his niece and nephew, surrounded by mangled and maimed animals woofing and chirping, lolling and prancing in and out and around the children as they played with boisterous unfettered glee.

Yeah, a home to envy. Only a home a woman could make. His father doesn't water the plants or bake the cookies, he didn't choose the warm blues and soft creams, he doesn't purchase the pleasant scented fabric softener, he sure didn't frame the family pictures and arrange them so lovingly along the mantel.

If his mother wasn't there, his father would be living in a cave. Basically like Hix himself was. Women make a house a home.

Hix glanced around again as he snatched his keys off a hook by the door. The image of his family's home compared to his glum apartment made him want to stay there tonight instead of hanging back here with the greys and tans, the dreary and dull. The empty. And again, the lonely.

It hit him like a frying pan to the head.

Hix realized he wanted to roll on the floor wrestling with the kids, he wanted to savor his mom's cooking, chat with his brothers, and, yeah, he wanted to spend time with Laurin. His body tightened at the picture of the blonde beauty lying so helpless and broken and scared in the bed in the pretty yellow room.

And, that's why he was going to stay away from his parents' place for a few days. Let Laurin and Benji settle and feel safe and loved. He'd check in with Kullen and his ma by text. Let them all chill without his dark presence hovering over everyone. Keep his sticky fingers to himself.

Phone to his ear, he took reports as he drove to the station.

In his office, Hix met with Prince, Kurt and Sinclair. Reviewing his email, he slumped back in his seat. "They found the source of the vecuronium bromide." He'd studied it enough now the drug's name rolled off his tongue. He had gone online to research everything about it.

The three men looked encouraged, then seeing Hix's frown, their smiles faltered. Kurt said, "Not good?"

"*Laa*," distracted, Hix lapsed into his native language. He bit his tongue and said, "Ah, no." He told them, "When Emilee had gotten nowhere at Saint Aubins, Mike Maverick had made an appointment with the director of nursing. It took some doing to get the director on board, but finally together they traced the vecuronium. It wasn't noticed before, because none was missing.

"But, due to our investigation and Kimi Consuelo's own death at the hands of the neuromuscular-blocking drug, Mike requested that the director have all the vecuronium pulled and taken to the lab and tested, and the director agreed."

"It had been fucked with," Kurt guessed.

His lip twitching, Hix turned back to read the email. "Not their words, but yeah. The solutions in many of the vials were dilute. They ran the records and Kimi Consuelo had signed in where those drugs were stored. She signed in to obtain saline drips but although she signed in two times she only took three saline drips one time, and nothing the second time.

"They figure the first times she removed the vecuronium stuff, then the second visit she put back the diluted liquid to mask that she'd taken any of the drug. She didn't have the medical clearance to remove anything narcotic, only passive items like the saline drip."

The men stared at Hix, their expressions pensive. Prince commented, "She stole the drug that he used to kill her. Do you think she knew what he planned?"

Hix shook his head. "Doubtful. A nasty way to die. If she was into erotic asphyxiation there are easier ways, less excruciating to play that."

Three pairs of eyes widened, two of the men snickered. Sinclair asked, "Really, Penn? You got something you'd like to share with your bros?" All three of them chuckled.

Rolling his eyes, Hix grunted. "No. I guess we'll never know how the perp talked Kimi into taking the drugs. Maybe he told her they would be playing some far-out BDSM games."

"Huh, way far out," Sinclair grimaced.

********

Later, Hix sat at his desk reviewing all the information regarding the three Poser murders.

Thinking about the last discussion with his team, Kimi Consuelo's involvement in obtaining the very serum that gruesomely killed her was a particular he was trying to figure out. How did the killer talk her into taking the vecuronium?

What the hell was Kimi thinking? Was she tricked into it, or forced? Unless the killer spills when he is caught, and there was no doubt in Hix's mind he would be caught, they would never know how he talked her into stealing the drugs.

They were pretty positive at this point that the killer was male, and judging by the videos, likely only one person.

There was supposition that the white-collar perp was the man seen on the videos and that a blue-collar person stayed back at home creating the slave box and chains.

But, the man had moved so easily with the pieces and put them together quickly, almost lovingly. He'd run his gloved hands over several pieces of wood after he'd hinged them together. A white-collar could have physical hands-on hobbies the same as the next guy.

Flipping a paper over in the file in front of him, Hix frowned. Howie Fernell was a dead end. Pun intended. Even though he was the one that purchased the wood and the paint sprayer and paint, they could find zero connections to him.

As he studied the information, Hix skimmed a few fingers down the dark blue tie knotted around the collar of his button-down white shirt. His suit coat hung on a rack by the door. Reading further, he rolled the long sleeves up his brawny forearms.

The people at Howie's crappy apartment complex said he never had visitors. The scant times he showed up at work the employees all claimed they'd never seen anyone meet with him.

He was such a skunky drunk that very few of the staff had anything to do with him, and that let out girlfriends as well. He was fat and smelly, obnoxious, a drunk, slovenly and poor.

Hix pondered if Howie was involved with the victims, if he had tortured and raped them along with the killer. But he doubted it, the killer was too smart to let Howie know too much about him, where he lived or kept the girls if they were imprisoned elsewhere.

Howie was a dumb alcoholic fuckup who would have eventually spilled all he knew either while drunk or trying to impress some chick. Or during interrogation with threats of life in prison.

Howie was probably kept in the dark about why he was paid to purchase the wood and paint, and too stupid to put two and two together when the news of the murders came out.

However, he would eventually connect the dots, especially when descriptions of the wood used to build the boxes hit the wires. He may not read the internet or watch the news, but everyone was talking about the murders. He would overhear the gory details eventually.

As they kept reiterating, the killer was smart, smart enough to take out Howie before he was traced to the wood, and before he blabbed about who had him buy it. Howie could have even tried to blackmail the killer and bought his own death with his foolish audacity.

The waitress at the diner was only going to do the dumb slob because he'd promised her he'd give her money. His bank account contained $5,000 in it with no trace as to where he got the money. He deposited cash, and used a debit card to pay for the wood and paint.

Rubbing his forehead, hearing a sound at his door, Hix looked up. His black brows turned down at the man standing in his doorway with his hand up as if he was about to knock.

Annoyed, Hix asked with asperity, "What the hell? Who let you in?"

The tall rangy man wore a beige trench coat that hung almost to his ankles and a fedora. He removed his sunglasses.

Hix fixed him for a G-man. A really corny G-man in that getup. When the man stepped forward, his ID held out, Hix's suspicions were confirmed.

"Hey, yeah, I sort of barged in, son, showed the ID at the front and they let me in. Didn't tell them where I was going, and they didn't ask. Anyway, Agent John Brewer with the CIA." He waited while Hix stood up, shuffled around the desk and took the ID, coolly studied it then handed it back to the agent.

"What can I do for you, Agent Brewer, that a phone call couldn't have sufficed?"

Brewer's forehead rippled at the insult that what the agent was there for wasn't so important it couldn't have been handled by phone instead of taking up Hix's valuable time.

"Ah," Brewer said, fixing Hix with a superior gaze, "I have important business to discuss with you."

"It have anything to do with the murders we're working on? The Poser murders?"

Brewer was taken aback, his small brown eyes blinked hard. A hint of confusion crossed his long face. "Uh, no, nothing about any murders, I-"

"I don't have time for any other *xara*, crap, Agent. I have three murdered women on my hands, if you're not here to offer some sort of help or information about them you need to take off. *Ma'is salāma,* goodbye." Hix gave him an impatient jerk of his jaw and started back to his desk.

"Ah, it's not about your shit, Detective, it's about mine." Brewer tramped several angry steps to Hix's desk.

When Hix didn't turn around or acknowledge his words, Brewer said gruffly, "It's about Laurin Ajanel." A smug smile lifted the side of his mouth at the stiffening of Hix's shoulders. The smile rose higher when Hix turned back to face him.

"What about her?" Suspicion and protectiveness cushioned Hix's harsh voice.

Moving further into the room, Brewer's lids lowered as he contemplated the detective. "That's an unusual accent. Where are you from?"

"What about Mrs. Ajanel?" Hix snapped, his ancestry was none of the agent's business.

Brewer's brows arched then lowered at Hix's rudeness. "I'm not at liberty to go into specific details, but Mrs. Ajanel needs to return to her residence." He wasn't prepared for the dark color that seeped up Hix's neck or the tightening of his jaw, the detective was formidable at any time, but right now he appeared downright fearsome.

Pinning the agent with a hooded, barbarous glare, his voice low and guttural and steeped in antagonism, Hix bowed his thick shoulders in a threatening stance and ground through gritted teeth, "She is not going back to that…Ajanel's mansion." His tone stated that was final and not up for discussion.

Brewer ignored his tone, and Hix's physically implied threat. "It is imperative that she does. Tell me where she is staying and I'll swing by and pick her up." He moved closer to the fuming detective.

"The hell you will." Hix stalked towards the agent. "Her motherfucking husband has been beating her, bad enough to break her bones. He has abused the boy as well, I'll be damned if I'll allow her and the child to go back to that hellhole."

Light brown brows rising again, Brewer sounded as if he was trying to be patient, "I don't care about the boy, he can stay where he is. He is only a tool Ajanel uses to keep his wife in line."

His small eyes thinned at Hix, his sarcastic grin crooked. "You fashion yourself that you are her white knight in shining armor, well, you can be that all you want when I'm done with her and get what I want. She will return to her home, immediately."

Top of his head about to blow off, Hix stated, "What you want?" His deep voice climbed, "Why the hell is it so crucial that she go back to that bastard who is assaulting her?" His hands clamped on his hips to keep from swinging at the abrasive prick.

One shoulder shrugged, the trench coat lifted on one side ruffling at Brewer's calves. "I said I am not at liberty to say, it is a need to know mission, and you do not need to know-"

"If I don't need to know your mission, then you don't need to know Mrs. Ajanel's location."

At an impasse, Brewer's tiny brown eyes narrowed in pique at Hix. He sneered a threat, "I will contact your superiors and have them force you to tell me."

"They can't make me tell any more than you can." Hix leaned his hips against his desk and crossed his arms over his chest, a bulwark against the agent's demands.

Red flushed his rangy face, Brewer shook with anger. "I will go to the goddamned governor, Hixman, and have your job if you don't tell me where she is!"

Crossing his ankles, Hix shrugged with bland indifference. "Go ahead. If I deny having knowledge of where she is staying, I can't be fired for not telling something I don't know." He would have thrown the prick out on his ear, but the agent had information Hix wanted.

Pushing back the sides of his coat, Brewer slammed his hands on his hips and leaned his gangly body towards Hix. Fury embroiled in his voice, his shoulders hunched with it. "You self-righteous bastard, you would be lying, you can be brought up on charges of perjury!"

Hix responded calmly, "Go ahead and try it, you little prick. Someone would have to come up with proof of my knowledge. And," his eyes darkened to stone-cold cinders, lids lowered over them in menace, "if I am working for an industry that thinks it's okay to throw a powerless girl straight into the clutches of a sociopathic sadist that beats her relentlessly, mercilessly, and brutally rapes her, then I don't want to work for that industry."

Brewer rolled his eyes. "Come on, Detective, speaking of proof, you have no evidence Mr. Ajanel hits her."

"The fuck I don't. I got hospital records you asshole. I've seen the damage. Hitting her is the least of his abusive actions. He whips her, breaks bones, rapes her-"

His eyes rolled again as if he found Hix tiresome and dramatic, Brewer sniped over him, "Give it a rest, Hixman, a husband can't rape his wife, it's her duty to give him what he wants." His plain face set in smug irritation, he started, "Now, you better-"

"You sick motherfucker." Hix pushed from the desk and stalked to him. Looming over the smaller agent, his fists clenched, he demanded, "You tell me right now why you put her in that house or agent or no, I'll beat you till you piss out your ass." Every shred of Hix's brutal military training and experience ground in his hard voice, it etched ferocity in every chiseled feature, his threat of violence was not a bluff.

And the blanching of Brewer's face indicated he took the threat as truth.

Brewer put his hands up warding Hix off, and took a self-protective step back from the enraged detective. "Okay, okay, calm the fuck down, okay already."

Expelling a fraught exhale, he removed his hat and dragged a sleeve across his forehead beaded with sudden sweat. Realizing the detective would not give him what he wanted without a little give and take of information, he gave in. "Back the hell up, hothead, and I'll tell you."

That Hix was struggling to hold back his rage and desire to beat the agent to a bloody piece of gristle on the floor was evident in his rigid body vibrating with tangible restraint.

He forced himself to step a foot back from the agent. "Speak," he barked to Brewer like he was a mangy mutt. Which Hix felt he was.

Sucking in a stabilizing breath, Brewer wiped his forehead again and worked to steady his voice. "The CIA has long suspected that Rádolfo Ajanel is a main player in the smuggling of weapons to Sudan that include rocket launchers, scud missiles and other deadly shit. He also trades in blood diamonds thereby making him a one-two punch. We have labored to obtain enough evidence to put Mr. Ajanel out of business and behind bars, but he has many lucrative enterprises here in the U.S. that help mask his dirty dealings.

"Witnesses that we ferret out are systematically killed or disappear before we can get solid statements from them, much less bring them to court to testify. Then there's the issue of his damned diplomatic immunity. We're working to find a way around that once we obtain the evidence we need to arrest him."

Hix crossed his brawny arms over his chest, his dress boots planted akimbo. "So what does this have to do with Laurin?"

Brewer's lips pursed at Hix using Laurin's first name. "Ah, I see that you are in close contact with her. Intimate even."

Hix bumped one shoulder, then he frowned. "So what. Doesn't prove I know where she is."

His lids lowered further, hooding the wrath in his dark eyes, he threatened, "Don't start shit about Mrs. Ajanel and me or any other man. She's had enough of that bullshit crap. Now, you were telling me how this involves her."

The agent paced a few steps, his head down, he slapped the fedora against his thigh. He turned back to Hix and said, "I, we, need evidence to put Ajanel away. My, uh, our idea was to plant Laurin in Ajanel's family, get her close inside so she could glean the evidence we need.

"I caught wind of Ajanel's plan to purchase a high-end, mail-order-bride for his shy, over-worked son, the doctor, and thought I could pass Laurin off as this said wife. She is clearly top of the line in looks and sex appeal, I figured Chevalier Ajanel would jump at her."

Hix was seeing red at Brewer's casual words of how he plopped an innocent defenseless Laurin right into a den of ruthless, greedy, deadly wolves. It was all he could do to not go right for Brewer's throat.

He seethed, "But she didn't marry the youngest son, she married Rádolfo, the lethal kingpin. Fuck's sake man, he's more than double her age." He lowered his hands to his hips.

A grin split the agent's gaunt face. "Yeah, great luck, right? The old man took one look at my pigeon and dove right for her. The best I had hoped for was that she would be around here and there to gather info, but it turned out a hundred times better that Rádolfo kept her for himself. I couldn't have planned that more perfectly," he gloated, proud of how his scheme worked out.

The fingers on his hips dug in or Hix would be throwing punches at the asshole. He said, "The story about Laurin cheating on Ajanel has always struck a false note with me. She is terrified of him, clearly there is no love, no affection on her part for the bastard, why would she take the chance to cheat on him? And with such a public figure, a married politician? Another older man? Was that yet another part of your lucky plan?"

Craning his neck, Brewer stared up at the ceiling. Raking a hand through his short hair, the fine strands spiked in the trail behind them, he sighed. "Ah, no. That entire episode was unfortunate." His eyes narrowed at Hix, he lowered his voice. "This is off the record, it doesn't leave this room, you hear me?"

"*Aiwa*, yeah, sure," Hix agreed, not. He owed the slug in front of him nothing but a fist in his mouth scattering his teeth around the room like bowling pins.

"Okay. Well, the Secretary of Energy, Woodrow St. Lawrence, was having an affair. It just wasn't with Laurin Ajanel. It was with his wife's niece, Caitlyn. Cattie was only sixteen.

"Woodrow's wife caught him in bed with another woman, but the girl, Cattie, had rolled off the bed and ran out through a patio door. It was dark, Marlene St. Lawrence couldn't see the woman, or girl actually, just that she was female and blonde. It was Marlene that attacked Woodrow with the fire poker."

Hix grunted, nodding for the agent to continue.

Brewer shook his head with mirthful disbelief. "These politicians, huh? The lives they live. Randy as shit, no morals. I could tell you stories-"

"Finish this one," Hix snapped.

The agent snorted at his terse command. "Yeah. So, after he took one to the noggin and was rushed to the hospital, word got out that Woodrow had been in an affair. His PR people jumped on it, covered up the fact that it was Marlene that popped him one.

"To keep her out of jail and to protect Woodrow's name and reputation, the PR people started the story that it was Laurin Ajanel that was the adulteress, hiding the fact that it had been an underage teenager. Screwing a minor would get him arrested and charged as a sex offender. They needed to throw water on the total firestorm."

"Laurin couldn't have been much older."

"True, but at least she was legal."

"The whole ordeal is wholly preposterous. Going with that story, what reason would Laurin have to try to kill him?"

"They put it to the media that Laurin had told Woodrow she was pregnant and when he denied being the father and told her they were through, she went nuts and clobbered him."

"But didn't the fact of the affair affect his reputation anyway?"

Smirking, Brewer replied, "Not really. He's a good-looking man, his wife forgave him, of course she enjoys the prestigious lifestyle his job allows them. Woodrow begged forgiveness from his constituents, said he had been drinking and Laurin deliberately seduced him, maybe even drugged his cocktail and took advantage of his weakened condition.

"Then she became enraged when he tried to break it off. He told her he would tell the police she tried to blackmail him with the baby. The story went out that Laurin Ajanel struck him in a blind jealous rage with the poker trying to kill him. That all made Woodrow the sympathetic victim instead of the lying, cheating spouse."

"No charges were filed against her."

"Of course not. That would have ensued an investigation and Woodrow couldn't have it come out that he had screwed his minor niece-in-law, his wife would have made him pay through the nose for that, and again, the legal repercussions."

"What do the Ajanels have to do with the sordid mess? Why would they agree to the story?"

Brewer gave him a salacious wink. "Rádolfo and Woodrow were fraternity brothers here in the States, and stayed close friends. The oily politician and the crooked ambassador. Word is that Woodrow asked a big favor of his friend. Knowing that Rádolfo would keep his confidences, Woodrow paid Ajanel a bundle as well as supplied wealthy insider favors to throw his wife Laurin under the bus."

"Rádolfo Ajanel is one of the most jealous possessive men I've ever come across. Why on earth would he agree to it being put out there that his wife cuckolded him?"

"Because, as I said, money, insider business and low bidding will pay long and well. The connections a cabinet member has would supply Ajanel with information and protection, and more contacts. Besides, Ajanel knows his wife wouldn't cheat, as you said, Laurin is petrified of the man. He keeps her trapped tightly under his brute thumb. She was forced to go along with the scandal."

"Has Laurin produced any worthwhile information?"

"No. That's why she needs to return."

"What is it that you have her looking for in the house?"

"She takes photos of people coming and going. I can possibly get a connection on a known criminal, foreign or domestic and go that route. She has searched his office, I taught her how to break in. She ransacked his desk, his files, his vault.

"Other than a ton of cash, jewels, passports and shit like that there was nothing of value to help my case. But, she finally found his laptop right before you whisked her away," he scowled balefully at Hix.

"I hardly whisked her away, you shithead moron. She was being beaten to death on the damned street because of that fake scandal, and I took her to the hospital to save her life."

"You can stop with the name calling, let's try to maintain our professionalism."

"*Tozz fiik*, fuck you. Professionalism went out the door when you tossed that innocent girl into that wolf's den. So, you have his laptop, what else are you insisting she be there for?"

"I don't have the laptop. She can't smuggle it out of the house, and I can't go in and take it, I have no probable cause. If she can get into the computer and find something I can use then I'll have probable cause to retrieve it. All I have to say is that she did it all on her own, came to the CIA with the information, we deny we even knew her. But, so far, she hasn't been unable to break his password."

"Ajanel has supposedly killed other witnesses or informers, he could, would, easily make her disappear with a snap of his fingers. How long do you plan on forcing her into doing your dangerous business?"

"As long as it takes. Ajanel is a kingpin in the weapons and diamond trades, thousands of lives are at stake. He is supplying rebels with machine guns, that could turn the tide in a civil war. One small girl's life isn't worth thousands. As well as the financial repercussions that could affect us here in the States."

"That is all bullshit, Brewer. At this point in South Africa, the gun trafficking has been clamped down by their own, and other corresponding governments. There are very few and small uprisings that the weapons trafficked could really affect. The worst is the blood diamonds, but then again, the government is clamping down on that shit as well. Tell the truth, you just want a big bust to further your own ignoble career."

Brewer's guilty gaze fell, he shook his head. "No, no, it's all true. I'm helping the poor indigent people in Afric-"

"Why did Laurin agree to the preposterous story about her and St. Lawrence?"

"Obviously Ajanel made her."

Hix nodded, of course the fucker would make Laurin do anything he wanted under the promise of a horrific beating, or threatening to harm the boy. "Why is Laurin going along with you? She's put herself at great harm, as well as her son. She isn't stupid enough to believe in your bullshit crap about civil wars. Why is she doing it?"

Brewer looked uncomfortable. "Ah, well, I, uh, we have her little brother Robert sort of stashed away in another country. They have no parents or relatives, only each other. Laurin will do anything to keep Robbie safe and bring him home to her. So," he shrugged, "when she brings me the bacon, her and little Robbie and the kid can all go off somewhere and live happily ever after."

No wonder their efforts of locating Laurin's brother had been to no avail. He was hidden away way outside of their purview.

"You motherfucking bastard." Hix charged at him, smashing his fist into Brewer's eye, the agent dropped to his knees with a howl.

His hand to his eye, Brewer cried, "I'll have your badge, you fucker, you'll pay for this, I'll have charges brought against your ass-"

Hix lifted his boot and put it to Brewer's head and thrust, slamming him into the floor. He crouched down, put his hands around the agent's neck and squeezed. Brewer turned red, gagged, clawed at Hix's hands.

Hix snarled in his face, "You won't do anything, you sleaze, because I'll bet your superiors don't know that you have forced a young vulnerable woman into living in a home of torture to get your dirt by holding her minor brother hostage. As well as there is another juvenile in danger in the home. You say a word to your people, or mine about this, and your world will go up in smoke. That's after I get my turn at bat with you." Hix paused, but kept his fingers tight around Brewer's throat.

Brewer choked, his eyes bulged as he struggled for air, he clawed at Hix's hands, kicked his feet.

"Who is the boy? Benji, who is he, where did he come from?" He slightly released his grip so Brewer could answer him.

Coughing, Brewer spat on the floor, choked out the words, "Kid's an orphan Ajanel bought from a sex trade show. He was going to use him to uh, buy some wealthy, influential perv's cooperation but then Laurin latched onto the kid and Ajanel realized he could use the kid to control her." He laughed then winced.

"Listen, Detective, I plucked Laurin from a shit boarding house where she was barely able to put food on her and her brother's table, and Ajanel plucked the boy from a sex slave auction.

"Technically, all their lives are better due to my interference. Laurin and Robbie are no longer starving, and Benji isn't some perverted deviant's sex toy. They should be thanking me, they should-"

Hix's fingers ground into Brewer's throat cutting off his words. He lifted Brewer's head and slammed it into the floor again and again then pulled his fist back and let it fly into the agent's face and head, blood spurted, Brewer screamed.

The agent's screams brought attention.

"Fuck, Penn!" At the shocking sight of Hix straddling the agent and pummeling him to mush, Prince and Kurt raced into the room. Each man grabbed one of Hix's arms and fought to pull him off Brewer.

Propped up on one elbow, a hand clasped over a blackened eye, Brewer howled through his ruptured mouth, "You broke my fucking jaw you bastard, I'm gonna have your ass, boy, I'm gonna fry you, you Muslim prick! You're through, you can kiss your job goodbye!"

Hix struggled to break free from his friends holding him back, he shouted, "Lemme go, I'm gonna kick the piss outta him! I'm gonna kill the fucker!"

Grappling with one arm, huffing with the exertion of restraining Hix, Prince spoke quietly in Hix's ear, "Cool it, Penn, you already hurt him bad, back off unless you want a murder rap."

Kurt strained to keep ahold of Hix's other arm as the detective twisted, and struggled, snarling his rage.

Breathing harshly, struggling to calm himself, Hix growled, "Little prick ain't gonna do shit. I'll dump his own career right in the toilet and flush him to hell," he sneered at Brewer as the man remained flopped on the floor.

The agent appeared too leery to try to get up with Hix still snarling and raging. He was too injured anyway to even sit up without help.

When his breathing calmed, Hix shrugged his friends loose and straightened his tie, stretched his neck making it crack. A brief snide glance at Brewer on the floor, he started for the door. He paused, looked back and the agent and said, "And I'm a Christian, you pissant."

Hix shook his shoulders as if shaking off debris, growled, "Thomas, take out the trash for me," and stalked out the door.

# Chapter Twenty-Six

Stomping into the room, teeth clenched, the man roared, "Goddammit!" and slashed his arm across the tools on the metal table. Knives and spikes, the curling iron flew out striking the wall then clattered as they hit the floor.

The small blonde woman tied naked to the huge wooden wheel whimpered. The ball-gag obstructed her words, but her screams were clearly audible. Straining and struggling, she fought to break from the ropes binding her to the wheel. All that did was tear the skin around her wrists, her ankles were shredded and bleeding.

Hearing her cries, he changed course and stomped over to the bound girl. He shouted furiously at her, "You stupid bitch, I didn't want you! But I had to do something, take someone, I had to!"

Big blue eyes as wide as truck tires shrieked her fright, drool leaked down the gag. Bare breasts bounced and shook, her hips thrust and twisted with her frantic struggles. When he stopped in front of her, every part of her froze except her skin that quivered with terror.

He frowned his dissatisfaction at the trapped woman. Then his head cocked and he smiled at her with vague disinterest. "Aw honey, I don't mean to hurt your feelings. I mean, sure, you're pretty enough, sort of sexy, but small tits," he cupped her breast as if weighing it. He gripped the soft flesh hard, then harder and leaned into her to watch her face.

Whimpers drooled as she grimaced around the gag while his grip dug in, squeezing hard, then harder with vicious merriment until she was panting with excruciating pain, and the breast in his savage grasp turned scarlet.

Watching her shake and cry, writhing to get away from the pain, he scowled. "No, I didn't want you. I wanted my prize. The first three were for fun, bide my time until I finally capture my prize. It's just," his bottom lip pushed up, he zoned out, absently squeezing, gouging skin and tissue with sadistic fingers, then he pinched a nipple with his nails, stabbing in. The scream behind the gag chafed out an agonized hoarse cry.

As if he wasn't standing there torturing a bleeding, bound woman, he serenely rattled on, "The one I want has been stolen out from under me before I could get my hands on her. Some fucking cop asshole has her under lock and key. Thing is," the serenity flashed into ire. He twisted her nipple, still gripping her flesh in punishing steel fingers, crushing it like her breast was a stress toy, he said, "I was all ready to snag her, bring her here to my playroom and enjoy her tender, sweet fruits."

He closed his eyes and smiled with dreamy pleasure. "Yes, I can picture my prize in her rose gold glory after I've had my time playing with her." Groping her other breast, he crushed both in fingers like sharp vices, squeezing, pinching, twisting. He pulled on them so hard it was as if he was trying to tear them right off her body. Hacking sobs racked her chest, tears ran with snot down her chin.

His eyes popped open, he said with a kind sneer, "You aren't her, my sweet," he gave her breasts a vicious squeeze, wringing her flesh as hard as he could. "But you'll do until I can get the one I want."

Shaking his head in remorse, he went on, "I was stupid, Tatum. I snatched you off the street with no prior plan. It was stupid, that's how people get caught, doing things spontaneously. You leave evidence, clues, witnesses, your picture gets caught on cameras." A beleaguered inhale lifted his strong chest, an irritated sigh pushed it out.

"I was just," he shook his head again, his smile wry, he muttered with self-rebuke, "I wanted her so badly. So badly I could fucking taste her, you know what I'm saying, hon?"

She couldn't answer him, but he got mad anyway at her lack of response.

Another crushing squeeze and he continued, "So, I lost my mind with frustrated rage and I hustled around to find…a replacement. You know, Tatum," his voice warmed like a scolding affectionate parent, "you shouldn't go to convenience stores alone late at night hon, it can be dangerous. You should at least park in front under the light and security camera instead of off to the dark side."

With a huge grin he gestured to the far wall near the doorway. "There, hon, at least you'll have the honor of joining my glorious collection."

The girl twisted her head fearfully to see what he pointed to. What color was left in her face drained, her body jerked rigid with terror.

The man had taken photos of the other women he'd captured. The pictures were enlarged so every detail of the females on their knees, chains clinched around their necks and their naked bodies shimmering with rose gold paint, was sharp and crystal clear. All three faces contorted in horror as they died in frozen agony.

Seeing the green nausea flowering her face, he slapped his hand over her mouth, pushing the ball-gag in further. "Oh no you don't, no puking allowed Miss Tatum."

She gagged and retched against his hand, but she had to swallow it down or she'd choke on her own vomit.

He kept his hand clamped over her mouth until he was sure she wasn't going to puke. She struggled so hard not to vomit liquid poured out of her nose.

With a smile, he praised her, "Good girl," and released her mouth. She gasped in air, swallowed convulsively, crying and coughing.

Snagging a towel off the floor, he wiped his hand clean, then bent to her chest and bit a nipple so hard blood spurted, he grinned at her shriek. Her body arched off the wheel in a spasm of pain.

He stepped back with a slight look of surprise. "Shit girl, thought I bit it clean off!" He dabbed at the bloody nipple shaking his head, tutting, "Sometimes I just don't know my own strength."

Tatum's screams diminished to hacking rasps scraping in her throat, her chest was soaked with her tears and drool and blood.

"Ah," he sighed, "I shouldn't let my frustration and anger out on you, babe. I'll keep that for my prize. When I get her, boy," the grin arced, "I will make her pay for forcing me to commit this sudden, unplanned snatch."

Cocking his head at her, but he didn't look at the girl as he said thoughtfully, "No, there'll be no 24 hours for my special treasure, unh uh," he shook his head. "Nope, I'm gonna keep my baby for weeks or longer if I can prevent myself from killing her accidentally.

"Fortunately," he smiled at Tatum, "I've had some practice now at it, I'm getting good, know exactly when to stop just before you girls keel, ya know what I mean, hon?"

Ignoring her whimpers, he mused, "Thing is, I'm excited to see the finished project. I can't wait to have her on her knees covered in my beautiful rose-gold glory, chain tight around her beautiful neck. Hmm," he pondered, "maybe I can still do that while she's alive. If I'm not quite as savage while impaling her with objects, and give her time in between to heal, yeah. Hmm," he looked up at her.

"Yeah, I think I can do that. If I'm careful I can keep her forever. Yeah."

Releasing Tatum's tortured breasts, he moved to the table he'd wiped clean in his anger and picked up the scattered items and placed them back on the table then wheeled it over to her, relishing the renewed terror in his victim's sobbing eyes.

He picked up a length of rope and moved to her and tied it under her ribs to the wheel.

"No more squirming and twisting, hon, I like you completely immobilized." He patted her drenched cheek, it bulged from the ball-gag. "I don't want you hopping around when I'm doing my art."

He gathered more rope to bind under her arms to help hold her body up and taut against the wheel.

Then, he leaned and grabbed up a thick iron rod that was propped against the wheel.

Her lids drooping from inexorable agony slammed back up at the rod he now held between her legs.

Digging his fingers into one of her thighs he attempted to spread her legs further apart. They were tied wide, exposing her sex. Pulling at her thigh, he lifted the rod to her entrance and chuckled at the way her belly quivered in hysteria.

Grinning at her, he said pleasantly, "We're going to have some fun, Tatum. Later, I'll introduce you to my favorite neuromuscular-blocking drug. But for now, I changed my mind, I do want to enjoy a bit of squirming and screeching." Tucking the rod under his arm, he removed her gag and tossed it aside.

The girl gasped in a deep breath. Before she could express relief that he'd moved the iron rod, he put it back and gripped her thigh again, tugging it as far apart as he could.

"Okay, you ready my sweet, to begin? A few thrusts with this first to warm you up, then I'll penetrate you with my penis, you'll like that, I promise. I'll show you a good time, I'm quite well endowed," he gave her a sly wink.

"Then, well, we'll see how I feel, what strikes me next. Maybe more rod in each hole, maybe," he glanced over at long, sharp, serrated instruments laid out on the table, "we'll see."

Without the gag, her hysterical screams ricocheted around the room.

# Chapter Twenty-Seven

Chelsea Brown and her husband William waited in one of the spacious conference rooms. Chelsea was suffering profound anguish, Hix didn't feel it was right to stuff her in a cold, tiny interrogation room. The couple clutched each other, Will wrapped a supporting arm around his bride.

Officer Emilee Rivera was sitting with them. She expressed her sorrow for Chelsea's loss and was giving the couple the preliminaries as to why they were there.

Hix and Prince entered the windowless large room. Part of the station was a relic, the conference room was old-fashioned wrapped in paneling giving it a refined stature yet felt warmly comfortable.

The Browns were nestled at one end of the long mahogany table. Grey cushioned chairs with wheels lined the table, a screen for PowerPoint presentations as well as dry-erase boards were affixed to walls. Several flip-paper stands were grouped out of the way until needed.

Chelsea Brown wore a demure dress with a large, white scalloped collar and low heels, her shoulder length blonde hair curled under. Will's long sleeved shirt was buttoned up to his neck, his dark hair combed neatly to the side, he wore black trousers and loafers.

"Mr. and Mrs. Brown," Hix said quietly as he took a seat at the table next to Will.

Chelsea sat at the head of the table with Will to her left. Emilee got up and moved down a chair so Prince could sit beside Chelsea.

"Please accept our condolences for your loss. I am Detective Hixman, this is Detective Princeton," he tilted his head at Prince. "Deputy Rivera," he said, nodding to Emilee.

Chelsea merely nodded as she blotted the tears cascading down her cheeks. Will nudged his chair closer to her and hugged her.

"Ah, so, Mrs. Brown, we need to ask you questions about your…sister." His gut quelled at the way Chelsea's face scrunched tightly in grief and more tears poured.

Hix spoke with rare gentleness, "Can, ah, you help us?" Normally he remained stoic, voice stayed at an even line. He blamed his new found softness on Laurin Ajanel. Every time he looked at Laurin, spoke with her, he felt his entire being ease of its own volition. She softened the jagged, rugged edges of his harsh warrior soul.

Voice husky with grief, Will Brown said quietly, "Anything we can do to help, Detective." He sucked in a breath filled with suffering like it physically hurt. "Chels and I were just married six months ago, you can imagine how devastated…" he broke off, his lips bunched to stop their trembling.

Hix leaned forward, clasped his hands together and rested them on the table. He looked to Chelsea then to Will. "First, have you any idea who could have…done this to your sister?"

The couple numbly shook their heads, Will mumbled, "No. Annalisa was as sweet as pecan pie. She taught Bible School on Sunday mornings, worked part time as an administrative assistant at an Audi dealership. She was enrolled at," his breath shook, he swallowed hard before continuing. "Um, Brevet Bay Community College. She wanted to- to-" he broke off as a sob trapped in his throat.

Her voice small, ragged and broken, Chelsea whispered, "My…sister, uh, loved animals. She wanted to- to be a vet."

Hix and Prince made notes. Hix looked up at the newly married couple. "Did Annalisa have any trouble with other students, professors? Co-workers, customers, boss at the dealership? She complain about strangers watching her? Any threats, perhaps an angry ex, or current boyfriend, maybe they had a fight? Was she seeing someone new?"

Pressing tissues against her eyes Chelsea shook her head. "No. No one would ever-" her chest thrust up and her head fell forward with a sob of despair cutting off her words.

Hunched around his small, bereaved wife, Will picked up, "Seriously, Detectives, Annalisa was pretty and kind hearted, she got along with everyone, always. She's only 23, she's only had two serious relationships and she told us they've both moved on to other relationships." At his wife's keening sobs, he tucked her under his arm and kissed the top of her head.

Prince ran down all the jobs, schools, churches, gyms, that the other victims had been connected to, but the Browns denied any knowledge of Annalisa having any contact with the women, their families, friends, or the places they attended.

"Current boyfriend?" Hix asked.

Chelsea started to shake her head but Will spoke up, "No, honey, remember she had just started seeing Sammy?" His wife nodded her head against his chest.

"Sammy's last name?" The detectives' pens poised on their notepads.

"Uh," the couple hummed, looked at each other. His brows drawn down in a frown, Will answered, "She never said. They had only gone out on a few dates."

Hix asked, "Do you know where they met?" His eyes widened when the pair lowered their heads and Chelsea blushed. "Mr. Brown?" he prodded.

At Will's hesitation, Hix said with slight suspicion tinging his deep, accented voice, "You appear to have known your sister-in-law as well as Chelsea did?"

"Uh huh." Will sniffed, his voice tight with emotion, he said, "Me and Chels are childhood sweethearts. I've known both girls almost all my life. Annalisa is, was, like a sister to me."

"Okay, so, do you know where Annalisa and this Sammy met?"

Will kissed the side of his wife's head, his lips brushing her hair. "Well, it's kind of, well, we don't want to, well, uh…"

"Mr. Brown, please. Anything you tell us will help," Prince prompted.

"Yeah, um, okay. Annalisa did have a bit of a quirky side to her." Will coughed with slight embarrassment.

"Quirky?"

Chelsea gave a short snort and leaned into her husband.

His head bobbing, Will's neck bloomed red, he cleared his throat, then explained. "Yeah, let's say, kinky."

"Kinky?" Emilee spoke up, then closed her lips at Hix's frown.

Will replied, "Yeah, Annalisa did like to fly along the um, wild side, uh, sexually. She was a member of Creamz."

At Hix's lifted brow, Will cleared his throat again and said, "It's a club. You know, a decadent club."

He said quickly, "Don't get me wrong, there is nothing untoward that goes on there, uh, I mean besides the kinky sex. My sis-in-law told us that there's no violence or seriously sick stuff. The members are all vetted so no criminals or freaks can join. It's just, well, Annalisa just likes it a little bit on the wild side."

Chelsea burrowed her head in his shoulder in embarrassment.

Hix and Prince shared a muted enthusiastic look. Hix asked, "Are you two members?"

Chelsea made a choking sound and Will's face burned bright.

With an adamant shake of his head, Will said quickly, "No, no, no, not us. We're just plain, simple people. We like our, um, sex, uh, you know," he gave a sheepish shrug, "straight vanilla, no whipping or handcuffs, just…uh…" he stuck a finger in his collar and awkwardly tugged at it as his Adam's apple bobbed under it.

Hix regarded the pair with his normal stony expression.

The Browns fidgeted and squirmed under his unwavering glare. Chelsea picked at the scalloped collar of her dress with nervous fingers.

Hix asked, "How long has Annalisa known Sammy? Is he a member too?"

"Sure." Will nodded. "Annalisa hooked up with him at the club, he's a dom." He blinked at the detectives' blank expressions.

"Ah," he explained, "that's a Dominant. Annalisa was a- a Submissive. She enjoyed being..." his face burgeoned red, "uh, spanked, you know, bound and spanked, obeying her Master's orders, kneeling at his feet, and...stuff like that."

A low sound emitted from Prince's chest, he shifted in his seat, his gaze shot up to Hix then to Emilee.

Emilee's eyes were bright and absorbed, her head nodded numerous times in succession, she was studying the Browns with acute interest.

"Uh huh," Hix murmured. "Have you met Sammy?"

The couple exchanged a glance then shook their heads.

"No," Will answered for them. "It was a new relationship and Annalisa hadn't brought him around yet to meet us. We had planned a dinner date but then Annalisa said Sammy was sick and we would do a raincheck when he was better."

Hix made a note, then asked them, "Can you locate a number for this Sammy fellow?" His eyes lifted to Chelsea then shifted to Will.

His IT people had Annalisa's phone but Hix had reviewed their findings and he knew there was no Sammy mentioned. But, just like the other victims, there were numbers they hadn't been able to trace to their owners. It seemed everyone had a burner phone these days.

"Oh." Chelsea glanced at her husband, then to Hix. "She had an adorable address book she's had since a child. It has puppies on the cover, she puts everything in it. She might have put him in her phone under a nickname, but he should be recorded in her book. I'll look for it and let you know."

The detectives asked a few more questions then Hix said, "I guess that's all for now. *Shukra*, uh," he frowned. He hated when his foreign words slipped in when he spoke. It happened more frequently when he was engrossed or angry, intense. It tended to make people nervous.

"Thank you for your time." He stood up. "If you think of anything that can be of help, please don't hesitate to contact us.

Officer Rivera will provide our contact information and see you out."

Prince shook hands with Will and nodded solemnly to Chelsea and followed Hix out of the room leaving Emilee to finish up with the Browns.

"Holy shit," Prince muttered as they trod down the hall.

"Yeah," Hix grunted.

"There's our tie in." Excitement bubbled in Prince's voice.

# Chapter Twenty-Eight

Kurt Klaus was waiting at Hix's office door for a scheduled meet. An iPad under his arm, he leaned a shoulder against the wall, his arms and ankles crossed. He was smiling down at a female officer whose head tilted up to him; she fiddled with a curl while smiling coyly at him.

Dropping the curl, she set her hand on his chest and cooed, "So, Kurt, when are you taking me for that beer you promised for the bet. Your Florida Panthers lost, you said-"

Spotting Hix and Prince, Kurt's smile vanished and he stood up straight. Muttering to the woman, he said, "Catch you later, Yasmine," and he turned his back on her.

"Hey, Hix, Prince, we got the rest of the member lists." He followed the detectives into the office, none of them heard Yasmine's affronted, "Harrumph, *men*."

Kurt swiped the iPad and punched some keys and handed the iPad to Hix as Hix was seating himself behind his desk. "You're in for a surprise, my man." Kurt grinned at Prince as Hix reviewed the information.

Prince smirked back. "Doubt it, brother." He and Kurt dropped onto chairs in front of the desk.

Kurt frowned at him then turned his attention to Hix.

A few minutes passed and Hix set the pad down on his desk. Lacing his fingers behind his head he sat back, his elbows winged.

Prince asked, "What we thought?"

Hix's nod was brief. "Yup. Kimi Consuelo and Eden Lombardo were members of Cuffs & Lace, and Annalisa Dominicci was a member of Creamz, both are adult clubs. We need to cross reference who else was present at the clubs the same times as the women were."

"Yeah," Prince agreed. "We have to see who knew them, who they…played with, anyone that had appeared angry or overly interested in the women in a stalking kind of way."

Hix said, "I spoke with Emilee about it since we know she also attended those kinds of clubs. Unfortunately, she's never gone to either of those particular clubs."

Lowering his arms and leaning forward, tapping the iPad, Hix commented, "I don't see Dante Lombardo's name on any of the lists. He was telling the truth that he didn't go to them. He was shocked when we called and asked him about his wife, Eden's attending. What about the Sammy that Annalisa's sister told us about? Let's see how many Sams pop up on the lists."

Kurt frowned at the two men that had usurped his surprise. Then, his smirk smug, he said, "Yeah, we already worked the Lombardo prospect. According to the manager of Cuffs and Lace, Ben Dover-"

Prince's snort was loud. "Seriously? That's a joke, man, *bend over*, ya know?"

Grinning, Kurt replied, "Seriously, I made him show me ID. He could go by Benjamin or Benny, but apparently he still thinks the sophomoric joke is still funny, especially considering where he works. Anyway, Dover claimed Dante wasn't a member, and his name doesn't come up on any of the other clubs' lists.

"We talked to some people that the manager said Eden tended to 'scene' with, and they all said Eden's husband was totally in the dark about the kink side of her. He always thought she was out taking barre lessons. She paid for her membership at Cuffs with cash."

"Bar?" Prince's brow wrinkled. "Another deviant activity?"

"Mind, gutter," Kurt pretended to scold his friend. "Barre as in ballet, fool. You know, the bar they practice with, it's called a barre," he spelled it out.

Prince mused, "Maybe old Dante got pissed that his wife was doing kink without him and he finds out, and like explodes and kills his wife. Then he takes out the other women as red herrings. Or to punish them for their immoral activities."

"Nope," Kurt told him. "We thoroughly checked out Lombardo's alibi. The guy had gone to his office even though it was a Saturday, there were other brokers there to verify it. He left at six to meet up with Eden at their country club for dinner, also corroborated with staff and his bar receipt."

"He took ballet too?" Prince joked.

"Ha, ha, you're a funny guy, bar ticket, not barre, fool." Kurt took a fake swing at the detective. Then he sobered. "We also thoroughly investigated Kimi's studs, they've all been cleared through alibis, including Troy Gardner, Kimi's friend with benefits and Troy's girlfriend Betsy Lou. I think our perp is a genuine whacked psycho who likes killing women of a certain type and exposing them in a grandiose way.

"He's killing fairly random women to get his rocks off and frighten and shock the public with his elaborate posing. I don't believe it's someone murdering because he's mad at one person and trying to cover his tracks with duplicate homicides."

"There's more to it than that, Kurt," Prince said. "The x's in a heart shape and the burn circles indicate a form of ritual."

Kurt replied, "Yeah, but, it's his MO. He's leaving his signature. It could just be something he cooked up to titillate, frighten, gross people out."

Prince's laugh was mirthless. "Yes, and to piss off cops trying to figure it all out."

Hix was bent over the iPad, his thumbs flying over the keys. He sat back after a few minutes and said, "Out of the two clubs in Brevet and the four in Alexandria, there are six Samuels. I'll have Mike and Emilee get on them." He turned to Kurt. "What about the Ajanels' alibis?"

Kurt answered him with a frustrated frown, "They're solid." He unclipped his phone from his belt and sifted through it. "Raoul was playing cards on the two weekends, the other players confirmed. They weren't happy with him, says he cheats. But, he still loses big and they'll continue to play with him because they get his money.

"Blane Ajanel was teeing off, and Chevalier had a patient rushed to Holy Point hospital in Alexandria and he was there with her during Eden's abduction." He paused while sorting through his notes.

"The old man, where was he?" Although disrespect and disgust were predominant in Hix's tone, his expression remained stoic.

Prince looked at him with a smirk. "Old? Heck, Penn, guy's only around 45 or something."

"He's 48 and he married his wife when she was still in her teens. He's a sick fuck."

Kurt and Prince regarded Hix, the anger in his voice made them both smile slightly.

Prince had been with him when they took the boy from the mansion, he was getting a good picture of Hix's design on the Ajanels, especially the missus. "She was not in her teens. Bro, you can't let this infatuation with Ajanel's wife affect-"

Hix swung on him in a flash, his face dark with anger, fists clenched. "I am not infatuated with the woman, I am well aware that she's married. I," he took a deep slow breath. "Laurin Ajanel was forced into marriage and forced to stay with that monster. She is a victim of domestic violence. She has endured vicious, brutal abuse. I'm merely trying to help her and her child out."

Prince blinked slowly while perusing his friend's anger. He spared Kurt a glance. Kurt shrugged.

Prince said coolly, "Maybe you should fully fill us in on what's going on. About why and how you got involved with her."

The two men waited, studying Hix's face as his lids hooded his eyes, his mouth flattened tight.

"Bro," Kurt said, "you know you can trust us. Whatever you tell us will stay between us, off the record, unless you say it's okay to put it out there. All right?"

Hix's gaze flicked from one man to the other, his shoulders ruffled with his sigh. Prince knew a bit of what was up with Laurin because Hix had told him why they were removing Benji from the mansion.

Hix looked towards the window then back to the men and explained in detail about the abuse, the talk with Laurin's doctor, and about Agent Brewer forcing her into marrying Ajanel and staying with him although he beat and raped her regularly.

He included the whole sordid, attempted murder, adultery tale with the Secretary of Energy.

Prince and Kurt were stunned. Prince's brows jerked up to his hairline. "Fuck me, Penn, what the hell? A CIA agent is holding an innocent boy hostage and coercing Mrs. Ajanel into putting her life and Benji's on the line? Doesn't he know how dangerous that guy is? He's a warlord for damn sake, a thug in a suit hiding behind his ambassadorship."

Hix paced a few steps jerking his hands through the hair on the side of his head. He ground out angrily, "He does know. He doesn't give a shit. He wants to move up in the CIA, get a promotion. Arresting an international crime lord like Ajanel will earn it."

Scratching his chin in thought, Kurt asked, "What about his diplomatic immunity?"

Hix bumped one shoulder. "The agent thinks he can get around that. At the least, get Ajanel deported to his own country. They find out what he's been doing, they'll be a lot more brutal to him than America's softer incarceration would be. That's if he makes it to prison, which wouldn't be likely. They'd probably never find what's left of his body." The thought of Ajanel being savaged the way he did his wife gave Hix a warm fuzzy feeling.

"So," Prince's gaze cut to Kurt and back to Hix, he asked, "what are you gonna do about it?"

Hix shrugged again. "For now, I'm keeping her and the kid in seclusion. I'm pretty sure Brewer is a rogue agent and he's not going to want his superiors to know what he's done. I think he planned on nabbing Ajanel then freeing Laurin and Benji, and returning Laurin's brother all without his superiors aware of exactly how he'd gotten the goods on Ajanel. I have no intentions of letting Laurin anywhere near Brewer or Ajanel, and Brewer knows it, so he's going to need a new plan."

He told them how Ajanel had bought Benji from a sex auction, and his plans for the young boy to be sold to a pedophiliac sicko so Ajanel could broker business deals with him.

"Holy hell," Kurt spat, his face twisted like he'd tasted something nasty. "Guy's a real tool. We need to get our cyber investigators on Ajanel, see if they can locate the sex trafficking ring."

"Already got them on it," Hix told him.

Prince eyed his friend with serious focus, he said, "Penn, regardless of how or why, she's his wife. And, I don't believe that you don't have…desire for her, feelings even. What are you-"

"That's my business," Hix snapped, not denying his interest in Laurin Ajanel. There was no point, his two friends could see how his attitude became defensive and protective when she was mentioned. "You were telling us, Kurt, about Ajanel's alibi?"

Kurt's lids flapped up and down as he struggled to pull back from the personal conversation, and the dirty little details of Rádolfo and the CIA agent's deeds. "Ah…" he glanced down at the phone in his hand. It had gone dark, he swiped it back on.

"According to his personal assistant, Rádolfo Ajanel was supposedly in South Africa during Eden's abduction. During Kimi's he was out to dinner with several men who manage some of his businesses. They claim the meeting ran deep into the night ending with drinks at a swanky bar."

"And Annalisa's abduction?" Hix asked,

"Rádolfo was out of the country again, and still is. It'll be quite difficult to verify those alibis of his being out of the country. He flies by private jet, he could easily bribe the pilot to lie that he was on the plane. I doubt if we fly over to South Africa that anyone is going to answer our questions. Ajanel is as dirty as they come, his counterparts are likely just as filthy and corrupt. His business associates would probably also lie for him." Kurt clicked off his phone and clipped it to his belt.

Hix's phone buzzed. He pulled it out, read the brief message and slipped it back into his pocket.

"Got another one," he said, heading for the door.

# Chapter Twenty-Nine

The scene Hix was driving away from hours later was just as horrendous as the others leaving a sick feeling in his gut.

The woman was found posed on her knees, hands bound behind her back, spray-painted rose gold, the chain around her neck holding her upright, and the same ugly pattern of the x's in a heart shape cut into her belly, and the burns inside the circle. The same type of handmade wooden box yet slightly diverse with different scrolling around the top trim and sides loomed a foot behind her.

Unfortunately, the person who found her put her picture on social media, so every scintilla of the scene was now public. The cutting, the spray-painting, all of it.

Doctor Burke, without his usual good humor advised Hix that clearly the girl had been raped, and sodomized and butchered while alive as Eden and Annalisa had been. It strengthened Doc Burke's theory that Kimi had only been sexually assaulted after she died because she had expired unexpectedly.

The doc revealed it was obvious when he examined the latest corpse at the scene, her vagina and anus were so heavily damaged, gouges and bruising on her thighs and her sex parts told him the suspect had used implements on her.

The damage was so extensive, so severe, Burke determined the perp had used various objects to penetrate her. Spermicide was present indicating there was also penile penetration.

250

As he climbed in his truck, Hix received a phone call from Mike Maverick.

When he answered, Maverick told him, "We located the Sammy that Annalisa Dominicci had dated. Sammy confirmed they met at the club. Annalisa was a popular submissive but Sammy was interested in seeing her outside the club."

"Yeah?"

"Not him, Hix. Samuel J. Trisdone has airtight alibis for Eden and Annalisa's murders, as well as the new victim. He has been in custody on drug trafficking charges since two days before Annalisa was found. We're checking Missing Persons to identify the latest vic."

"Goddammit," Hix cursed, pounding his fist on the steering wheel in frustration. "Another victim, we need to find the son-of-a-bitch before he gets another one."

Mike didn't respond, it would be redundant.

"Ah," Hix groaned. "Keep me updated," he hung up. He was headed to his parents' house. He told himself he just needed to check up on their guests. But, he knew he was craving to see the little blonde. Since he first met her, she hadn't been far from the back of his mind.

Now that he knew she had been basically forced to marry Ajanel, he was going to bring up the fact that Laurin could get the marriage annulled. Immediately.

Which reminded him. Hix scrolled down his phone and located the number he'd entered for Agent Brewer, and pushed it.

"Special Agent Brewer here," the voice was wary, the agent didn't recognize the number.

"Yeah, Brewer, Detective Hixman here, remember me?" He chuckled to himself at the dead silence on the other end of the line.

Brewer's words were slightly slurred, lisped, shunted, because he was speaking through the wires supporting his broken jaw. As Hix figured, Brewer had not made any complaint against Hix, not a word was breathed.

Hix was curious what story the agent had come up with to explain the injuries to his face and body. Brewer couldn't out Hix without what he'd done coming to light.

The CIA finds out Brewer forced Laurin to get married and spy on Ajanel knowing Ajanel was capable of killing her without a qualm, and also allowed the child Ajanel had purchased from the cybersex trade to stay in that violent home. Notwithstanding that the agent didn't even submit the sex trade issue for investigation.

Not to mention kidnapping and imprisoning young Robbie, not only would Brewer's career would be over, he'd be facing criminal charges.

When the silence remained, Hix said, "I'm calling to tell you to release Robert Cerridwen to his sister's care. You tell me where he is and I'll either retrieve him, or you have him brought to the station. What's it gonna be, Agent?"

More silence. But Hix could hear the slushy breaths Brewer made through the wiring. A foul sound came through, then Brewer said, "All right. The kid is not in this country. It will take a minute to retrieve him, get him a ticket and get him to me. The orders," his s's came out as sh's, "from me to his…guardians, were that he is only to be released to me in person. I have to go there and get him myself, and," his breathing a thick rasp, "currently, because of you, you bastard, I'm in the hospital for at least another week or more. So, fuck you."

Hix pondered his words. "Okay. You will contact me the second you are released. If you fuck this up, Brewer, I will speed dial your SAC and tell him or her what the hell you've been up to. You hear me?"

Hix didn't share that he had plans to tell Brewer's SAC, Special Agent in Charge, everything Brewer had pulled anyway, he owed the bastard nothing. But he needed to make sure Robbie was safely in Hix's hands first. He didn't trust the slimy agent to somehow double-cross him using the boy.

The sun was low in the sky when Hix pulled into his parents' driveway. A sense of peacefulness rolled over him as he looked over the big white house with green shutters surrounded by a vast hedge of budding forest. Smoke spiraled from one of the white brick chimneys, the setting was like something out of a fairy tale.

Not that he knew much about such things, just what he'd read to Holly and Michael. Children under the military's thumb were not given picture books to read. He learned about valiant knights and Rapunzel right along with the kids.

He climbed out of the truck and breathed deeply. The crisp minty air flowed from the thrush of evergreens flanking the house.

The smoke from the chimney and earthy scent of the damp grass added to the illusion that Hix had stepped into one of the colorful pages of the magical books. He'd pay a fortune to see unicorns and dragons come barreling out of the forest.

Shaking the fanciful thoughts out of his head, he opened the front door without knocking. He didn't need his key either, the door was unlocked.

Kullen stood only a few feet away. He grinned at Hix's frown. "What's the prob, bro? You ever plan to clear that brooding scowl from your acerbic face? We know you're dangerous, you don't have to keep broadcasting it."

"Door was unlocked, K, that's unacceptable. Laurin and Benji are here because they're supposed to be being kept secure. That-"

After a mocking guffaw, Kullen trod to his brother and clapped him in a brief hug. "Due to the security, we knew the second your truck neared the first gates. I unlocked the door so you could come right in, you ungrateful bastard."

"Kullen!" Vageline hurried into the foyer and moved between her embroiling sons. "You know there is no cursing in this house, especially when the children are here. Darling," she fussed as she hugged Hix and kissed his cheeks, three times.

"Okay, Ma, cut it out." Hix stepped from her embrace not seeing his mother and Kullen share a grin.

"Come dear, we're just getting ready to sit for dinner. I'll get another plate." His mother took his arm pulling him towards the living room.

"Sorry about not calling ahead, Ma, I didn't know if I was going to be able to get away and I didn't want to-"

She squeezed his arm. "You never have to call, honey. I've told you, this is your home too. You come and go as you please. You have your own room, and you know I always cook enough for an army. With you big strapping boys popping in here and there I have to make sure I'm stocked up!"

The trio wandered into the living room and Hix saw his father relaxed in his big recliner. Benji was curled on his lap, his little head set against Kresskin's big chest. He appeared to be asleep.

Kullen said to Hix, "Dad, Cliff, and I showed the little guy how to catch a ball. Did it for hours. He was so discouraged when he couldn't catch it. But, he stuck with it until he finally did it several times. Kid's a natural. Tuckered him out though. Pa was reading the newspaper to him when he knocked off." Kullen's smiling gaze rested affectionately on Benji nestled in his brawny father's huge arms.

Hix's face fell. "Shit, I wanted to be there with you guys. I wanted to be in on teaching him stuff like that."

"Language, Penn," Vageline scolded. "There will plenty of things to teach the boy, and if he's anything like your brothers, he'll beg to play catch every day." Her smile diminished at the sad look that flickered across Hix's face.

He had missed out on all those things little boys did growing up. She caught the way his eyes traveled continuously around the room and towards the staircase.

"She's in the kitchen, honey." Vageline smiled again.

Hix turned to her with a frown. "You put her to work? She needs rest, she's healing for God's sake."

Vageline and Kullen laughed.

Vageline told him, "It was her idea. The girl is used to helping out the staff at her...home. She doesn't like to be idle. Go on now," she gave him a nudge.

Without a word, Hix left his mother and brother standing grinning as he strode off towards the kitchen.

He hesitated under the large arched doorway to the kitchen.

Laurin was poised at the wooden part of the island and appeared to be frosting cupcakes. Flour spotted one cheek and her chin, her hair was tied back in a ponytail making her look about 10. Her tiny pink tongue stuck out the corner of her mouth as she concentrated on her task. All the tension in Hix's body poured out of his body at the sight of her.

All day he feared he'd been dreaming that he had taken her to his folks' home. She was continuously on his mind as he worked. But now, not only was he feeling relieved, there was a tightening in his gut at the sight of her.

It was all he could do not to stalk across the kitchen, lay her out on the table, strip her bare and make love to her. And the fact that he thought of the words 'make love' was what scared him.

Laurin pushed a hunk of loosened hair out of her face with the back of her hand leaving another spot of flour.

Hix said quietly, "Laurin."

It showed the gentle care his family had bestowed on her, and the cheerful busyness of the household that she didn't jump at his voice. She turned to him, and smiled.

"Detective, hi." She set down the spatula she was using to frost the cakes.

Hix bit back his frown at her still addressing him by his title. But, she had smiled naturally at him, that soothed his tense gut.

He stepped slowly into the room and moved to within a few feet of her, he didn't want to undo all the work his family had done at putting her at ease, by jumping at her.

With a mix of elation at the sight of her, and anger at her possibly harming herself by getting around too soon, he stuffed the angry bark and said coolly, "You, ah," he gestured to the cupcakes, "you okay to be standing like that?"

The wounds to her face had improved since he'd last seen her. Still, the injuries she had incurred were internal as well as external.

Her smile softened with warmth. Damned if she was already the most beautiful thing he'd ever laid eyes on, with her gorgeous smile, Hix's head felt light, her lovely brilliance dazed him, knocked all intelligent thought out of his thunderstruck brain.

She untied the apron around her waist, folded it and set it on the counter and came out to stand a few feet from him.

"I'm fine. Your mother has been sort of a bulldog keeping after me to take my medication and to get rest. Until the doctor cleared my concussion, your mother set an alarm to go off every two hours all night and either she or your dad would come and check on me. It should have been…annoying. But," her lashes lowered, then her eyes rose to his, she wore an abashed smile.

"It was actually nice to have someone take care of me like that. I can't ever remember a time that-" She broke off and the lashes covered her embarrassed eyes again.

"Laurin," he started to speak, lifting a hand to brush her cheek but dropped it.

"I mean, Benji deserves that kind of…caring, but not me, I deserve what-"

This time he did caress her soft cheek, lightly touching the spot of flour. He cut her off, "You are as important as anyone, Laurin, anyone. You've been dealt a raw, dirty deal in life, and it's time you were treated like the sweet, compassionate, brave young woman that you are."

"Huh," her laugh short, "brave?" A brow rose. "I don't think so."

Hix stopped himself before he moved closer to her, did something he shouldn't, like pull her into his arms and lay his lips on those pink puffy petals. "Brave, Laurin, and I know how much. The truth is showing itself, little one."

Her dubious eyes cut up to him. Their gazes caught, neither blinked for a moment. Then she said, "Detective," her voice soft, smile sweet, "I want to thank you for what you've done for Benji and me."

Shaking his head, Hix muttered, "You don't need to thank me."

Now she stepped closer, however clearly her intent was innocent unlike Hix's tamped down desire. She set a hand on his forearm. "But I do. If not for you, I fear what would have happened to us. My husband…" the smile left, sadness filled her blue eyes.

Hix laid his big hand over her small one on his arm. He shifted close enough he could see the different shades of blue in her gorgeous eyes.

"Laurin, first, can you please call me by my name? I don't want to be just a detective to you." He could have slapped himself for saying that. He couldn't be more than a cop to her, she was a married woman. But, maybe they could be friends.

His stomach soured, he wanted more than that from her. Now that he's freed her from Brewer and thereby Ajanel, she could obtain an annulment or divorce and live her life the way she wanted to. Hix only hoped that would include him.

The smile returned, she said, "Okay, um, Penn. Your mom calls you Penn. She talks a lot about you, you know."

His face cringed. "Ah, yeah. Sorry about that. She just…worries."

Her smile shone brightly and she giggled. "That's her job, Det-um, Penn. That's a mother's job to care and worry." Her gaze lowered to their hands on his arm, but she made no motion to move hers.

She looked up at him. "It's more than just worry, Penn, she is so very proud of you. Your whole family thinks the world of you, what you've endured, and the great job you do now."

So many years without his family, Hix found it difficult to let anyone in, and that included his doting mother. But, she pushed, his father and brothers and sister pushed, they all just continued easing their way around the wall he'd built around his heart.

When fighting in deserts and jungles, he killed others, and, many of the men, boys, he'd trained and lived with were also killed.

He couldn't let grief tear him apart. He had to stay coldhearted, merciless, ruthless to survive. Changing modes wasn't easy. Yet, if he had an incredible woman like Laurin at his side... Damn, he can't go there. Not yet.

"Listen Laurin, can we talk a minute?" He forced a smile to lighten his harsh face.

"Um, of course. I thought we were talking…" A small giggle tinkled out. Made his heart quicken.

"Yeah, well, let's go sit somewhere. Or," he glanced at the cupcakes, "do you need to do more to them?"

She shook her head and dropped the hand she'd set on his arm. "Nope. They're done. You might want to take one because if your mother doesn't come in and hide them before dinner, they'll disappear in a blink. And, your family won't be wolfing down your mom's fantastic fried chicken, and she'll get mad and tell them all off." Laurin grinned up at him.

Hix's heart warmed, she was filling herself with his family, he couldn't have hoped for more. Well, he did in the back of his bad, bad mind. "My brothers are chow hounds, she'll have to hide them."

"Not just your brothers, your dad packs away the cakes and cookies I make, and the kids," she rolled her eyes with a tender smile. Snapping her fingers, she said, "Gone in seconds. I swear, those children can smell out sweets baking from ten miles away! With Benji here, your sister has let the children come more often on the weekends and some afternoons."

Hix grabbed up two cupcakes and stuffed them in the pantry behind the olive oil. "There," he grinned, "I got mine. They look delicious even if they do have pink frosting."

Her hands slapped on her hips, head tipped back to look up at him. "What's wrong with pink? They're pretty."

"Un huh, come on, let's go to the back den where we can talk in private." He lightly wrapped his fingers around her arm and turned her to the doorway. His hand left her arm and lowered to the bottom curve of her back.

He ushered her down a back hall so they didn't have to pass the rest of the people in the house. He wanted her to himself.

# Chapter Thirty

Hix led her to a room done in shades of brown and gold. Walls were lined with bookcases stuffed messily with books. A brown brick fireplace took up half of one of the walls. The furniture was large and casual with thick cushions.

He moved to the sofa and motioned with his hand. "Here, have a seat."

Laurin sat down gingerly, suddenly wary of what he had to say so privately to her. She smoothed the jeans over her thighs with her palms then tugged at a few buttons on the lacy white blouse. She wasn't wearing shoes, she pulled her legs up, curled her knees and tucked her socked toes partially under one of the couch cushions.

Hix stood for a second watching Laurin get settled, but he was picturing her lying down on the big sofa, with him on top of her, nestling between her legs. Her bare legs. "Uh, would you like something to drink?" The vision in his mind made his voice come out awkward and scratchy.

"No, I'm fine. What is it you wanted to talk about?" Suddenly her expression tightened, "Are, I mean, is it time for me to go? You're taking me back to my husband?" Tremors constricted her voice; she shifted her legs back down to put her feet on the floor.

"I understand," she said with a breaking voice, "it wasn't to be for so…long. But," her fingers twined in prayer on her lap, she looked up at him. "Please, if you could help me find a safe…place for Benji. He can't, he just can't go back to the mansion. Please, Detective-"

Hix shrugged out of his suit coat and laid it on a chair and loosened his tie. He moved and sat down on the sofa keeping a good twelve inches between them. Unfortunately, he didn't trust himself to sit close enough to inhale her fresh scent, already he could barely keep his hands off her.

He half-turned towards the beauty, one leg pulled up, his knee bent, the other foot anchored to the floor. "Calm down, Laurin. You aren't going anywhere. I told you that you were staying here until you can get on your own feet. There is no rush. My folks love having the both of you here. Please, just, relax," he took a breath watching the fright pale her complexion.

Laurin chewed her plump bottom lip in consternation. But, at his sincere stare remaining level at her with calm compassion, her fingers lightened their stranglehold on each other.

He noticed her slender shoulders lose some rigidity, yet she still gazed at him with uncertainty, her fingers locked together on her lap. Well aware his normal mien frightened some people, Hix worked to soften his harsh features, even tried a smile.

He quickly gave up on the smile, forcing the relatively unnatural act would make him appear more suspiciously malevolent than kind. Although, he was hoping the more time spent with his niece and nephew, and Benji and Laurin, he would start to smile much more easily and naturally.

He said quietly, "I know everything, Laurin."

Her lashes blinked in confusion, the smile left. "Everything, um, about what?"

Clearing his throat, Hix looked directly in her eyes. "Everything about you."

The swift inhale she took was loud. "Me?"

"Yeah. Listen, Laurin," he scooched an inch closer to her. He said, "I met with Agent John Brewer," his lips twisted with disgust.

Her eyes grew wide, then fear flooded them, she cringed back from him. "I…don't understand, why…"

Seeing the distress inkling back in, Hix said quickly, "It's okay, Laurin. Everything from now on will be okay. You and Benji and Robbie, you will all be safe and taken care of."

The yellow lashes flew up. "Robbie? You know about Robbie?"

He nodded, inched closer. "Yes. Agent Brewer came to see me. He told me all about Ajanel. How Brewer kidnapped your little brother and stashed him away. How he set you up to be the mail-order-bride, how Ajanel got his hands on little Benji. How Brewer forced you to stay in that house and spy on Ajanel.

"He even told me about the fucking scandal with St. Lawrence, how your... how Ajanel threw you under the bus to take the blame. How they all allowed you to suffer the shame and degrading insults from the public."

She blinked rapidly, the pulse at her throat pounded. Her chest rose and fell with quick short breaths. She clutched the top of her blouse, the agitation taking her over.

Hix said softly, "Laurin," he was now only a few inches from her. "Sweetheart, it's all over. Brewer and I had a...discussion and he is bringing Robbie home."

"Home?" As if afraid to get her hopes up, Laurin asked quietly, "When? When can I see my brother?" She squirmed, about to get up to go seek out her brother.

Hix set a hand on her thigh holding her. "It's going to be a couple of weeks. Robbie can only be released to Agent Brewer and," he took a breath, "at the moment, Brewer is...incapacitated."

Her brows wrinkled down. "Incapacitated? What does that mean? What is wrong with him?"

Hix's neck reddened, he lifted his hand and rubbed the back of it. "Uh, well, when we had our...discussion, I got a little bit...angry."

She stared at him trying to comprehend. "You- you hit him?"

Murmuring, "Hmm," he rubbed his neck nodding. "A few times. He's in the hospital."

Gawking speechless, her lips parted in surprise. Then, her mouth curved up slightly. She smoothed the grin away and said firmly, "I don't condone violence, Penn."

"Ah," he scowled, "he kind of made me do it. Prick. Anyway, as soon as he's released, he will retrieve your brother and I will take Robbie from him and bring him to you."

Laurin sat back, a heavy breath released slumping her chest. For once in such a long time, a hint of hope brought color to her pale face. She pushed to sit up straighter and that brought the couple within a few scant inches from each other. She looked up at him.

Hix felt his body swelling, heating, her breasts had almost brushed against his chest. He inhaled her fresh scent, her head tilted back causing her lids to lower. Blue shimmered out, her lips parted. To Hix, she looked like a woman who wanted to be bedded.

Of course that was just wishful thinking on his part. Still, he couldn't stop himself from caressing her soft cheek. Her lashes lowered demurely but she didn't move from his touch or lower her head. They held the moment, then, Laurin blinked and shifted back from him.

Doubt clouded her eyes. "Is this a sure thing? Is it really going to happen? Or," she crossed her arms protectively over her chest. "Is this a- another trick to get me to do something?"

She squinted in suspicion. The accusation came out, "You are working with Brewer, you want me to spy on Rádolfo." Tears suddenly shone with her lips turning down in disappointment. "It's just another-"

"No." Hix grasped one of her upper arms and lifted her close to him. A growl burned low in his chest, the primordial need of a male animal for a female was posturing its rutting head.

The years of surviving as basically an animal with other like males living and fighting in virulent filthy jungles or infinite sand-stormed deserts where there were few rules, no courtesy and zero mercy, were a huge part of him.

Blink wrong and it could cost you your life. That existence turned men into barbaric gorillas that took and killed ruthlessly and without remorse, even with each other. A single slight and the suddenly offending headless body would be tumbling to the ground.

Hix had been an embedded aboriginal part of it. And now, with the scent of Laurin filling his nostrils, the craving want of her was overwhelming every one of his senses. The killing, mindless beast was rising in him, Hix could feel it blinding, deafening him to the civilized world, turning him into that razing animal.

He grabbed both her arms, lifting Laurin up against him, his mouth lowered to begin his devouring of her, all of her.

"Please," the whispered breath hushed over his prowling mouth, stalling him. Her tiny fingers gripped his shoulders.

Even as her body melted into his, under heavy lids her eyes a smoking sultry glow, her luscious lips misted and parted to receive him, resistance elbowed aside the blossoming desire.

Laurin's body wanted him, her heart too, maybe, but her brain's moral compass kicked in. Her palms had moved down to place flush against his chest, she was trying, futilely, to push him back.

Hix's fingers ground around her slender arms like steel pliers, it was like he was holding her so he wouldn't use his weight to push her onto her back and rip her damned clothes off.

Shaking his head like a dog, trying to throw off the base animal instincts that had seized him, it was a battle to gain control of his damned self.

His eyes scrunched tightly, they were sitting in his mother's house for Pete's sake, what the hell was wrong with him? He never should have left the squad in Egypt. As much as he tried, worked hard to become a normal civilized man, he couldn't shake loose the beast inside that the raw armed forces had created.

Keeping his eyes shut tight, he growled, "Laurin, I'm sor-"

But she cut him off, he tensed at her soft fingers that stroked the side of his face. "No, Penn, you always stop when I ask you to, you don't have to apologize. You've been pretty clear about your…um, interest in me."

He started, blinked, his head lowered and he peered up at her. He had been expecting her rebuke, cries of rape, reminders that she was a married woman, not the soft smile, warmth dusting her big blue eyes.

She wriggled gently and he realized he was squeezing the life out of her poor arms. He instantly released her and dashed his palm up his forehead pushing back the dark hair. His head cocked quizzically at her, he shifted from her to give her breathing room.

"Laurin, I…" he pushed the hair back again in consternation. "I don't know what comes over me when I'm around you. I turn into a brainless rutting animal." The corner of his mouth edged up sheepish. Then he frowned.

"I want you, desperately, I have to put it out there. I've fought it, but, I have very real feelings for you Laurin. I mean, you're safe here, I promise, even from me. I will stow my…feelings and shit for you, I swear. You are only here to be protected, to heal, and to get on your feet. And only those things."

His mouth tightened into a slight grimace. Damn but her fingers felt amazing on his skin. He didn't move a hair not wanting her to become aware she was still stroking him and stop.

She smiled, her hand dropped from his face to set on one of his hands. "Penn, um," her shyness overshadowed, yet she went on, "I would be a liar if I said I wasn't…" a rosy blush filled her round cheeks.

Enjoying the pretty color staining her face, the corner of his mouth edged up further into a half-smile. She wasn't angry, or scared, possibly slightly embarrassed. He moved his head closer to hers, nudged, "You what?"

Her lashes fluttered covering her eyes. Hix curled a finger under her chin lifting it so she had to look at him. "You what, Laurin?"

"I…I think I have…feelings for you, too, Penn."

His brows shot up. "You think, or you do?" He turned his hand over to twine their fingers together.

She murmured, "Um, Penn," her smile ebbed, lowering her head she tilted it and looked up at him with a serious expression.

"I've never had a…real relationship, even a boyfriend. Our parents passed when I was sixteen and we stayed with an aunt for a few months then she passed. It was only Robbie and me. I managed to keep us both in school and worked several jobs to keep food and shelter, but," one shoulder lifted then lowered sadly.

"It was barely enough. We lived in one room in a boarding house. I had to keep us sort of…off the books so the school and CPIS didn't find out we were living alone underage. They would have taken us and separated us."

Her lips pinched as the past engulfed her memories. Hix squeezed their fingers bringing her back to the present. She let out a heavy sigh. "Um, so, there was no time for frivolous things like going out and dating, so, I've never even kissed a man except for... Rádolfo."

The edges of her mouth curved down, she turned away from Hix in her humiliated angst. Her mumbles almost inaudible, "Things...sex, with Rádolfo," she cleared her throat, voice small she explained, "was never wanted, or- or normal.

"My experience with men is...well, that. So I have nothing to compare, to base things on. Our parents were working on a divorce, we seldom saw them together so there's no...role models."

Her head stayed lowered. "However, um, I can't have you thinking your advances are unwanted, that your interest isn't reciprocated. I have to admit, I think... about you." Pain crinkled around her bleak eyes, the breath she took was aggrieved.

"But, I'm not normal, Penn, I don't think I ever will be. Even if- if Rádolfo is out of the picture, I don't think I can ever uh, like sex, or- or know how to be a...woman." She peeked up at him quickly, her lips bunched then she quickly lowered her gaze.

Hix curled his hand around the side of her face again to keep their eyes connected. He smiled, tough to do but for her he'd force it. "Baby, you've only known brutality and perversion. Natural sex, love-making," his smile twitched, "ah, it isn't like that. It isn't painful. People that...like each other, want to make each other happy. Not hurt, not terrorize, not force. When," he sifted tendrils of light hair off her cheek, "when we get rid of Ajanel," his features firmed, "and we will, when he's gone, if you let me, if you want me as much as I want you, then I'll show you what real...caring, intimacy is about."

Hix had never experienced it himself, but he wasn't about to tell her that. He knew the way he felt about her that every part of his being wanted only to cherish, worship Laurin, protect her, take care of her, love her. He would learn, read, talk to his parents, he would ascertain how to make her happy and feel treasured.

His parents were still wildly in love. On more occasions than he'd like to remember, Hix had caught his father prowling his mother, and their laughter, heated gasps and contented sighs drifted through their closed bedroom door. The way they still gazed at each other, they were the perfect model of a couple in long lasting, deep love for Hix to learn from.

Laurin sniffed back tears, she tilted her head into the cradle of his large palm and peered thoughtfully at him. "Right now I…can't help feeling guilty. I mean, legally he's my husband although he's an evil wicked man that I was coerced into marrying, still, until the marriage is…dissolved, I wouldn't feel right having, you know," she blushed, "relations with you."

"After Ajanel is arrested or deported or just out of the picture, you can get an annulment. Then, if you want to, it's all about what you want, Laurin, we can start slow, real slow. Let me take you out, there's a neat restaurant in Alexandria on the wharf I think you'll really like. I have a sailboat; we can go for a sunset sail on the weekend on the Potomac. Benji would love that too.

"What do you say, when you're ready? But I won't pressure you, honey, if you don't want to. If you say no, I won't push you, I'll back off, you have no worries. So, what do you think?"

Chuckling at his words and the eagerness in his voice that negated his promise to not push her, Laurin smiled shyly. "I'd, uh, I think I'd like that, Penn."

He smiled down at her then pulled her into the curve of his arm. Gently curling her against his chest, Hix held her, stroked her back.

"Okay. We have something to look forward to. Until then," he set a finger under her chin and lifted it to him. "Let me take care of you, I won't pounce on you, I just want to hold you, is that okay with you, Laurin? Just holding you in my arms makes me feel…hell, on the top of the world. Safe, happy, content, like home."

She nodded, smiling. "Yes, that's okay with me, Penn. I can't remember the last time someone…held me."

"Good." He lightly brushed their lips together then tucked her back against his chest and they just sat there, with his arms embracing her. Penn heard her sigh of relief, of finally being able to depend on someone else to take care of her, to fight for her, to value her.

Kullen entered the kitchen and pulled a soda from the fridge. At the sink, Vageline twisted to turn and look at her son. One brow arched. "You were going to tell Penn and Laurin to get ready for dinner."

Taking a few slugs, Kullen grinned at his mother. "Ma, you saw how little Benji was all curled up safe and toasty on Daddy's lap?"

The other brow rose. "Of course. Every day when Daddy comes in from work Benji flies to him and Kresskin lifts him up, carries him to his recliner, sets him on his lap and reads to him until the little guy nods off in his arms."

Vageline's smile broadened. "It's so beautiful, so sweet, I've taken pictures of them. The child has changed, thank God, from the tense, terrified, skinny waif he was when Penn brought him here." She frowned. "What about them?"

Kullen grinned, swigged more soda, wiping off his mouth with the back of his hand. "Well, picture them but put Penn and Laurin in their places."

Her frown bunched to confusion, the brows now drew down. "What are you talking about? How can-" she blinked, then smiled. "Ah, you mean Penn is holding her, and she's letting him?"

"Yeah." Kullen crunched the empty soda can in his hand, moved to the pantry and tossed it in the recycling bin then grinned harder at his mother.

"But not in a sexual way, just, cuddling, it's sweet as shit, uh, I mean sugar. Never thought I'd see the day Penn lost his heart to a female. And certainly not a tiny delicate, fragile one like Laurin Ajanel."

Vageline crossed her arms and leaned a hip against the sink. "She's fragile, but has a spine of steel, honey. She's stayed in that den of horror to protect both Benji and according to Penn, her little brother as well. She's self-sacrificing, and hasn't murmured one complaint about her horrible life, or the pain she's still suffering from her husband's beatings and that terrible mob assault."

Shaking her head, she dropped a wooden spoon into a pot on the stove. "Not a hint of complaint. Just keeps asking me what chores she can do to help me out when she can barely stand for more than ten minutes."

Kullen agreed. "Yeah, she's small, almost frail, but she's strong enough to hold up to Penn. He needs a strong woman who can stand up to him. He has a lot to learn though, he's used to whores, uh, sorry Ma. I mean, he's used to tough women like him. Even that bitch he foolishly got himself engaged to. Little Laurin's going to give my brother a run for his money. It's great, I can't wait to watch her spin him around her little finger, eh?"

Vageline slapped his hand when he stuck a finger into the pot for a taste. "She's already done that, Kullen. You've seen the way he looks at her, like she's priceless crystal."

Licking his finger, Kullen nodded. "Priceless crystal he wants to touch. Yep, our boy is up shit's, uh, sorry, sunk."

Rolling her eyes at his cursing, Vageline said, "Go on then, go get them, but," she reached out and held his arm, "do it gently. Okay?"

Wiping his palms together like the evil villain, Kullen grinned and said, "Sure, no prob." He swung around and hurried out of the kitchen.

# Chapter Thirty-One

At work a few days later, Hix struggled to pay attention to the videos playing on his screen. He was reviewing all the interviews they'd done. There were hundreds. Not just the Ajanels and the victims' friends, spouses, relatives, employers, co-workers etc., but seemingly unending amounts of members of the sex clubs.

Hix pinched between his eyes, if he'd been able to focus and keep attuned to the videos he would have gone blind by now. His already messy office duplicated the murder board.

Pictures of the crime scenes and the victims were pinned to his walls. It took every modicum of effort to keep his mind off Laurin and on work.

When they caught the killer then he could daydream about her all he wanted. He'll get Rádolfo Ajanel out of the way and then his daydreams will become real.

He fast-forwarded through frames and returned to the interviews of the Ajanel clan, now absorbed he didn't look up when Prince came in.

The detective pulled a chair over next to Hix and plunked down beside him.

Following what Hix watched, Prince commented drily, "Penn, you keep circling back to the Ajanels. Come on, you see you've got a damned grudge for Rádolfo. You want our sick killer to be him so you can get rid of him. You know what the chances are it is him, or one of his sons?"

Prince snapped his fingers. "None. Zilch. Nada. Get real. A wife-beating ambassador, a married doctor with an infant, two married, wealthy Ajanel sons, are not going to run around town stealing women, killing them and painting them gold. There's another sicko out there, we need to keep reviewing the films we have of the perp, we'll find the clues there."

Hix's eyes flit back and forth as he continued studying the interviews conducted on the Ajanels at the station. His lips pulled in, he tugged the bottom one then scratched at his short beard, grunted. He clicked some keys on the keyboard and hit enter.

Another screen came up. It produced videos of the crime scenes, the victims, all angles of the women and the boxes. He scrolled through them and on to the autopsy tapes.

Beside him, Prince's gaze revolved dizzily over the screen as he studied the images with Hix. "Man, we gotta have this shit memorized by now."

Nevertheless, they studied the information all over again for a couple of hours when Hix said, "Wait." He hit on the arrows scrolling back up until he stopped on the twine found tied around the victims' wrists.

He muttered, "The wires were painted gold too. He painted them before tying them around the women's wrists after they were dead and posed in front of the wooden boxes."

His brows low over darting blue eyes staring at the photos, Prince asked, "What? What else are you seeing?"

Hix sat back in his chair and tapped a knuckle on the screen. "The twine, the knots are identical, it's a sailor's knot."

"Huh," Prince chuckled, "like the restaurant?"

Hix sent him a glare. "No, asshole." He clicked on a web icon and typed in "sailors' knots." Dozens of pictures came up.

Hix scrolled through them then stopped. "There," he said, pointing at one. "I recognized it because I learned knots in the army and use various ones when sailing."

Prince leaned in to look closely at the picture.

"It's a constrictor knot," Hix told him as Prince read. "It has a lot of uses. It can be a temporary whipping for a frayed rope, it can tie the neck of a sack, it can be used as a hose clamp, to hold things together, in this case, wrists.

"It doesn't work on a flat surface, it requires a curved surface for the bindings to grip. Wrists are curved. And," Hix glanced at his friend, "it is usually tied with twine and can only be cut apart, can't be untied."

"Huh." Prince continued reading about the knot Hix had pinpointed. "Doc Burke said he had to cut the binds off the women. Forensics wanted them to be carefully untied, taking photos of each step so they could reproduce them and weren't happy when they found they couldn't unwind them. They had to let Burke cut them so they could remove and study them."

"Okay," Hix said, reaching for his phone, "let's find people on the list that have boating or military, mainly Navy backgrounds."

"Hey." Kurt stepped into the office, his phone in his hand.

Prince grinned up at him, said, "Take a load off, bro."

Used to Hix ignoring people, even his friends, Kurt smiled at Prince and sat down.

Prince filled him in on what they'd just discovered.

Kurt leaned back in his chair and said, "Oh yeah? Good work, Penn." Hix still ignored him as he continued perusing the computer.

"You got something, Kurt?" Prince asked, motioning to the cell in Kurt's hand.

Brought back to his own news, Kurt looked down at his phone then grinned up at Prince. "Yup. It may mean nothing, but," he swiped the phone on and tapped on a picture. "Doc found this stuck to the back of the latest vic, Tatum Nichols' knee. It was glued on by the gold paint, but when Burke peeled it off he saw the other side of the fragment was preserved against her skin." He held his phone out for them to see.

Hix shifted his chair to get a view of the image. Kurt lowered his hand so they could both see it.

Kurt said, "It's just a piece, a tiny fragment. It appears to be from a magazine. Our computer program identified the words as isiZulu. South African. I googled for those kinds of magazines. What I discovered was the font, the wording, it only matches a few magazines not common around here. I couldn't obtain them online, I'm going to check out the bookstores around, like Barnes and Nobles, Books'aplenty and Good News is Good Reading." He stood up. "I'll let you know what I find out." He grinned at the pair and left the office.

Prince held a hand up. "Don't say it."

"Don't say what?" Hix smirked.

"Ahh," Prince groaned, "just because it's South African, doesn't mean it's Ajanel."

"Too coincidental, Thomas."

Prince argued, "The killer has been smart, careful, diligent, how could he make such a mistake to leave evidence like that on the vic? Maybe it's a frame. Someone who knows Ajanel is on the CIA and FBI's radar."

Hix shrugged. "No, I don't think so. I think he laid her out, stood her up, whatever, while he painted her. Somewhere along the way, in his car, home, lair, whatever, at some point when she was prone, the fragment stuck to her leg, perhaps he painted over it before he could notice it. The freak is smug, he thought he was in complete control, made him careless."

He grabbed up his phone. "I'm gonna tell Kurt when he finds the mag to get sales receipts and surveillance films."

"Hell, Penn, that's farfetched. The guy could have purchased the magazine directly in South Africa."

Dialing, Hix agreed, "Yeah, could have. Still need to check."

After hanging up, Hix returned to viewing the tapes on the computer. He was scrolling through when he paused at the video of the killer when he set his palm on the top of the post.

"Hmm," he made a low growl of curiosity then clicked to his phone. Like he had with the wire, he held the phone up next to the computer screen and compared them.

Noticing Hix's intense interest, Prince asked, "You see something?"

With a grunt, Hix nodded to the phone. "Look at the killer's hand on the post."

"Uh huh." Prince stared at the stilled frame.

"Okay, now look at this guy's hand." Hix motioned to the computer.

Prince leaned closer and squinted. His gaze ping-ponged between the pictures, then he whistled. "Hell, that is some creepy odd as shit stuff."

"Yeah," Hix muttered and took the phone. He dialed Doctor Burke.

Burke answered, "Hello Detective, what can I do for you?"

"Listen, Doc. I'm sending you a couple of pictures, tell me what you see. If it's as odd as we think, tell me if there is a…I guess a diagnosis?"

"Uh, okay," Burke's voice faded as his phone pinged alerting him he had mail.

*********

At the Hixman home, Laurin was outside with Vageline hanging laundry on the line.

Vageline finished clipping a shirt to the clothesline, she ran her hands down the damp shirt to ease out wrinkles. Before reaching for another piece of wet clothing, she glanced with affection over at Laurin who was copying her albeit much more slowly.

Reaching her arms up still pained her. Laurin was breathing heavily and her face was pale, her eyes tight with fatigue.

"Honey," Vageline said gently. "I've told you, you don't have to work to pay your way here. You are still recovering, why don't you run inside and lay down for a bit?"

Laurin clipped a pin to a pillowcase. "No, really, I'm fine. This is so nice, the weather is still cold but I love the smell of laundry that has dried in the fresh air. The pine trees add a crisp minty scent." Reaching up to pin the other end of the case, she winced and lowered her hand to clutch at her side.

"Okay, that's enough, honey." Vageline dropped the pins she held into a clothespin bag hanging on the line. "You get yourself inside right now and just lay out on the sofa and take a breather. Kresskin took Benji to the park, it'll be quiet. Take a few winks."

"No but-"

"No buts," Vageline insisted. She caught Laurin's shoulders, still too thin but she'd gained a needed pound or so, which made Vageline smile with satisfaction. She turned Laurin around and gave her a little push to the back door. "Go on now, I refuse to allow you to do any more today."

Her head down, Laurin begrudgingly trod to the house. It was mortifying that she was too weak to pull her own weight. Although all of the Hixmans insisted they didn't want or need her help, she still felt like such a burden.

For heaven's sake, they were even taking care of Benji. Feeding him, reading to him, playing with him, going to the park, the zoo.

Vageline even took him for a dental checkup and a physical because he'd never had one. She scheduled for him to have the inoculations every regular child had.

Traipsing into the house, Laurin headed for the living room.

She lay down on the comfy powder blue sofa and stared at the ceiling. Restlessly rolling back and forth, she reached over and grabbed the remote off the coffee table and turned the TV on.

Flipping through channel after channel, nothing interested her, she wasn't big on television. Randomly clicking on a news show, she plumped a throw pillow against the arm of the couch and settled back into it.

Laurin put the sound on so low she couldn't really hear it, she just stared at the news reporter, it was mostly about The Poser murders. Her eyes glazed as her mind traveled.

Everything she'd been through in her young life reeled through her thoughts like a movie. Her family had been dirt poor, every time her father got a job he'd manage to get into a brawl at the pool table in the local dive bar. He'd get injured, stabbed mostly, land a lengthy stay in the hospital and the bills would pile up.

Her mother picked up clerical positions through a temp agency. The jobs didn't last long, just enough time for her to have an affair with the best looking male there. When the affair was over so was the job. Not that Marcy cared, working interfered with her sleep. She wasn't an early riser, usually because she stayed out late most nights drinking and carousing with her slutty girlfriends.

At a young age but nine years older than Robbie, Laurin had to care for her younger brother. See that he was fed and clothed and got to school. She was the one who helped Robbie with his homework.

When she was sixteen and Robbie eight, their folks died in a car wreck leaving no insurance and no money. Her father had lapsed making payments on their auto insurance.

Laurin and Robbie were evicted and ended up in the boarding house dump where they'd lived for the past seven or so years. Laurin went to school during the day, worked in the evenings, and kept Robbie in school. She had no time for fun or friendships much less a boyfriend.

Who knew things could go from bad to worse? Agent Brewer had spotted Laurin in the market and stalked her, learned she and her brother were orphans. He decided she had a preternatural beauty that would strike a man deaf and dumb, so he swooped in and kidnapped her and Robbie.

And the saga continued. She had been forced to suffer Rádolfo's brutal beatings and vicious rapes. The only light was when Rádolfo had brought poor Benji home. He had bought him and planned to sell him to a freak that liked little boys who could help increase Rádolfo's businesses.

But when Laurin tried to protect Benji from Rádolfo's big fists when he was angered by the boy, Rádolfo realized he could control Laurin using Benji. Rádolfo wasn't stupid, he knew Laurin hated him and would attempt to flee the first chance she got, so he kept Benji to keep her in line.

When Laurin had balked at being the scapegoat for the St. Lawrence scandal, Rádolfo held little Benji up off the floor by his neck. It was horrible. Rádolfo gloating, taunting Laurin. Benji thrashing, gagging, his face turning red, Laurin screeching for mercy, the servants hiding behind doors, none brave enough to come forward and help.

She had to give in, do whatever her husband said. She and Robbie and Benji were living in a real live nightmare. Until now.

She pictured the valiant detective who stuck his nose in, and rescued them. They weren't in the clear yet. Not until Robbie was home and Rádolfo was put away could Laurin take a deep breath. She couldn't wait to see how things progressed with her and Penn.

The first time she saw him at the charity event, he terrified her with his dark violent looks, the tough expression, strapping body. But he had helped her and she tried to thank him.

He had been mean to her that day, he had heard about the scandal and believed it like everyone else. Yet, he never stopped trying to help her, even when he thought the worst of her.

Sure, his violent appearance still frightened her, it was like having an ancient warrior glowering down at you, she smiled at the image. But, as hard looking as he was, he was just as handsome. Penn was kind, and gentle, and could kiss like a maniac. Making her want more, more of everything with him.

Her finger absently pressed on the remote, and people running and shouting flashed by her blank stare.

Blinking hard a few times, she tuned into the show. "Hmm, a cop show. What else is on…" she started to flip through the channels again when she heard one of the characters say, "Ambassador Livingston." And she sat up straight.

Again she stared at the show unblinking as something struck her… Laurin sprang to her feet. "That's it, that's what it is."

She glanced around. "I need to go, how am I going to get to-" She spotted Vageline's purse. Feeling guilty as sin, Laurin took out some cash from her wallet then quickly wrote a note telling the wonderful mother that she'd stolen…borrowed some money and she'd pay her back as soon as she could.

Not wanting to use up any of the minutes she might need on the cell Penn had given her, she went to the kitchen where the Hixmans had a landline. Laurin called 411 and got the number to a rideshare service and requested a car to come pick her up.

Then, she grabbed her jacket out of the closet by the front door and fled from the house.

# Chapter Thirty-Two

She waved at the guard at the gate as he opened it for her to pass through. Thankfully, apparently the word wasn't out yet about her leaving the mansion. The driver accepted his fee and tip and he drove back out of the gate.

One of the side doors to the mansion was usually unlocked during the day for the servants to go back and forth from the house to the yard. Thanking her lucky stars none of the Ajanels' cars were in the driveway or the garage, Laurin slipped inside.

Since she was no longer present in the home, there were few monitors activated watching the house. They had only been necessary to ensure that she and Benji did not leave the mansion.

She scurried down the carpeted hall all the way to Rádolfo's office. She picked the lock, opened the door, took a peek behind her to make sure no one saw her, slid inside and closed and locked the door behind her.

She went immediately to the bookcase, dropped to kneel on the floor, and pulled out the books covering the wall safe. Pushing the lever to release the door, Laurin stuck her hand in and pulled out the laptop. She moved to sit on the carpet and placed the computer in front of her on the floor and powered it up.

It took 30 seconds and the screen lit.

"Okay, Laurin girl," she coached herself, "let's see if you're right." Her fingers clicked over keys, mumbling aloud, "Let's try Ambassador number one." Nothing, *incorrect password* flashed at her. "Hmm, how about Number One Ambassador?" *Incorrect password.* "Darn, am I wrong?"

Shaking her head she deliberated for a minute. "I was so sure it was Ambassador. With Rádolfo's massive ego, it has to be something all about him."

Laurin stared hard at the screen as she pondered, "It wouldn't be anything to do with his criminal deeds, or his family, or me, huh," she snorted. "Nothing was as important to Rádolfo as Rádolfo." She tried putting Rádolfo Ajanel number one, and variations of that, but *incorrect password* continued to mock her.

"Oh well, I tried." Her finger on the power button, she was about to shut it down, when she thought, "Let me try one more." She typed in #1Ambassador- and- "Yes!" She clapped her hand over her mouth. Files sprung up all over the monitor. "Oh my God, I can't believe it worked."

Laurin crossed her legs and settled in for a while to transfer copies of the files as well as the entire email file with contacts included to the email address Agent Brewer had given her. She included where he could find the laptop if he wanted to retrieve it for evidence.

She didn't want to press her luck by taking it with her. If she ran into anyone, a guard or a servant they would prevent her from leaving with it and instantly put her in lock down.

Finally, after some time, she shut down the computer, stashed it back in the safe, stood up and stretched her numb limbs. She moved to the door and peeked out. The coast was clear.

Closing the door quietly, she crept towards the stairs. She'd hidden a small album containing photos of her family in Benji's room. This hopefully, would be the last time she had to enter this Godforsaken hellhole.

She dashed silently up the carpeted stairs and hurried to the room. Letting out a sigh of relief that she didn't run into anyone on the way, she hopped inside and rushed to the closet. Way in the back, up on a shelf under a spare pillow, she pulled the album out and tucked it under her arm.

Before she left, she trod to the window and peered out to make sure no one had arrived at the mansion. Raoul, Blane and Chevy and their wives all had keys to the house, and often came and went as they pleased.

They all had their own pools, but Rádolfo's pool was magnificent. It was enormous and spectacular with a grotto and waterfall. The Ajanels loved to lay outside tanning while servants ran drinks and food hither and thither to them.

Laurin stood at the window and looked down. The window was above the patio area. Visions of the last time the men had been in the pool passed in front of her eyes. It was heated, so even though it was still chilly outside, they enjoyed swimming and playing in the water. Splashing their wives and otherwise making nuisances of themselves.

That last day, the men fooled around in the pool, the women lounged on lawn chairs, and Shona flashed her bare breasts to all and sundry. Laurin and Jewel had left shortly after that for Jewel to go visit her lover.

Laurin had felt so bad that day. Chevy was standing there dripping all over the marble floor, giving his wife a tender kiss when Laurin knew full well his wife was on her way to a rendezvous with another man. Still, he-

The image of that scene was suddenly transposed over with the news show she'd just seen. Her heart started racing, she muttered, "No, no, it can't be…" Laurin snapped her eyes shut to focus on the news report she'd just watched, the pictures of the victims, and she flashed over to the scene in the foyer.

Her eyes flapped open, she cried, "Oh my God, oh my God," and ran to the parlor where there was a landline and called the car service. Then she raced out the door.

**********

At the station, Hix still stared at the surveillance videos waiting for the doctor to call him back. Prince was in his own office doing research.

Now Hix finally knew what the something was in the back of his mind that had been bugging the shit out of him.

He watched transfixed at the video on his phone of when the killer had placed Annalisa Dominicci's body at the posing location, then dropping his glove on the way back to the black van.

Hix pulled up the film of the interviews of the Ajanels. He held the phone beside the computer as he stared, his eyes bouncing back and forth between the two screens.

"Yo, Penn." Daron Sinclair slapped the side of the door to alert Hix he was entering the office.

Hix raised a hand acknowledging him.

The sergeant dragged a chair over next to Hix and sat down to observe what the detective was watching.

"Come up with anything?" Sinclair asked. He sat back, stuck his long legs out and crossed his ankles. He wore cowboy boots, went along with the Stetson he normally wore but left in his car. Today, his scrolled braids glinted under the fluorescent lighting. He twined his fingers and set them over his flat belly.

"Huh," Hix grunted. "Fuck yeah." His eyes narrowed to a sharp squint at the computer and the phone he held in his hand. He turned both so Sinclair could easily see them.

"Tell me, wait-" he clicked until he had stills of two images and placed them side-by-side. "Okay, tell me if anything pops out at you."

"Hmm, okay." Sinclair uncrossed his ankles and leaned forward to get a good look at both screens. His gaze flit from one to the other, back and forth, back and forth, then- "Holy shit, Penn, holy shit."

Hix sat back and grinned. "Yeah, oh yeah, I think we got him."

"Got who?" Kurt strolled in with papers in his hand.

His eyes on the papers, Hix said, "You tell us first what you have."

"Okay, sure." Kurt grinned cheerfully with a bit of smugness. He handed the papers to Hix. As Hix read them, Kurt said, "Chevalier Ajanel's alibis don't hold up." He nodded at the papers Hix was reading.

"Yeah, he did have a few emergencies at the hospital, but each one he used as his alibis didn't pan out. We talked to people, viewed surveillance videos, journal entries of nurses, and conversations with the doctors as well as Ajanel's patients."

"Do tell," Sinclair said, moving to peer at the papers Hix was reading.

Kurt snapped his head with a grim smile. "Yeah, the bastard was there, but only briefly, just enough to have it on record that he was in the hospital. I think he snatched the vics and stowed them, then went to the hospital for a short time to visit one of his ill patients that happened to be there, then he returned to torture the women all night, and drop them off the next day at the locations where they were found."

"That's great, Kurt, but not anywhere near enough to bring charges," Sinclair remarked, yet his dark eyes lit with excited interest.

Hix handed the papers back to Kurt. "What about his background? You find anything regarding boating or Navy or something like that?"

Kurt nodded vigorously, his grin broad and triumphant. "Yes to that too. He did a short stint in the Coast Guard. Get this, he was dumped out because he failed the psychological tests. Tended to go psychotic when he got angry. Hurt people."

"And," a voice came from the doorway as Prince strode in. "That ain't all. He was kicked out of several of the sex clubs for excessive violence and brutality. Put a few women in the hospital. He liked to brand them without permission and that's a no no."

The three men turned to Prince as he took a seat. Kurt said, "Yeah but, they said the same about all the Ajanel males."

Prince shook his head. "True, but, the others received warnings, they weren't kicked out and their memberships revoked. But Chevalier's was. He took a couple of women home and broke bones, sliced skin open with knives, and he loved to burn them. With, get this," he grinned as the other men leaned towards him with intent curiosity. "He didn't burn them with cigarettes, boys, he used a curling iron."

Before anyone spoke, Kurt told them, "I'm waiting on a video from a local Barnes and Noble on the South African magazine. The only store in the state that carries it. I found the magazine. I had the receipts located and then the film of those days pulled, I have Emilee reviewing it to see who purchased the mags. I'm-"

The other men's brows rose almost comically, then lowered with his comprehension.

"Oh hell, the curling iron," Kurt said, "that's what made the circles on our vics." He frowned. "But that's still not enough to arrest him. The lack of alibi and lying about it, the knots, his beating and disfiguring women with a curling iron, even the magazine if we can tie him to it, all totally circumstantial, a lawyer will say coincidence."

Hix's phone rang, it was Burke. While Hix spoke with the doctor, Prince turned his phone on and brought up a copy of what was on Hix's phone, and he showed Kurt the comparison of the cell photo and the computer screen.

Kurt's eyes bulged wide. "Holy hell."

Prince nodded. "You said it, bro."

Hix said into the phone, "Doc, could those burns on the vics have been made from a curling iron?"

A grunt then, "Yepper. That'd be it. Good job. Now, let me tell you about those pictures you sent me."

Before he had the last word out, Hix was already on his feet and grabbing his keys and jacket, he ordered, "Let's go."

*********

On the way to Chevalier Ajanel's home, Prince received a call from Emilee Rivera. He put it on speaker, "Go," he said in answer.

"Nice," Emilee groused.

"In a hurry here, Em, just give it." Prince rolled his eyes at Hix who was driving. Sinclair and Kurt were in the back. Kurt was calling for backup to meet them at Chevalier's house.

"You guys are all alike, you know," she complained, "no finesse, no manners-"

283

"Goddammit Rivera, enough of your shit," Hix barked from the driver's side, "give us the info."

There was silence. Then, her voice stilted and small, Officer Rivera said, "The receipts for the magazines were paid in cash, but Chevalier Ajanel is clear as a bell on the cameras purchasing them. The clerk even remembered him.

"He told her he was buying a subscription for his father's birthday and was going to wrap up one of the magazines as a gift. It's not conclusive evidence, Princeton, the fragment could have been from any magazine at anyone's house. It could have transferred from one of his brothers or his father, even one of the wives, I think that-"

Prince disconnected and stuffed the phone in his pocket. "Okay, Penn, you spoke with the doc then we all raced out here, tell us what Burke said."

His thumb tapping on the wheel, Hix's mouth twisted in a crooked grin. "Okay. I noticed when I watched the video of the killer setting his hand on the post, something niggled in the back of my mind. So I reviewed the tapes of the Ajanels, that's when I saw it. I compared the pictures, as I showed you. Both the killer and Chevalier Ajanel had strange thumbs. They were noticeably shorter than would be normal, but only one thumb, not both."

Prince remarked, "Totally weird."

Nodding, Hix said, "I thought maybe they both *coincidentally* got the tips lopped off at some point, but, I studied them hard and sent the pictures to Burke. They weren't amputated, the thumbs grew that way."

"Did Burke say what caused it? Or what-"

"Patience, Daron," Hix tossed back over the seat behind him. "Yes, the affliction or whatever you'd call it is called Brachydactylic type D. Type D unilateral means only one thumb. Some people have it in both thumbs. They're born that way, they're stub thumbs. In the old days they called them, get this, Murderer's Thumb. How's that for apropos?"

Kurt said from the back seat, "How rare is it? What are the chances that it's, again, coincidental that both men have the condition? Can we use it in court?"

Hix nodded with a half-grin. "Oh yessir, you bet we can. It's rare, but not as much as you'd think. Megan Fox the actress actually has the disorder. But, with the stub thumbs and the partial print on the post, hell, that's enough for a warrant. And I'm damned sure with the match, along with the twine sailor knots, the fragment from the magazine, the false alibis, he flat out lied, the DA can start building a case."

From behind them Kurt grunted. "Megan Fox, eh? Hell, I was always so busy checking out that face, that body, who would look at her hands?"

# Chapter Thirty-Three

As she raised her hand to ring the bell the door opened.

Chevalier Ajanel grinned at her. "Hey, honey, to what do I owe this lovely surprise?"

She had thought of a cover story on the way there. "Hey Chev, I thought I'd catch up with Jewel on the shower for Dottie's wedding." Laurin knew Jewel wasn't home, she had told the family a few weeks ago she was going out of town to visit her sister who'd just had a baby. She brought their own baby Channing with her.

Laurin had called Chevy's practice and learned he was not there, that he had returned home because he'd forgotten to bring his cell with him to work. She had hoped to see him alone.

Chevy stepped aside, gestured. "Come in, Laurin." He waited until Laurin passed him then he shut the door. "Why don't we go to the living room?" He escorted her from the foyer and down a wide hallway then turned and walked through a large open archway.

"Oh!" Laurin exclaimed as she strolled across the burgundy carpet. Pointing above the fireplace. "That's new, Chevy, it's fantastic!" Carrying her album she hurried over to admire the painting hanging over the mantel.

"Yes," his voice right behind her, very close behind her made her heart skip a beat. Without turning around, she took a step towards the fireplace.

He moved to stand next to her. "We bought that little beauty on our last trip to Paris. I found it striking." He sighed. "Jewel thought it would be a good investment. The artist is up and coming but quite elderly." He chuckled. "Jewel figures he'll produce only a few masterpieces, then he'll die, then we can sell this one for a fortune, eh?"

"How, um, clever of her." Laurin spun around and pretended to take a survey of the room so she could put some space between them. She set the album on a table.

Chevy clasped his hands behind his back and gazed at her with a benign smile. "Can I get you something to drink?"

"Um," Laurin smiled and replied, "I don't think so. I just wanted to speak with Jewel," she glanced around as if looking for her.

His arms dropped, Chevy said, "She isn't home. Her sister had a baby, Jewel is off in Kentucky helping her. But then, didn't you know that? She talked about it several times while we were at your home for dinner. Don't you remember? She went on and on, complaining about how her sister had married a true blue blood." His laugh a grunt, mouth pursed.

"Yep. Jewel says although the Ajanels are wealthy, I'm a doctor, and Rádolfo is quite prestigious with his ambassadorship, but," he huffed and shook his head in annoyance. "Her sister married *real* aristocracy and that can't be bought no matter how wealthy you are."

"Chevy-"

He kept on, his face hardening, eyes narrowed, "No, Jewel thinks we Ajanels are just peasant immigrants from a poor, shithole of a country. We were all born in South Africa, she mocks our Portuguese accents even as mild as they are, oh," he smiled dourly, "not in front of Rádolfo of course, she's not into suicide." A coarse laugh cracked out as he shook his head again.

Seeing he was growing angry, Laurin said quickly, "Um, now that you mention it, I do recall Jewel mentioning the trip. I'm so sorry to have bothered you, I think I should go." She looked towards the doorway.

His head cocked up and tilted, he stared at her through thinned lids. "How are you here, Laurin?" He straightened and took a step to her. His smile rose in a mean slant, he said callously, "Everyone knows my father refuses to allow you to ever leave the mansion without him present or with a guard. You've never been here before without being on his arm." Resentment wreathed through his words, brows the color of coffee lanced down.

Laurin continued facing him but she backed away. "It's, uh, he's out of town, so I thought, I'd uh, visit Jewel. I'd forgotten that Jewel would be away. I-I thought it's a lovely day, maybe we could all lounge out on your patio, it's still too cold to swim," she laughed awkwardly, "uh, well for me, you men don't seem to mind as long as the pool is heated. I thought-"

Chevy moved to his doctor's bag sitting on an end table and removed something from it then he stuffed his hands in his pockets, one of them fisted inside.

Two steps and he was less than a foot from Laurin. He still looked benign but his lids lowered, hooding his eyes, his smile rose with a foreboding slant. His voice soft and oily he said, "You finally put two-and-two together, sweet little Laurin."

The smile widened as he shook his head. "You must have seen the news and remembered that day at your house, when Blane and I had been swimming. You came here today to see if what you think you saw was true. You'd hoped to get me to take my shirt off."

His head angled in thought, but he smirked lamentably. "I'm always so careful, the others tease me for wearing a shirt, even in the pool, alas," he shrugged, "I was remiss that day."

"I, um, I guess I should go, Chevy, you're right. I slipped out, if Rádolfo gets word that I came here, and well," her weak smile false, "he would be furious."

He sidestepped her and blocked her forward movement. "No one else noticed."

His tone filled with self-pity he said, "No one ever really looks at me, they never have. Not when my brothers beat on me when we were growing up. I tried to show my mother my bruises, ha, she didn't give two fucks. My wife insists on sex in the dark, she says my figure is displeasing. I should be more muscular she tells me, like that Thor character. Cripes. I've told her he's padded but she believes what she wants."

His mouth twitched wryly. "We were not a love match. She wanted money, and I wanted…" he stared at Laurin under low lids.

"Listen, Chevy-"

"Yeah, I'm insignificant. No one pays attention to the mild, geriatric physician. Except you, my beautiful Laurin. Because you're so sweet and treat everyone with supreme kindness, you noticed, because unlike everyone else, you really look at people. You really see them."

Her head down, Laurin started for the door but Chevy moved and blocked her way again.

He growled bitterly, "You were supposed to be mine." His voice grew louder, harsher. His thumb jabbed at his chest as he repeated, "*Mine*. My father bought you for me, but," he frowned with contemptuous anger, "he stole you from me. Kept you for himself." He set his hands on his hips. He wore jeans and a flannel shirt.

A small smirk played at his lips. "If you couldn't talk me into going into the pool, what else would you have done to get me to take my shirt off? Would you have tried to entice me? Seduce me to get my clothes off? Would you have gone that far, little Laurin?"

Adamantly shaking her head, blonde hair swatted across her back with her denial, "No, of course not. I'm married to your father, I wouldn't think to, I mean you're wrong, uh, about whatever it is you're thinking. I came to see Jewel, and like I said, I really must be going." She made to go around him but he stepped right into the doorway. She jumped back.

"Is this what you wanted to see, my Laurin?" Chevy gripped the sides of his shirt and ripped it open, buttons flew in all directions pinging off tables and lamps. He jerked his shirt out of his jeans and pulled it completely open.

Her eyes round with horror, Laurin saw what she had hoped she had imagined, what she'd hoped were just marks and scars with no real pattern. Her breath sucked in swiftly, her hands covered her mouth dropping open in fear.

On Chevalier's displayed abdomen were marks, but they did have a pattern. A bunch of x's in a heart-shaped circle with big round burn marks in the center.

"Oh my God, Chevy, what, how did that happen?" She couldn't drag her horrified wide-eyed gaze away from the cruel torture that was carved and burned into his skin. The white X's were faded, they were old, the burn marks dark red circles, wrinkled in unforgiving scars.

He ran a palm over the scars, an onerous sadness clouded his eyes. He wasn't seeing Laurin right now, he was somewhere else. Laurin's panicked breaths brought him back to the present, his morbid smile brought deeper panic to her soul. He lifted a hand to cup her face but she turned her head away. His mouth pinched, eyes tapered in anger.

"I'll tell you, Laurin, I've never told anyone else ever before. I tried to show my dad, only once." His eyes closed. "He made me regret telling him about them. Like I said, no one ever noticed them, or would have cared if they had. But," this time he did grasp her jaw to hold her from moving from him. "I'll tell you because my long desire, dream for the past 18 months, has been to inflict these very marks on your lovely porcelain skin."

He grinned wickedly at the terror that flung her eyes into panicked saucers. She tried to twist out of his grasp but he had fingers like thick daggers.

"Yes, my darling." He moved his face close to hers so he could watch the fear blaze in her blue eyes. "Yes, that's what the old man calls you, *darling*. Now, you are my darling, as you always should have been, right sweetheart?"

When she didn't respond, he moved her head up and down in an agreeing nod. "That's right, darling. So, you wanted to know how this," he waved at his belly, "occurred? I'll tell you."

She garbled through her taut jaw, "No, please Chevy, I don't need to know."

Holding her face, he pulled her over to the large, thickly cushioned couch and pushed her to sit. He flopped down right next to her and set his big hand on her knee holding her down.

"Okay now, my father's first wife, my mother, was mentally unstable." He snorted. "Understatement that, hon." His face crunched up as he drew up the memories.

"No, she was sick as shit, deranged, a holy terror on two feet. Schizophrenic they'd labeled her. They took her away every so often, locked her up for a few months, gave her meds, proclaimed her stabilized and then released her back home.

"Home...to where I was, defenseless, powerless, a voodoo doll for her enjoyment to play with, get all her anger out, stabbing pins in me like she believed she was stabbing people she hated. Like my father. Thankfully, most of the pinholes have faded. Mostly." He squeezed her knee.

Her arms wrapped around her body protectively, Laurin tried to squirm away from him but he squeezed her knee so hard she yelped in pain.

"Now, now," he said, patting her leg then gripped her knee again. "Be a good girl. We're going to be spending a lot of time together. So, as I was saying, my childhood. Well, childhood makes it sound soft and innocent, my youth was anything but.

"Every time she returned from a stay at the hospital, at first, she was calm, tranquil, she'd be drugged up to her eyeballs. She was like a zombie, which, was a break for me. Bad thing was, after a few days she'd stop taking her meds, and blam," he clicked his fingers, "she was the wicked witch of hades."

Laurin wrenched her leg from his grasp and went to leap to her feet, Chevy threw his arm around her shoulders and jerked her back down.

"Stop it," he growled, "I don't want to hurt you yet. We haven't started our playtime. Now," he winked at her, "where was I? Oh yes, dear Mama. She had long blonde hair, it swept over me when she...played with me. Her hair dresser liked to put some sort of glitter in her hair, gold glitter that shimmered while she carved those X's in my belly."

At Laurin's cringe, he gave her a hug. "Yep. She claimed they were signs of her love, you know, the X's and O's, hugs and kisses." Chevy chuckled with angry mirth.

He sat back pulling Laurin with him. "She wore this rose-gold colored kimono, it would drape down, flow so softly over me, like satin, so incongruous with the torture she was inflicting."

He paused as the memories gripped him, then went on, "When she tired of slicing the X's into my gut, she'd heat up the ol' curling iron and burn these round marks in the center of the heart-shaped circle she'd make. You know, the X's were the kisses, the circles the hugs. Inside the heart shaped circle because she just loooved me so much."

Laurin pushed and pulled, shoving at him but contrary to Jewel's declaration, he was quite muscular and held her as if she was a weak little bunny.

"But, that wasn't all, my sweet, nope," he said gaily giving her a strong hug. "No, back to the voodoo doll. She'd made a real one, but Dad found it and tossed it out. That made her mad, well, madder. So," he heaved out a sigh and smiled, "she decided I'd make the perfect little voodoo doll. Every time she got angry at someone, anyone, for any real or imagined slight, she stuck a big old needle in me. Later I'll show you my back, some of the scars still remain along with the other slices and dices and burns."

Trying to twist from his grasp, Laurin's voice was soft and sympathetic. "Chevy, it was horrible what she did to you, an unprotected child. Did you tell your father? Your teachers? Anyone?" Her expression was rife with compassion and sorrow for the young child that had been so horribly tortured.

"Huh," he snorted inelegantly. "I told you, I told my Dad. Once. Only once. He beat the living shit out of me, more than my brothers ever had, or even my mom when she was on a particularly long cruel roll.

"Dad told me if I breathed a word of it to anyone he'd see that I disappeared. And not like out of town or something, really disappear, not exist anymore. He didn't want the reputation of having a messed up family spoil his lucrative businesses, or his great ambassadorship."

"Oh, Chevy, that's awful." He held her smashed against him with one arm, she set her hand on his other arm in sympathy. "But now, now you can get help for your tormented memories. You can speak with someone, I can-"

"No!" he roared and crushed her against him harder.

Laurin couldn't draw a breath he held her so tightly, his arm like a steel log.

He gripped her jaw and jerked her to face him. "You see, my Laurin, I could have dealt. I did. I'd tucked the memories, the abuse way back in my brain. But, then, my father, your husband," he shook his head swallowing down the rage that threatened to boil over.

Sucking in a deep breath, letting it out with a loud huff, he said, "He bought you for me. I was…enamored. The second I laid eyes on you, darling, I was in love. You were a glorious vision, and you were going to be mine. All mine."

He smiled tenderly and wrapped his other arm around her and hugged her tightly. At her hands clawing his shirt and her gasps for air, he slightly loosened his grip.

"Anyway, you were snatched out of my grasp. He stole you, he fucked you in the mansion even when he knew I was in the house. He did it to taunt me, the bastard. I was so enraged, I couldn't think. I stupidly ran right out and married Jewel. I felt, somehow I had to be even. Ha," he snorted, "that's a laugh. My whoring greedy wife compared to you, all precious innocence and child-like eyes filled with wonder, not even close. But, Dad was killing that wonder in you, he was destroying you."

Laurin fought to get away but her efforts were in vain. He was too big, too strong. He just cuddled her closer. He told her, "You know Jewel's girlfriend, her best friend was one of the women that got me kicked out of my favorite decadent club. Sure, I was a bit rough, I didn't mean to slice her leg open, I didn't mean to strangle her until she passed out, I didn't mean the broken ribs, really," he raised his shoulders sheepishly.

"Then the topper was, Jewel got pregnant, I thought, yes, finally, something of my own. I was denied you, but now I could have a piece of me, but," his lips pulled in, head lowered in pain.

Then he lifted his head and looked at Laurin, egregious despair burned in his brown eyes, he blinked back a tear that eased out.

Bone-jarring rage scraped with bitter betrayal in his voice, he went on, "The topper was, Channing isn't mine. My whore of a wife got pregnant from one of her copious lovers, she says she doesn't even know who his father is. Well, that was it. That took the cake, you know what I mean?"

"Chevy, please, let me get you some help." Tears sprung out he was squeezing her so hard.

"That tipped the scale, the straw over the camel's back, I was finally done with it all. They kept taking away what was mine, so I took them back. Those girls, Laurin," he cradled her jaw and gazed lovingly into her compassionate eyes.

"They were you. Not really you of course, just, replicas. Toys until I got the real thing. I'd always planned to take you back one day. It was difficult because my father had you locked up like Fort Knox. Isn't it funny, darling," he paused and kissed the tip of her nose.

Resting his forehead on Laurin's, he said, "That I needed to get my hands on you and it was so hard. You were never allowed out of the mansion, and when you were, you had guards or my old man alongside. Then, when I finally thought, hey, just go in and snatch her out when my father's away, you were gone, Laurin. Gone. Out of my father's possessive grasp. But, I *still* couldn't get to you because that damned cop stole you and hid you away."

He suddenly leapt to his feet and yanked her up with him. He clutched her arms and shook her. "Yes, again, something of mine taken from me. I was plotting how I could find where you were, when," his smile suddenly bloomed bright and cheerful.

"Here you are, darling. You walked right into my den. Right into my hands. And, there are no witnesses. None. I can have you for as long as I want. Where I'm taking you, you will never be found. Never, my sweet."

"No, Chevy, please, listen to me, don't do this, please-" her words cut off in a shriek as he jammed his hand in his pocket, withdrew a syringe and stabbed it in her neck.

He stared into her eyes as he watched her pupils dilate.

"Yeah, that's it. I got you baby. God I love watching you girls go under, and you my Laurin, you were worth the wait. You are the juicy ripe cherry on top I've waited so long for," and he caught her as she collapsed.

# Chapter Thirty-four

With Prince, Daron and Kurt around him and backup officers covering the rear of the house, Hix banged his fist on the front door. He knocked again, louder, called out, "Brevet Bay Police! Open up!"

He was about to kick the damned door in when it slowly opened partway. Hix could see the frightened white face of a female peering around the door at them.

"Mrs. Ajanel?" Hix asked as he pushed the door open, forcing her to move to the side or get steamrolled. He stomped inside looking around, his hand on the gun holstered at his hip.

"Huh? Huh? Yes, that's me," the woman choked out. Her hand at her throat, she jumped out of the way as the officers barged inside behind Hix with guns drawn.

"Spread out, people," Hix boomed his order. "We're looking for Chevalier Ajanel and anything that could tie him to the murders."

"M- murders?" the woman squawked, her hand pressed harder against her throat, eyes as wide as freakin' satellites dishes.

Hix turned to her. Pulling a paper from his inside coat pocket, he unfolded it and stuck it in her face. "We have a warrant, Mrs. Ajanel, for the arrest of Chevalier Ajanel, and we also have a search warrant to search the premises. You may sit down there," he pointed to a divan, "don't move, and keep your mouth shut unless you want to tell us where your husband is."

Then woman staggered backwards, the backs of her legs hit the seat he'd indicated and she fell onto it with a puffed out, '*oof.*' Her hand still at her throat, she cowered from the fierce detective stammering, "My- my husband? He- he's at work."

"No he isn't, we just came from there, they said he was here at home." Hix could hear his people shouting out, "Clear! Clear!" Indicating their search for Chevalier Ajanel was not coming to fruition.

Whispering, "No," she blinked, tugging at a button on her flowered blouse. It was tucked into a matching full skirt that stopped a few inches below her knees. "No, I just left him twenty minutes ago at the office, he's there."

Hix marched over and lowered to set his hands on his knees and got in her face. "Stop lying, Mrs. Ajanel, he is not there. If you harbor him, or refuse to tell us where he is, you will be arrested as an accessory."

He leaned in so close he could smell her flowery rose perfume, it made his nose wrinkle. "Do you hear me? Now, where is Chevalier Ajanel?"

She blinked at him, her mouth worked but nothing came out except, "Ah, ah, ah." Her eyes bounced from Hix to the other officers tromping through the home and collided back with Hix's fearless, ruthless glare. "Uh, Chevy? Why would I know where Chevy is?"

Now Hix blinked with angry consternation. "Because you're his wife, Mrs. Ajanel. I'll ask you one more time, where is your husband?"

She raised her hand and set her palm on her forehead that was beading with sweat. "Ah, ah," she croaked again, then cleared her throat. "Chevy is not my- my husband."

Hix's spine turned rigid. "You are Mrs. Ajanel are you not? You said you were when you opened the door. You are in Chevalier Ajanel's home, is that not right? Ergo, he is-"

Her fingers clutched at the front of her blouse she squeaked, "My brother-in-law. I- I am Geraldine Ajanel. My husband is Raoul Ajanel."

Hix froze, blinked rapidly as he took in her words. "What the fuck are you doing here then? You people playing musical homes? Wife swapping and that shit?"

Her brows disappeared into her hairline, her mouth dropped wide open in refutation. Hix could see the majority of her lower teeth. They were artificially white. "What? No!" she shouted in horror. "Absolutely not!"

Hix inhaled in a long, deep breath, let it out slowly, but it didn't dispel his impatience. "Then," he said slowly, carefully, as if she were a dull child, "why the hell are you here alone then?" He stood up straight. His movement caused her to cower again into the divan.

"I- I," she gulped, tried to swallow, her mouth was dry from fright. "Jewel is out of town for a few weeks." That was all she said.

"Yeah, and so, you came here to keep her husband company?"

Her lashes flew up again. "What? No! If Raoul ever thought his little brother and I...well, you know," red flushed her pallid complexion. "He would kill us both. Seriously. He would put us both in a grave. Raoul doesn't allow anyone to touch anything of his, including his wife. Um, me."

Dragging both hands through his hair, Hix tried to calm his voice, he repeated, "Tell me why you are here? Be specific," *for fuck's sake* he muttered under his breath.

Geraldine clutched her fingers in her lap to still their trembling and told him, "When- when Jewel goes out of town for any length of time, I come and check on things. I water the plants, check that the maids and lawn maintenance are doing their jobs. With no one here to watch them sometimes they slack off." The side of her mouth pulled in with disgust she complained, "Lazy people they are, you know?"

Hix wouldn't know. Didn't want to know. "Dr. Ajanel can't take care of his own house?" He glanced around. They were in a grand foyer standing on sparkling, black-and-white diamond-shaped tiled flooring.

The walls were octagonal with antique white wallpaper that was streaked with gold. A chandelier hung right over a marble table in the center of the room that held a vase flowing with a bouquet of colorful flowers.

Around the room were black and gold divans, with small glass tables near them. Hix could hear his people shouting back and forth and heavy footsteps pounding on the stairs and across the floors.

Geraldine shook her head with a droll smile. "No, Chevalier is seldom here. He spends long hours at his practice, and Jewel says he's out many nights, all night. Besides, he wouldn't lift a finger to water a plant or correct a staff. That would be beneath him," she sniffed.

"Why aren't there any servants here now?" Hix asked her.

She turned towards an open hallway and frowned at the voices traveling down it. "With Jewel out of town, Chevy sometimes sends them all home. He hates having anyone underfoot if she isn't here to run interference."

Hix silently regarded the woman. He could have slapped the side of his head, he was an idiot. He'd spent hours reviewing the tapes of interviews conducted at the station. He'd paid little attention to the haughty obnoxious Ajanel wives. He remembered they were loud and flashy. Who knew which one was married to which Ajanel son?

This one, his eyes narrowed at her, was dowdy. Her hair a swirling mess, the dress didn't fit her right, her hair was a disheveled brown. Yeah, now he recalled her, she was so plain and mousey he hadn't paid her much attention. He recalled she was married to the eldest Ajanel son.

"Okay," Hix said, "do you know where we can find Chevalier Ajanel? He is not at his practice."

Geraldine shrugged one shoulder. "I really couldn't say. I wouldn't know where he spends his free time."

"Does he have a girlfriend?" Prince strolled up.

Geraldine's unladylike snort came out derisive, she glanced at him and shook her head with an amused half-smile. "No. That's how that girl, that gold-digging slut came into our lives."

Hix wanted to smack her talking about Laurin like that, but he bit his tongue as Geraldine continued talking.

"Chevy was so busy, so shy, he just didn't have the time, and he was so reserved and terribly introverted, he found it difficult to talk to women. At the clubs he could hide behind the mask and playact a role. He reveled in it, or so I hear. We wives weren't allowed at the clubs," she said that with envious regret, and an embarrassed blush.

She looked up at Hix with a sigh. "I am much like Chevy. Shy, retiring, I would have liked to have done what he did, go in disguise and become someone else. Live a different, flamboyant, sexy, maybe dangerous life for a night." Her eyes danced away from Hix as the blush darkened, filling more of her fair skin. She fidgeted, smoothing the skirt of her dress.

Hix stood stoically listening to her, Prince now beside him, and Kurt was striding across the floor to join them.

Geraldine simpered, her lashes fluttered at him, "You, Detective, do you ever go to the clubs? Perhaps I could tag along sometime with you."

His stomach turned, the bitch was flirting with him. Prince snickered in his ear. And she called Laurin a slut. Jeesh. "Mrs. Ajanel, you just got through telling me your husband would kill you and any man you were with if he caught you."

Her shoulder rolled up coyly to her ear, the smile was now coquettish. Peering up at him under her fluttering lashes, her heated gaze tramped all over his big strapping body, she gushed, "Oh but that's the thing, Detective, we wear masks. We could tell him you were taking me into the police station for more questioning. He would never know-"

"We gotta go. Prince, Kurt, tell the officers to keep looking, search every square inch of the house and the grounds, any outbuildings. There's a boat out back, have them check it out." Hix grit his teeth and stomped out the door to his truck.

He jerked the door opened and threw himself inside and slammed the door. "Damn," he cursed pounding the steering wheel with his fist.

The passenger doors opened and Kurt, Sinclair and Prince climbed in, and Hix drove off towards the station.

"It's all good, Hix," Sinclair said from the rear. "At least we know who we're looking for. We got a bolo out on him. We'll get him."

"Yeah," Hix grunted. "But will it be before he takes another woman?"

The men sat in morose silence the rest of the way to the station.

As he parked, Hix's cell rang. "Hixman," he barked into the phone without looking at it.

"Honey?" It was his mother.

"Yeah, Ma, kinda busy right now." Well, he wasn't really, they didn't have a next step yet. Maybe forensics would find something useful at Chevalier's house to indicate where he was holing up. Every bar, restaurant, shop in town would be hit by an officer. This case took priority, every free officer was on it.

"Of course dear. You have Laurin there with you?"

His heart stopped. "Laurin? No. She's home." Silence. "She is home with you, isn't she, Ma?"

"Um, well, oh dear…"

"Fuck, Ma, tell me what's going on?"

"Don't you curse at me, young man, I'll wash that mouth right out," she threatened him.

"Ma, please," his heart was still not beating.

He heard her take a deep breath then she said, "We were outside hanging up the laundry when I noticed she was in pain and growing weary. I insisted she go in for a nap. But, well, when I came inside and went to check on her, I discovered she wasn't in the house."

"Fuck, Ma," he groaned, his fingers raked through his hair, panic surged up his throat.

"Penn-"

"Skip the lecture, Ma. Where could she go? Maybe Kullen or Dad or Cliff, what about Suzetta, maybe one of them came by and took her out for lunch or shopping or something."

"No, honey, they wouldn't do that. They have your orders she's not to leave the house. They are quite aware of the danger she's in. Benji was with your father at the park riding the carousel. There was a, she left a," her inhale was audible. "She left a note, Penn. She borrowed some money from my purse and apparently called one of those car services."

The panic was digging its fingers into his throat, he could barely draw a breath. "What did the note say?" Surely she wouldn't be foolish enough to go back to Ajanel? Didn't she trust Hix by now, that he would bring her brother home and keep them all safe?

He heard rustling, then, "Um, it says, 'Dear Mrs. Hixman, I am so sorry but I needed to borrow some money. Please forgive me for taking the money, I swear I'll pay it back. Regards, Laurin Ajanel.'"

Hix started to speak but she rushed over him. "Then she called and left a message. She, oh, dear, honey, she said she saw a news report and it triggered a memory. She thinks… she might know who that- that killer, The Poser is, and she's going to go check him out. She said she didn't want to bother you and call you, but she didn't want us worrying about why she wasn't here. Honey, my goodness, I was outside a long time, she may have been gone for hours by now."

His heart started beating again, but now it raced. Hix felt his insides just flow down his body in cascading, drowning terror. "Oh, God," he groaned. Prince looked over from his front passenger seat.

"I pushed the callback number she dialed but it didn't go through. I'm so sorry, honey."

"Ah, okay, Ma, let me know if she calls, or comes home, or…anything." He hung up, his shoulders hunched.

"Penn?" Prince said his name quietly.

Hix turned his head to face him but his eyes were blank. "It's Laurin. She thinks she figured out who the killer might be, and the damned fool went to see if she could prove it."

"Uh, Penn," Kurt said from the backseat. "We were at Chevalier's home, neither he nor Laurin were there, so she likely thinks it's someone else and she's safe."

Hix ran his hands through his hair then scrubbed them down the front of his face, "No. His work said had gone home. He was here. He took her somewhere. She's a smart cookie, I'm sure she figured out it was that fuck. She must have gotten here before Geraldine

Ajanel and us. I'll get a dump on my folks' phone to learn the car service she used and confirm where they drove her."

The men sat taking in this information, while Hix called an officer at the station to get the number and info and told him to contact him right away when he gets the information. Concluding his call, they had arrived at the station. He opened his door and sprang out. The others followed on his heels.

"What are you doing now, bro?" Prince asked, jogging after him.

Pulling out his phone, striding fast, Hix muttered, "He's gotta have a second home, a cottage, cabin maybe. We need to contact the wife and the brothers, even the old bastard Ajanel himself to see if they know. We can check property deeds, find something in his name." They hurried inside to get to work.

Hix called other counties requesting extra help from their officers to help track down information. Now his heart was climbing up his throat, he thought he'd suffocate or puke, didn't know which was first his fear was so great.

Grousing out loud he promised, "That damned little girl, what the hell was she thinking? When I find her, and I will, she's gonna get a paddling she won't ever forget!"

Ignoring his friends' grins at his announcement, he got down to work.

# Chapter Thirty-five

Laurin came around slowly, her limbs felt like they weighed two tons and she couldn't open her eyes. *What on earth*? Had she relapsed, was she back in the hospital? Benji must be beside himself with worry. She tried hard to move, and moaned when the effort was to no avail.

"There you are darling, I've been waiting forever for you to wake."

The male voice was familiar, but her ears were buzzing, her head fuzzy, eyes gluey. She turned towards the voice. "*Where...*" came out in a sigh, it was all she could say. She felt a large warm palm stroke her forehead.

"There, there darling, take it slow, it'll be a few minutes before you shake off the effects of the sedative."

Her eyes crinkled in a wince. "Drugs? Am I back in the hospital?" Her voice faltered, so dizzy, she concentrated just on breathing in and out.

"No, my Laurin, you are here with me, in my special place."

The words crept eerily into her ears, causing goose bumps to pop up her arms with a foreboding chill.

Her eyes fluttered as she struggled to open them, she could barely feel her dry lips as she licked them. "Your...place?" she eked out hoarsely.

"Yes darling. Take your time, I don't want you to harm yourself," he paused as she tried to move her arms and legs, "that's my job," he said with a little giggle.

She froze. She must have heard him incorrectly. Blinking hard, she forced her eyes open and saw an amused, blurry, Chevalier Ajanel peering down at her.

"Oh goody, finally," he crowed, clapping his hands together. "I've been so eager for you to come alert so we can play."

"*Play?*" voice a rasped whisper, her lids drooped, it was work to force them to open. He looked different, somehow.

His gaze didn't shyly dart away as it normally would, his mouth was loose in a macabre grin. She remembered. She had gone to his house to see if she could get him to take his shirt off so she could see if he had the scar pattern of the serial killer they were seeking.

*Oh Lord, Chevy was The Poser*! She hadn't really believed he was, at least she had hoped she was just being overly imaginative, that's why she didn't call Penn and tell him of her suspicions. Her stomach clenched when the full extent of her predicament hit her.

Berating herself, she should have called Penn anyway, no one knows where she went, or where she was now. She was pretty sure they were no longer in Chevy's home. Her body squirmed with adrenalin caused by the sudden panic that gripped her.

If she couldn't get away from him on her own, he was going to savagely torture her, and eventually kill her.

He saw her blanch. "Ah, my sweetheart, you are recalling what happened." His lips pushed out in a chiding frown. "It was naughty of you Laurin," his voice roughened, "and dangerous to confront me alone. I thought you were smarter than that. Are you just gorgeous angelic fluff?" He lifted a lock of her hair and toyed with it.

"Chevy, please," she gasped for air to fill her lungs, wheezed out, "this isn't you." Closing her eyes for a few seconds to regain her strength, she opened them, and saw pure evil, triumphant, lust-filled, vile evil.

His head fell back with his loud clap of laughter. He chuckled for a minute then wiped a brown eye and smiled at her. "That's the thing, sweetheart, this is the real me. Those years they allowed that sick bitch to inflict her torture on me, yes, they created me. You know," he pulled a chair over and sat down so they were more eye level.

Laurin was lying flat on her back on something that was cold and hard, like on a sheet over steel.

Even sitting down he still loomed above her. He looked down at her and said matter-of-factly, "The Gold Girls weren't my first kills." He grinned at the horror that struck her beautiful face.

"Yep." He nodded proudly. "I started years ago when I traveled. Paris, Germany, Italy, crowded places where the police would be seeking a local resident as the killer. Sure, I played with some animals as a child, but people started getting suspicious so I had to stop."

Setting his hands on his thighs, he rubbed his palms on the coarse jean material, his face stiffened. "Those women were just for fun. But the Gold Girls," his expression relaxed back to smug, he explained, "those were, as the shrinks will say, my killing my mother in effigy over and over. I can't deny it. I thought the slave boxes were a nice touch, hmm? Let my creative side show?" He grinned, pleased with himself.

He had replaced the shirt he'd torn with a black thermal. Chevy was a handsome man, well-built, strong jaw and nose. His dark brown hair, clipped fashionably with the top cut longer than the sides was combed neatly off his broad forehead.

Thrilled to have a captive audience, he went on, "Jewel, my whoring wife slunk out with gigolos that took her to the sex clubs, not the ones my brothers and father and I attended, heaven forbid she'd run into one of us. She used a false ID to make sure I didn't find out. The boxes, the naked kneeling, the chain, kind of a slap in the face to my lying, conniving, cheating wife.

"When I'm done killing my mother over and over, that will end with you my sweet, I'll get to her. The torture my Gold Girls suffered will be nothing compared to what Jewel will endure." His mouth tightened, eyes slit in fury.

"I plan on removing each of her limbs. One at a time over a period of time, and keeping her alive so she can be fully aware of every agonizing second she suffers. She'll rue the day she cheated on me, and the ignominy of bearing some other man's bastard child. Bitch. Wish I could have done that to my mother. Queen Bitch."

"But," Laurin drew in a thick breath, she whispered through her scratchy throat, "your mother died. You were free."

He stood up so quickly she flinched. His face was thunderous, his hands clenched in tight fists. "Not until I was grown up, you idiot. My father could have gotten rid of her earlier, when she was abusing me, but no," he paced back and forth shaking his head. "He waited until she got on his nerves with her folly then he finally put her down."

"Pu- put her...down?"

Chevy shrugged negligently. "Yeah. My father. He couldn't be bothered to do something about her when she was torturing, menacing me, it wasn't until he found out she was feeding information to the police about some of his businesses. She was schizo, believed herself to be a spy. Thought she was an international special agent or some such shit. Woman was totally delusional, off her rocker, shoulda been in a cage."

"But-"

Ignoring her wide-eyed disbelief, he went on, "So yes, Father had to take her out. It was listed as a boating accident. Those are notoriously the easiest to create so there's no suspicious hint of homicide."

Laurin's brain was spinning, this had to be a dream, she had to be dreaming. She clamped her eyes closed tightly as if she could make him disappear. He laughed.

"Sorry darling, you aren't dreaming. That's the first thing the other women thought too. Prayed."

He came back and leaned over her. "No, you are wide awake, but yes, I'm gonna be your worst nightmare. Come, I need to put you in position so I can play with you. I want to take you on a tour first, though. I'm very proud of my special place, my artwork."

As she felt pins and needles coming alive in her arms and legs, Laurin became aware she was restrained.

Chevy reached down and first unbound her ankles then her wrists. He rolled his arm under her back and lifted her to sit. She was horrified to realize she couldn't sit up by herself. Her struggles were useless.

She was still under the power of the drug, and he was a large, strong man. She'd have to wait to find her chance to surprise him to make her escape. She realized there would be no rationalizing with him, he had gone around the bend. Years of ghastly abuse had taken their toll.

"Don't worry," he said with a tender smile as he lifted her in his arms. "I'll take care of you, my Laurin. Good care. I plan on keeping you for a very long time, so I need to be careful."

He mumbled under his breath, "Keep the cutting fairly shallow, stay relatively light on the burning. No muscle-blocking meds for a while." He looked down at her, his gaze trailed appreciative over her soft beauty.

"Yes, I want you alert, active, I am so anticipating you fighting me. You're small, delicate, still rather frail, but, I'll plump you up so you can take it. You are a very brave, strong girl to endure what you have with my father to protect Benji, a child that isn't even yours. We both know your struggles and fighting to get away from me will be futile, but nonetheless exhilarating! I am so excited to get started!"

*******

Hix and Prince went back to Chevalier's house to speak with the neighbors and Geraldine Ajanel. No one answered when he knocked and there were no vehicles in the driveway.

Standing on the front porch, Hix called dispatch and got Geraldine's phone number. She had already been contacted to see if she knew of any other property any of the Ajanels owned.

Geraldine answered the call with nervous breaths and wariness, "H-hello?"

"Mrs. Ajanel, this is Detective Hixman, why did you leave Chevalier Ajanel's premises?"

There was a moment of silence, then, "Uh, I felt uneasy after you police left and went home. One of your people called me only thirty minutes ago. Detective, like I told them, I am not aware of any property any of us could possibly own. You need to call our husbands and stop harassing me." She ended not on an assertive note, but a testy one.

She was showing her Ajanel colors, by insemination, but she was an Ajanel, and they had high-powered lawyers, they were not to be harassed.

"This isn't about that. When you arrived at Chevalier's house today, were there any other cars there? Was anyone else in the house?"

Another long moment and a deep sigh before she answered, "No. I told you when you were here that when I arrived no one was home. I had called Mrs. James, the housekeeper, and she told me that Chevalier had sent the staff home. Apparently something caught his attention at the end of the driveway by the street and he told the few staff that were there to leave. He insisted they go out the back door."

She was on speaker, Hix and Prince exchanged a glance. Chevalier must have seen Laurin arrive and cleared the house so there were no witnesses, and no help for Laurin. Hix already had other officers contacting the housekeeping and lawn staff to see if they saw or heard anything.

"All right, Mrs. Ajanel, if you think of anything, please call me," and Hix clicked off. He nodded at Prince. "Let's check the neighbors."

They knocked on a dozen doors before anyone answered. It was daytime and people were at work, or lunch or shopping. Chevalier's home was a mansion as were all the others on the oak-canopied street, therefore there was a lot of space between domiciles.

At one of the homes they noticed two cars in the driveway and car parts laid out on a blanket beside them. Maybe they'd catch a break and they'd get a witness. Hix banged his fist on the door.

Within a second, as if he had been watching them, a tiny elderly man opened the door, his fuzzy white brows arched in question.

Hix flashed his badge and announced, "Good afternoon, I am Detective Hixman, this is Detective Princeton," he tipped his head at Prince. "We would like to ask you a few questions if that's okay?"

The man gazed first at Hix then Prince and nodded. He looked like a wizened elf. Spindly with thin, curved limbs and spine. A thatch of pure white hair topped his head like a snowy bush.

He grinned, there were spaces between his teeth. "I wuz'a wonderin' when you'd git to me. I seen you hit the other houses. No one is home much durin' the day, ya know."

Hix and Prince tried to not glance at each other, the little guy was a character, had to be at least a hundred.

Prince pulled out a notebook and pen, flipped a page and asked, "Can I have your name, sir?"

The tiny wizard squinted an eye at Prince, looked at him from head to toe, then said, "Rudy Valentine."

Prince's bottom lip pushed out like he didn't believe him. He opened his mouth to ask for ID but Hix stopped him.

"Yeah, so," Hix said, "Mr. Valentine, do you know the Ajanels down the street?"

Nodding vigorously, the white bush bounced up and down he replied, "Sure do, sure do. Stupid folks, them."

Keeping his expression from showing surprise, Hix asked, "What do you mean by that?"

Scrawny bent shoulders shrugged. Valentine squinted one bright blue eye at Hix. "What are you, you look kinda fierce, like one a them Eye-talian gladiators that should be inna arena fighting man-eating lions."

Used to the question, Hix's face remained impassive. "Can you explain what you meant by the comment about the Ajanels?"

The old guy shrugged again. "Sure'n nuff. The missus, nasty piece of work. Rude as shit. An talkin' about shit, she don't think hers stinks. She thinks the whole neighborhood don't know what a whorin' trollop that she is.

"Even did my son an one'a his friends. Sleeps wit any fella got a dick. Hell, I even hide my damned mutt when I see Miz Jewel on the loose. Maryanna Dupree down yonder," he motioned with his head towards the street.

Hix and Prince followed his gesture not knowing what he was indicating then looked back at the elf.

"She got pritty sick ways back. No insurance an no family or man to help her. A few of us went about wit a basket to help wit her medical expenses, an trimmed up her lawn, brought her casseroles, cleaned her house an stuff.

"Miz Ajanel had just got outta her car with tons'a shopping packages. I ask her can she spare some bucks for Maryanna, maybe provide a hot meal. Bitch don't even acknowledge me. Swoops right on past me like she wuz a queen, goes inside an slams the door in my face. Bitch." He spat on the ground.

Prince jerked his foot back to avoid the gob of saliva.

Hix asked, "What about Dr. Ajanel? Can you tell us anything about him?"

Chevalier's patients had little to say about the doctor. Said he ran hot and cold, mostly cold. He foisted the majority of the patients off on his assistants and aids and actually didn't spend all that many hours at the practice.

Valentine's wizened face wrinkled up more with distaste. "Weird kinda fella. Keeps to hisself but I seen him talkin' to hisself, a lot, as he works on his van. Piece'a shit the van is. Buys parts offa my son."

Now they did share a glance. Hix asked, "Van? Can you describe it?"

Crossing his skinny arms over his concave chest, Valentine sounded like Hix should already know, "It's a big black van with blacked out windas. He's up to no good 'cause the van ain't actually there much an he keeps mud on the tag. His ride is normally a Jag. His bitch drives a Mercedes."

Hix turned his head towards the direction of Chevalier's house. The images the videos had captured were of a black van with tinted windows. They knew the killer had obscured the plate.

He pictured Chevalier's back yard when earlier he and Prince and other officers had patrolled the entire plot looking for anything that could help them with the case. He said to Valentine, "There's a boat in the back of Ajanel's property, you ever seen him go out in it?"

Shaking his head, the wad of white hair flopped back and forth. "He took it out once or twice years ago, but not since. Pussy. Probly gets sea sick watchin' his bitch douche."

"Hmm," Hix didn't want that image in his head. "Today, did you see any activity at the Ajanels'?"

White bush bobbed up and down. "Yessir. Got nothin' to do all day but spy on my neighbors. Boring assholes they are. Early in the AM the doc left the house. Less than an hour later he come back. He was inside a few minutes or so when a car pulled up out front an the most breathtaking female you ever gonna see got out. Tiny thing, but so hot even at my age my dick went up," he said pragmatically.

Another picture he didn't want in his head. Hix felt energy burn his chest, Laurin had positively been there. "Then what happened?"

"Ah, not much. All'a sudden seen all the remaining help run out the back, hop in their autos an flee down the back exit drive. By the time the young honey git to the door the doc had it opened an ushered her inside. The car droppin' her off left."

"You see what happened with the woman after that?"

He shook his head. "Nopers. Never seen her leave. Only seen the black van pull up to the far side door, park for a minute a so, then it left. A while later that other bitch, the frumpy one goes inside. Nothin' else 'til you cops show."

The information didn't help, it only confirmed what they had already assumed. Laurin was in Chevalier's sociopathic clutches.

Pushing his coat back, Hix set his hands on his hips and dipped his head to the elf. "I guess that's all the questions I have. Prince?" He looked to his friend.

One shoulder bumped up. "I have nothing else." Prince handed the old man a business card. "Anything comes to mind, sir, please don't hesitate to call us, even if it doesn't seem important. The littlest things can have the most significance. Of course call us immediately if you see anyone come to these premises."

Valentine took the card and stuffed it in his worn jean's pocket. "Okey doke, pleased ta meet ya flatfoots. Come by any time."

Hix and Prince said goodbye then started to walk away, when Valentine said, "You catch that fucker, The Poser, I'll be havin' a big celebration barbecue an you folks are invited. Once you lock that asshat doctor up for his abominable deeds we'll have us a party!"

Hix swung around. "Are you talking about Chevalier Ajanel? Are you saying he's The Poser?"

The elf squinted at him like he was dull. "Well, duh. He's creepy as shit, slithers around all sneaky like. He got kicked out of them sex clubs for excessive violence, seriously hurt alotta women. You can see it in his sick eyes he's evil incarnate. Wuz wonderin' when you flatfoots were gonna come take him away."

Moving back to the elderly man, Hix set a palm on a beam that attached the porch to the roof. "Are you saying you knew all along Ajanel was the killer and you never called the police?"

Valentine gave him a sour look. "Fuck right, son. Ain't got no evidence to alert you cops. I'd git laughed right off'n the operator."

Hix pondered that then said with ire, "But the black van. Pictures of it have been all over the television and net, you could have-"

The old man leaned towards him with his bright eyes all squinty as if Hix lacked a brain. "Yeah, right. I'da called, said, 'Hey, come check out this rich prestigious doctor, he's gotta black van like the one all ya lookin' for. Sure, youd'a come right out.

"If they did, take one look at me," he chuckled, "laugh themselves silly they would. Only afford this neighborhood 'cause my dearly beloved wife, Sophia, had inheritance. She passed ten years back." The loss still shadowed the old guy's eyes.

Thinking about it, Hix realized he was right. They'd received hundreds of sightings of black vans, none were viable. However, Hix would have definitely investigated it just because it was an Ajanel and they were looking at the whole clan as suspects.

But, Valentine wouldn't have known that. And, just the old guy's instinct wouldn't have been enough proof to move on Ajanel.

But it would have put the doctor more quickly in Hix's crosshairs. Damn, the time wasted, and they might have put an officer on him, tail him, and Laurin would be safe. Coulda shoulda woulda, Hix couldn't beat himself up or anyone else.

The air in his lungs expelled in a flat sound. "You're right. I apologize for getting on you. Anyway, if you think of anything, or if Chevalier Ajanel or anyone shows up, please give us a ring."

Hix would call and have an officer put on detail watching the house, but it didn't hurt to have another pair of eyes on it. Especially a canny guy like this elf was.

"Shore nuff, son. You boys have a good day, an find that sick fucker, ya hear?"

Hix and Prince headed back to the station. Hix's heart was so heavy it pained him to take a breath. That butchering freak had Laurin.

# Chapter Thirty-Six

He spoke to her with his lips against her hair on the top of her head, "Look, darling, this is where I first bring my girls to inspect them."

Chevy pivoted slowly so Laurin, held snug and caged in his arms, could see the room. It was the size of a bedroom but only contained the gurney she had been lying on and a table with items on it.

Laurin stared at the table feeling her gut pinch. There was a pair of scissors, two knives, rope, a hammer, a roll of electrical tape and an open box that she could see contained bottles of pills, and an assortment of other things that she closed her eyes to.

"Yes," he said, "I bring them here and put them on that table so I can intimately examine them. Usually they're like you were, unconscious. But some are more robust than others and start to waken sooner so I have to tie 'em up and gag 'em. Didn't have to gag you, my love," he grinned proudly down at her, "you're so delicate the sedative still has control over you."

He gestured with his head to the table. "I cut off their clothes here, but sometimes I wait until I get them on the wheel to cut them off."

Laurin didn't dare ask what he meant by the wheel, she feared she'd know soon enough.

He went on, "The knives are because sometimes I get eager and want to start slicing on them right away."

A laborious sigh and he said, "Those are usually the prostitutes I pick up. No one notices when they disappear, or they don't care. It's like having an army of ants at my pleasure. I just scoop one up when I'm in the mood for cutting, and, well, there you go. I play with them while preparing for my Gold Girls.

"The prostitutes aren't good enough to be a Gold Girl, and they don't look like you. You know," he chuckled, "the vast ocean makes a great burial ground. Easy peasy, no digging, burning, chopping into pieces."

She lifted her head to look up at him, then quickly lowered it at the intense lust radiating from his dark eyes.

"You know of course, my love, that I chose each Gold Girl because they resembled you. It's all about getting back what's mine, and doing what I please with it." He said gleefully, "My old man will choke on it when he finds out."

"Chevy," she rasped with a puff of his name, "those are real people." She drew in a tight breath. "Real women with families. You're hurting," she breathed in again, "real people."

He grinned cheerfully. "Yes, I know, isn't it great?" He swung around with her and ambled out the door, muttering, "Give back what I got in spades."

He tramped down a hallway to another room. This one was clearly a bedroom. A massive bed in the center was surrounded by gold. Gold on the plush furnishings, the door handles, an antique desk, dressers, the carpet was rose with gold fibers in it. The bed was covered in a rose-gold duvet.

Chevy squeezed her tightly against his chest. "Yep, later you and I will be here. You'll be chained of course, but you'll be with me and you'll be so thrilled. You will see that I am ten times the man, a hundred times the skillful cruel lover that my father is."

His words made her gag, her stomach recoiled but she kept her mouth shut. She didn't want to anger him when she was still so helpless. Draped across the foot of the bed was a rose and gold satin kimono. The low golden light in the room shimmered over the soft design on it.

Chevy watched her taking everything in with a satisfied smile. "No need to be jealous, sweetness, none of the others ever shared my bed. Bitch of a wife doesn't even know about the yacht. I bought the bed for you and me exclusively. I want you sleeping in my arms every night. Don't worry, I'll have your wounds tightly bandaged, there won't be any blood on the sheets. They're silk, you know."

Yacht? She was on a boat? What were her chances of escaping when they were on the water? It took every bit of strength Laurin could muster to not puke, not pass out from the terror of it all. All that awaited her.

"Okay." He grinned as she curled more tensely in his arms from her fear.

Leaving the room he headed for some stairs. "You don't need to see the kitchen or the deck, you won't be near them. Not that you won't be bound at all times 'cause you will, but the kitchen has knives and the deck is escape. Of course we're out too far for you to swim to land. Besides, hypothermia would get you first. Let me show you my workroom."

He moved down a hall and stepped inside a large room. Wooden tables were covered with tools; carving, polishing, sawing, drilling, cutting, hammering tools, and cans crammed with nails. In a corner was a setup of paint cans and a paint gun.

What looked like blue tarps were stacked against a wall, and next to them was a big pile of wood, long beams. The wood had a rosy-hue to it.

She saw a giant box, or pen, made out of the wood, the rest of the room faded away as she saw her name on a piece of paper taped to the top of it. She'd seen the wooden boxes on the news. Fear bombarded like an ax into Laurin's mind, her brain about short circuited from the sudden intensity of it.

"Now I'm going to show you my pride and joy, sweetie," he told her and carried her back out and went to the stairs. There were four steps going down.

Once down the stairs, he walked a short hall and entered a room. An enormous room. A room of horrors.

Even as tightly as he held her, Laurin's body twitched with such fright it ate at her bones. There was a giant wooden wheel painted straw colored in the center of the room, and there was a table beside it containing some of the same things as the one upstairs, but this one had more, so much more frightening implements.

On one wall hung a variety of whips, chains, serrated metal rods, and what was either a cattle prod or a Taser, she wasn't sure which. She was too terrified to take in anything else.

He jostled her roughly to get her to raise her head. "Look baby, my wall of splendor, showcasing my work, my girls." He beamed proudly.

"I know you're excited to join their gilded glory. Not right away because I want a long time to play with you, but, eventually, you'll be up there. I'll put you at the top because you're my extraordinary prize, my rose-gold goddess. But you'll have to be patient." He sounded like he was scolding a child, a smirking grin tempering the reproach.

Her mouth fell open in dismay. On the wall hung four framed pictures of women. Laurin knew who they were, she recognized them from the news shows. The news only showed their faces. The photos on the wall depicted the full scene.

The kneeling women were naked, their wrists bound so tightly behind their backs their spines arched sharply inward, forcing their breasts to thrust up. A chain lifted their heads, and they were painted rose-gold. And they were all dead.

Behind each girl was a huge wooden box like the one she'd just seen with her name attached to it. Each box resembled the others except each had its own unique scrolls of art carved along the top and side trim.

"Yes darling," Chevy boasted proudly. "I see you are impressed with all of my artwork." He moved closer to the pictures so she could get a better look, and bragged, "I did all that, my love. The building, the carving, the staining, everything. Aren't I quite the skilled one?"

As if her eyes were tacked wide open, Laurin nodded. She couldn't look away from the victims, she didn't know what to say to the monster cawing like a diseased demon how great he was. Budding sexual sadists could learn from Chevalier Ajanel, he is the epitome of the term.

"Isn't this wonderful, my darling? This is where I do the best part of my work." He moved so she was facing the huge wheel.

"I bind my girls to the arched side of the wheel, cut off their clothes, then wait for them to wake up. The first awakening, and realization of their situation is the best part. I don't like to miss it."

He chuckled with delight. "Sometimes it takes them a while before they really become aware of what's going to happen to them. It gives me a kick, like watching one of those movies like, oh The Chainsaw Massacre, The Saw, love those flicks, don't you?"

Laurin was too numb to react. She could picture a woman tied to that monstrous thing and him torturing her without the victim having any way of defense.

He stared with self-satisfied marvel at his work. Then he smiled down at her. "Okay, sweetie, I feel you limbering in my arms, I think more of the sedative is wearing off. Let's get you tied up so we can start playing. We'll save the wheel for later, I have other fun stuff we can do." He started moving.

He spoke as he walked, "Knowing you'll be on the wheel at some point will keep your anticipation burning, kind of like foreplay, huh? Besides, when I fuck you I want to be able to toss you around in different positions, I have chains on the ceiling and the walls, the floors. Good times ahead, my pet, eh?"

Laurin could feel a meagre bit of strength returning. She considered fighting him, but he was unbelievably strong and his arms gripping her against his body were like iron vices. She'd do better to save her energy and wait for an opportunity to get away from him when he was distracted.

He carried her back up the stairs and into another room. Despair slammed into her as they entered the chamber. It was actually pretty all done up in blush and peach colors, but what was inside was ugly, pulse-stopping ugly. A weird contraption was in the center of the room.

It was like a sawhorse with a horizontal beam to sit on, and at one end another beam attached at a vertical incline. More beams with hinges on them lay a few feet away by the wall. Laurin could only guess that they were designed to be attached to the machine so it could be changed around for different positions. The rose colored wood was the same as the big boxes were made of, and highly polished.

What was frightening were the handcuffs attached by chains at both ends. Different sized iron rods lay on a towel on the floor beside it along with several whips. And knives.

More chains attached to the walls and ceiling, and there was other apparatus but Laurin's attention was glued to the sawhorse.

The beams of the sawhorse were rounded apparently to protect the captive from hurting themselves on the sharp edges. Considering the alarming equipment next to the chair that seemed farcical.

"Okay, sweetling, time to get situated. As soon as you're restrained, I'm gonna get a bottle of my favorite wine and some glasses. I've never given someone something to drink while chained to the horsie. But, like I said, you are special and I want to share this entire experience with you."

He stared musingly at her. "I think I'll like serving you. Some of the submissives only like to be a slave while playing, but I think you'll make a wonderful 24/7 slave for me. Hmm," he looked at the sawhorse. "I guess first things first, let's get you naked. Okay?"

He smiled at her like they were lovers and she was enjoying this as much as he was. "I want to get those jeans and blouse off you ASAP. I'm dying to see what kind of lingerie my darling wears. Don't worry, my scissors are sharp, I'll only nick you a little here and there while I cut everything off you. Scarlet drops of blood will absolutely shine against the foil of that beautiful pearly skin of yours."

His tongue swirled around his lips as he gazed down at the lovely package in his arms. "I can't wait to open you up, sweetheart."

Chevy carried her to the sawhorse, Laurin struggled, but the sedative was still in her system making her limbs more like a wet noodles. Thrashing her head, her cries terrified pleas, "No, please, Chevy, don't do this, please!"

He set her down on the sawhorse and reached for a cuff. "Now, now, darling, shh, I'll take care of everything. You're mine now to cherish and take care of. I am in charge of everything regarding you. I control your food, your sleep, your tears, your pain, your pleasure, your very breaths belong to me. I decide when you can draw a breath, and," he licked his wickedly grinning lips, "when you can't."

He pulled her arm back and slapped a cuff on one wrist. When he let go of her arm, it flopped but the chain held her arm not quite behind her back, but there wasn't much leeway to move it.

Laurin thought he did it on purpose, let the chain have a little give so her struggles would have more mobility for his amusement.

Grabbing the other wrist, he did the same then sat down on the end of the sawhorse, straddled it facing her and beamed at her.

Laurin was splayed with her spine braced by the tilted back of the chair. Chevy lifted her legs and placed them on either side of his legs so her knees were straddling his.

Utterly helpless, her legs were spread so wide she couldn't lift them to kick or fight, her chained arms were also useless for defense. Scowling at him, she summoned her strength and yanked at the chains, but her futile efforts only brought a delighted grin to her captor's cruel face.

"Ahh, there's the fight I so love seeing in you." He frowned. "Granted, at first I thought I'd scared the spirit out of you, but," he grinned, "my valiant little Laurin is back." He set his hands on her thighs smiling at the twitch in her legs at his intimate touch.

"And, you know what? I think I'll take a picture of you like this and send it to my fucking father. It'll piss him off so much he'll roar and bite his tongue and threaten to kill me. He'll search for us, he has the means and the men, but," his grin lengthened in glee, "he will never find us. Trust me."

"Chevy, please-"

321

"No, no, sweetheart, don't start begging yet. You'll want to save that tender throat of yours. You'll need it for screaming. Okay?"

He leaned forward, running his hands up her thighs stopping with his thumbs brushing her sex. Laurin flinched and tried to shift her hips out of his grasp but he laughed in enjoyment and stroked his hands up to palm her breasts.

A deep groan reverberated in his chest. "God, Laurin, I've waited for so long to touch you, so goddamned long."

Suddenly the room tilted oddly, the rods on the floor rolled a little, then the room sort of swished then settled back. "What on earth-" Laurin cried.

Grinning with his brows arched, Chevy said, "What's it feel like?"

"Like- like-" she swallowed, eyes flapping in distress, "like we're on water."

His grin wide, he nodded, fondling her breasts. "So astute. Yes, my darling. We are, and that's why no one will ever find us. That's why those bozo cops haven't been able to find The Poser's lair. Ingenious, right?"

She had hoped when he'd earlier talked about the yacht that they were still docked, but the rocking motion increased and verified they were sailing. Laurin could do nothing but blink at him in desperate fright.

Squeezing her breasts roughly, he smiled at her wince of pain. "You're mine now and I can touch you all I want. So," he patted her breasts then lifted her legs off his letting them drape down to straddle the horse and he stood up.

"Time for wine. I'll get it, it's a great Burgundy, dry but with a hint of citrus, you'll love it. I'll give you a few sips then it's on to cutting off those darn clothes."

He swung his leg off the horse and ambled to the door.

Chevy paused in the doorway and looked at her, his head tipped to the side, his smile sweet and loving. "Finally, my darling, you are finally mine. Be right back!" He spun and left the room.

Laurin swallowed the petrified screams that crawled up her throat and she wrenched at her arms. She lifted her legs to add to the gravity of the pulls but her fighting was in vain.

There was no way she could break the chains or dislodge them off the horse.

No way.

She was trapped.

# Chapter Thirty-Seven

They had researched every piece of property and holdings the Ajanels owned, including the businesses. Hix sent teams out to every place they found to search for Laurin.

Everyone came back empty. He dragged a hand through his hair and hunched over his desk, his elbow on the desk, his forehead propped in his hand.

He felt so fucking impotent. That freak monster had his girl and God knows what torture the perv was wreaking on her. Hix didn't even know if she was still alive. The back of his mind was primed for the call that they'd found her, kneeling outside one of those goddamned wooden boxes.

"Anything?" Kurt asked from the doorway as he strolled in. From the bleak look on Hix's face, Kurt's question was superfluous. They were both wearing casual clothes, black jeans and jackets. Kurt dropped his jacket on a chair.

Hix shook his head, he was too numb with dread to speak. It was a labor to even think. But he had to, he had to figure it out. Tapping at keys on his computer, he sat and scrolled through frame after frame rehashing all of the evidence, the videos.

Kurt dragged a chair over and sat beside him. "Two pairs of eyes are better than one." At Hix's nonresponse, Kurt said quietly, "We'll find her, Penn, we just keep putting one foot in front of the other." His gaze went to the monitor.

Prince wandered in, looked as defeated as Hix and Kurt. Rubbing his eyes with a yawn, he walked over to stand behind them to watch the screen. "Hell," his sigh thick with exhaustion, "at this point, my brain is totally awash. Like I got nothing but a lake sloshing around inside my skull."

Kurt nodded, agreeing with him. "Yeah, totally." He stared solemnly at his friend and boss and said, "Sorry, Penn, you've been at this with no rest. You gotta be feeling even more brain dead than us." He tried to lighten the mood. "You got brain flood too?"

Pawing his short beard, Hix grunted, his eyes on the monitor that flashed scene after scene on a roll. "Yeah, pond brain," he muttered then blinked. "Pond, lake, river..." he mumbled as his fingers flashed over the computer keys.

"Huh?" Kurt glanced at Prince who shrugged. "We're all past exhaustion. He doesn't know what he's-"

"Wait." Hix started hitting the keys faster.

"What?" Kurt asked, as he and Prince leaned forward at the sudden interest in Hix's demeanor.

Hix pounded at the keys then paused, he bent his face to the screen. "The fucker's a sailor, prior Coast Guard, he has a boat in his back yard..."

Prince said, "Yes, but the neighbor said he never took it out."

Hix jabbed his finger at the screen. "Yeah, but, he's wealthy, he can afford a much bigger boat than the one in the yard." The screen not giving him any marine holdings on the Ajanels, he snatched his phone off his desk and dialed.

Kurt and Prince watched him with confused wariness.

But the phone rang before he finished dialing. "Hixman," he barked into it.

"You asshole, it's Agent Brewer. We got the bastard, got him solid!"

"What the hell are you talking about?"

"Huh," Brewer grunted. "Laurin came through. She broke the password on Ajanel's computer and it was a fucking treasure chest of incriminating information. I have men out there now bringing the bastard in. You tell Lau-"

"Call me immediately the second they have him. That's an order, Brewer," and he disconnected then dialed again.

"Blake," he said when it was answered. "Get officers to every marina in Brevet Bay and Alexandria. They need to grab video surveillance and canvass the people there for any sign of Laurin Ajanel, Chevalier Ajanel, and anyone that knows the Ajanels."

He growled at the response, then barked, "I know there's a fucking million of them, take a million cops. Call me the second you have anything."

He couldn't just sit there and wait, Hix stood up and grabbed his jacket.

"Where we going?" Kurt asked as he and Prince followed him.

"Considering his giant ego, we're going to the biggest, fanciest, closest marina to Chevalier Ajanel's home."

The trio raced out to Hix's truck, and Hix was barreling down the driveway before the last door was closed.

Peeling out of the parking lot, he said, "Kurt, call the Coast Guard, tell them we need a boat. Have it waiting for us at Starvista Marina." Hunched over the wheel, his fingers gripping it, he blinked hard as something popped into his brain.

"Thomas, have Mike Maverick go to that old guy's house, that weird little elf, Valentine. Tell him to find out where his son gets his auto parts from. When he finds out, tell him to grab a team and go there, look for Laurin."

********

"Here we go, darling," Chevy cooed as he entered the room carrying a bucket in one hand and a wine glass in the other.

Laurin was just as he'd left her. Except, "Tut, tut, baby," he scolded, "mustn't fight so hard, you already have red rings around your pretty wrists. They're so thin, fragile, I'd hate for you to start out with broken bones."

In answer, Laurin groaned as she tugged as hard as she could on the restraints, again, to no avail.

Clucking a reproach at her efforts, Chevy set the bucket on a small table and put the bucket and glass on it then lifted a bottle of wine from the bucket.

He had a towel over his shoulder that he drew off and wrapped around the bottle, then pulled a corkscrew out of his pocket. Whistling a tuneless yet cheerful tune, he stuck the corkscrew in the bottle, twisted it and removed the cork with a pop.

"Hmm," he regarded the corkscrew thoughtfully then his eyes slid over to Laurin. His gaze lowered to between her legs. "Never tried this before, might be a fun new toy for us to explore. I could shove the cork up you and try to get it out with the corkscrew. Sounds like a cool game, what do you think, darling?"

At his intimation, Laurin bit back a cry and resumed squirming frantically to free herself from the cuffs.

Chevy poured a dollop of wine in a glass, lifted the glass to his nose and sniffed. Swirling the liquid he took a small sip then beamed. "Excellent! You'll love it, darling. We'll drink out of the same glass, that'll be more romantic and intimate than us each having our own wineglass." He filled the goblet with red wine then lifted it to Laurin's lips.

She considered refusing it, but this wasn't the moment to reject him. She took a tiny sip then Chevy swigged the remains then refilled the glass. The goblet was overly large for a wineglass. He set it on the table then turned to Laurin.

Rubbing his palms together he grinned. "Okay, sweetheart, finally, you and me." He picked up the scissors and moved to her. She tried to shrink away from him but that only made him laugh.

"I'd hold still if I were you, sweetling, you don't want me to damage that porcelain skin of yours yet, do you? We have long fun days ahead of us, I'd like you to last as long as possible." Without waiting for her to reply, he stepped to the horse then lifted a leg to straddle it.

Sitting down, he faced her. He placed his legs outside of hers, and chuckled again when she tried to lift her legs away. He pressed his thighs against her knees to trap them against the wood beam. "You have nowhere to go, babydoll, just sit still so you don't get hurt. Yet." He moved the scissors to her and snipped off the top trim of her long sleeved t-shirt.

"No, Chevy!" she cried out and thrashed her chest to the side, wrenching her wrists in the cuffs, the chains clanked against the wood.

His laughter rang out loudly, with the scissors in one hand, Chevy grabbed both sides of the top of the shirt and slowly pulled them apart. The material rent down the middle.

As if she was rich ice cream, his eyes gleamed with hungry desire, the pupils glowing. "Oh yes, my precious. Let's see now," he hummed, pushing the torn shirt apart to see beneath it.

A huge grin lit his face. "Nice. Figures you'd wear something so innocently sexy with lace and peach silk." He stroked the pads of several fingers over the slopes of her mounded breasts and groaned.

"Yeah," he murmured, inhaling deeply with a lick of his lips like she was aromatic honey he couldn't wait to taste. "Let's check out the undies, see if they match, okay?"

Laurin wriggled about and jerked her arms as hard as she could but Chevy cut away until he'd gotten her jeans off. He tossed the remnants to the floor.

His appreciative eyes as wide as plates, he nodded with a pleased grin. "Yes, matching set. You are so feminine it's ridiculous. I love it!"

Her shirt spread open exposing her lace-trimmed bra, Chevy held her legs immobile so she couldn't squirm as he studied her figure barely concealed in peach silk. Bucking her hips, frenzied shallow breaths billowed her chest in rapid hitches as Laurin pleaded with him to let her go.

Ignoring her cries, he muttered, "You're still too thin, hon, but we'll fix that. Doesn't skimp on those luscious curves though." His gaze ate up her jiggling breasts, then lowered to her panties where his tongue lolled out of his slack mouth.

Staring unblinking at her body for a moment, then he snapped out of his haze of lust and said, "Oh wait, a picture for my beloved pater. I'll take a pic at every juncture, it'll be like a movie for him. Almost like he was here, but unable to do anything except watch."

He drew his cell out of his pocket and stood up, moved back and took a picture of her splayed out half-naked, then grinning like a gloating jack-o'-lantern, he sent it to his father. "I'm sure I'll get a nasty reply quickly. He's gonna be slightly pissed."

Chuckling at his understatement, he put the phone in his pocket and slid back onto the sawhorse and reached out and grasped a bra strap. "Now this," he moved the scissors towards it.

"Wait, Chevy," she cleared her throat, tried to sound calm, sexy. "You said wine, you, uh, said we could drink together? Make it…romantic." That last frightened struggle to get loose was so frantically rough she felt her skin shred from the metal, but her one hand was almost out of the cuff.

He paused, observed her terror so body-shaking acute she couldn't hide it. Goose-bumps sprung up over her body, her nipples budded against the silk.

Chevy smiled. "You're stalling, my sweet. But," he shrugged, "what the hell. We have the rest of our lives, well yours anyway, there's no time limit. You're right, let's enjoy, savor this first time together."

Chevy got up and retrieved the wine glass then sat back down with his long legs stretched around hers. He moved the glass to her lips and tilted it slightly so she could take a sip.

After she did, he pulled it back and took a big gulp. "Wow, I'm liking this, Laurin, it's so romantic," he gave her more to drink. "I should have thought of candles and music, make it a perfect first date."

They drank while Chevy regaled her with stories about his job, his youth, the women he stalked and killed. Whether he spoke about sadistic murder or taking a patient's blood pressure, his tone never changed, it all sounded as if he was calling in a dinner order. Though, he clearly enjoyed telling her about the women he'd ravaged, but when he started on his mother he grew tense.

"That manic bitch," he snarled through a clenched jaw, slugging down the entire glass of wine before speaking again. He refilled the glass and tossed back half of it. Chevy's eyes were glassy, his nose red, he was angry but his words slurred. He'd drunk more than two thirds of the bottle, whereas Laurin had taken only tiny sips. When he tried to press more on her she demurred stating she wasn't used to drinking.

"You don't want me to throw up, Chevy, do you?"

"No, gross." Taking a huge swallow he complained bitterly, "Anyway, the bitch that spawned me would come in acting all motherly loving. She'd pet me, stroke my back, slick her fingers through my hair," his lids lowered, his voice grew heavy remembering the brief bliss. Before the rest.

"Ah." He guzzled the goblet, wiped his mouth with the back of his hand. His glassy eyes stared blankly over Laurin's shoulder.

"She'd get me all cuddled up on the bed, she would-" he broke off, suddenly bewildered. He frowned at the glass in his hand in disorientation as long buried memories suddenly plowed in a whirling turmoil into his head.

"What, Chevy?" Laurin needed to keep him distracted, keep him talking as she worked to get her wrists free. She could feel the blood sticky on her skin, the sting of the tearing flesh. "Tell me what happened next."

He finished the wine and set the glass down, stared blankly at her, he was lost in the past. "She helped me take my clothes off then she would…play with me."

Laurin froze. "Um, you mean like…"

Nodding as if he was in a dream state. "Yes. Sexually. Then she removed her clothes, and wriggled our bodies together. She'd be all giggly and humming while she played with me, with my…genitals. She put my hands on her breasts, taught me how to caress them, suck them. She liked me to suck rough, said she liked the hickeys I made all over her breasts. She said the darker the better, she liked the pain. Even had me bite them sometimes."

He took a breath, it came out shaky. "She kissed me on the lips, her tongue…" he winced. "When I was older and could get an erection, she'd sit on me and- and take it." His face was screwed up in confusion, his mouth contorted as if swallowing nausea that crept up his throat.

"I…these memories, I've forgotten about this, her." He shook his head in disbelief. "I've repressed them. What a sick bitch, you see where I get my deviancy from."

Laurin said nothing as she kept tugging, twisting her wrists in the cuffs.

His head hung slightly, dark hair flopped over his eyes, he noisily sucked in a heavy breath. Raising his head, he peered blindly at Laurin, still seeing the past, not her.

"Then, after we…played, as she called it," he snorted. "She would change. Change from the wanton hussy into…a monster. She would tie me down and that's when she would cut me, burn me. Said she was giving me hugs and kisses that I could carry with me for life. X's and O's. Put them in a heart-shaped circle, said it was so I could see how much she loved me. Huh."

He rubbed his belly over the scars. "And she was right, I have carried them my whole life." From the bottom of his abdomen to the top of his chest were hundreds of scars, she'd carved and burned one right on top of another.

His eyes closed as he relived the blend of revulsion, the shameful incest, the agony of his mother's torture. The confusion of a loving mother that screwed him one second and maimed him the next gashed hideous abomination in the twist of his lips, the flare of his nostrils, the pain flowing from his dark eyes.

Lungs harsh with tormented air, he muttered miserably, "I tried to tell Dad, but, he just, whacked at me. While slapping me, he ordered, 'Buck up, you're a man, count yourself lucky the whore favors you with her body. You got experience at a young age most boys would give their right arm for. You can take a little pain, for cripe's sake, quit your whining.' Then he'd laugh and laugh…and laugh. Bastard." His head hung lower, a tear spilled on his pant leg. He lapsed into silence.

Keeping the rest of her as still as possible, Laurin worked the cuffs, biting back the pain, she didn't speak, maybe he'd fallen asleep.

And he had. A snore erupted from him. His head joggled but he didn't straighten, his legs fell limply to the sides.

A wrist slid free. Laurin gripped her still restrained arm and using her full strength, she wrenched and twisted and 'pop' she almost fell off the sawhorse when she sprang free.

She didn't dare look at her torn wrists, she didn't need her stomach revolting any more than it already was. Carefully, slowly, holding her breath, she slung her leg over Chevy's and slipped off the sawhorse to her wobbly feet.

*Darn*, she hadn't counted on the sedative to still be in her system and mixed with the wine it was throwing her off balance. She grabbed the back of the sawhorse to steady herself. Taking a glance at Chevy, his head was still down and soft snores blubbered from his lips.

Laurin set her hand on the table to keep her balance and started to move around the table, away from him. Her eyes on the door, if she could get out maybe she could lock it from the outside, or push something against it to keep him from coming after her.

She wasn't looking at the table and her hand hit the empty wineglass, it tipped over on the table landing with a clack and rattle.

Chevy's head shot up with a snore cut short in a snort. Blinking in drowsy confusion, he saw Laurin freeze, terror etched across her pretty face. His eyes narrowed, he lashed a hand out to grab her, she was within arm's reach.

Laurin screamed. Her hands scrabbled at the table behind her. She grasped the bottle of wine and swung it around and slammed it into his head as hard as she could. Wine spewed across the room, with a howl of pain, Chevy slumped to the floor.

Not wasting any time, she raced to the door and out. Slamming it shut, she was chagrined to find no lock on it. There was nothing in the hallway to push against the door. She ran for the stairs.

Hurrying up the stairs, she looked left and right as she hurtled out and felt the sun on her face, the brisk breeze instantly chilling her. Chevy hadn't lied, they were on the water. The boat was enormous, it was a yacht.

The wind whipped the torn shirt and stung her bare skin, she was standing there in her underwear and barefooted. He had removed her shoes and socks. Didn't matter. She ran over to the railing, if they were close enough to land she could jump and swim to it.

Gripping the varnished wood, her panicked breathing rushing loud in her ears, she leaned over it and peered out. Blonde hair flying in her face, she pushed it back with both hands, and she felt like an elephant stomped on her gut. She could see nothing but water. Endless miles of water.

Quickly, she swung around, then hurried around the railing to see all sides. Her heart sank, water everywhere, not a speck of land to be seen, not another boat.

"What do I do now?" Plucking windblown locks out of her eyes, she spotted another set of stairs. "Ah, the bridge. I've never driven a boat before, but how hard could it be? Turn the key, pump the gas," she raced to the stairs, her bare feet smacking the wooden deck.

A few feet from the steps, her hands reached out to grasp the metal railing- something caught her flapping shirt.

"Oh no you don't you little bitch!" Chevy grabbed a fistful of her shirt and threw her to the ground.

Slamming down on the hard wood, Laurin cried out as her hip and elbow hit the deck. She rolled away as Chevy bent and grabbed at her. "No, you don't Laurin, goddammit," he stepped on part of her shirt halting her escape.

Her skin scraped and burnt across the wood as she continued to scramble from him. But, he dropped down on all fours over her, fencing her in. He was beyond enraged. His face ballooned dark red, eyes bursting with animosity, his teeth bared with his snarl of fury.

He pushed Laurin onto her back. She pummeled at him with her fists, kicked with her bare feet, her fighting only infuriated him more. He punched her jaw and she fell slack.

Leaning over her, sweat fell from his forehead splatting on her cheek. He heaved at her, "You fucking bitch. I was gonna hold off on the extreme torture for a while. Show you how good things, sex with me could be. But after you hit me and ran," his head shook side-to-side, he gripped her upper arms and dragged her to a thick pole shooting up six feet from the deck.

He jerked a chain from his jacket pocket. His hand gripping around her neck, he slammed her against the steel pole and slapped a clamp around her neck. A chain was attached to the clamp. Chevy clutched the end and stood up straight jerking the chain upwards, yanking Laurin's head with it.

Gagging, Laurin curled her fingers around the clamp trying to keep it from choking her. Her head was jolted back as her neck was wrenched up hard, hard enough she had to stumble to her feet or her neck would break from the force of his pulling the chain. "*Chevy*," her cry gurgled, "please!"

His face blistered with rage, he looped the end of the chain around the pole leaving a slight slack in it then put his hand on her shoulder and shoved her down to her knees. Pain shot up her knees and the chain wrenched and tore at her neck as he tugged on it.

Chevy secured the chain around the pole then crouched behind Laurin and gripped her wrists. Yanking them roughly behind her back, he wrapped a piece of twine around them tying her wrists together. She tried to stand to relieve the pull of the chain, but he shoved her back down with a snapped, "*No.*"

He stood up and moved to the front of her and studied her form. "I need to secure your legs so you stay in the pose. I'm not ready to douse you yet with a paralyzer." He bent over and slammed his fist into the side of her head.

With a tiny groan, Laurin toppled over, but was yanked back up by the neck before she hit the floor, the chain keeping her from falling prone.

"That oughta hold you for a minute," he muttered, stomping across the deck and down the stairs.

Her hands bound behind her, still on her knees but having fallen sideways, Laurin hovered awkwardly, painfully, from the chain holding her partially up. Dizzy from the punch, she struggled to stay conscious. If she passed out the clamp around her neck would choke her to death.

She could feel the yacht moving fast again. Chevy had taken the boat off auto pilot and was now at the helm.

It seemed an eternity when she felt the boat slow and then come to a stop. After a few minutes she heard his feet pounding across the wood as he approached her.

"There, good girl, you stayed as I ordered," he chuckled, "not that you had much choice. I wanted to put a few more miles between us and land. Here, let me help you." He wound his hands around her arms and positioned her back on her knees. Then he pulled very thin chains from his pocket and several extra-long nails.

"This'll keep you the way I want, sweetheart." He wrapped the thin links around her ankle then reached behind him and took a hammer he had stuffed in the back of his belt.

He hammered a nail into the deck, then hit it until it bent like a hook. He stuck a loop of the chain through the nail then hammered the other end into the deck. Spreading her knees apart he did the same with her other ankle. Laurin's ankles were secured to the deck making it impossible for her to move from her kneeling position.

Chevy stood back to admire his work. Smiling with a satisfied nod, he said, "Now you can't move, or fight me. But," he frowned and rubbed at his chin in thought. "I can't very well fuck you like that now can I? Hmm." He circled around her as he pondered positions.

Tears streaming down her face, Laurin wriggled, straining at her bindings. He had positioned her like he had the women he'd killed. On her knees, her hands tied behind her back, a chain clamped around her neck attached to the top of the pole, legs secured. Profoundly captive.

He snapped his fingers. "I got it, babe. I can spread those knees further even though your ankles are attached and bend you back, arching your spine. It'll hurt like hell, for you, not me, but I think I can get my dick in you in that position.

"I can also twist you around, eek, that will really hurt when the metal scrapes your ankles. However, I think I can get you on all fours, ha," he snickered, "make that on your knees and face because your poor hands are bound behind your back."

Laurin squirmed harder, the skin on her knees rubbing raw along with her wrists and ankles, and her neck. She was choking on the gush of tears as well as the chain.

"Yup." Chevy grinned at her. "I can flip you around and bend you over and take you from behind. I think we'll start with my first idea though, I'm kind of curious to see how much you can arch your back before it…snaps."

He loosened the chain attached to the clamp around her neck so he could maneuver her then knelt down and gripped her knees. He shoved them apart so hard her pelvis made a cracking sound.

"Oh!" His brows rose with his grin, he exclaimed, "I do like the sound of that," and he put his hand on her chest and started pushing her, bending her spine, arching her neck. Her shirt fell wide open.

He paused to put his mouth on her upper breast, mumbled, "Yeah, Mama," and he sunk his sharp teeth into the lush flesh, and she screamed.

# Chapter Thirty-Eight

As he drove, Hix and Prince and Kurt all held phones to their ears. Hix and Kurt were receiving information on the marinas. So far, no one admitted to knowing the Ajanels or seeing Laurin.

His foot pressed hard on the gas pedal, Hix floored it all the way down Riverview Drive. Chevy Ajanel's phone had been shut off so they couldn't trace it.

His cell at his ear, Hix answered another call. It was Sergeant Daron Sinclair.

"Brother, we got a pic on surveillance film of Chevalier Ajanel at the Starvista Marina. Witnesses said he pulled up in a black van and removed a bundle and carried it onto his yacht. He raised anchor about an hour ago."

"Thanks, Brother." Hix suppressed the hope clamoring in his chest. "We're almost there. I thought that might be the one. The Coast Guard is sending a boat for us. You game to go hunting?"

"Hell yeah, bro, I'm already on my way."

Hix disconnected and called Agent Brewer.

Brewer answered with an annoyed, "What now, Detective?"

"You got Ajanel yet?"

There was a bunch of chaotic noise in the background. Brewer told him, "Yes, about twenty minutes ago. I know I said I'd call you when we got-"

"Ask him if he knows of a yacht his son might have. Chevalier Ajanel is holding Laurin captive on a boat that isn't registered in his name. If Rádolfo knows anything, ask him if it has GPS. Tell him we'll consider taking the death penalty off the table for his cooperation."

"What the fuck, Hixman, this is a federal case. You can't finagle that."

"I know that, pretend it's from you."

Brewer grumped with a huffy, "I can't do that either. And I won't. I'm not making any promises I can't-"

"Just do it, you asshole. He doesn't know you can't do it, just get him to talk. We don't owe that fuck any promises. His damned son is likely the serial killer we've been looking for and Laurin may be his next victim. Do it now. I'll wait. Don't make me come after you, Brewer, because you know damned well I will. And last time we met will seem like a picnic."

Hix pulled onto the long drive leading up to the marina. He sped right to the wharf and slammed the brakes so hard the truck jostled back and forth. Sirens wailed in the distance.

The three men jumped out and Hix looked around until he spotted a male dressed in a dark blue uniform. He was with the Coast Guard. They hurried over to the officer.

Hix barked quickly, "I'm Detective Hixman, I called you. I need a boat, we have a kidnapping, time is of the essence. Do you-"

"Yessir," the man replied, nodding sharply. "It's all ready for you. We'll drive." He glanced at Prince and Kurt. "Everyone coming?"

"Yes," Prince and Kurt said in unison.

"Follow me," the officer said and took off at a jog towards the water.

When they reached the dock, the officer told them, "I am Lieutenant Commander Lon Shephard. We have a 45-foot Special Service Craft waiting. It has 400 horsepower, we use it for chasing down drug smugglers. We have several more at the ready."

Tied to a post attached to the dock, a large boat bobbed in the rough waters.

More Crafts rocked and rolled behind it. Three more officers were waiting on board the first boat, the engine was running, smoke tailed out from the stern.

Lon said, "Climb aboard." He stepped back as Prince climbed onto the boat followed by Kurt.

Hix was next. He put his hand on the railing and heard shouting behind him. Daron Sinclair was sprinting across the lot. He reached Hix, huffing and puffing. "You were gonna leave without me?"

Hix growled out a dark laugh, clapped him on the back. "No way. Go ahead, hop onboard." He motioned for Daron to go ahead of him. Sinclair jumped into the boat, then Hix followed.

Lon untied the moorings and then came aboard. "Raise anchor!" he called out.

He introduced the other three officers. "This is Ensign James McDonald," the young blond man bowed slightly. "And Lieutenants George Ballard and Ronald Morrow." The men nodded in greeting but said nothing.

"Lieutenant Commander Melinda Briggs is driving this heap." Lon made a hand motion up towards the bridge. Then he held his hand extended indicating for Hix, Prince, Kurt and Daron to move to the center of the boat.

They took one step and the boat surged from the deck, did a quick turn then burst out over the river leaving a spray of water cresting behind them, every male managed to keep his balance. The roar of numerous other crafts thundered in the background as they followed.

"Go ahead and have seats, gentlemen," Lon offered. "What direction once we clear the inlet, Detective Hixman? When you requested the boat you didn't signify where we were going."

All of the men declined to sit. Hix said, "I don't know yet. I think our perp is on a yacht, we're presuming he's heading downriver, maybe to Chesapeake Bay then onto the ocean where he can find a zillion places, and eventually countries to hide."

Lon said, "Hard to hide a yacht. Once we spot him, there are a number of sites along the river we can possible track him by land."

Hix replied, "Problem is, we don't know what the name of the boat is, what kind or what it looks like. Plus, he's had an hour head start."

"You mean we're chasing a ghost?" Lieutenant Morrow's brows arched.

"Yeah," Hix glowered at him. "You got a problem with that?"

Morrow shook his head rapidly. "No sir. We love an adventure. A challenging manhunt is right up our tree. We're all adrenalin junkies."

Hix's phone rang, he pulled it out and swiped it on. "Hixman," he snapped.

"Brewer here. The guy is threatening all kinds of things, says he ain't speaking until he gets his lawyer."

"Shit," Hix exploded with frustration. He forked his fingers through his hair. "I know we're not allowed to torture suspects, but waterboarding-"

"Wait, slow down, boy. He's outraged at being hauled in, but, when we told him about his son being the serial killer and he has Rádolfo's wife trapped on board, Ajanel became cooperative. Says the name of the boat is named Ambassador One. Says it isn't Chevalier's, it's his. Registered under one of his shell companies." He described the yacht and its VIN number.

"Okay, Brewer, ask him if there is GPS on it."

There was a pregnant pause, then, "Yeah, already did. That's a no. Allegedly the boat is used for…let's say likely nefarious deeds, so they disconnected the GPS."

Hix slapped his palm on his forehead cursing, "Motherfucker." His phone was on speaker so the other men heard the conversation. Smothered groans made the rounds.

"Ah." Hix tried to think. "Ask him if he'd have any idea where his son might go to hide." Boots akimbo, Hix wore black jeans and a bomber jacket over a beige thermal. One hand on his hip, he tapped the phone with his fingers as he waited. No one said a word. The only sound was the waves as the boat thrust through them.

Several minutes and Brewer returned. "Sorry, man, says he has no idea where the puny pussy coward would go, his words. Has no friends, no girlfriends. His wife barely speaks to him. Rádolfo says his son asked to borrow the yacht like almost a year ago and never returned it. As far as he knows, Chevalier has no other property in or outside of the country. We turned up nothing on our searches conducted earlier in our investigations into all the Ajanels."

Nodding his head while dragging consternated fingers continuously through his hair, Hix grumbled, "Yeah, we didn't find anything either." He drew in a heaving breath and said with a sigh, "Okay, if you learn anything, call me. Right away this time you asshole."

"Wait, Cop," Brewer called out.

"What?" His annoyance harsh.

"You ain't gonna like it, but, Chevalier Ajanel sent a photo to his father."

Hix was afraid to ask. "Yeah?"

Clearing his throat, Brewer told him, "It was of Laurin. The creep has her on some kind of contraption, like a sawhorse with an inclined back. Her arms are restrained behind her back, legs spread over the horizontal beam she's sitting on, and, uh…"

"Spit it out, asshole." Hix's heart clenched.

"He's torn her clothes off her. She's in her bra and panties, but I don't think for long. She's," he took a shaky breath, "she's obviously terrified, face streaked with tears. He sent the picture to goad his old man. But, man, at least she's still alive. Well, at least twenty minutes ago she was still breathing."

His voice tight, Hix growled, "Send me the pic and call me with anything else," and clicked the phone off. He knew he didn't want to see the picture of Laurin, but there could be something in the photo to give an idea where she is.

Turning to the others he said, "Well, we know the name of the boat. Maybe the guy was too cheap or too stupid to change the name or paint it."

"How do you want to proceed, Detective?" Lon asked.

Stretching his neck back until it cracked, Hix thought hard. He heard his phone ping, the photo was received. "For now, head downriver. We have officers stationed along the roadways and bridges although he's probably long past the local ones. He's likely already out in open water.

"Kurt, call dispatch, tell them the name of the yacht and the style of boat, get it out to every law enforcement officer on and off the water, including the Coast Guard and other patrolling units."

Kurt whipped out his phone and dialed.

"If I may ask," Lon's hands clasped behind his back, "why didn't you request whirlybirds?" One of the lieutenants made a call to inform the Coast Guard of the name and design of the yacht.

"I did. We've got them coming out here, thing is, if he slipped down a tributary some are so heavily canopied by trees and thick brush, they would likely miss him. He's had a big head start. Also, I'm afraid to get them too close, I don't know what kind of firepower Ajanel has on that thing, I don't want the choppers shot down. Right now I'm using them for long distancing views."

The men grew silent, each one moved to the railings to peer out over the water in hopes of catching a sighting of a large yacht. Ensign McDonald handed out binoculars to everyone. Hix took his and made for the stairs. He wanted the highest location he could get to.

When he reached a spot, he opened his phone and steeled himself to see the picture of Laurin. He hated to have anyone else see her like she was, but they needed all eyes searching for anything of note.

Struggling to keep his mind professional, Hix thrust down all agonized thoughts of the way Laurin looked. Vulnerable, helpless, terrified. A red mark on her face denoted he'd struck her. A blank wall was behind her, there was nothing to indicate anything revealing about the boat.

He texted the picture to the others. Just what he always wanted, sending a photo of his girl in her lingerie to other men to scrutinize. He hears one comment about her body and the beast will come out and attack.

Time went by, officers called in. Several had stopped large boats and investigated them, but nothing yet.

Hix paced in front of the bow, his stomach tied up in knots tightened more fiercely the more time went by.

Prince wandered over to him keeping his eyes on the water. He knew better than to offer platitudes. They didn't know the condition Laurin was in now, and to say everything will be okay when she was in the clutches of a sadistic serial killer would be ludicrous.

Prince's phone rang. He answered it quickly, his eyes on Hix. Hix's gaze was fixed on his friend. "Uh huh," Prince mumbled shaking his head. "Yeah, thanks, Mike." He hung up.

Hix could tell by the negative slant of his mouth it wasn't good news. "What?" His stomach tensed to hear what Prince had learned.

Prince held a hand up. "Nothing, it's nothing, Penn. Mike talked with that Valentine dude. Got ahold of his son. Son buys his parts and scraps from Anderson's Salvage Yard. And, you figured it right, there's a ton of that metal The Poser used for the chains, that palladium shit.

"Son says he's sold a load of it to Chevalier Ajanel. Mike and Teague took some uniforms and raced over there. Owner never heard of or ever saw any of the Ajanels, only ever dealt with Rudy Valentine's son, Mitchell. More evidence against Chevalier, but they searched every nook and cranny of the lot, no Laurin."

"Didn't expect she was being kept there. Too many other people around. He's out there." Hix nodded over the water. "He's got her on a boat. That's why no one could find The Poser or any place the Ajanels owned." His hands on the railing, Hix's shoulders hunched, binoculars hanging around his neck, his head rotated as he studied the water around them.

He glanced at Kurt who joined them, then blinked. "Fuck me," he growled.

"Huh?" Kurt's lips pushed out.

Hix snatched his phone out of his pocket and started tapping on it.

"What is it?" Kurt asked.

Staring at the phone, Hix told him, "Remember I took that tiny phone from you? I gave it to Laurin. I'm praying she has it with her somehow, unfortunately it isn't likely he let her bring her purse. But maybe, just maybe..." He put his finger on the phone's screen, found the GPS link and pushed it around. "Hell yeah, bro, hell yeah, come on," he raced to the stairs to the bridge.

When they burst into the bridge, the female at the wheel inclined her head in greeting but kept her eyes peeled on the river.

"I have coordinates, Lieutenant Commander," Hix told her.

"Hit me." She grinned.

Hix told her the coordinates that the tracker in Laurin's phone was indicating.

Kurt asked Hix as he came up to stand beside him, "How do you know it's with her and not at your folks' home, or Chevalier's, or her pukey husband took it from her and it's with him?"

Hix aimed one of his rare smiles at his friend, "Because all of that is north of us, and the tracker is moving south, and it's not stationary."

"South Southeast, sir, and it's traveling damned fast," Lieutenant Commander Briggs informed him glancing at the phone. Then her eyes focused on the water directly ahead of them.

Hix ordered Kurt, "Call dispatch and give them the coordinates where we're heading." Then he left the bridge and made his way back to the bow. Phone in his hand, he lifted the binoculars to his eyes and searched.

It seemed like they were just racing on and on and not getting closer to the yacht.

"He's moving fast, Penn," Prince said joining him. His sandy hair flew in all directions from the wind. "But we're moving faster." Kurt came up to the railing, his eyes narrowed at the horizon.

His heart in his throat, Hix couldn't speak, he wondered if he could hold his breath until they got her. Wouldn't do her any good if he passed out on the deck. He looked down at his phone and took a breath before speaking, "He's slowing down, looks like he's coming to a halt."

Hix called up to the bridge, "We're gaining on them, the boat has slowed to a stop." The bad thing was they couldn't accurately judge the miles between the two boats.

The Craft's engine roared as they tunneled down a tributary. Just as Hix thought, the bastard was sneaking to Chesapeake Bay then gonna hide in the vast ocean.

They continued on, their bodies rocking and rolling and bobbing with the motion of the boat and the swells of the rough water.

It was a tributary, but it was hundreds of feet wide and bracketed by thick forests and coves lending many places for a boat to hide in. Now they had to be careful they didn't pass it- someone jabbed him in the side.

Kurt's arm was rigid, he pointed up ahead and to the right. A dot rolled up and down with the waves.

Prince turned his phone on and called dispatch, he gave them the information.

Hix ran for the stairs and raced up, stuck his head in the bridge shouted, "Up ahead," and ran back down and to the deck.

The Coast Guards gathered around the officers, three of them held a phone to their ear. Lon said brusquely, "Tell us what you need, we'll do it."

Hix gave a brief nod, he squinted across the water.

Lieutenant Morrow said, "We don't have confirmation it's them."

Hix glanced at his phone, a grim smile nicked in the side of his mouth, he peered back over the water. "It's them."

The Craft zoomed slicing through the water. As they got closer, Hix said, "Weapons at the ready, we don't know if he's armed or he has confederates. Just remember he has a hostage on board. Don't fire unless he shoots at you and make sure what you are firing at."

Everyone pulled their guns from holsters and held them at their sides.

Lon recommended quietly, sternly, "We should wait for the other vessels, Detective."

Hix replied, "There's something I need you to get for me."

# Chapter Thirty-Nine

Chevy sucked at the bite wound he made on her chest. In the awkward painful position he forced her in, Laurin twisted as hard as she could but he held her inert with his heavy body, he licked across a soft mound of flesh.

His mouth sucking and biting red marks on her skin, he smiled and stated, "Love it when you scream, sweetheart. See, I told you we'd make a great couple. Let's consummate our new relationship."

Laurin's back bent in a curve, he held her in an n shape. It was agony, she felt her spine was going to snap in half from his weight pressing on her.

Her ankles bound to the wooden planks, hands tied behind her, her neck arched so far back her head almost draped the floor. With the pressure of his body, Laurin couldn't raise her head to look at him, much less fight him off.

She was way past terrified. Her entire body shook and shuddered with desperate fear. She had defied him, hurt him, and ran from him. Already a psychopath, he had now entered his punishing, killer mode. She could see it flashing in his crazy eyes while he slobbered on her.

His lips still sucking and nipping at the tender skin of her plump chest, Chevy put his hands on her thighs and dug his fingers in, pushing them as far apart as he could without snapping her legs from her hipbones.

He knelt between her thighs holding them wide and palmed her sex over her panties. "You wet for me, my darling?" He cooed soft words and growled with lust, but Laurin could see the insane wrath burning in him as he stroked her intimately.

Shoving his hand inside her underwear, he bit her breast again and she screamed from the shocking pain.

Chevy murmured gleefully with his teeth stabbing her flesh, "We'll fuck first, then I'll introduce you to some lovely serrated rods I have. The other girls just squealed with delight when I used the rods on them." So involved in Chevy's assault, a thick finger poised to thrust into her, they never heard the other boats arrive.

Words roared from a loudspeaker, "Chevalier Ajanel, stand up with your hands above your head!"

Chevy froze. The loudspeaker repeated the words, "Stand up with your hands above your head!"

Unlatching his teeth from Laurin's breast, he lifted his head and blanched. The front of his yacht was surrounded by dozens of boats, and two helicopters were buzzing in from both directions coming fast at them, a third one zipped from behind a tree line.

He straightened on his knees. As the boat rocked, over the bobbing railing around the bow, he could see a million weapons aimed at him.

"Fuck that," he spat and whipped a knife out of his boot and shifted quickly to lay it across Laurin's neck. She went stock still, confined in the taut arch, her chest heaved in fright. He lifted her off the ground to an upright kneeling position and moved behind her.

Staying crouched using her as a shield, Chevy shouted out to the boat directly in front of the bow that seemed to be in charge, "You all need to back up the bus and get the hell out of here or I'll slit her throat. I mean it, I have nothing to lose!"

Laurin squirmed but he pressed the blade against her throat. He threatened her, "Hold still, darling, I'll cut you. I've proven I have no qualms with slicing and dicing women."

He lifted his head and shouted, "I'm not playing here, you fuckers! Get the hell out of here or I'll kill her! You have ten seconds and then I'm gonna- *oof-*"

Something slammed into Chevy from behind- knocking his body hard onto the deck. He was so busy watching the lead ship at his bow that he didn't hear the man board the boat from the stern.

A fist bashed into his face again and again, and Penn Hixman glowered over him with his fist raised to hit him until he had no face left. He bellowed, "You bastard, I'm going to rip you apart!" Footsteps pounded across the deck.

"We got him, Penn, see to Laurin," Prince said in his ear. He and Kurt leaped forward and tumbled on Ajanel.

Dozens of men and women jumped on board and spread out to search the vessel.

Chevy wailed and screamed, cursed and threatened, he was suddenly silenced when Kurt slapped a strip of electrical tape across his flapping mouth. He and Prince flipped him on his belly and they handcuffed his wrists and bound tape around his flailing ankles.

Huffing his rage, chest expanding with heaving furious breaths, Hix turned his attention from Chevy to Laurin.

Without Chevy holding her up, her body had fallen sideways towards the deck, she was strung up, trapped in a tremendously painful contorted pose, her breasts billowing with frightened frantic breaths as she was slowly strangling.

"Oh God, baby!" Hix moved to her. First he rolled his arm under her back to lift her back to a kneeling position, get the tension off her neck.

They were quickly surrounded by Coast Guards, the police, some were Hix's people, their feet stomping over the wood deck while they shouted from one to the other, another chopper joined the three already buzzing above the yacht.

Propellers whirled loudly in the darkening night. The sun had almost set, the cold wind slapped sharper, the swells rippled higher making all the boats bob harshly in the coarsely flowing river.

An officer said, "Sir, I'll get a hammer or screwdriver to remove those nails from the dec-"

Hix ripped the nails right out of the wood with his fingers and unwrapped the chains from around Laurin's ankles. He slipped out his knife and cut the twine binding her wrists then stood so he could get the clamp off her neck. Thank God it was only latched on without a lock. He ripped it off her neck and threw it, the chain bounced clinking and clanking against the post it was tied to.

Laurin crumpled to the deck.

"Okay, baby, I have you," Hix whispered, dropping down to sit. He wrapped his arms around her and gently cradled her against his chest. Her body was jelly, she couldn't sit much less stand. He sat with her huddled against his broad chest. Laurin wept on his shoulder, her sobs hitching and hiccupping, soaking his shirt.

"Shh, Laurin," he murmured quietly kissing her temple. "It's over. All over. You're free. You and Benji and Robbie are free. I'm taking you home."

He cupped her chin and kissed her trembling lips. Hix winced at the damage Chevy had wreaked on her tender body. A bruise darkened along her jaw, another at her temple, her wrists, ankles and knees were raw and bleeding. He couldn't even look down at her breasts, the maniac had chewed all over her leaving ugly red marks and nasty bites.

When she moved, whimpers of pain escaped her trembling lips and her legs shifted oddly. Chevy had probably manhandled her so hard he'd strained her hip muscles. Hix had to rub her arms to help her regain motion and feeling back into them from being so harshly restrained behind her back for so long.

All around them people still shouted and bustled. One officer yelled out, "Hey, you guys gotta see the damned contraption, a giant wheel he built below deck!"

Hix drew Laurin's shirt closed and removed his jacket and placed it over her shoulders. He tugged her arms inside the sleeves, zipped it closed, then pulled her back into his safe embrace.

The yacht was secured and, with a huge smile, Lieutenant Commander Melinda Briggs drove them back to the marina with the other boats following. The helicopters flew back to their bases.

When the yacht was tied and anchor dropped, Hix lifted Laurin in his arms and carried her to a waiting ambulance. He laid her on a gurney and leaned over, kissed her carefully. "I'll follow the ambulance, Laurin. When you're declared okay by the doctor, we'll go home. All right?"

Lying on her back as the paramedics strapped her down, she stared up at him with those big blue eyes blurred with tears, still in shock, and nodded.

# Chapter Forty

The doctor insisted Laurin stay in Imperial Summit Hospital for a week. He was worried about the bite marks becoming infected, and at first he thought her legs had been broken, but they were just severally sprained, same as her arms from being so tightly bound.

On the eighth day, Laurin whined, "I know I'm being a crybaby, Penn, but I want to go home. I want to see Benji. I think I can get Robbie back now too and I'm anxious to get started."

Hix was sitting on a chair beside the bed holding one of her hands. Machines beeped and whooshed behind them. He lifted her hand and lowered his head to kiss her knuckles, he laid her hand back down gently and questioned, "Hey, I wondered why Chevalier didn't find your phone?"

"I was darn lucky," she replied, her grin derisive but carried gratitude. "He was so anxious to cut my jeans off me he never noticed it in my back pocket. He just heedlessly let the pieces of my pants drop to the floor and paid no attention to them."

"Thank God you stuffed the phone in your pocket, it was the best move you ever made."

"I heard your voice in my ear telling me to take it when I went to Chevy's place. I owe God a bunch of thank you's." The grin slid to a sultry smile. "I especially owe you, Penn for giving it to me. It, you, saved my life. I can never thank you enough."

His head ducked with her thanks. "It was nothing, Laurin. I told you, it's time someone took care of you."

351

Her smile became a questionable purse. "I don't understand why you even came after me. Or, oh," her cheeks reddened, "you were after Chevy, The Poser." The full lips curved down.

"Hey, baby," he said, squeezed her hand and kissed it again. "Of course we wanted, needed to catch the serial killer, but," he bent over her and kissed her lightly on the cheek.

"The only thoughts in my head the entire time I learned you'd left my folks' house and might be confronting the killer was to get to you before he hurt you. The fact that when we rescued you we also caught that bastard, hell, that was just the frosting on the cake. You were the cake, little one."

Laurin quirked one eye in disbelief at him, but was met only with the sincerity in his eyes and the determination in the set of his strong jaw.

He said quietly, "I will never lie to you, Laurin, and I will always come for you. I promise you, I would die for you." They stared at each other without blinking, studying the thoughts and feelings that shimmered over their faces.

Laurin blinked first and looked away. "Um," she swallowed awkwardly then said, "I'm ready to leave, Penn."

His face relaxed into affectionate tolerance. "You know the doc's orders, baby, we want you strong on your feet before you leave. Besides, Benji doesn't need to see you all broken and bruised again."

Her lips pushed out in a pout, then firmed. "You're right. But the bruises and lacerations have faded, they're almost gone. I've been walking with you around the atrium every day. I'm good to go."

His smile tender as he gazed with love and desire at her, he said, "Well, letting you in on a secret, Doc Rothschild signed your release papers this morning, that's why I urged you to dress. We're only waiting on the wheelchair."

"Oh!" She frowned. "Why didn't you tell me right away?"

Dark eyes traveled over her gorgeous face and down the blouse and back up, the smile broadened, lazy heat filled his eyes. "Because you would have pestered me all day asking when are they going to get here. Honey," he leaned over her and softly kissed her plush lips. "Trust me, I'm as anxious as you are to get you home."

She returned his warm smile and sat back against the pillows. "Once I'm out of here, I swear, Penn, I hope to never have to darken a hospital's doorways again."

"I agree. Except for when…"

"When what?" Blonde brows beetled together.

He leaned over her again, this times his lips were parted for a real kiss. "For when you are having our children."

Lauren leaned away from him with shock. "Our children?"

His big hand gently cupped her healing jaw. "I know it's fast, Laurin. But you feel our chemistry, our connection. I know how I feel about you, I've fallen hard for you and want to spend the rest of my life with you. I want to be a father to Benji and your little brother, and I want more children with you. I want us all to be a family, a big happy family."

He sat back, twined his fingers and set them in his lap, watched the emotions play across her face.

When she opened her mouth to speak, Hix said quickly, "I won't pressure you, honey. You need time. You can stay as long as you want at my parents, Benji and Robbie too of course. Then, if you feel you need to be on your own, I'll help you get your own space. I just hope," thick lids lowered over the desire in his eyes, "that you'll give us a chance, give me a chance. I'll court you, whatever you need. If it's not what you want, I'll back away.

"It'll be the hardest thing in the world for me to do, but," he sighed, "I love you, I want you to be happy. And if that has to be without me, I'll understand. You've been under Rádolfo's cruel fist for a long time. You might not want to jump into another relationship right away, so I'll-"

Laurin cut in, "If you'll shut up for a second," she smiled at the big hard man that would scare the beejesus out of most people just by his looks alone. "I've never heard my rough tough detective talk so much." She laughed when his lips snapped closed in surprise.

Laurin swung her legs around to hang off the bed as she sat on the edge, her legs dangled between his. His hands automatically went to set on her thighs.

"I know what I want, Penn. I know I want opposite to what I've had. When Chevy had me on that boat, all I could think about was I'd never see you again. We could never…be together," her cheeks pinked at her implication.

Hix hitched to the end of his chair and tucked his knees around her dangling legs. He slid his palms up her thighs and leaned closer.

She said, "I…so want to be with you. Yes, I think we should move slowly, get to know one another, but," she blinked shyly, "I think I might love you too, Penn, or at least I'm falling there."

Scooting to the edge of his seat, Hix reached his arms around her and pulled her close. "Oh yeah? Only falling? You need to catch up with me. Okay, my apartment is small, I would feel the most comfortable if you stayed at my folks. They can help you with the boys, and get a job, or school, whatever you desire. But," he slid her off the bed and onto his lap, her legs straddling his hips.

"What I really want, Laurin, is us to all be together as a family. Until then, I'll have to make excuses to secret you away to make slow, languorous, or fast and hot love to you." He grinned at the blush that covered her face. He cupped the back of her head and pulled her to him and pressed their mouths together, he moved his lips until hers opened, and he slid his tongue in to taste and conquer.

Their kiss, hot and heavy, passion steamed off the couple in waves. Hix slanted his mouth to seal them tighter and his hands roamed her body. He cupped her butt then stroked up to palm her breasts. Their deep, shared moan was interrupted by a clearing of a throat.

A nurse stood in the doorway dressed in green scrubs, her hands on the back of a wheelchair. "You aren't ready to go home yet, Mrs. Ajanel?" She winked with a smirk. "I can come back later if you-"

"No!" Laurin tried to scramble off Hix's lap but he held her still with a chuckle. She turned and frowned at him.

Hix stood up with her legs still wrapped around his hips and he deposited her in the wheelchair. "There you go, baby." He smiled at the nurse. He was doing that a lot lately, smiling, and he really, really liked it. Made his stomach soften. "Okay, go on," he said to the nurse, "I'm right behind you."

As the nurse wheeled her down the hall, Laurin smiled up at her and said, "It's not Laurin Ajanel, it's Laurin Cerridwen."

Behind them Hix murmured, "Soon to be Laurin Hixman." He glanced at Laurin to see if his words bothered her, but he was met with her happy grin.

# Epilogue

**T**wo months later, Benji and Laurin, Hix's brothers Kullen, Clifford and Aven, his father Kresskin, and Brett, Suzetta's husband with their children Holly and Michael were teaching Benji how to play tag. The children were shrieking with laughter, the adults shouted and laughed as they all chased each other.

Off to the side, Vageline smiled with dear affection as she watched them. The picnic table was almost completely set with cold cuts, huge sourdough buns, cheeses, potato, macaroni and tossed salads, chips, baked beans and sodas.

Hix had gone to the station.

Next to her, watching the kids and adults play, Suzetta sighed. "I think Hix fled because he couldn't stand the shadow of sorrow that lingers in Laurin's pretty sapphire eyes. Laurin had hoped her little brother would arrive, but day after day has gone by and no word about the boy. It takes the shine off her new happiness."

"True," Vageline agreed, wiping her hands on her apron. "But she is flourishing surrounded by the love and joy of all of us. She's happy and she's enrolled Benji in pre-K and he loves it.

"Laurin herself has enrolled in the local community school studying for Neonatology Assistant. She plans down the road to maybe go for her own MD. She had been taking a few classes online before Agent Brewer got his claws in her. Then Ajanel refused to let

356

her continue with her studies. All her attention, Ajanel had demanded, according to Laurin, was to be on him."

Laurin had explained neonatology is a subspecialty of pediatrics that consists of the medical care of newborn infants, especially very ill or premature newborns that have low birth weight, congenital malformations, and a host of other calamities.

Suzetta laughed. "Remember how her eyes lit up when she received her acceptance to college? Hugging the document to her chest she'd danced around the house with unbridled glee. We had all gone out to dinner to celebrate."

Nodding with a smile, Vageline said, "Now that Rádolfo Ajanel along with his felonious sons are incarcerated, Laurin is finally safe and at peace. Hix told me that the feds had wanted them deported to South Africa where they could suffer a harsher fate than in America, but the District Attorney feared with all his connections Rádolfo could escape justice."

Suzetta said, "Right. It was all due to Laurin and her brave investigating that got the Feds the goods."

Vageline agreed with her daughter. "They had found proof in the information Laurin had scored from his computer that he and his sons had dealt with terrorists. They were responsible for untold deaths.

There is no diplomatic immunity for terrorists, and the Ajanels were charged with terrorism and face the death penalty. It was assumed they would eventually all take pleas of life in prison to save their sorry skins. Their wives had been arrested as accessories."

A frown pulled Suzetta's mouth down, a line cut between her brows. "That sick, horrible Chevalier Ajanel is taking his chances at trial. Good luck to him. Once he's sent to prison, due to his infamy with the savagery he dealt to his victims, the other convicts will see to his care. Poor guy." Her sarcasm told her real feelings.

"I'm going to grab the condiments and pickles, Suzy, why don't you put ice in the glasses?"

Vageline started for the house to bring out the condiments, a soft smile curved up her pretty face. Laurin and Hix usually spent most of their time at Hix's apartment. Benji stayed mostly with the

Hixmans because it was closer to his school. He spent some nights at Hix's.

Gazing over the shrieking running people on her lawn, her heart thumped with joy, soon the couple will get engaged. Hix had been fairly bursting with his need to tie Laurin to him, and by the way Laurin looked at Hix, the way they couldn't keep their hands off one another, a wedding planning is in the near future. Hix had convinced Laurin to start house hunting.

Vageline sighed. Soon her full house would be almost empty again. "Oh well," she smiled, "I'll just have to plan a lot of family parties."

Just as Vageline approached the house and reached for the screen door, Hix's truck rolled up the drive. She paused as he parked.

The driver's door opened and Hix slid out and slammed the door shut. He trod around the front of the truck and to the passenger side as the door slowly opened.

The passenger appeared shy to leave the truck. Vageline could see Hix speaking quietly to whoever was inside, then he grinned and opened the door further.

A young teenager hopped out. He had bright blonde hair that gleamed in the sunlight, just like Laurin's-

At that moment Laurin had tagged Kresskin. Laughter on her lips, she glanced over at Hix, and she came to a dead stop. Her eyes grew wide, she covered her mouth with her hands, and even from her distance from Vageline, Vageline could see tears spring in her eyes.

Laurin shrieked and went running across the lawn to the truck. To the boy.

"Robbie!" she screamed, then gasped when her breath caught with emotion. Robbie grinned at her and held his arms out when she flung herself at him. The siblings hugged, both crying tears of joy and relief.

Hix stood off to the side to give them their moment. He turned to look at his family, they were all beaming with delight at Laurin and her brother. He turned back to Laurin and Robbie, and Laurin peered around her brother's head at Hix, the tears streamed, she mouthed, "Thank you."

Hix grinned back, mouthed, "You're welcome." He added, "Marry me," and chuckled when she stuck her tongue out at him.

When everyone calmed down, and Robbie was introduced, they sat down to a spring lunch with flowers blooming in vibrant colors and trees budding pops of green all around them. The air was still slightly crisp but smelled pleasantly fresh and woodsy, the sun shone down on them from its blue cradle.

Laurin and Hix spent the next several nights at the Hixmans' house so Laurin and Robbie could relink and catch up. Because of the children, Vageline had insisted Hix and Laurin sleep in separate rooms. Laurin still shared a connecting room with Benji.

The fourth night, after dinner, Laurin put Benji to bed and read him a story. When the little guy was in snoozeland, she set the book down and turned to see Hix standing in the doorway leaning a hip against the frame, his arms crossed and a smile on his rugged face.

He wiggled a finger at her indicating for her to come to him.

She grinned at him, then stood up, leaned over, kissed Benji on the cheek and pulled his blanket up to his tiny chin. She made her way to where Hix waited.

He slung an arm around her and plundered her sweet mouth for several minutes. They broke apart, both breathing heavily and smiling like silly lovebirds.

"Come on, baby," Hix said as he guided her out of the room and to the hall. "We're going to my place for the night where we'll have privacy. I still need to teach you what real lovemaking is like."

Laurin giggled up at him. "You've been showing me that for a month."

He hugged her to him and smiled, gave her a tender kiss. "There is so much more to learn, baby. I need to work harder to get you to agree to marry me."

They continued down the hall, Laurin said softly, "As soon as I see Robbie has settled knowing he's safe and loved, we'll talk about it."

Hix lit up. "You mean it?" He bent and swung her up in his arms and kissed her hard. His mouth against hers he said, "Let's go to my place and start making plans."

Her arms sliding up around his neck, their lips bumping, she whispered, "Hurry."

She didn't have to repeat herself. Hix strode swiftly down the stairs and through the house.

He flung "Goodnights," to his family as he passed them without stopping. He had his own little family nest he wanted to start.

He already had two new sons, Benji and Robbie, and he couldn't wait until he and Laurin made it legal and they could get their own house and bring the boys home to stay while he and Laurin got busy making them siblings.

Once he and Laurin were married Hix planned to adopt both boys, and Laurin could make Benji her legal son. The engagement ring he's had for two months was burning a hole in his pocket.

Maybe if he told her they could honeymoon in Hawaii she would finally agree to be his wife.

She had told him about her bucket list. She wanted to learn to scuba dive, surf, go parasailing, ride a mountain bike. She had read where in Honolulu there was a volcano that they would fly you in by helicopter, and you could sleep overnight inside the crater top of the volcano then ride the bikes down the steep volcano in the morning with dawn breaking overhead.

As long as she was happy, that's all Hix cared about. He would give her anything and everything to keep her happy. For now, he could wait for her to agree to marry him.

But, he was impatient to make her his wife, give her his name, put his ring on her finger to claim to all that she was his. His to love and protect.

Oh yeah, all was right with his world. Hix never thought he'd see the day, never thought he would know true happiness and peace. Never thought he'd be a dad, have a wife, have a decent life. And here it all was, blossoming around him.

Smiling with grateful serenity, when they reached his truck, he bent his head to kiss Laurin; love was safe in his arms, she was his life.

# The End